Bitter

RE de Jauregui

Books by Ruth de Jauregui

Novels
Bitter

Bitter Sins

Bitter Dreams

Nonfiction
Ghost Towns

100 Medical Milestones That Shaped World History

The Soul of California ~ Cooking for the Holidays

50 Fabulous Tomatoes for Your Garden

There Is No Conflict (as George H. Stone)

Connect with Ruth
Ruth's Sneak Peeks: http://www.ruthdj.net

Alien Star Books ~ Science Fiction and Fantasy for Teens and Young Adults of Color:
http://www.alienstarbooks.com

Table of Contents

Bitter Blood

Bitter made her way past the flashing blue and red lights, past the yellow tape. She didn't show her badge to the hovering blues; they knew who she was.

A smudge of brownish-red marred the grey cement as she stopped to put disposable booties over her shoes. She grimaced at the staid practicality. There was a time she'd have worn high heels, forensics be damned. Now her knees protested as she ascended the steps and heels? Heels were impossible.

The young officer at the door did stop her. "Detective, I don't think you…."

Bitter stared him down as his words faltered and trailed away like the long years since she'd joined the force. He stepped out of the way.

The carpet squished as she picked her way past the overturned sofa and stepped into the kitchenette. He was sprawled across the floor under the open window. Death's indignities softened the limp muscles; the body was face, well, chest down. Jagged skin ripped across the remains of his neck. She didn't think he was a young man, but it was hard to tell—his head was gone. A quick glance revealed that his fingers were also missing. Judging by the torn remnants of his khaki pants, he was probably missing other parts as well.

"Prints?" Despite the wide pool of blood congealing on the tile and splattered on the wall, Bitter's voice was dispassionate, detached from the scene.

One of the techs glanced up at her. Sweat darkened the edges of his mask, though the night was cool. "No, none yet."

"Identifying marks?"

He pointed silently at the faded tattoo on a bare shoulder, barely visible under the spattered blood.

Bitter glanced, then stepped forward, nearly treading in the blood. Emergency lights flashed through the window, alternately painting her face blue and red, as she paled. She swallowed and the tech looked up at her face.

"Are you all right?" His voice was puzzled. She'd seen worse during the drug wars. A headless man was nothing new or unusual in this city.

She stepped back and turned away, hiding her face. "No," she choked out. She took a deep breath as she dodged past the sofa, out the door, and rumbled down the stairs. She paused at the bottom.

"Bitter?"

"Call the Chief. He needs someone else from Homicide. Here. Now." Her voice was urgent.

The tone in her voice drew the attention of the blues. Conversation stopped as they turned toward her. She took a few more steps and turned, leaning against her car, hands over her face.

The blues parted like the Red Sea as Sgt O'Malley emerged from the darkness of the alley. He looked around and suddenly all were busy with notebooks and crowd control.

"Bitter?"

She looked up at him, tears shining in her eyes, reflecting the flashing lights.

His voice softened, but he didn't reach out to her. He knew better. "Bitter?"

She shook her head and turned away, shuddering with rage. She looked up at the darkening moon, drifting behind the black clouds as a single tear streaked down her carefully rouged cheek.

"It's my ex."

O'Malley opened his mouth and paused as Bitter turned back toward him, fists clenched, her face twisted in anger. Furiously, she swept away the tear, smudging her makeup, as she began pacing beside the car.

"Why would that fool come back here? What would make him come here, of all places, and finally get himself killed? Lord knows he dodged enough bullets here."

O'Malley winced. A few of those bullets were his.

Bitter stopped pacing and stripped the booties off her shoes. She glared at the blood dripping down the stairs.

"Okay. Until the Chief sends another detective, you know the drill. Coroner, forensics, take witness statements, run a list of suspects. Lots of pictures—I want every inch of that flat and the body photographed before anything is moved. And you and I are at the top of the list of suspects, don't leave anyone out, and don't touch any of the evidence yourself. Get one of the blues to bag it and tag it." She turned abruptly toward the alley. "Did you find anything in there?"

"Only ghosts."

Bitter looked back at him, her deep umber eyes black in the dim light.

"You don't have to believe me, you know." A trace of Irish lilt touched his voice, then faded back into his normal rich baritone.

Bitter shook her head, "Yeah, yeah, I know, you're the sixth generation of seventh sons, so you don't have the full Sight, but you can see ghosts. Whatever. Speaking of, did you see his head? It's not near the body."

"No. And his ghost wouldna' be speaking to me anyway. There's no love lost between us and death wouldna' change that." His voice was bitter and unforgiving.

Bitter choked down a shred of sympathy. It was, after all, O'Malley's wife who'd been foolish enough to be caught with Sal on his last escapade before the divorce. Yet, O'Malley stayed with her because he was Catholic or something. At least she kept her twitchy tail home now. Bitter shrugged it off—old news and not her problem—especially not tonight.

"Let's take another look at that alley. Fire escape?" She looked around for a blue uniform. "Sapp!"

"Yo!"

"Sapp, grab some gloves and evidence bags. We need you to document the evidence—if we find anything."

She saw the side-eye to O'Malley but ignored it.

The rain arrived just ahead of the coroner. Fat drops splattered across the windshield as he peered through the smeared glass. Bitter changed direction, the two cops trailing her.

"One. Upstairs. And Joe, I think it's my ex."

He tipped his head sideways and frowned, his face pallid under the yellow glare of the streetlights. Bitter waited impatiently.

Finally, he shook his balding head. "It's not your ex."

"But..."

"He has hands, right?

Taken aback, Bitter nodded.

He nodded back, firmly, "Then it can't be Sal. He's dead. A drug deal went bad. His body never surfaced after his main competition tossed him into the river. Knocked him in the head and cut off his hands to prevent identification if the body floated to the surface." He peered through thick bifocals at Bitter's face.

"Vice found the hands in the perp's freezer six months or so later during a raid. I got enough of a thumbprint to positively identify him. Nasty stuff." He shook his head and turned toward the stairs.

Fists clenched, Bitter turned to O'Malley.

"It wasn't me, Bitter." He protested, "The man nearly destroyed your career after he fed you those shrooms when he was trying to kill you. Then you were in the midst of the divorce and on leave, taking care of your mother. So Chief Brown ordered us to keep it quiet. And when you got back, we had that serial murder case and, well, no one thought..." His voice trailed away under her disbelieving glare.

Bitter closed her eyes and gathered her rage, stuffing it into the black abyss where she stored her emotions. Time for that later.

Both men stepped back when she opened her eyes, but she just pointed with her chin. "Alley."

The flashlights lit one item at a time, casting deep shadows behind the dumpsters and trash piled in bricked up doorways as they cautiously dodged broken bricks and bottles. O'Malley stopped and breathed deeply, looking at a particularly dark shadow beside a spilled trash can.

"Ghosts?" Bitter's voice conveyed her disbelief even as she asked the question.

He took another deep breath. "Maybe. It's barely here now. They fade, you know. They're just shadows left behind, not the soul."

Bitter didn't know. She only tolerated his obsession with ghosts.

A dripping spot caught Sapp's attention as he looked up the fire escape. "Y'all see that?" He reached up to touch it before Bitter knocked his hand away.

"It's slime. Put on your gloves, take a picture, and then a sample." She kept her flashlight on the viscous smear. She had to take a deep breath to steady her voice before she continued. "Sal specialized in exotic hallucinogens. Like imported botanicals, mushrooms, amphibian skins, and slimes. Trust me, you don't want to touch it."

Sapp sputtered, "But you're talking like that body was Sal. You heard the coroner. Sal's dead!"

"Is he? They never found his body."

"Strange," O'Malley muttered as he looked around the alley, flashing a light into darkened corners.

"What?"

"Where are the homeless people? There's usually at least a half dozen back behind that dumpster, huddled with their dogs and shopping carts inside that old doorway; sheltered from the rain and wind. And rats. Where are the rats?"

"Scared away by the action?" Bitter asked.

Sapp glanced behind the dumpster. "Naw, old Mumbles never moves for anything. He's so far gone that he wouldn't notice a cop if one stepped on him." Sapp paused as he sealed the evidence bag, "He used to trip on acid and angel dust, but later he got into meth. Last time I saw him, he was going on about tunnels and giant lizards or alligators or something."

O'Malley chuckled, "Giant lizards? Well, now."

Bitter didn't laugh. She trained the flashlight into the doorway, where a darker shadow led into the building. "Maybe they just found a better place to shelter from the weather."

She bent to peer inside, then jumped back when she looked down. A few more glistening spots, and a wide, weaving line of slime surrounded by several tiny trails led into a deep hole in the old building's floor. A filthy khaki rag fluttered below, caught on a brick that was just out of reach.

O'Malley flashed his light into the hole, carefully avoiding the slime and the crumbling bricks around the edges. "Hey, there's water down there. What do you think of that?"

"I think we have a problem, O'Malley. The underground city is right below us and I suspect that water is an old cistern or well, left over from the Gold Rush era. The river connects with the passages when the groundwater rises high enough. Anything could be down there."

Sapp shook his head. "Like what, Bitter?"

Bitter sighed. "Anything. The Gold Rush era brought men from all over the world to California, and this is where it all started, here on the American River. They all brought their own cultures and vices, everything was sold here, from opium to prostitution to, to," she stopped for a moment, "to their favorite foods…"

"And ghosts," O'Malley said firmly. "There are ghosts down there too. I've seen them many a time, shadows hiding in corners during the summer tours."

"I wasn't thinking of ghosts." She said sternly, looking down at the light reflecting onto the walls from the rippling water below. Something glittered beside the round hole, but when she followed the movement with the flashlight, it was already gone, fleeing into the deeper shadows below street level. Maybe it was a rat.

"Both of you, come on. I'm not climbing into that hole. There are stairs two blocks over that lead into the underground city."

Before they left the alley, Bitter looked long and hard at the open window above. A few dark smears stained the windowsill. They looked suspiciously like blood, but the rain was quickly turning them into dribbles of pink as they dripped down the old brick walls.

The crowd of spectators had grown, with a few posturing for the news cameras. Bitter groaned and slipped behind the taller officers, trying to avoid the reporters. Luckily, the cameras were facing away from the alley as the handsome men and women gestured toward the bloody steps, excitedly repeating any rumor that fluttered past their eager ears.

"Sapp?"

"Yo."

"Can you pull up the Internet on that fancy phone of yours?"

He pulled the phone from his pocket and hit a few buttons. "What do you need to know?"

"Bitter! Wait!"

Reluctantly, she turned but breathed a sigh of relief when she saw the coroner hurrying toward her. "What's up, Joe?"

He looked furtively behind him, at the cameras. Bitter took his arm and tugged. "Come on, let's keep moving so they don't notice us."

"Bitter, there's something wrong with that body."

"More than just a missing head, fingers, and a few other parts?"

"No, no, it's not that. The hands aren't right."

"What do you mean, the hands aren't right? What's wrong with his hands?"

"This is not to be discussed," he looked sternly at O'Malley and Sapp. They nodded silently in agreement.

"The texture of the skin changes at the wrists. Also, the palms are a little too small in relation to the size of the body. It's, it's as if another person's hands are attached to the arms."

"Like they were grafted on?"

"No, no, the scarring doesn't indicate grafts. Have you seen lizards that are regrowing a tail? More like that. I'll go over this carefully at the morgue when we do the autopsy. I want to run some tests. But there's something weird about this whole murder." He held up a hand before anyone could respond. "Yes, more than missing body parts. I have a bad feeling about this, Bitter. You be careful. Your father would come back to haunt me if I didn't warn you that there's more to this than it appears."

"Tell me about it." Bitter snorted.

He scurried back to the van as the EMTs carried the body bag out on a stretcher.

The blaze of cameras and flashing lights were blinding as Bitter turned away, shielding her eyes to protect her night vision. The trio slipped around the corner into the shadowed downtown streets, where layers of graffiti obscured the plywood that covered long-broken windows. The drenching rain dropped like a waterfall from sky to street to sewers far below.

"Down here," whispered Bitter, unlocking a metal door and leading them down a rotting staircase. "No loud noises and keep the flashlights on the ground, so you can see where you're putting your feet. There's debris and holes in the floor."

"Say Bitter, you wanted me to look something up online?"

"Later, Sapp. No time now."

Picking her way over the uneven floor, Bitter led them deeper into the maze of tunnels beneath the city. The stench of decaying wood and mold grew stronger as they followed another staircase down to a moisture-laden passage. Water trickled over the stone and brick walls and crumbling mortar. Bitter stopped when the tunnel divided again. She looked right, then left. Biting her lip, she flashed the light quickly down each passage before she turned right. Abruptly, she stopped and dug into her pocket for a small tube. Quickly she drew an arrow on the wall, pointing back the way they'd come.

"Lipstick?" O'Malley whispered.

She rolled her eyes, nodded, and put it back in her pocket. Motioning them forward, she slowed the pace as patches of slime appeared on the walls. Odd rumbles echoed from somewhere ahead. Three semi-automatics cleared the holsters at the sound. Adrenaline, dark passages, and an unknown murderer ahead will make any cop paranoid.

A loose stone turned under Bitter's foot, but Sapp caught her arm before she fell. She gave him a tight smile and limped on, her knee throbbing in rhythm with her pounding heart.

A sign peeled from the wall beside them, the faded Chinese characters nearly obscured by black mold and dirt. As Bitter paused, a small dark shadow passed in front of them. O'Malley hissed at Bitter. He pointed with his chin and frowned at the faint, blurred figure that trembled in his flashlight's glare. Bitter raised her eyebrows questioningly; she couldn't see the shade. He pulled one eyelid into a squint with a finger. It took a minute before she realized what he was saying.

"Chinese?" her lips shaped the word. He nodded.

She nodded back grimly. They were getting close.

A few steps more and a wide doorway opened on the left. The wooden door lay in rotting ruins, covered with more slime. It led into a storefront that had lain empty since the heyday of the Forty-Niners. Today the air was dank, rolling out of the hole and warning of stagnant water.

"It's here," O'Malley said in a bare whisper. "He's pushing me away."

Bitter motioned him back to silence, but a clatter of falling bricks and a grumbling growl drifted from inside the old store. Two 9mm and a .45 Glock pointed steadily at the doorway as they backed away, up the tunnel. Another brick clattered and then a third as something heavy moved in the dark. Slowly a huge, greenish-brown head appeared. Slime dripped from the thing's skin, oozing down the wrinkles of its blunt snout. A long, wide body carried by four short, webbed feet followed, with one claw dragging a scrap of khaki that occasionally caught on a rock or brick. It matched the pants on the body three floors above.

It raised its ugly nose, smelling the air currents as it looked for the intruders. The tiny eyes were unblinking as three flashlights centered on the amphibian. Bitter backed up and stumbled again on the uneven floor. Its head swung toward the noise. Miniature versions of the slimy creature swarmed around and under the giant, working their way up the tunnel in a slow-moving wave.

"Look at that," muttered Sapp as he continued backing up, "it's at least ten feet long."

"Twelve," said Bitter softly, "and we'd better move a little faster, the babies are faster than the adults.

"What the hell is it?"

Bitter's lips twisted in a grimace. "I was going to have you look it up. The Chinese consider it a delicacy, but I never thought they'd have brought a breeding pair over here." Her eyes narrowed. "Unless the legends of giant salamanders in the rivers are true, and an imported one mated with a native…"

"What?"

"I told you that Sal specialized in exotic hallucinogens. That looks like a Chinese giant salamander—except it's way too big. They're usually only six or eight feet long. But I suspect that the slime mixed with brandy makes an excellent high for the jaded druggie with money to burn."

The great head swung back toward the tunnel as it crawled ponderously forward. Bitter took another step back and stepped on another loose brick, losing her balance and falling backward onto her butt. She was already scrambling backward as she shouted, "Don't..."

O'Malley fired as the salamander swiftly lunged forward, snapping at Bitter's legs. The shots slammed the giant amphibian back, but the little ones flowed forward, wide mouths snatching at each other and Bitter's sturdy shoes.

Sapp and O'Malley grabbed Bitter's arms and jerked her to her feet. They turned and ran back up the tunnel, stumbling over debris as they dashed away from the salamander's nest.

Bitter was puffing hard as they climbed back up the last set of stairs and burst back through the doorway, out into the raging storm.

"Nobody's ever going to believe this," gasped Sapp, as he leaned against the wall.

"No, they aren't," said Bitter, "and you aren't going to say anything either."

O'Malley looked at her sharply. "We aren't going to say anything?"

"Nope. The damn things are endangered in China, and if you killed the largest specimen ever seen..."

"But they're eating people."

Bitter smiled, bitterly. "Maybe. We haven't heard of any missing homeless. They could've migrated to the shelters. Or moved to San Francisco. It's been a long, cold, wet winter. And maybe it's just a certain person who was stupid enough to disturb the creatures. Or lure them by feeding them from his kitchen window so he could harvest the slime." She paused, then continued slowly, "And I'm not too sure that it ate his head."

O'Malley spat to the side. "You think he..."

"Sal liked to experiment with drugs. Even on himself." Bitter smiled cynically. "Salamanders can regrow missing limbs. You probably didn't kill the mother, but it should take her a while to regenerate the damaged tissues. And they're both carnivores and cannibals. Don't be surprised if the body is missing from the morgue tomorrow."

O'Malley opened his mouth, then closed it again.

Bitter continued, "No, I don't know. I don't know anything for sure. Even if he did survive being tossed into the river ten years ago, I think Sal's done for this time. At least, I don't think Sal's body can grow a new head. But then again, we didn't find his head, now did we?"

As Bitter relocked the door and pocketed her set of master keys, O'Malley and Sapp looked at each other. O'Malley shook his head slightly and Sapp dropped a bare nod. Bitter knew that by morning, they'd start rationalizing the whole confrontation. By nightfall, they'd deny they'd ever seen a giant salamander under downtown Sacramento.

The cameras and crowds were thinning as the trio made their way back to the crime scene. Yellow police tape flapped in the rising wind. One end tore loose by a gust as the storm intensified. Lightning and thunder crashed together over the old house, adjoining narrow alley, and remaining police cars. Only one marked car's lights were still flashing, eerily synchronized with the wild white flashes from the towering clouds above.

Favoring her right knee, Bitter walked stiffly back to her sedan, leaving the two men to write the report. She would review it tomorrow—and delete any parts that'd bring the psychologist sniffing around, ready to make his case for mass hallucination instead of accepting the cold, hard facts as they stood. She'd had enough of his poking and prodding and incessant questioning about the hallucinations she'd suffered eleven years ago after Sal poisoned her, and she wasn't going to listen to the doctor's nasal voice droning on and on.

She'd never tolerate it again.

Slowly, Bitter limped up the wet steps of her tidy Alkali Flats bungalow. A soft drift of Mariachi music wafted across the water-laden air from the apartments down the street as she pulled the keys from her bag. Her knees still ached, complaining about their abuse tonight and warning of more rain to come. The lock stuck like it usually did in damp weather, but she patiently worked the key until the door finally opened. Carefully, she took off her suit and hung it neatly in the entry, where the cat couldn't shed on it, and put on her favorite robe. She made a mental note to drop her dry cleaning off in the morning and to recommend O'Malley for sensitivity training. *Ayyy, using a finger to make a slant eye. Really?* She rolled her eyes in disbelief.

Bitter considered her message for a few moments before she lifted the receiver of the vintage phone on the desk and dialed. Voicemail, of course. "Harry? This is Bitter. Give me a call when you have a chance; I came across some interesting exotic wildlife tonight. Your colleagues at the university might want to secure it, but it won't be easy." She paused. "Don't say anything to anyone until we've talked about how to handle it quietly."

Her duty done, she shook her damp hair out of what remained of the tight bun and poured a glass of wine before hobbling down the hall.

She paused in front of the family portraits and raised her glass, saluting the man that cheerfully greeted her every day, her black hair matching his tight curls, unruly despite his neatly clipped cut.

"Papá, you were right. If I could raise that cold-blooded bastard from the dead, I'd kill him again."

Black shadows gathered in the dark corners of the house as she plodded into the bathroom. She didn't see the golden glint growing in her father's eyes, nor the shadow that slid from his portrait to the front door, ready for another night of guarding his beloved child—Juanita Bitter.

15

Bitter Nights

Chapter 1 ~ And It Begins

Barely visible under the flickering streetlights, a shadow appeared in the garden. A second and third shadow pulled darkness from the corners of the landscape, materializing like black smoke and solidifying just as a lumbering figure crossed over the property line. Hissing gasps produced a foul stench, forming a colorless but deadly cloud that kept the ever-present mosquitoes away as he clumsily searched through the bushes. Slowly, more shadows slipped past the windows and under the door, gathering on the porch until a dark cloud concealed the chubby old cat hiding behind the vintage peacock chair.

A clear, piercing whistle cut through the night as the screen door opened, and the cat leaped across the porch and inside to safety.

Bitter stepped out, muffled in a dark bathrobe and slippers, with her Walther PPK/S ready in her left hand.

"You!" Her voice rang out clearly in the quiet Alkali Flat neighborhood. "What are you doing in my yard again?"

No one answered.

The black and white cruising by slowed and pulled up to the neatly tended walk. The bright white spotlight disbursed the shadows gathered between the porch and the hunched figure.

"Bitter?"

A familiar voice. "O'Malley?"

"Got a problem?"

"Same one. He won't stay out of my garden. He's trying to catch my cat."

A loud sigh emerged from the squad car, followed by O'Malley's long legs and scowl. "Jean. You canna go in her yard. Get out here where I can see you."

"Mine."

"Jean, if I have to come over here one more time and take you out of Bitter's garden, I'm going to arrest you."

O'Malley glanced up toward Bitter and hesitated. The shadows behind her grew darker and more threatening. He shook his head before he looked back toward the garden. His voice sharpened, "Out, Jean. NOW." Reluctantly, the man scuttled out of the yard, but not without a last lingering look under the bushes.

"Jean, do not go in her garden again. Do not bother her cat. Do you understand me?"

"Mine."

Bitter stood on the porch for several long minutes after the trollish figure disappeared down the street. "Any suggestions?" she asked dryly.

"Put a lock on the gate. Call your cat in before dark." O'Malley looked again at the shadows gathering protectively around Bitter, as she stood silhouetted against the porch light, her long, curly hair floating in the light summer breeze. "And plant something strong and sweet-smelling, something night-blooming, here by the gate. The stench out here is terrible."

As Bitter turned and went back inside, the cloud of shadows followed her into the tidy bungalow. O'Malley pursed his lips and considered the ghosts as they faded from sight. A familiar shadow, the last one, looked back at him and nodded before slipping in behind Bitter.

O'Malley nodded back grimly. His grandmother told him to always be polite to ghosts. Especially the ones he knew…

Bitter quickly brushed her hair up into a bun and grimaced. *It's my day off, I don't have to do this.* She looked in the mirror again and shook her hair loose. It was longer than she expected after she applied the hair gel "guaranteed to hold every curl under control" and braided it into one long braid. A few brushes of blush and eyeliner, a bit of mascara, and a touch of lipstick.

Time to go. She'd already packed up the lumpia and sweet chili sauce so there were no more excuses.

She clipped her badge to her purse and slipped her personal carry gun into the holster tucked into the small of her back. It filled that loose spot in her jeans' waistband nicely. She turned once more, examining herself in the full-length mirror. "Ayyyy, Mamá, I got your bootie and Papá's hair," she sighed as she adjusted the soft folds of the silk blouse to cover the Walther .32.

No more delaying. Time to go.

She looked at herself one more time. The turquoise silk suited her coloring. She added her mother's favorite hoop earrings and her grandmother's silver and turquoise crucifix before she was finally satisfied.

Careful of her knees and the insulated carrier, Bitter slowly went down the bungalow's steps. She paused at the bottom and looked across her lawn. "Jean Petit," she said sternly to the slumping man lurking by the fence, "do NOT go in my yard after the cat. He is my cat and I will hurt you if you try to take him."

He straightened and turned toward her; his pasty face swollen in the late morning sun.

"Mine," he slurred.

"No. Mine," she said clearly and firmly, "and if you go into my yard, I will have the police go to your house and take you to jail for stealing my cat. You have already been told to stay away from my house." She glared at him until he slowly stumbled down the sidewalk toward the corner house that belonged to the old woman who kept him.

Bitter held her breath as she stepped through the gate and locked it behind her. The air still stank foully of an unclean body and worse, something dead and rotting. *Maybe I should ask O'Malley to do a welfare check on the old woman. Jean's stench is getting worse every day.*

Sapp's broad smile lit up his face when he saw Bitter arriving with the insulated carrier. "We were wondering if you were coming." He sniffed the air as he held the door open. "What did you bring this time? Homemade *tamales*, fried chicken, *sarmi*?" he asked hopefully.

In spite of herself, Bitter cracked a smile at his enthusiasm. "No. Papá's favorite, lumpia with sweet chile sauce, just the way Lola made it."

Sapp rolled his eyes in ecstasy. "No! You make lumpia too?"

"Aye, yes she does," O'Malley said from the break room, "and you'd best get out of the way before the stampede."

Bitter picked her way through the crowd of blues. She took a tray out of the carrier and set it on the middle table with the rest of the potluck favorites. Behind her, she could still hear Sapp joshing with O'Malley about Irish cuisine.

"What, you don't have any traditional Irish foods?"

"None that you'd want to eat," growled O'Malley as he stared past the overloaded table into a shadowy corner.

Bitter paused and shrugged. O'Malley was always seeing ghosts in the shadows. Sapp leaned down, murmuring, "You should ride with him at night. If I hear one more time about him being the sixth of seven sons—"

Laden with a large silver coffee urn, one of the dispatchers staggered into the room. Bitter couldn't remember her name. Maybe it was Candy. The high heels, flowing white dress and overdone makeup made her think of a perky young woman named Candy anyway. "Hey, hey, let me get that," someone said swiftly and several of the younger officers jumped to help her.

"Thank you," Candy said as they put the pot next to the industrial-sized coffeemaker.

"What is it?"

"Oh!" She gave Bitter a wide smile. "It's chaga tea. You'll have to check it out, it tastes sorta like coffee. And it's organic," she finished brightly.

Turning away so Candy couldn't see his expression, Sapp gave O'Malley a quick side-eye, then sent an expressive eye roll in Bitter's direction. Just then, a huge platter of stuffed mushrooms arrived, and Sapp started making a space on the main table.

"No, no, no, over there." Bitter pointed at the side table.

"What?"

"Allergy-producing foods go on that table. Peanuts, shellfish, mangos, and mushrooms go over there."

"Mushrooms? Who's allergic to mushrooms?" Sapp asked curiously.

She looked at him grimly. "Me."

Sapp sobered. "Really?"

"Yes, really."

Sapp looked down at her sympathetically, remembering a late-night tale told by O'Malley about how her ex-husband poisoned her once with shrooms. He didn't say anything more. He knew better.

Bitter looked at the potluck line and sat down at one of the long tables. The uniformed officers went first since they had to hurry and get back on patrol. Behind them, a long line of off-duty cops and staff waited. O'Malley and Sapp sat down across the table from her, still bantering about food. Neither was on duty, and they worked nights anyway. There was no hurry.

"Ah man, the lumpia will be all gone by the time we get there," groused Sapp as a blue went by balancing a fully loaded plate with at least a half dozen lumpia teetering on top of his food.

O'Malley gave Sapp a Mona Lisa smile.

"What are you smirking about?" Sapp demanded.

"You're talking about Bitter here. Do you really think she put it all out at once?" O'Malley countered smugly.

Sapp turned to her, eyes filled with hope, and Bitter couldn't help herself. She laughed.

Behind her, the room grew still in shock. Bitter hadn't laughed in a long time. Years. Before the silence grew too long, Candy popped up next to Bitter with a steaming mug in her hand.

"I wanted you to taste this chaga tea." Her voice was too high, more toward the annoying little girl pitch than the breathy Monroe image that she was trying a little too hard to emulate.

Bitter politely took the steaming mug. Candy's hand lingered a moment too long, until Bitter gently pulled the cup away. "Thank you."

Candy still hovered, so Bitter gave her a brief smile and a nod. She sniffed at the slightly bitter scent rising from the brew. "It smells—interesting." A quick sip and a grimace sent her to the coffee urns looking for sugar and creamer, while Candy retreated to her entourage of admiring blues.

"Whew, this is strong even for a cop brew," Bitter commented to Sapp as she sat back down, with the tea properly sweetened and lightened.

"What is it again?" O'Malley asked.

"Some organic tea stuff," Bitter replied, taking a swallow. "It's not bad once you add sugar and cream to it. Sort of a cross between tea and coffee. A little bitter."

Bitter took another sip and began fanning herself with a napkin. The room suddenly felt stuffy.

"Is it warm in here?" Her words slurred as she started gasping for air.

Sapp stood. "Are you all right, Bitter? You don't look good."

He reached across the table, too late, as Bitter fell to the floor, the tea splattering across the worn linoleum. Voices rose and fell, fading in and out of the fog that surrounded her as she struggled to breathe.

"Call the paramedics."

"What was she drinking?"

A shrill scream echoed through the room.

Sapp's frantic voice rose above the babble, "Oh Lord. What was that tea called again?" Something in the back of her mind paused to wonder at his tone, even as a wave of darkness approached.

Sapp shouted, "I need an EpiPen. Here. NOW!"

The last thing Bitter felt was a sharp pain in her thigh as she slipped into a black sea of nothingness.

Chapter 2 ~ Tuesday

Bitter slowly opened her eyes as far as she could force them—a bare slit. The oxygen mask and slow beeps chirping in rhythm with her heartbeat told her that she was in the hospital. Late afternoon sunlight slanted across the room, golden dust particles dancing in the air as voices rose behind her.

"No! She is not for you. She is one of us." A woman's voice, speaking in Tagalog. A soft murmur answered her, but Bitter only knew that it was a man's voice. She couldn't make out the words, though she strained until the beeps grew faster, betraying her wakefulness.

A familiar smiling face came into view, and for a moment Bitter thought she was seeing Lola as she was in her younger days, when she'd met Bitter's grandfather during the waning days of World War II in the Philippines. Then memory returned, reminding Bitter that Lola had walked on a few years before Papá's untimely passing.

"What happened?" Bitter whispered.

"We nearly lost you this time."

"What?"

"Your mushroom allergy. You went into shock."

Puzzled, Bitter tried to remember those chaotic moments when she couldn't breathe, and everything went black. "I didn't eat any mushrooms."

"No? What do you think chaga tea is?"

"What? That herbal tea?"

"Steeped from dried chaga mushrooms."

Bitter closed her eyes, furious at her weakness.

A gentle hand patted hers, carefully avoiding the IV. "Do you have enemies?" she asked in Tagalog.

"Yes, but I was at work, with my coworkers. I should've been safe there," Bitter replied in the same language.

The woman with Lola's face shook her head. "You have enemies everywhere, my child. But you are safe for now. I will watch."

Bitter tried to keep her eyes open but sleep again overcame her as the woman faded back into the shadows.

"I will watch."

A bird perched outside the window, its clear song rising in a series of chirps and twitters that flowed through the morning air like a hymn. Bitter lay for a while, listening to the song, before she finally opened her eyes. All the whispers that fluttered to her ears, an undercurrent in the bird's song, ceased abruptly.

Tired. She was so tired.

"Good morning," O'Malley's cheerful voice echoed in the empty corners of the room. "Ready for some breakfast?"

Bitter's stomach churned at the thought of food. She wasn't sure if it was nausea or hunger until the smell of a smuggled Cinnabon reached her nose. *Definitely hunger,* she decided.

"Coffee?" she whispered.

"Hot, sweet, and light, just the way you like it." Sapp set a steaming cup lightly on the bedside table.

The buzz of the bed lifting Bitter's head and shoulders until she could reach for the cup obscured the bird's song. Her hand trembled. She pulled it back and rubbed it for a minute before reaching again.

"Here, let me get that for you." Sapp placed the cup in her hands and held it until she had a firm grip.

"Sit down." Bitter took a sip and breathed a sigh of relief. "Thanks for the coffee and roll."

O'Malley glanced at Sapp. "It was his idea. I didn't think you'd want any company until you were looking better."

Bitter tried to frown, but her face wouldn't crease. She closed her eyes for a long moment. "How bad?"

"Well," O'Malley replied cheerfully, a bit of Irish lilt entering his voice, "you look a lot better than the last time you were in the hospital. Good thing Sapp realized that you were having a reaction whilst you were still breathing."

Bitter's deep brown eyes darkened. The last time, her ex had tried to kill her.

"Mirror," she demanded.

Sapp bit his lip as O'Malley said, "No mirrors. Doctor's orders."

"Liar." Bitter couldn't raise the energy to sit up, but her anger filled the room.

"Easy now," O'Malley murmured, "The blasted psychiatrist is sniffing around. He was asking if you were hallucinating this time."

Bitter glared at him until she finally got herself under control, breathing slowly until her fury faded into exhaustion.

A touch of air, as warm as a breath, touched her cheek. She relaxed, comforted by the touch, until she saw O'Malley stiffen and stare above her head.

"What?" she said impatiently.

O'Malley shook his head. "Shadows. Just shadows."

The warmth faded and Bitter lay back.

"Look, we'll come by later when we go off shift," Sapp said swiftly.

Bitter nodded, too tired to speak, as Sapp pulled the room's curtains closed, blocking out the bright sun. Shadows crowded into the darkest corners as the two men left.

Shadows. A memory stirred.

"Wait," Bitter called, barely able to raise her voice, "please wait."

O'Malley turned.

"My Walther?"

"In your office, in the bottom drawer of your desk." O'Malley hesitated. "I used your keys."

"My cat?"

"Aye, yes, I checked your house and made sure he was inside myself."

Bitter nodded. "Good. Thank you."

Despising her weakness, she opened her mouth again to ask a favor, but Sapp interrupted her. "I'll go by and feed the old boy tonight. He won't get out. Cats like me." He glanced at O'Malley and tipped his head toward the older man. "But I don't think your shadows like him."

O'Malley shook his head and stalked out of the room, as Sapp winked at Bitter and stepped softly out behind him.

The smell of the Cinnabon rose seductively from the bedside table. She ate it all before she went back to sleep, savoring the sweet cinnamon treat one small bite at a time.

The soft stirrings of a hospital at midnight echoed down the hall and through the open door. Somewhere out on the floor, a woman sobbed, quietly and bitterly.

Bitter woke with a start, reaching for a weapon that wasn't there.

"Who's there?" she whispered, still barely able to move.

A nurse bustled into sight. "Just checking your vitals." She busied herself, checking the machines and IV.

"Bathroom?"

The nurse hesitated.

"I'm not using a bedpan. Can you help me get to the bathroom?"

The nurse pressed the call button. "Antonio, can you please come to Ms. Bitter's room? I need your help."

Bitter nodded. "Thank you."

A short, slight man entered. He and the nurse carried on a rapid conversation, and Bitter finally said impatiently, "I have to go to the bathroom. I'm not going to use a bedpan. And I understand what you're saying. I speak Tagalog."

They turned to look at her. The nurse's face darkened in embarrassment.

"Yes, I know, I don't look Filipina. I need to go now." Bitter said in Tagalog.

"I'm sorry. Antonio, please help me get Ms. Bitter into the bathroom."

Dizziness descended upon Bitter as soon as her feet hit the floor. The room spun in a whirl worthy of a carnival ride. The nurse and orderly kept her from falling until the spinning slowed and stopped.

Once in the bathroom, Bitter took a deep breath and reluctantly looked in the mirror. Though the swelling was slowly going down, her face looked like she'd been in a barroom brawl with a three-hundred-pound behemoth that had soundly beaten her with an ugly stick. Dark circles under her eyes, swollen eyelids, and lips that resembled a Botox mistake didn't help her appearance any.

She hissed when she touched the bruise on her cheekbone. It must've happened when she fell on her face in the break room. And her hair was a tangled mess, half out of the braid. *So much for the guarantee on that hair gel.* With fingers that felt like sausages and knees that didn't want to bend, she managed to handle her business and with a little help got back into bed without falling.

The nurse lingered after Antonio left.

"You're Filipina?" she asked curiously, looking at Bitter's hair and face.

Bitter sighed and replied in Tagalog, "Half. Lola married Abuelito and came over to California. A war bride."

"Ah, I see."

"No, you don't," Bitter replied as firmly as her body's weakness allowed. She knew that the nurse was looking at her closely, seeing the warm, dark olive skin and brown, nearly black eyes, tipped up slightly at the corners, and comparing it to the cloud of kinky black hair escaping the braid.

I'm not going to enlighten you, Bitter thought, ornery in her exhaustion. *It's none of your business who the rest of my grandparents were.*

A buzz interrupted the nurse's scrutiny and she dashed off to the next patient, leaving Bitter alone in the room.

Again, sleep weighed down Bitter's eyelids and she slipped into dreams of long-past days when Abuelito bounced her on his knee, and Lola brought them lumpia, adobo, and as a special treat, sweet tres leches flan made Mexican-style—just the way Abuelito's Mamá had taught Lola.

Chapter 3 ~ Wednesday

A voice woke Bitter. It was still dim outside, but doctor's rounds start early. She kept her eyes closed for a few minutes while the rumble of voices sorted themselves out in her sleep-drugged mind until she realized they were in her room.

A gentle hand patted hers, a familiar touch, and she opened her eyes to see a doctor bending over her. He busily scribbled on her chart as a crowd of doctors, interns and medical students stood waiting.

"Ah, Ms. Bitter, I'm sorry to wake you so early, but we rarely have someone with your particular allergies available for the team."

Bitter sighed. *At least it's not the psychiatric team.*

"The hospital psychiatrist, Doctor Kezar, and his team will be by later, although we understand that this time your reaction was to chaga tea and not a hallucinogenic species."

So much for that, she thought bitterly.

He turned to the group, "*Inonotus obliques,* known as the chaga mushroom, is commonly believed to have medicinal value, however, no studies have shown—"

His voice droned on and on. Bitter stopped listening. The sky grew brighter outside the window, but the room felt dark with shadows, although the lights were on. A sudden silence caught Bitter's attention. "I'm sorry? You said something?"

"Yes, I noted on your chart that you're also allergic to penicillin and have seasonal allergies to molds. Do you have problems with cheese? Blue cheese perhaps?"

Bitter glanced at him, distracted by the woman with Lola's face standing on the other side of the bed, opposite from the doctor. "No, not blue cheese."

"You must be careful not to eat blue cheese, gorgonzola, Roquefort, or Stilton cheeses. They all use the penicillin mold in the aging process."

A student tittered when Bitter replied dryly, "Oh, damn."

The doctor lowered his head and peered at her over the top of his trifocals. "Ms. Bitter, you must take this more seriously. You stopped breathing. If it weren't for the quick thinking of Officer," he looked at his notes, "Ummm, here we are, Officer Sapp, who realized that you were having a severe allergic reaction, you would have died."

Bitter took a deep breath and her eyes darkened as she looked at the doctor, boldly meeting his faded blue eyes. A soft touch on her hand reminded her that she wasn't alone with the doctor and his crowd of white-coated followers.

At last, she broke the silent battle, "Feta?"

The doctor's mouth twitched in what almost looked like a smile, "Yes, yes, feta is fine. Just avoid moldy cheeses."

Bitter barely nodded as he turned back to continue his lecture comparing mushroom allergies and her reaction versus the more common peanut allergy patient. When he finally left, his contingent trailing behind him with notepads and pens clenched close to their white coats, Bitter closed her eyes and sighed in relief.

"I thought they'd never leave."

Bitter forced her eyes back open as Sapp pulled up a chair.

"I know you're too tired to talk right now, but when you get better, we need to talk about your neighbor."

"Jean?"

"Is that what they call him?'

Bitter slowly nodded, her eyes drooping.

"I saw him searching around your fence and I smelled him." Sapp frowned. "It's been a long time since I've seen one like that. Don't worry, your cat is safely inside your house, and Jean is locked out of your garden. O'Malley stayed by the gate to keep Jean out and your shadows inside while I fed the cat. They really don't like O'Malley, do they?'

Bitter rolled her eyes, too tired to even speak.

"Yeah, I thought so. I'll check back in after work and let you know how your cat is doing."

This time Bitter's eyes didn't open.

Sapp stood and looked down at her. His frown softened as he looked around the room. "Watch over her," he whispered in Tagalog as he left, closing the door quietly behind him.

Bright silvery light filled the darkened room as the whispers rose and fell with the rhythms of a hospital at night. Bitter lay in a well-lit path, the hospital bed aligned so she faced the full moon's face through the window. She woke slowly, blinking in the moonlight, as the whispers intensified. Suddenly, the curtains whisked closed.

"How did your bed get turned around?" the stocky bleached blonde nurse asked as she pushed it back into position.

Bewildered, Bitter replied, "I don't know. I just woke and the moon was shining in on me."

"Well, I'll fix that." The nurse briskly locked the wheels on the bed. "No roaming for you," she said to the bed as she patted the blanket.

"Bathroom?"

The nurse sighed. "You aren't supposed to get out of bed until tomorrow."

"Bathroom," Bitter repeated firmly.

The nurse just shook her head as she helped Bitter out of bed and shuffle across to the bathroom. "You're just as stubborn as you were the last time," she said as Bitter closed the bathroom door firmly in her face.

Bitter took care of business first before looking at her face and hair. "I'm a mess," she sighed and opened the door. She paused, finally paying attention to the nurse's words.

"The last time?" she asked.

The nurse already had Bitter by the arm, guiding her back to the bed. "Yes, I was here the last time. You were in pretty bad shape." She pursed her lips. "Well, you were in pretty bad shape this time too, but at least you weren't thrashing around screaming about lizards and shadows and crazy stuff about tunnels under the city running with blood."

"Is that what happened?" Bitter said quietly.

"Oh yeah, honey, it was terrible what that man did to you. He definitely was trying to kill you." She looked at Bitter curiously. "You don't remember?"

"No, not really. Sounds like it's probably a good thing."

The nurse nodded, her soft blue eyes sympathetic. "And that awful psychiatrist. We had a terrible time with him. He simply would not get out of the way." She patted Bitter's hand, a familiarity Bitter allowed as the woman kept talking, "But don't you worry honey. I got Doctor Leon and he came right over to tell that man to leave you alone. He ran Doctor Kezar and his colleagues right out before he managed to wake you up. We weren't having it this time. They could wait until you were awake." She lowered her voice, "That pack of ghouls were hovering over you like you were going to die, and they'd be glad for it."

"Really?" Bitter's curiosity rose. "And why is he so eager to see me this time? I wasn't hallucinating."

"That's exactly what Doctor Leon asked him. He didn't answer, just muttered something about following up on your condition and walked away."

The nurse bustled about, taking Bitter's vitals and noting them on the chart. "I'm sorry we keep waking you in the night, but Doctor Leon is crazy strict about vitals. Especially after using an EpiPen, it can make your blood pressure shoot sky high."

The room grew silent, and a low sobbing echoed down the hall.

"It's okay," Bitter finally said, breaking the silence, "but who's crying? I heard her last night too."

The nurse straightened with a jerk and turned toward Bitter. "Crying?" she asked. "There's no one crying."

"But," Bitter stopped abruptly.

The nurse eyed her and glanced toward the door. "There's no one crying. Do you hear someone crying?"

Bitter didn't reply.

Looking nervously out the door, the nurse closed it and turned back to Bitter. "You aren't the first patient to tell me that someone's crying. But I don't hear anything." She shook her head slowly. "I never hear anything. Just the patients snoring and the custodial staff when they start cleaning early in the morning."

"Are you the only one here at night?"

"No, there's usually another nurse and several orderlies, but Rosie was called away to another floor just a little while ago. They needed someone who spoke Tagalog to help with one of the geriatric cases upstairs."

"Does the other nurse hear someone crying?"

The nurse looked at the door again, not noticing the shadows leaning in from the corners, listening closely to the conversation. Bitter ignored them. *They're just shadows.*

"I think so. She nearly always has music playing at the nursing station. She says it's to keep her company at night. But if a patient buzzes for a nurse, she makes one of the orderlies go with her to the room. Especially if the room is near the emergency exit."

"I see. And she always takes an orderly?" Bitter asked.

"Yes, usually it's Antonio."

Bitter nodded slowly.

Looking down at Bitter's pensive face, the nurse smiled gently. "Don't worry, I won't mention it to the psychiatrist."

"Good," Bitter said, "I don't think he can do anything to fix it, anyway."

A phone rang at the nursing station and the nurse dashed out of the room to answer it.

Someone's crying, and no one can hear her? Bitter's thoughts drifted as her eyes closed and she slipped back into sleep.

Chapter 4 ~ Thursday

Morning light splashed onto the walls around the edges of the curtains when Bitter woke and stretched.

"Ah, and a beautiful morning it is," said O'Malley.

"What are you doing here?" Bitter asked grumpily. Tired of being in bed and tired of being tired, she wasn't in the mood to hear a cheerful Irish lilt.

"They're letting you get up today, so Sapp here brought you some things from your house."

Bitter opened her mouth and then saw her pajamas, robe, slippers, toothbrush, and the book from her nightstand in a clear tote bag. Grudgingly, she cracked a smile. "Thank you."

"I hope you don't mind, but we took your car home last night. O'Malley didn't think we should leave it out in the parking lot. I locked it in the garage. One of us will pick you up when you're discharged."

"He was right. Thank you."

Sapp grinned. "Yeah, and my sister is coming by later to do your hair."

Her smile disappeared.

Sapp didn't flinch. "Don't even try to say no, Bitter, I knew you'd be mad. But if you saw your hair—"

She muttered ungratefully, "I've seen it."

"Well, she'll be by in a while to fix it for you, so don't tire yourself trying to get it back to normal. And no worries, she knows how to do our hair." Quickly, he changed the subject before her glowering frown became a storm, "Oh, and your cat is fine too. I took care of the litter box and made sure all the windows were still locked before I left. You're getting low on cat food, so I picked some up already. I checked the brand and don't worry about it."

He rushed along before Bitter could interrupt him, "So, gotta go. O'Malley needs to get to his sensitivity training."

O'Malley's smile vanished.

Before Bitter could speak, both disappeared down the hall. If she didn't know better, she'd think they were fleeing.

The lukewarm water sluiced down Bitter's swollen skin, relieving the itchy hives that still covered most of her body. She reveled in the water, soaping up with the vanilla verbena body wash that she'd found in the bag with her clothes. Finally, rinsed and clean, she shut the water off and slowly patted herself dry. Long experience had taught her that briskly rubbing an outbreak of hives meant hours of misery. Sapp hadn't brought any shampoo, so she untangled the remnants of her braid and finger-combed her hair.

She frowned as she slipped into her favorite black satin pajamas, wrapped herself in the oversized robe, and wiggled her feet into her slippers. *He has nerve,* she thought, *to ask his sister to come and do my hair.* She shuffled back into the room and sat with a sigh in the chair, conveniently positioned in front of the window. Her book lay on the table. She frowned again. *Didn't I leave my book on the bed?*

She shrugged. This room was as busy as a Bay Area freeway during rush hour. One of the orderlies had probably moved it while she showered. The bed was freshly made, so someone had been in here.

Settled in with her book, her feet propped up on the second chair, Bitter slipped back into the world of Bram Stoker. She only read a few pages before a visitor intruded.

"Gurrrl, look at you," the cheerful young woman purred as she carried in a tote and plopped it on the table. Tipping her head, she eyed Bitter's tangled mass of damp curls. "Yep, bro was right. I've got some work to do here. I can't believe no one did your hair for you."

Bitter tried to scowl, but the sister's unrelenting smile disarmed her.

"So, I'm Gema."

"Everyone just calls me Bitter."

Gema gave her a quick glance. "Okay, then. Now Jasir said you normally wear your hair in a bun for work, but right now I think it'd be easier to put it in two braids. Just until you get home. What do you think?"

Bitter hesitated. She hadn't worn her hair in two braids since she was twelve.

Gema shook her head, the gold beads clicking in her mane of long black braids as they swung freely down her back. "It'll just be for a couple of days," she said persuasively, "and they'll be easy to keep tight so when you get home you can take them out and fix your hair yourself."

Bitter sighed and nodded.

Gema wasted no time in pulling the chair away from the window and whipping a towel around Bitter's shoulders. Her hands were gentle as she set to work conditioning and teasing the tangles out. "Gurrrl, you have good hair. You should see what they do to mine when it's time to redo these braids."

Bitter flinched.

"Oh, sorry. You're tender-headed, aren't you? Bet you never let anyone do your hair." Gema laughed quietly as she smoothed and whipped the first braid into place, her practiced fingers flying down the long strands. "It's longer than I expected." With one side completed, she stood back and surveyed her work.

"Excuse me," Gema said as she dodged past a shadow, "you can look from the other side. You're in the way."

Bitter stiffened.

"Dang girl, you must have hecka family, as many as follow you around."

"I don't know what you're talking about."

Gema stopped and put her hands on her hips. "Now, don't tell me that you can't see them. They practically fill the room."

"No," Bitter said firmly, in a voice that didn't allow more questions, "no I don't see anyone here except you and the nurse that looks like Lola, my grandmother. I don't know her name. I can't see her nametag."

Gema looked at her doubtfully. "But you see Lola?"

"No, the nurse that looks like Lola."

Gema sighed, "Whatever you say, Bitter. Just trust me, they're here, and there's a lot of them. More than there should be." She paused and looked around again. "Way more than there should be."

"I don't see anyone else in this room," Bitter repeated testily. She looked around the room. The nurse was gone. It worried her that she didn't see the woman. "I didn't see the nurse leave."

"Don't worry about it, Bitter," Gema said gently, "she'll be back when you need her."

When Gema finally finished, she pulled out a hand mirror. "Whatcha think?"

The cloud of kinky curls was tamed and sleekly braided, lying flat and neat over Bitter's shoulders, emphasizing her high cheekbones and large dark eyes. "It looks fine," Bitter said.

Gema hesitated, "Can I ask you a personal question?"

Bitter looked at her warily. "Depends…"

"Are you Native American? You have that look."

Bitter didn't speak.

"Well, I was just wondering," she went on cheerfully, not letting Bitter's dark mood stop her. "We're Gullah and Louisiana Creole. Mostly."

"Really?" Caught off guard and despite her determination to never share any personal information, Bitter found herself relaxing with this friendly young woman. "I'm Creole too."

"Creole?" Gema said, surprised, "I thought Jasir said you were Filipina."

Bitter shot her a questioning look. *How would he know?* "Half. Mamá was Choctaw, Roma, Louisiana Creole, and half Filipina, and Papá was Mexican, mostly indigenous, and half Filipino. I'm a registered member of the Choctaw Nation." She paused, then continued, "I identify as a Choctaw citizen first, then Filipina, Black, and Latinx, mostly."

"Oh, so your Mamá was Choctaw? And your Papá was Mexican?"

Unlike most who questioned Bitter's ethnicity, Gema's questions felt genuinely curious, so Bitter settled in to share a little history lesson. "Mexican is a nationality, not a race. Papá's *familia* was mostly Mixtec and Mayan with a splash of Spanish blood. Maybe a little Basque mixed in too, along with the Miwok and Maidu, after they came north to the valley. It's hard to say."

She paused. "My sister-in-law is into genealogy. She has records going back to old Mexico and Spain—or so she says." Bitter shrugged and winced with pain. "Of course, she also thinks she's Cherokee even though her family is from Illinois and New York, and before that England, Ireland, and Germany—and she glows in the dark."

Gema cringed sympathetically.

Bitter paused again, considering her words before she continued. "To be fair, she loves my brother with all her heart, and he tolerates her delusions. Skin color isn't really relevant anyway, citizens of the Cherokee and Choctaw Nations come in all colors. Though our high-blood Choctaw citizens tend to be darker complected than the Cherokee. Maybe that's why everybody and his cousin thinks they're Cherokee."

She finished with a swirl of sarcasm in her voice and a sweeping motion toward her own face and kinky hair, "Can't be too dark you know, somebody might think that you're Black or something."

Gema gave Bitter a wry smile and a nod at her facetious tone.

Bitter took a deep breath to center herself, a bit surprised at how angry the thought of those pretending to be Natives made her, and continued, "We do know that Papá's family has been here since before the Gold Rush. His *ancestra* arrived with the Spanish in the late 1700s, but not by choice. Her," she paused, "Ummm, I guess husband is good enough. He was Spanish. He was a hard man and there were few women, so he did what men do—" her voice trailed away in her reluctance to continue.

"Oh, I understand. You don't have to explain any further. Our Gullah ancestors worked in the rice plantations in the Low Country. And Creole, well, you probably know more about the Creole than I do. We survived and we are still here," Gema smiled, "and so are you. But now I see where you got your beautiful coloring."

Despite herself, Bitter blushed.

"And why my bro was talking about you."

Bitter's hot flash of anger showed in her voice, "Sapp was talking about me?"

"No, no, don't take that wrong. He just mentioned that one of the homicide detectives—that's you—was in the hospital and asked me to come by and fix your hair He said you're a proud woman and would be embarrassed for any of your coworkers to see you with a hair out of place. That's all."

Bitter forced herself to relax, releasing her anger. "All right, as long as he's not going around talking about me."

"Bitter, it's not my place to say this, but you need to get out more. Meet some nice people for a change."

Bitter lowered her chin and gave Gema a dark look.

"Okay, okay, girlfriend, I'll mind my business. Jasir says I talk too much anyway," Gema called over her shoulder as she washed her hands in the bathroom.

She picked up the hair products, gel, picks, and combs quickly, glancing at the clock on the wall. "Gotta run, time to go to work." She paused, and then dug in her purse. Pressing a business card into Bitter's hand, she said, "Call me if you want your hair done or need to go get a drink. Lord knows I need to escape my teens some nights. We could go to this little place downtown—no driving—and the appetizers and music are to die for!"

She lofted the tote and said, "Excuse me," to a shadow that crossed her path. In Tagalog.

Before Bitter could control her surprise and ask the questions that suddenly crowded into her thoughts, Gema was gone.

Bitter looked at the card in her hand and blinked. It read *Gema Sapp, Attorney at Law* with a downtown address near the courthouse.

Night slipped into the room slowly, the golden glow of sunset fading to the blues and purples of night, lit here and there in neat rows by yellow halogen streetlights. Bitter picked at the pot roast, green beans, and salad. It tasted all right, but a little bland. A single packet of ranch dressing lay untouched on the tray. *No blue cheese,* she sighed. *Tomorrow I get to go home. Finally. I am so tired of this place.* Her thoughts returned to the sobbing in the hall. *Tonight, I'm going to find out who's crying,* she resolved.

The shadows crept closer, sweeping in a dark mist between Bitter and the half-open door into the hospital corridor.

Bitter looked up and down the hall. The dimmed lights didn't prevent her from seeing the Filipina nurse and orderly rushing into the room at the far end of the hall. *Good,* she thought, *I won't have to worry about them for a minute.* She'd heard the patient come in, screaming and out of his head, just after they'd taken her vitals at midnight. He'd finally quieted down a little, though now his low moans echoed down the hall. She padded toward the rooms closest to the emergency exit. She'd thought about getting dressed but she didn't have her street clothes and it seemed less suspicious to be wandering the hospital halls in her pajamas and robe. She could always say that she couldn't sleep.

It wouldn't be far from the truth.

Bitter stopped in front of the exit door and listened, holding her breath. *No sobbing. That figures.*

Irritated, she cracked open the fire door, looking down the staircase and then up. She didn't let go of the door. Sometimes emergency exit doors don't open from inside. She didn't feel like walking all the way down to the lobby and then taking the elevator back up to her room. Her swollen knees twinged painfully at the thought of several flights of stairs.

Thoughtfully, Bitter stepped back and carefully closed the door to prevent it from banging against the frame. She paused and listened again, ignoring the shadows that followed her down the hall, slipping from darkened doorway to doorway, avoiding the dim lights overhead.

"What are you doing out here?"

Bitter swung around, reacting swiftly to the threatening tone in the familiar voice.

"I'm walking in the hall, stretching my legs. What are you doing here in the middle of the night?" she demanded.

The psychiatrist stepped back, raising his palms to each side. "Just checking on my patients."

"I am not your patient, Doctor Kezar," Bitter snarled. She clenched her fists inside the depths of her robe as he smirked down at her, his eyes icy cold in his fish-belly pale face, a stark contrast to his thinning black hair, mustache, and wiry beard.

"Really, Bitter? Are you sure?"

Forcing herself into a semblance of calm, she took a deep breath and stepped forward, forcing him back another step. "Yes, I'm quite sure that you're overstepping your authority."

He smirked again, and Bitter clamped down on her temper. Now was not the time to have a confrontation with the psychiatrist. He could keep her in the hospital longer. Home and her own bed called for her.

A movement behind him caught her attention. She smiled.

"Doctor Kezar, what are you doing on this floor? You have no patients here." The nurse's accent grew stronger as she bustled forward.

"Yes, Doctor," Bitter's dark tone made the title a slur, "I haven't been your patient for eleven years and I'm not starting now."

The nurse stepped between them, breaking the standoff, and forcing the doctor to step back yet again. "Ms. Bitter, are you, all right? Why are you in the hall?" She continued in Tagalog, "Come back to your room where you're safe."

A second nurse, the one that looked like Lola, took Bitter's other arm as they brushed past the psychiatrist. Antonio stepped in behind the trio and kept the doctor from following Bitter and her escort back to her room, his slight body a barrier to the taller man.

For a moment, Bitter thought she heard a hiss. *Was that Antonio?* But the air conditioning clicked on and the sound of the fan covered the small noises that the orderly made as he moved to block Doctor Kezar.

"Bitter, you must sleep. You don't want Doctor Leon keeping you here because you've fallen, or your vitals aren't good."

Bitter didn't argue. She felt the psychiatrist's eyes boring through her back. *What does he want? Why is he haunting me?*

The nurses had her back into bed before she could protest. It wasn't until the door closed and she heard a chair bump against the wall that she realized that Antonio was standing guard outside her room for the rest of his shift.

The nurse with Lola 's face sat in the side chair and put her feet up, fading back into the shadows that surrounded the bed. "I will also watch."

Despite her rage at her weakness, Bitter's eyes closed as she fought and lost the battle against sleep.

"Do not worry, I will watch."

Chapter 5 ~ Friday

Slowly, one step at a time, Bitter climbed the stairs to the porch. She grimaced in pain as a stabbing pain shot through her knee. Gema, hovering at her elbow, pretended to not notice.

It was already noon. Despite Doctor Leon's prompt release that morning, it still took time for Sapp and Gema to find Bitter's clothes and check her out of the hospital. They made two trips for the flowers and potted plants that filled a corner of the room. And then Bitter insisted on going to the station to pick up her carry gun.

Bitter grimaced again at the thought of the station. Luckily, Candy wasn't assigned to the main building, so she didn't have to listen to any sniveling excuses, though her fellow officers offered handshakes and, in a few cases, hugs. The emotional response surprised her. She never fit into the good old boy network that once filled the department. She didn't think she had any friendly coworkers, let alone friends among the detectives and blues.

Times really have changed, she thought, *maybe for the better.*

The screen door slammed open just as she reached the porch.

"MOM!"

Sapp and Gema stepped back and down a step, as the tall young man leaped forward and gathered Bitter up in his arms. He bent his head over her, the tightly trimmed black curls matching hers, as he hid the sudden glistening in his eyes.

"Mom, thank God. I got the word yesterday morning and it's been two hops, Amtrak, and a taxi to get home. And you weren't here." He paused, looking sharply at the siblings and back down at Bitter. "Who are these people and what are they doing here?"

"Easy, easy, son. I'm fine." Bitter's muffled voice emerged from the protective bear hug.

"No, no, you're not. You damn near died this time."

Bitter pushed him back and glared up at her youngest son. "I said I'm fine."

His exasperated sigh disputed her words.

Sapp grinned and stepped up onto the porch. "Nice to see you again, José. How's life treating you?"

Gema gave Sapp a quick side-eye in surprise.

"Wait," snapped Bitter. "How do you know my son?"

Sapp laughed as he stepped forward and thrust out his hand. "Air Force. I was his first shirt at Minot."

"Holy shit, it is you!" José took Sapp's hand, stepped closer, and slapped him heartily on the back. "How are you doing? How's retired life treating you?"

"Well, it's been interesting."

"And who is this beautiful lady with you?"

"Don't think it, dude, she's my sister."

Bitter and Gema exchanged looks, and Gema rolled her eyes expressively.

"Why not Minot?"

"Freezin's the reason."

Laughing, the two men fist-bumped before José turned back toward Bitter. "Mom, of all people I'd find helping you up these steps."

"Son, why are you here? You're using up your leave time."

José sobered as he interrupted her, "Mom, let's go inside. You're not all right, you damn near died, and if O'Malley hadn't emailed me, I still wouldn't know that you were in the hospital."

Bitter opened her mouth, but José carried on angrily, "And don't tell me that I didn't need to know." His voice softened, "I haven't forgotten about Sal, Mom. Sometimes even strong women like you need a little help," he lifted both hands at her glare, "but just for a minute. I know!"

A cell phone rang.

Sapp jerked his phone out of his pocket. "Sapp."

He frowned. "Yes, we left about eleven-thirty. No, we were never apart at the station. Well, except when Bitter went to the restroom while I was talking to O'Malley, but my sister was right there. Why?"

He hesitated and looked at Bitter. She swayed a little, so he waved for José to take her inside. She jerked away when José gently took her arm. "Come on Mom, he'll tell us inside."

Bitter gave him a look, so he wrapped an arm around her shoulders instead.

"No! Seriously? When?"

Gema raised her eyebrows, but he waved her to silence.

"No, she's barely out of the hospital. I'm not bringing her back to the station. You can come here if you need to interview her or it can wait until tomorrow." He paused. "We're at her house right now. We can wait." He turned off the phone.

Vibrating with impatience, Bitter demanded, "What?"

Sapp closed his eyes and shook his head. "They found Candy."

Bitter frowned.

"Candy, the blonde that poisoned you. She was found dead in the stairwell. Blood everywhere. Coroner's on the way now."

"And?"

"Tom, you know Tom, the janitor, he found her right after we left the station."

"And?" Bitter demanded.

"Well, they want to talk to us."

Bitter's frown deepened. "Why? We weren't anywhere near the stairs. There are cameras. They can see that."

Sapp sighed, "That's the weird thing, all the cameras were borked. Nothing but static."

Bitter turned to go back down the steps.

"Where are you going, Mom?"

"Back to the station. Where else would I be going?" She barked. "It's a homicide."

Sapp looked at Gema and shrugged. He pulled his phone out and dialed the station.

"Just a minute, Bitter," Gema said, "I have to change."

Puzzled, Bitter stopped to look at Gema. "Why do you have to change?"

"Jasir, my extra suit is in the car, could you get it?" she said firmly before turning to Bitter. "You aren't going back there without a lawyer. And I'm certainly not going in skinny jeans and a tank top. It's," she took a deep breath, "it's unprofessional."

Bitter paused and nodded somberly. "José, take the cat in the house. Please stay here."

"Mom, you are not—"

"Yes, I am. And I need you to stay here. Someone needs to watch the house. Get the shotgun from the gun safe, you might need it. Be careful. It's loaded with steel buckshot. The silver loads are in the boxes on the left. They're marked with an S. Rock salt loads are marked with an R. Check all the doors and windows, especially the basement door. Make sure it's locked and the bolt is on. Don't let anyone in, even if you know them. And don't let Gato out."

"Don't let the cat out?"

"Jean has been trying to catch Gato for weeks. I don't know what he does with the cats but he's not taking Gato."

José shook his head, muttering, as he scooped up the fat old cat. Only Sapp was close enough to hear him after he kissed Bitter on the cheek and started into the house, "Jean died years ago. Why is he hanging around now? And why does he want Gato?"

The lingering shadows slipped inside after José, disappearing in the gloom of the old bungalow.

Bitter labored up the steps of the station, just ahead of the media pack crowding the sidewalk. Sapp had dropped them off at the corner and then pulled around the station to park in the large lot on the other side, pulling the reporters' eyes away from Bitter and Gema. They would've tried for the back door of the building, but the reporters were hovering in the parking lot. Bitter had to sign Gema into the building anyway, so they made a dash for the lobby, past the blues fending off reporters and cameramen.

"How did they find out already?" she muttered to Gema.

Gema rolled her eyes. "There's always somebody who knows somebody." She sighed, "Makes my job harder. Sometimes they muddy the case so much that I don't have anything to work with. And then the media frenzy contaminates the jury." She shook her head as a flash highlighted the gold beads interspersed through her braids.

"Oh damn. They got a picture of us."

Gema grinned, "Just our booties going up the steps. Could be worse."

"True that," Bitter said grimly.

The lobby was empty, unusual since there were always people filing reports or waiting to speak to a detective in an ongoing investigation. Bitter looked around the room before sliding her key card across the sensor.

"In here, quick, before the reporters overpower the guys outside and swarm in." The rookie at the desk looked Gema up and down, noting the expensive suit, silk scarf, and briefcase. "Lawyer?"

Bitter nodded.

"All right, let's get you a visitor's badge so you can go with Bitter down to the interview rooms. O'Malley is already there, so it might be a while. Things are a little crazy today." He hesitated, "I don't have to tell you not to cross the yellow tape."

Bitter gave him a scorching look and he quickly looked down, avoiding her glare. Bitter and Gema exchanged a glance before Bitter shrugged and led the way down the hall.

The battered hall, painted in standard institutional blue, led them to a waiting area. Yellow tape closed off the hall past the chairs. An officer had dragged a chair over and was sitting just inside the blocked off area, sipping from a chipped mug and watching everyone in the waiting area. Bitter noted that he was a blue from West Sac, over the river. After a quick nod to acknowledge his presence, she ignored him.

Sapp was dozing, slouched in one of the uncomfortable chairs with his feet up on an end table. He opened one eye, nodded, and closed it again. Cops who work nights take their sleep where they can get it, even in ancient waiting room chairs.

"I see they've touched up the paint since the last time I was here," Gema said, looking around the room. "Fixed that hole in the wall too." Her lips twitched in an amused smile. "That was one of my clients. Lucky he missed me."

Sapp drawled, eyes still closed, "Didn't help his case any."

Gema gave her brother a look that would've intimidated any juvenile delinquent. Not that he noticed with his eyes closed. "No, it didn't, but not because I didn't do my job. He didn't listen to me, his lawyer, so off he went, back 'home' again. Of course, trying to attack the judge in court didn't do his case any good either. There's only so much I can do for determinedly dense clients."

Bitter sat down across from Sapp and yawned, covering her mouth neatly with one hand, her eyes heavy. She shook her head grumpily to knock away the cobwebs threatening to overwhelm her. She looked around the room, trying to stay awake, but there was nothing new to see. It was still the same dingy waiting area. Except this time, she was the one waiting for interrogation. Despite herself, her eyes closed.

"Whooo, that was a close one!"

Bitter heard Sapp, but it took a few minutes for her consciousness to swim back up from a comforting dream that she didn't want to leave, with Papá and Mamá hugging her under a warm summer sun.

She reluctantly opened her eyes. She felt as tired as she had at the hospital, with a stiff neck and knees complaining about steps and a long day. Gema was talking to Captain Morales, taking notes and motioning toward the stairwell at the far end of the hall.

He saw Bitter's eyes open and strode over to her, waving Gema off impatiently.

"We need to test your carry gun."

Bitter stood, painfully, and glared up at him. "Why?"

"Candy was killed with a .32."

"And?"

He frowned unhappily before he replied, "We think she was killed with your weapon early this morning. Most of the officers carry 9mm pistols. A couple of the younger guys carry Glock .45s. We know you carry a Glock 30S .45 for work and a Walther PPK/S .32 when you're off. You weren't on duty when you came to the potluck, so you were carrying the .32 that day, right?"

Shocked, Bitter stared at him, and then looked at Gema behind him, motioning and mouthing, "Give it to him."

"I was still in the hospital when Candy was killed. And I picked up the Walther from Property."

"Yes, yes, we know. But we need to know which gun killed her." He shook his head. "We know yours was in the building. And as far as we know, you're the only member of the department that carries a .32 regularly, either on or off work."

Bitter looked at him for a long minute before she pulled the Walther from its holster. Her eyes never left the Captain's. "Don't misplace it, Papá's carry gun is my favorite."

When Morales broke eye contact, she looked back down the hall, toward the emergency stairs. She'd never noticed it was so dark inside the building before. Shadows filled every corner.

The bungalow was dark as Bitter slowly limped up the steps. Shadows flowed around her, but never in front, where they'd block her view of the house. She paused and sighed, *Maybe I should've let Sapp help me up the steps.* She shook her head slightly. No, she could make it on her own. *I don't need help.*

Bitter unlocked and opened the door slowly, flicking the light switch on and glancing into the living room quickly. She frowned. *Where is my son?* All was quiet, except a soft flow of jazz streaming from the back of the house.

She put the bucket of fried chicken on the kitchen table before she went out onto the back porch.

The steep little back steps strained her knees, but the rail was sturdy. Light spilled from between the narrow strips of the lath house and the music grew louder as she carefully stepped down the last two steps. The door stood slightly open, so Bitter peeked in. José sat on Papá's old wooden chair with his back to the door, in the middle of the orchids, gently touching an arching spray of orange and red brilliance.

"Son?" said Bitter gently.

José leaped up. "Mom, damn, you startled me. Don't sneak up on me like that."

She grinned, amused at her son's reaction. No one but her boys ever saw that smile. "Son, what are you doing down here in the middle of the night?"

"Thinking. Talking to grandpa and Lola. Looking at grandpa's orchids." He gently touched the delicate blossoms. "This one is new. Where did you find it?"

Bitter shivered a little in the chilly humidity of the lath house, "Oh, that's a Masdevallia. It's a cloud orchid from South America. There's a little nursery up on the coast, in Elk that sells salvias and orchids online." She put her hand on José's shoulder. "Papá would've loved this one. It's very rare." She grimaced a little. "And hard to grow. I had to adjust the automatic sprinklers and install a swamp cooler, so it doesn't get too hot in here."

José put his hand over Bitter's. "I've also been wondering why you've installed metal mesh over the entire interior of the lath house and hardware cloth over the floor. And added a padlock." His voice grew sharper, "Is there something going on here, Mom? Do I need to come home for a while?"

Bitter paused, considering what she wanted to tell her youngest—and what he'd accept as truth.

"Is it Sal? Has he come back to bother you?"

She gave a short, snorting laugh.

"No, the Coroner told me last winter that Sal died ten years ago."

José looked down at her, and she recognized that look. She bridled and then relaxed. *The apple doesn't fall far from the tree*, she thought, *I can't be mad at him for being just like me.*

"Seriously, son, he was murdered by a rival drug gang and thrown into the river."

"Are you sure?" he asked suspiciously.

"Well, the Coroner is sure." Then honesty forced her to tell the rest, "I'm not sure though. I mean, I'm not sure his death was ten years ago."

José's eyes narrowed. "Ok, then tell me."

"Inside." Bitter turned off the lights in the lath house and looked around the moonlit garden. A black shadow obscured the silver light for a moment. *It's just an owl.* She snapped the lock closed. "Inside, I don't want anyone to overhear."

Bitter sat back in the recliner, waiting for José's reaction. The tale of a headless man sounded even stranger now, safe in her cozy bungalow. Of course, she skipped over the part about a giant salamander. José didn't need any reminders of Sal's habits.

Her son's steady regard caught her attention, dragging her back from dark thoughts of the past.

He sighed, "Okay Mom, now tell me the rest of the story."

Steadily, she looked at him. "There is no rest of the story."

"Oh, please Mom, you think I don't know that look? You never were going to tell me the whole story about Sal, but I have a right to know. Remember, I was here too, me and Roberto and Nana, when they rushed you to the hospital." He leaped to his feet and began pacing around the small room. Bitter drew her feet back, out of his path.

"Nana locked the door and wouldn't let him back in the house after the ambulance left. Luckily, O'Malley answered the 9-1-1 call. He told Sal to leave and never come back. And then Sal just disappeared, while you were still in the hospital," he hesitated and plowed on, "raving about monsters in the underground city."

Bitter shrugged.

"Mom, don't be so ornery."

She tightened her lips and looked darkly at her son.

José flopped onto the sofa. "Okay, okay, I get the message. So, if you won't talk about Sal, what's going on with Jean and the cat?"

Bitter glanced around the room. "Where is Gato?"

José grinned. "I locked him in my bedroom. Otherwise, he'd be out the door and hunting for mice outside. You know how he is."

"Well, I don't know what's going on with Jean, but he's been catching the neighborhood cats. I don't know what he does with them. He keeps insisting that Gato is his cat."

"Hmmm, maybe the old woman is using them."

Bitter frowned. "Using them for what?"

"Oh Mom, surely you know she's a *bruja*?

"A witch? Son, who told you that? Abuelita?" Bitter's sharp disbelief showed in her voice.

"And Lola too. She warned me to never go near the old woman's house. She told me to stay away from Jean because he can only do what the *bruja* tells him to do."

Bitter shook her head.

José sat up and leaned forward earnestly. "Mom, how long has that woman lived there? And how long has Jean looked like that?"

"As long as I can remember," Bitter admitted reluctantly.

"See," said José triumphantly, "If she's not a *bruja*, she's something *other*. I don't know what, but Mom, don't go over there alone. Please."

Bitter shrugged. "As long as he stays off my property and leaves my cat alone, I have no need to go down there. Although," she said thoughtfully, "Jean is getting pretty rank. I was thinking that I should ask Dispatch to send someone out to do a welfare check on the old woman. For all I know, she's dead. I haven't seen her in a long time."

José huffed, "Tell them to send at least two officers. Don't go in there alone. You need backup."

"Son," Bitter cautioned.

"Okay Mom, I know that you know your business." He held both hands up. "I'm not trying to tell you what to do."

Bitter yawned as the clock struck midnight. She couldn't keep her eyes open much longer.

Shadows scattered as she rose. "Goodnight son. Your bed is all made up, but it might be a little dusty in your room. Just put your plate in the sink, I'll wash up the dishes in the morning."

"No worries, Mom. I'm going to sit up for a while longer."

She leaned over and kissed him on the forehead. Slowly she limped down the hall to her bedroom, while shadows trailed behind.

Chapter 6 ~ Saturday

Bitter sat at the kitchen table watching the morning news updates, steam rising from her coffee cup. She slowly sipped it as she watched the media frenzy in front of the station's stairs. She'd forgotten her hair was still in braids when she and Gema went into the station, but the media had no trouble identifying her—and her lawyer. The earnest face of the reporter stayed somber as she pointed out that Bitter had been in the hospital for several days, for reasons unknown, but there was a rumor that the deceased was a factor in the hospitalization. The cameras zoomed in on Bitter's profile, catching a good shot of the bruise on her face and the lingering dark circles under her eyes when she turned her head to speak to Gema.

Impatiently, Bitter clicked the remote and turned the TV off. *Nothing new, just more speculation.*

Overhead, she heard thumping and bumping from José's room. He was in the closet, judging by the sounds, searching for something. She turned the TV back on, checked the date and time, and sighed as she got up and limped to the stairs.

"It's in the downstairs closet, under the stairs," she shouted up the narrow stairwell.

José clattered down the steps, kissing her on the cheek. "You're the best!"

He pulled the hockey bag out and started searching through it. Bitter shook her head.

"Son, it's all freshly washed. Do you want your roller blades or ice skates?"

"Ice."

"Look on the shelf to your right, inside the closet. The sticks are on the left."

She went into her bedroom and pulled out a sweatshirt, a heavy jacket, and a blanket. Without her .32, she felt naked. She thought for a moment, then went to the gun safe in the hall closet. *The Sig Sauer P320 will have to do.* She sighed sadly. *I'm not taking any of Papá's pistols.* After she loaded the 9mm, she slipped it into the holster in the small of her back.

"Okay, I'm ready."

José looked up from his gear and smiled eagerly. "Stick time starts at noon, so we have time to get to the rink in Roseville. Lunch afterward?"

"Only if you shower. And no fast food." Bitter stepped into the bathroom and pulled out the heavy-duty shower gel, specially formulated for athletes. "Here's your stink-off. Let me get you a fresh towel." She tossed the bottle to him.

He snatched it out of the air and laughed.

The summer morning was already sizzling, waves of heat rising from the tumbled brick walk, as José carried his gear into the cool darkness of the garage. The misters in the lath house were already cycling on and off, keeping the humidity high in the enclosed space.

He looked to the left as he loaded the hockey gear into the open trunk of the vintage Maverick Grabber. "Not the Dart?"

"No, the a/c works in the Maverick and she gets better gas mileage." Bitter patted the bright apple green paint. "She still runs great."

José said, "And you'll park a mile away from the rink, so nobody dinks her."

Bitter limped painfully around to the driver's side as José opened the garage door into the alley. "Well, maybe not today. I'm still a little tired."

The little inline-six engine purred.

"Lock the garage."

José sighed, "All right, Mom." He paused, "Let me drive?"

Bitter turned her head slowly and gave him a look before pulling out into the narrow alley.

The little diner was nearly full, packed with parents and hockey players. Bitter impatiently adjusted the roll-down blinds to block out the slanting afternoon sun. Its heat radiated through the window, overwhelming the air conditioning.

"Drinks?" asked the waitress, her face pink and damp with sweat. A loose hair straggled from her tightly twisted bun.

"Strawberry lemonade, please."

"Make that two," said Sapp as he sat down. Gema squeezed in next to José, and several teens that looked suspiciously like Gema parked in the next booth over. Now that they were out of their hockey gear, Bitter could see the family resemblance, though one was fair, one medium-complected, and the other two sported tight black curls and rich complexions that matched their uncle's.

"I didn't know you played hockey," Bitter said.

"Oh, at why-not-Minot, there's not a lot to do, so I took up ice skating," Sapp paused to smirk at Gema, "and then moved on to ice hockey. A manly sport."

José burst out laughing.

"Don't let him kid you, Mom. He kept falling over the toe picks."

Sapp shrugged. "They don't have toe picks on inline skates. It was easier to learn to play hockey on ice than to deal with toe picks."

He glanced sideways at Bitter. "Ready to go back to work?"

"The doctor will probably release me for duty on Monday. So, after I take José down to Travis Air Force Base at o-dark-thirty and then see Doctor Leon at nine, I'll check in with the Captain."

Sapp looked at José. "Catching a hop back?"

"Yeah, the first shirt, he wants me back ASAP. Have some new airmen, just out of training, and he said they're my responsibility."

Sapp snickered, "Really? They trust you with new troops now?"

José gave him a look that Bitter recognized. She managed to keep a smile off her lips as she changed the subject. "So Gema, how long have your kids been playing hockey?"

"Ever since their favorite uncle sent them a picture of him in full gear," she sighed. "There was no stopping them once they discovered hockey. It's been about eight years now, every weekend either at the rink or off to a tournament." A loud laugh echoed behind them. "Knock it off," Gema said over her shoulder to the tallest boy, "we all saw your sister block that slapshot, so don't even go there."

Sapp chuckled, "Gema, I never would've thought your girlie-girl would become a goalie."

"And a fine goalie she is, too," José bantered, "Tasha blocked shots I never would've thought she'd been able to reach."

"Blocked your shots too," bragged Gema's youngest child, and only girl, before she turned back to harass her brothers again. The beads in her braids clicked together as she gave the boys a triumphant head dip and shoulder shake.

"Hey Bitter," Sapp caught her eye, "What's the deal with the Walther? It's a bit unusual for a cop to carry a .32. Most of us carry a 9mm or the ever-popular and very manly .45."

José burst into laughter.

"Oh," Bitter looked at her son sternly, but he kept snickering as she continued. "Papá was a fan of Ian Fleming."

Sapp raised his eyebrows. "Who?"

"James Bond." She smiled as realization dawned on Sapp's face. "He started watching the movies when they were released on VHS. His favorite was the first movie, 'Doctor No.' It was when 007 gave up his Beretta for the PPK." She shrugged. "He loved that scene."

"'This damned Beretta again,'" interrupted José, quoting from the movie, "and then M told Q to give Bond the Walther. It was great. Grandpa laughed every time he watched that part of the movie."

Bitter continued, "So he bought a Walther PPK/S as his personal carry gun."

"Ahhh," said Sapp. "It was a good choice. The Walther is a sweet little pistol. I tried one at the range at Minot, but the P99 had a little more oomph."

"He liked the P99 too," José said. "What Mom didn't tell you is that she doesn't like the Bond movies. I remember she told Grandpa that Bond was a sexist pig and he shouldn't be letting me watch that garbage." He shrugged. "Grandpa just laughed and said, *Mija*, they're movies. People watch them for entertainment and to escape their boring lives. In real life Bond would probably be sporting a black eye most of the time.' And then he'd wink at me and say, 'Especially if he tried that with your Mom.'"

Bitter took a sip of her lemonade to wash down the sweet potato fry she'd nearly choked on. José sounded just like Papá when he was at his snarkiest best.

The exuberant noise in the diner nearly drowned out the small voice behind her, "Excuse me."

Bitter twisted around to look at the chunky blonde teen in the next booth.

"Excuse me. Were you on the news last night?"

Bitter sighed, "Yes, I'm afraid they did get a shot of me as I went into the station."

The teen's face brightened, "I knew it! I've seen you on TV before. You're Bitter!" She blushed. "I mean Detective Bitter. You're famous. I have clippings of all your cases. The best story is the one where you found the little boy that everyone thought was dead. How did you know he was still alive?"

Sapp put both hands over his face and bent forward over the table, trying not to laugh at the teen's obvious hero worship.

Bitter smiled patiently at the girl's enthusiasm. "Yes, I'm Bitter. I wasn't sure the little guy was alive, but I was hoping he was. I was just following a hunch. And what's your name?"

"Jennifer. Jennifer Black." She gushed on, "I read all the news stories about you. I'm studying criminal justice—I want to be a detective too!"

Sapp quickly slid out of the booth, fleeing to the men's room before he burst out in laughter at Bitter's discomfort.

"Um, well, yes. It takes time and a lot of work. It's not an easy job." Bitter paused, "Excuse me, but our waitress is back." She paused again as disappointment filled Jennifer's face. "Maybe we can talk later before you leave?"

Jennifer flashed Bitter a huge grin. "I'd like that, thank you."

José shook his head in mock dismay as Bitter turned back to the table. "You can't fool me, Mom. You put on that tough exterior when you go to work, but we all know you have a heart of mush."

Bitter sipped at her strawberry lemonade and ignored his teasing as she ordered a cheeseburger with no onions and sweet potato fries with mayo and mustard on the side.

"Mom? No blue cheese?" José's eyes widened in surprise.

Bitter lowered her head a little and gave him her best mom-quelling-son look. "Against doctor's orders."

Gema pursed her full lips as she looked at the menu and pretended not to notice José's question and Bitter's response. The waitress waited patiently as Gema ordered milkshakes, cheeseburgers, and fries for the four teens in the other booth, and a salad for herself.

"So," Sapp asked as he slipped back into the booth, "who's going to work Candy's case?"

Bitter shrugged, "Not me. It's a conflict."

"I dunno, Bitter. You might be the only one."

Startled, Bitter looked at Sapp.

He ordered quickly without looking at the menu, "A burger and fries for me too, please. No onions, no cheese. Medium rare."

"What are you talking about, Sapp? This should be investigated by another jurisdiction. It's a conflict for me to investigate it. We work for the same agency."

"Well," Sapp leaned over and spoke quietly, "rumor has it that Candy had several office romances, and not just at our station. And her father is a Captain with the State Police, so that's a conflict too. There's talk that with the amount of publicity and conflicts of interest among the different agencies, plus pressure from her father, the Chief is just going to assign the best homicide detective to her case, conflicts be damned. And that's you."

"Oh," Bitter paused, biting back stronger words as she remembered the teen behind her, "Oh, well dang."

"Exactly."

"I think we'd better not talk about it here." She glanced behind her quickly, but the girl was texting, her head bent over the phone, and plump fingers flying over the screen.

Gema followed her glance and quickly changed the subject. "So, you're coming over for the Juneteenth celebration on Sunday afternoon, right?"

Bitter hesitated a long, uncomfortable moment and José nudged her under the table before she finally gave a quick nod.

"Jasir is still complaining that he didn't get any lumpia at the potluck if you're up to making some."

José grinned at Bitter's reluctance, and then moaned as Gema's words sank in, "Noooo, I'll be back at Minot and you'll all be enjoying homemade lumpia." He shook his head. "It's just not fair."

"Life isn't fair, get over it," Bitter's and Gema's words came in unison.

Sapp leaned back and laughed, "Son, you're being tag teamed by the Moms. Better stop while you're ahead."

Chapter 7 ~ Monday Already?

The sun was just peeking over the distant Sierras as Bitter pulled into the station parking lot. A few independent news crews loitered in the empty parking lot across the street. The nearest reporter had his back to her, too absorbed in his steaming coffee to notice the vintage dark blue Dodge Dart Swinger passing through the security gate.

Bitter parked at the far end of the parking lot where the huge Modesto ash trees shaded the cars through most of the afternoon. The deep shade and a cooler car after a long day at work made the extra steps and a few bird plops worthwhile. She sat in the car for a few extra minutes, listening to the morning weather report. "It's going to be another hot one," she sighed, reaching for the ignition key.

"And in breaking news—" Bitter jerked her hand away from the key and turned the radio up. She didn't notice the news crews leaping into their vans and screeching away, toward the river. All her attention was on the announcer's tense voice.

Body parts.

Found floating in the river.

The police declined interviews on the ongoing investigation.

Bitter shuddered. She turned the ignition off and got out of the Dart, automatically checking her Glock and straightening her jacket. She wasn't officially on duty until Doctor Leon cleared her, but she wanted to check a few things on the computer before her appointment.

Now she wanted to talk to the Coroner too.

She checked her face in the side mirror and patted a stray curl into place. *No, no one can see the bruise.* Her young fan hadn't noticed. At least, she didn't think the girl had noticed, but the teen was quick with questions about old cases and what to expect when applying for a job with the department. Bitter sighed again. She wasn't sure how she'd agreed to come to the girl's school and talk to her criminal justice class.

I'm getting soft. Ayyyy, soft in the head. Nothing but career and family for years and suddenly I'm speaking at schools and going to a coworker's celebrations.

Inside, the building was quiet in the way of all twenty-four-hour operations. It was the space of time between the last of the evening's drunk driving arrests and the first of the morning rush of reports—auto accidents, fights, and break-ins. Voices were hushed. No one was screaming, yet, and shift change wasn't for another hour. She heard a laugh from the break room. O'Malley was in early from patrol. She wondered briefly, then shrugged. Probably had a report to finish and since he'd spilled coffee on his keyboard, he'd taken to writing reports long-hand in the break room and scanning them on the copier.

She shook her head. *These old-school cops, you can't break them of old habits.*

Bitter contemplated stepping into the break room for coffee, then reconsidered after looking at her watch. Quickly, she ducked around the corner to the elevator before anyone noticed that she was in the building. Technically, she was still off-duty, and she didn't want to talk to anyone about Candy or the case yet. At least, not until she'd had a chance to review the files and talk to the Coroner.

Naturally, as she stepped out of the elevator, Morales nearly mowed her down in the dimly lit hall.

"Bitter! You're back?"

"Not until later, after I see Doctor Leon. I'm just checking my computer."

Morales took her by the elbow. "I have a few things to go over with you."

Bitter looked at his hand, pale against her navy jacket, then up into his eyes, unsmiling. He let go quickly. She caught a glimpse of a splotchy red rash on his right hand as he pulled it back.

"Come with me to my office."

"I don't have a lot of time. I have a 9 a.m. appointment with the doctor. I'm not on duty."

Morales frowned. "This will just take a minute."

Bitter reluctantly followed him to the elevator. The early morning sun was already beating into his office on the third floor. Windows on two sides let in more than the normal amount of sunlight. He sat at his desk and motioned toward a chair. "Sit down." He began shuffling files, ignoring her.

She glanced at his aristocratic Castilian profile, then stepped to the window behind him and closed the blinds. He pretended he didn't notice what she was doing, though she saw the glint of his eyes under his eyelashes as he watched her movements. She moved the chair at an angle to the desk in case he decided to reopen the blinds and blind her with sunlight. As she sat, a glance took in the pictures on his desk. The picture of he and his wife was gone. *I wonder if that poor woman finally filed for divorce or if he's just on the prowl again.*

He frowned as Bitter perched on the edge of the chair, ready to leave as soon as possible. She knew that he deliberately put his desk in that exact spot to intimidate underlings. She didn't allow him that liberty.

"Bitter, I'm assigning you to Candy's murder," he said abruptly, as he carefully moved papers from one side of his desk to the other.

"Why?"

"Her father requested you specifically."

"It's a conflict. Someone from another department should investigate."

He shook his head firmly. "No, I'm assigning it to you."

Bitter leaned forward. "No."

Morales looked up in surprise at her vehement reply. "What?"

"No. Absolutely not. It's a conflict. You know that I can't work this case. The girl nearly killed me a few days ago and now you want me to investigate her murder? No."

With a sinking feeling, Bitter watched Morales' face change from surprise to triumph.

"You don't have a choice. It's either work the case, disciplinary action, or resign from the department."

Bitter looked down at her clenched fists and smothered her rage at his smug expression. She breathed in, out, in, out, controlling her expression carefully as she considered his threat. Then she boldly looked him in the face.

"Fine. Put it in writing, with the justifications. And my objections." She stood. "I'm not on duty and I have an appointment. I'll expect the paperwork when I return to work," she paused, "with the Chief's signature and a copy of the letter from the State police specifically asking that I work this case. I'll have the Union rep and my lawyer look it over."

Morales pushed his chair back and stood. He held out his hand.

Bitter looked at him, looked at his hand, turned, and walked out, closing the door quietly behind her. *As if I'd shake his hand after that little power play.* Shadows lurked in every corner as she stopped and waited several feet down the hall, beside the next office door.

Bitter smiled with dark satisfaction when she heard the chair crash against the wall. Morales never did like anyone contradicting him.

Doctor Leon turned away from the computer and faced Bitter. "How are you feeling? Still tired?"

Bitter reluctantly nodded.

"Fortunately, the allergic reaction to the chaga tea has subsided. You'll probably be tired for a few more days. The EpiPen is hard on the body. It also looks like your iron is a little low. I'm going to prescribe iron pills—"

Bitter grimaced.

Doctor Leon ignored her frown and body language, arms crossed in negation, and continued, "—an antihistamine, and an anti-inflammatory. I want x-rays on those knees before I release you for work. We need to see why you're in so much pain."

"How long will that take?" Bitter asked impatiently.

Doctor Leon looked at her patiently over his reading glasses. "Not long. I already sent the order to radiology and your prescriptions to the pharmacy. After the x-rays, I want you to come back so I can review them before I release you." He smiled, "It won't take long, and then you can get back to work. I'm sure you're looking forward to investigating the body parts in the river."

"Nope. Not my case. They washed up on West Sac's side of the river, near the I Street Bridge. That one is Yolo County's problem." Bitter huffed a sigh of relief.

"Ahhh. The job isn't easy, eh? Are you feeling stressed or isolated? We can arrange for discreet counseling if you're having any difficulties."

"Oh no," Bitter said hastily as the pinched face of the psychiatrist flashed through her mind. "I'm fine. My youngest son was just here, he left this morning, and I'm going to a Juneteenth party on Sunday."

Doctor Leon looked at her doubtfully. "Juneteenth?"

Bitter seized the opportunity to turn his attention elsewhere. "Yes. Juneteenth celebrates the date that the slaves in Texas learned they were free. The news didn't reach Texas until Union soldiers landed in Galveston on June 19th, 1865, two and a half years after the Emancipation Proclamation."

He nodded thoughtfully. "People have parties celebrating the event?"

"Yes, it's traditional in the community. There's a parade and a huge festival on Saturday. Families have weekend celebrations down by the river and private parties at their homes. I'm going to a coworker's barbecue. My son knows the family. They all play hockey."

She saw his suspicious look.

"I'm fine," she repeated.

Bitter saw Doctor Leon purse his lips as she stood. He didn't miss how she pushed down on the armrests, taking some of the stress off her knees as she rose. She briskly shook his hand, "I'll be back shortly."

"Walk at least thirty minutes every day, and don't sit for more than forty-five minutes at a time. Get up and walk around the office every hour. I'm not going to order physical therapy, but I want you to follow the exercise routines on this handout." Doctor Leon looked sternly at Bitter. "You have a lot of inflammation in your knees. Are you sure you don't want shots to reduce the swelling?"

Bitter stubbornly shook her head no.

"Swimming, walking, bicycling are fine. No running, no high impact aerobics. And no sitting all day. I'll fax your work release over to HR, with a request to have the ergonomics specialist from Risk Management take a look at your work area."

He handed Bitter several papers and the handout. "Here's your copy."

"Thanks."

"Bitter."

"Yes?"

"I know you're eager to get back to work, but I also want you to spend some time away from the office. I'm worried about burn out. You need a hobby."

"I have a hobby."

"And it is?"

Bitter cracked a small smile. "I grow orchids."

"I'm not talking about a few plants in the window."

"Neither am I. I have a lath house filled with orchids in my backyard." Doctor Leon's eyes widened in surprise. "And I'm speaking at a high school in a couple of days. Don't ask me how that happened," she paused, assessing his response, "I do stay busy."

Bitter shook his hand and left while he was still speechless. She almost made it to the elevator before someone called her name. Bitter turned and saw the blonde nurse dashing for the elevator. Bitter didn't want to talk but pushed the button to hold the doors open anyway.

"Thank you," puffed the nurse, "I just got off and I need to get to my daughter's school to talk to her teacher. And I'm late."

Bitter nodded politely and looked at her nametag to memorize her name: *Angie.*

"How are you feeling? Better?"

"Yes, thank you."

"Back to work? Going to work that body parts case?"

"No. That's on the West Sacramento side of the river. I have other cases waiting for me when I get to the office."

"I saw you on the news the other day." Angie ignored Bitter's dark look and plunged on, "You looked terrible."

Bitter bit her lip and then changed the subject. "Have you heard any more sobbing at night?"

"No, but I think Rosie and Antonio heard something last night. She was talking to him in Tagalog and they were both looking down the hall. I never noticed how dark it gets at that end of the floor before. It was so dim. I couldn't see anything except the exit sign."

The elevator stuttered to a stop as the bell dinged.

"It was nice seeing you again, Ms. Bitter. I'm glad you're feeling better."

Bitter stood out of the way as Angie raced out of the elevator toward the lobby. *I have to come back to check on the sobbing, but not tonight.* She shook her head impatiently. *I don't like this. I don't like it at all.*

Chapter 8 ~ Still Monday

Bitter pushed back her chair and stretched when the computer dinged gently. *Forty-five minutes already?*

Carefully she pushed down on the chair arms, lifting herself without putting too much pressure on her knees. She flexed one knee and then the other before venturing to step away from the desk. A mountain of paper lay scattered across the desktop, tagged with colorful sticky notes. Pacing slowly back and forth across the narrow confines of her office, she shook her head as she pondered the evidence. A sheaf of photos lay next to the computer. She paused and leaned over her chair, using the mouse to enlarge the digital image on the computer screen until it began to pixelate. The mark on Candy's forehead hadn't had time to bruise, and the livid finger marks on her arm were red and angry. Like the mark on her forehead, they hadn't started purpling before she died.

Ayyyy, I should've been here to see the scene. Not just look at the pictures and papers. Her thoughts were sharp with frustration as she picked up the Coroner's notes and skimmed over the dry facts. Cattee (Candy) Maria Soto. Female, Caucasian, five feet nine inches, one hundred and thirty pounds, twenty-six years old. Cause of death: gunshot wounds.

The overhead lights flickered. Impatiently, Bitter opened the blinds to let in the afternoon sun and drive the shadows back into the corners. Heat migrated into the room. It made the window too hot to touch. Bitter turned her small fan away from the desktop and set it on high to keep the air circulating.

Coffee. I need more coffee. Her stomach grumbled. *Maybe an iced coffee and a sandwich.*

When she left her office, Bitter double-checked the door to make sure it was locked before she limped to the elevator. She didn't need any more cards or flowers. It had taken her twenty minutes to clear her desk before she could even look at the files piled on her chair. She wondered briefly who had left her the lovely moth orchid. It didn't have a card or note attached to the hot pink foil wrapped around the pot. She shrugged. Perhaps it was from one of the old-timers who once resented her presence. *But why would one of them leave a gift? And how would they know to give me an orchid?*

The elevator door was already sliding open when she paused and looked down the hall at the steel fire door. Forensics hadn't missed anything, but still... She walked slowly to the stairway door and looked up at the red exit sign, then over her shoulder at the camera trained on the door.

Why was Candy in this building? She was a dispatcher. She worked over at the Dispatch Center. Was she meeting someone here that morning?

Bitter frowned as she turned the knob.

"Bitter!"

Reluctantly, Bitter turned away from the stairwell.

Morales strode down the hall toward her. "Bitter, Chief Brown wants an update on the case."

Incredulously, Bitter stared at him. "An update? An update on what? She was found dead in the stairwell. Shot to death. That's the update right now."

"Doesn't matter. The Chief wants you in his office right now."

Bitter took a deep breath and stuffed her anger down into the dark place before replying, "Fine."

"Good."

Morales reached for her arm as if to escort her. Quickly, Bitter stepped back before he could touch her. Dark shadows rose behind her threateningly, but Morales only grimaced and turned away.

Back at the elevator, Bitter stabbed the up button. She caught a glimpse of Morales coming down the hall. Luckily, the doors closed before he could get to the elevator and ride up with her.

The sun shining through the windows at the end of the hall, past the Chief's office, made a pattern of glowing light and contrasting dark. Unwary visitors were alternately blinded by the bright sun and unable to see in the darkest spots. The sun's rays didn't reach the elevator. It stayed dim and still at that end of the hall. Bitter shaded her eyes with one hand as she made her way to the Chief's domain.

"Bitter." The Chief's secretary hefted herself from the chair and hugged Bitter when she entered the office. "Thank God you're all right. We were so worried about you."

Bitter awkwardly patted the plump, blonde woman on her shoulder as she disengaged from the tight hug. "I'm good, Sally. The Chief wanted to see me?"

"The Chief?" Sally blinked in surprise. "Oh, he told Morales to send you up when you had an update on the case. But you just got here, why would that man send you up right now?"

"Good question."

"Let me see if the Chief is available."

"Wait. Sally, I want to ask you some questions."

Sally paused, "Me?"

Bitter nodded. "I need the gossip. Now I know you're not like that, but everything passes over your desk eventually. I need to know if there was any scuttlebutt about boyfriends, love triangles, stalkers, sexual harassment allegations—anything that might relate to Candy's personal or professional life."

Sally hesitated.

Bitter smiled gently. "The gossip can wait until after work if that makes you feel better. You can come down to my office and help me gather all the cards and candy and plants to take to the car."

Sally sighed in relief and nodded. "Yes, I can do that. I'll bring a cart down after the Chief leaves at five, is that all right?"

"Perfect." It was Bitter's turn to hesitate, "Nothing about this case can be off the record. I'll have to document every detail."

Sally nodded somberly. "Yes. Poor Candy was a popular young woman. There will be a lot of details."

Before Bitter could ask Sally any questions, the Chief's door swung open.

"Bitter! Updates already?"

"Not yet," Bitter said.

The Chief harrumphed unhappily and then opened his door a little wider. "Come in. Let's go over what you have so far."

The office was cool and dim, with only an LED desk lamp lighting the Chief's papers. "Whew, it's hot out there, Bitter. Must be one hundred and ten in the shade today."

She nodded as she sat down.

"Coffee?"

"No thank you, I'm going to lunch shortly."

He poured himself a cup before sitting down. Bitter's stomach churned at the vile scent of the brew. It had been on the burner far too long to be drinkable by anyone other than a cop.

"Bitter, I really appreciate you taking on this case. With the ins and outs of the departmental conflicts and her father's personal request, we wanted our best investigator on it. I know it's a conflict, but we need someone familiar with the department and, well, you're known to the public. They have confidence in you." He sighed, "The press is having a field day with this case. One of our own murdered in the stairwell. I suppose you saw the horde out front?"

Bitter grimaced, "They have the story on the news feed twenty-four seven. Rotating with the body parts in the river, a two-headed turtle, and frying an egg on the sidewalk."

He chuckled before sipping at his coffee. "I know it's too soon for a progress report, but is there anything that's caught your attention?"

Bitter shook her head. "Too many questions at this point. What happened to the cameras? Who was in the building? Why was she even in the building?"

He pushed the coffee back, away from the papers scattered across his desk. "I have the IT guys working on the server now and a video guy working on the camera end of it. I'll send it over as soon as I have their reports."

"They don't have it yet?"

The Chief shook his head. "I'm starting to wonder if they're going to get anything at all. If the cameras were borked before she was murdered, we may never know who was in that stairwell."

"But we know who was in the building?"

"Yes. It's in the file. Date, time, who entered the building by using the key card readers. And we're still working our way through the staff to make sure no one held a door open for another employee." He pulled a tissue from the box and blew his nose. "Blasted allergies," he muttered, then sighed heavily, "Hopefully someone will fess up to it. Against regulations, you know."

Bitter nodded. Nearly everyone broke that rule at least once by holding the door open for a colleague carrying in Starbucks coffee and the fixings for a meeting, a box of Krispy Kreme donuts, or an armload of paperwork. Not everyone leaned in close enough for the key card to register on the reader while entering the building.

So much for a secure building.

"She's still down at the morgue if you want to see her."

"She is?" Bitter asked in surprise.

"The Coroner's office hasn't released her to the family yet. Joe said something about waiting for the investigator."

Bitter stood as quickly as her knees allowed. "I need to go see Joe, then. Today."

The Chief rose to shake her hand. He didn't release it. "Bitter, it's good to have you back. Let me know whatever you need to get this case solved." His voice hardened, "Nobody commits a murder in my station and gets away with it."

She nodded as she gently pulled her hand free of his calloused grasp. The red marks on Candy's body were already consuming her thoughts.

Bitter barely paused at Sally's desk. "Sally, can we talk tomorrow? I need to get to the Coroner's office this afternoon and I might not be back before five."

The door closed behind Bitter before Sally could reply.

Chapter 9 ~ Monday Afternoon

Bitter tapped her fingers impatiently on the hot steering wheel. The air conditioning labored as she crept through the afternoon traffic, past Capitol Park, and through the one-way streets toward Broadway. Waves of heat shimmered off the sedan's white hood, distorting the view of the lifted black truck ahead of her car.

I wonder what he tows. That's a pretty hefty hitch.

"Breaking news," the radio suddenly blared, interrupting the flow of classic jazz, "breaking news on the murdered police dispatcher case."

Bitter tensed.

"The Soto family has announced that Sacramento's own Juanita Bitter will be working to solve the murder of their beloved Candy. The well-known homicide detective with the Sacramento Police Department—"

Bitter hit the off button. *Well damn. So much for staying off the press' radar and getting the job done.*

The taillights of the truck flared and Bitter hit the brakes, stopping only inches from the trailer hitch. She took a deep breath and then her head slammed back against the headrest, and forward again as the sedan smacked the hitch and bumper ahead of her.

What the? Bitter looked in her rear-view mirror, only to see the sedan's crumpled trunk lid. It blocked the view of the bright pink Honda CRX that had been trailing her since she'd turned off J Street.

Just what I need today. She reached for her phone to call the accident in to Dispatch.

Startled, she nearly dropped the phone at the sudden banging on her window. An agitated man pounded his fist on the lightly tinted glass. He pulled at the door handle and pointed back, behind the sedan. She turned to look, then grabbed her purse, briefcase, and suit jacket off the seat as she scrambled out. Smoke obscured the Honda.

"Is the driver out?" Bitter demanded.

The tall man nodded, "My friend got her out. She's over there." He pointed at a young woman with purple and pink hair sitting on the curb. Bright sunlight glinted off the assortment of metal ornaments attached to her face. Bitter noticed that the girl's nose was bleeding.

"We need to get everyone away from the cars," she said and pointed at the truck.

"That's mine," he said. "We're okay, you barely touched the bumper. The hitch is stuck in your radiator though."

Bitter glanced at the growing crowd and pulled out her badge. "Back. Everybody back. Get away from the cars."

The dispatcher finally answered the line in her usual cool, calm voice. Bitter interrupted, "This is Bitter. I need the fire department right now on 19th, one block south of O Street. Accident and car fire. She rear-ended me. Better send EMTs too, she hit me hard and may be injured."

Bystanders milled in the street with their iPhones poised as they filmed the black smoke billowing from the front of the little car. Two workers from a nearby construction site ran up with fire extinguishers and began spraying the hood of the Honda.

Bitter took the phone away from her mouth before she shouted, "Out of the street. Now!"

A few phones turned toward her as she shooed the lookie-loos out of the street and away from the crumpled cars, and then more phones appeared as the crowd realized who was shouting at them.

Sirens wailed as police, fire and rescue, and an ambulance slowly pushed their way through the packed street. With a practiced eye, Bitter judged at least ten to fifteen more minutes before the emergency vehicles could work their way through the three blocks of traffic on 19th. A battered white and green news van was trailing the ambulance.

I hope they get a ticket for that maneuver.

A patrol car pulled up on O Street and parked. Bitter waved the blue toward the battered cars before she walked over to the curb. She leaned over the stunned driver of the Honda. The silver ring in the young woman's lip had blood on it. "Are you all right?"

"*No, no sé. ¿Chica? ¿Donde está Chica?*"

Bitter straightened and looked at the pickup's driver. "She was alone in the car?"

"Yes, except for her dog. We got it out too. Damn Chihuahua. The little shit bit me, but she's settled down now. Barry has her wrapped up in a towel. She was just scared."

Bitter looked at the bloody rag wrapped around his hand, sighed, and handed him her card. "Make sure you get that looked at as soon as possible. I have fire and rescue on the way. And an ambulance."

She leaned down and gently patted the young woman on a tattooed shoulder, "*Tenemos Chica. Está bien.*"

He took the card and glanced at it. Then his eyes widened, and he looked at Bitter. "Are you—?"

She gave him a wry smile, "Yes. That's me."

"Wow," he grinned, "wait until I tell the guys at work who ran into me today."

Bitter made a face. "Well, technically I stopped in time. But she didn't."

He stuck out a calloused hand. "I'm Glen. Sorry to meet you under these circumstances."

She took a deep breath and pasted on her public face – gentle with a slight smile. She shook his hand firmly. "Nice to meet you, Glen."

The approaching siren cut off as the fire engine stopped, blocking the street, and firefighters leaped out to extinguish the flames. A pair of blues wheeled up behind the firetruck, lights still flashing, and began shooing the bystanders away from the scene.

Bitter looked at the sedan's crushed hood and trunk. Antifreeze dripped from the front of the car. *Well, so much for talking to Joe today.*

"Bitter?"

Bitter turned at the shout. The reporter leaped out of the van and ran toward her. The cameraman was at his heels, camera rolling as they approached.

She raised one hand, fending him off. "No. No comments at this time."

The blue taking statements looked up when the reporter shouted. He stepped between Bitter and the pursuing reporter. "Out of the street and away from the accident." He pointed at the curb across the street. "You can film from over there."

"You can't—"

The officer straightened to his full height. Sweat glistened on the blue-black highlights of his bald head when he removed his hat and wiped it with a handkerchief. He stuffed the cloth into a pocket before he looked down at the reporter and replied, "Yes, I can. You can get out of the street and film from over there. Nobody is infringing on your right to report the news, so get onto that sidewalk before I have to notice you disobeying a lawful order."

The cameraman stepped back as the blue loomed over the pair.

"To the curb. I'm sure there are witnesses you can interview while we take care of the accident."

"I want to know your name and badge number," the reporter blustered. Bitter noticed that his bald spot was turning red. Whether from rage or too much sun, she couldn't tell. She hadn't noticed it during his reports on the evening news.

The blue smiled grimly as he handed the little man a business card. "I'm sure you do. Now we're busy." He pointed and his face grew stern. "Over there."

He watched the pair scuttle to the far curb before he turned toward Bitter. "We'll take your statement in a few minutes. Would you like to sit in the car? The air is on."

"Thank you," Bitter hesitated as she read his nametag, "Officer Khalid. But I'd better just go stand in the shade. They're filming."

The blue nodded. "Let me give you a water then. It's too bloody hot out here. And just call me Khalid."

"Thank you," said Bitter as he handed her the icy bottle. She pressed it against her face for a moment, relishing the cold, before she twisted the top off and took a deep drink.

A cell phone rang.

Bitter hastily swallowed before she answered. "Bitter."

"Nita, we have a problem."

Bitter pulled the phone away from her ear and looked at the caller ID. "Julio?"

"Yes, yes. Nita, my wife just called me. She's waiting on the house phone. Her cousin called her at work. Her cousin's daughter was in an accident. Can you find out what's going on?"

Bitter sighed. *Family.*

"Where was the accident?"

"By midtown, I think. The girl was pretty hysterical. I guess she hit a cop."

Bitter closed her eyes briefly, then looked over at the young woman. "Is her hair purple and pink this week?"

"Just a minute." Bitter heard her brother's muffled voice, then he uncovered the phone, "Yes. How did you know?"

Bitter sighed again. "Julio, tell your wife to tell her cousin it'll be all right."

"Bitter?"

"Yes, she hit a cop. But I'm fine. What's the deal? Why is she only speaking Spanish?"

"She has an anxiety disorder. When she gets upset, she loses her English until she calms down." He paused, "Wait a minute. You're okay? What do you mean you're okay? Where are you?"

"Julio, tell your wife that she might've broken her nose, so I'll have the ambulance take her to the hospital and check her for injuries. Someone will have to pick her up later. The car looks like a total loss."

Muffled voices drifted from the phone before Julio came back on the line, "Nita, she has a companion dog. Is the dog with her?"

Bitter took a deeper breath of overheated air. It smelled like exhaust fumes and hot asphalt. "Yes. We have Chica."

"I know you have a cat, but would you mind taking care of Chica until someone can pick her up? Liz has already clocked out and she's ready to head for Sac, but she can't bring Chica here. The last time, that little stinker went after my pittie and tore up the old boy's nose before I could grab her."

Khalid touched Bitter's shoulder. "She wants to talk to you." He pointed at the curb where the young woman was sobbing.

"Julio, I have to go. What's her name?"

"Rosalia."

"I'll get the dog. Don't forget to pick it up. I don't think Gato will appreciate a dog in his territory."

"As soon as we can. Thanks, Sis."

"*Es familia*. Okay, Bro. I'll talk to you later."

"Wait, wait, my wife reminded me. The car?"

Bitter glanced over at the blackened hood. "It doesn't look good."

"Ah, but Hondas are easy to fix. Can you store it at your house?"

Bitter sighed deeply. "No, Julio, I'm not storing that broken little car at my house. I'll have it towed to my body shop. They can probably get a good deal on a rebuilt engine for it. If they can't fix it, no one can."

"*Gracias*, Nita, we'll take care of the bill, whatever the insurance doesn't cover. She loves that little car."

Bitter motioned to the tow truck operator.

"Call me later, Julio, I need to take care of the car and Rosalia now."

The driver climbed out of the truck. Sweat trickled down his round, sunburned face.

"I need you to take the Honda over to Martinez Custom Auto Body on Watt."

He grimaced, "Not the junkyard?"

"Nope. Take it to the shop." She wrote her cell phone and Julio's home phone number on the back of a business card before she handed it over.

He shook his head as he pulled his burly bulk back into his rig and maneuvered it behind the little car.

Bitter walked slowly through the shimmering waves of heat rising from the pavement. She gently touched the young woman's shoulder. "Rosalia. I just talked to your mother's cousin's husband. He's my brother. You need to go to the hospital. I'll take care of Chica."

Heads snapped around, and the EMTs and officers stared at Bitter. She shrugged a little sheepishly, "Family."

Khalid shook his head, "Of all the luck, to get run into by a relative."

"*¿Tía, tía. Tienes Chica? [Aunt, aunt. You have Chica?]*"

"*Un momento, mija. [One moment, my child.}*"

Bitter looked around. The duo from the truck stood in the shade of the oak that towered over the east side of the street. She walked over, sighing in relief as she passed into the shade.

"Hey, you're limping. Did you get hurt?" The taller man asked, concern on his face.

Glen. She thought, *Don't forget his name is Glen.*

"No. Bad knees," Bitter said. "So, I'm going to keep the dog for a few days."

They stared.

"It bites." The driver ventured.

"She'll be fine, Glen," Bitter reassured him. She saw the disbelief in both men's faces. She let her smile grow a little, "Just my luck, to get run into by one of my brother's relatives."

Glen groaned, "Seriously?"

"Seriously."

She let Chica sniff the back of her hand. When the little dog stopped growling, Bitter took her gently from his arms. "Do you need your towel?"

"Actually, it was in the CRX. I just grabbed it to wrap up the dog."

"Thank you. Call if you have any trouble with the insurance." Bitter nodded at the two men and walked back to Rosalia. The EMT was helping her into the ambulance.

"*Gracias. Gracias.* [*Thank you. Thank you.*]"

"*De nada. Familia es todo, mija.*"

Bitter fumbled in a pocket for a business card and handed it to Rosalia before the ambulance doors closed. A bead of sweat trickled down the back of her neck.

"Ok then, Bitter. Ready to make your statement?"

Bitter looked up into Khalid's dark eyes. "Let's move into the shade. And watch out for Chica, she's snappy."

He chuckled, and for a moment he sounded like Barry White, "She won't bother me." He carefully let Chica sniff his hand before he patted her on the head. "Dogs like me." Chica wagged her tail and wiggled enthusiastically. Bitter took a firmer grip on the little dog.

Bitter glanced over at the news crew. They were filming as the tow truck tugged the Honda away from the sedan. It dribbled radiator fluid and firefighting foam as the winch pulled it up onto the flatbed. The fluids hissed as they hit the hot pavement.

Bitter shuddered slightly, thinking of things under the city that hissed—and ate people.

"Bitter, you need to sit down. You look a little pale."

She nodded and finally let Khalid lead her to the idling patrol car. Chica panted happily as he reached into the back seat and grabbed a dog treat. The air conditioning was set on high, but it barely cooled the car interior.

"I think that'll do for now. It's not like I don't know where to find you," chuckled Khalid. "Now, we're about finished here. Do you need a ride?"

"No, I'll get a taxi."

"Seriously, I can drop you off. It's on the way back to the station."

"No, I can get a taxi." She gave him a slight smile, "It's got to have better a/c than this heap."

"Don't forget you have to stop at Occupational Health for a blood test," he said, "to make sure you hadn't been drinking or anything."

Bitter turned slightly toward Khalid, then took a deep breath before she bit his head off. He was just doing his job. "I'll be fine," she said firmly, "and I know I have to make a stop for testing."

Khalid opened his mouth to argue. Brakes squealed and the sound of crunching metal stopped him.

They both looked over in time to see the little reporter jumping out of his van.

"You idiot. You hit my van," he shrieked.

The cameraman leaped out of the passenger door and jerked out his camera to film the scene.

"Well crap," grumbled Khalid. "There goes the rest of my shift. And some overtime too."

Bitter glanced at him. "Do you need my statement for this one?"

"I'll call you if we need it. Now I have to take care of this fool." He sighed heavily as the reporter started kicking the side of the delivery truck.

A tiny redheaded woman in brown swung out of the truck. "Who are you calling an idiot? Don't you look before you pull out into traffic?"

Nose to nose, they shouted as another crowd gathered. Then the reporter pushed her.

Bitter shook her head. "That was a mistake. She's pretty mad—and a redhead on top of it."

"Oh, Lord, here we go," Khalid groaned, "I'd better go save him from himself."

Before Khalid could haul himself back out into the afternoon heat, the fiery woman hauled back and punched the reporter in the nose. He went down hard as the crowd groaned and cheered. Bitter saw money passing from hand to hand. The bystanders were busily laying bets as the driver proceeded to haul the little man up by his lapels.

"Nobody pushes me, fool," she hissed in his face, "Nobody." And she punched him again.

While the cell phone cameras stayed focused on the fight, Bitter slipped out of the car. Blues converged on the pair. Khalid snatched the reporter by the collar and lifted the little man out and away from the fight. He held the delivery driver back with a muscled arm. Sweat dripped down his forehead.

"Well, Chica, I guess I should take you home before I do anything else." Bitter hit the speed dial on her phone. "This is Bitter. Is Gian available? I need a ride from 19th and O to my house." She nodded absently. "Oh, he's just around the corner? I'll meet him there. Traffic is still backed up on 19th. Thanks."

Chica licked Bitter's cheek. "Ugh, little dog, could you not lick me," she muttered grumpily as she limped toward the waiting yellow taxi.

"Bitter!" said Gian with a smile. "Welcome to my taxi! And what's this, you have a dog?" Sweat darkened the edges of his navy turban as he opened the taxi door.

"Thank you, Gian. Yes, I'm afraid I'm puppy-sitting for a little while. *Es la familia.*"

"Ahhh," said Gian. "Home?"

"Would you mind swinging past Safeway so I can pick up some dog food?"

"*No problema,*" he grinned, "I was in the mood for Panda Express anyway. I'll pick up my dinner while you shop. I'll go to the drive-thru so you can leave the little dog in the car. I'll keep the air on."

Bitter smiled in spite of herself. "Thank you, Gian. Don't feed her any people food now."

Gian laughed, "Ah, Bitter, you know me so well."

Bitter slowly ascended the steps, carrying Chica, while Gian followed close behind with her bags. "Thank you for your help, Gian."

"*No problema,* Bitter, call dispatch any time." He set the bags on the porch. "Are you sure you have everything?"

"Yes, thank you. And Gian, I was distracted. How's your latest novel coming along?"

He gave her an evocative grimace, then smiled. "Well, it's getting there. I think the rewriting is far worse than getting the first draft done."

She shifted Chica to the other side, "Let me know when it's out. It's the sequel to your last book, right?"

"Yes," he said cheerfully. "You'll be the first to know."

"Great, thank you. If you don't mind closing the gate behind you?"

"See you next time." Gian gave Bitter a quick wave as he closed and latched the wrought iron gate.

Bitter set Chica down as she fumbled for her keys. The little dog snuffled around the porch, but as soon as the door was open, Chica darted into the cool, dim hall.

"Chica!"

Too late, Bitter grabbed for the little dog. Gato was just inside, waiting to dash out into the garden. Yapping madly, Chica stopped and crouched, ready to leap toward the cat. Shadows gathered, looming over Gato as he glared at the barking Chi and spat.

"Chica, no," Bitter said firmly.

Chica glanced up at Bitter and danced closer to Gato, still barking. Gato reared up and as Chica closed in, he swatted the little dog, once, twice, three times. Chica tumbled back, yipping, as Gato turned and swished his tail across the dog's nose.

Bitter bit her lip, trying not to laugh, as Chica backed into her legs. She scooped up the Chi and checked for scratches. "He didn't even use his claws, Chica, he must like you."

Gato stopped halfway to the kitchen and, tail still twitching, watched as Bitter turned on the light. Shadows retreated from the bright light. "Okay now, you two are going to have to get along for a little while."

Bitter retrieved the dog food and bags from the porch. "Food, water, puppy pads, and a dog bed," she muttered as she quickly moved the cat food into the hall and shut Chica in the kitchen. "That will have to do for now. I need to get that blood test and then see Joe before he leaves for the day." She glanced at the clock and sighed. "Not enough time to go pick up another sedan from the station. I guess I'll have to take the Maverick. At least the a/c works better than the Dart's."

"I wasn't sure if you were going to make it over today," said Joe. He pulled the sheet away from Candy's pale face and torso. "The family has been very patient, but they're trying to arrange for the services. I think they're going to have a full Catholic Mass for her."

"Sorry it took so long. I got rear-ended on the way over, so I had to stop by Oc Health for a blood test."

Joe's face reflected his concern. "Are you all right? Feeling any pain?"

"No, no," she said absently as she focused on Candy's body, "I'm fine."

Candy's perfectly made-up face and red lipstick seemed garish under the bright lights. With the blood drained from her features, the foundation was too dark, and the carefully blended blush was obvious. Her blue eyes, outlined in smudged kohl, stared unseeing at the ceiling. The almost peaceful look on her face, despite a large red blotch on her forehead, contrasted with the marks of violence on her body.

Bitter focused on the marks on Candy's arms and walked to the other side of the table. "So, these marks?"

"Ah, those marks on her arms?" Joe pointed at the livid red blotches. "They would've been bruises in a few more hours if she'd lived. Bodies generally don't produce bruises once the heart stops beating."

Bitter nodded.

"Someone violently grabbed her by the arms, shortly before she died. Probably a man, or maybe a woman with large hands." Joe peered at the body through his thick glasses. He adjusted the bright lamp over the body, muttering, "I don't know why it seems so dim in here."

"And the cause of death?"

"Three bullets to the chest, from a .32." He used a probe to point out the obvious bullet holes. "Plus, even if she'd survived the gunshot wounds, her neck was broken when she fell down the stairs."

Joe frowned. "I can only speculate, but I believe that she was pushed back violently and shot, and between the shove and impact of the bullets, she fell backward down the stairs. You can see where she tumbled, and her forehead hit the wall. The marks on the body indicate that she'd been in a struggle recently, probably minutes before she was shot since they didn't bruise."

"So, she was on the second floor and fell to the bottom of the stairs?" Bitter frowned. Her office was on the second floor.

"Yes. Forensics took pictures of the blood spatters and the angle of the bullets through the body show that she was tipping backward after the first shot. One went through her heart, the second, slightly higher, went through her chest but at a steeper angle, and the third, probably while she was falling, hit her just below the collarbone and went out the back of her neck. The bullet pattern on the stairwell wall behind her shows a tight pattern consistent with the rapid firing of the weapon."

"Do you have a time of death?"

Joe took off his glasses and wiped them carefully with a cloth. "Estimated time of death is between 5 and 6 a.m."

Bitter considered the time frame. "A little before shift change, and early enough that there'd only be a few people in the building."

Joe nodded and put his glasses back on. "And I understand there was a problem with the cameras?"

Tightlipped, Bitter gave a brief nod in return. "I'm waiting on IT to see if they can recover anything, but I'm not hopeful. We don't know who was in the building or on the stairs that morning. And I don't know why she was in the building. She worked over at the Dispatch Center."

Joe paused, "No backup system?"

Bitter walked back around the body. "Nope. It's an antiquated CCTV system hardwired into the building with a video recorder and monitor system packed into what used to be a closet, so no backup to the main server or the cloud." She shrugged. "It's scheduled for updating next year. It wasn't a priority item in this year's budget."

"Well, that's not going to help then."

"Nope."

"There are also indications that she'd had sex recently. I've sent the samples out for sequencing."

"Really?" Bitter said. "How recently?"

"The night before or early that morning."

"Consensual?"

Joe frowned. "It's hard to say. I think so, though the finger marks on her arms," he led Bitter back around the body, "indicate that she had her arms raised when these occurred as if she'd been held face down or up against a wall." He pointed and Bitter saw that there were several sets of marks on the young woman's arms. "These are a little older than the second set, they'd started to turn purple, while the other set is fresher and still red. Those look like she was grabbed from the side or front by someone taller and stronger."

Bitter looked again at Candy's face. "So, she'd applied the makeup after the first set of bruises?"

"Why yes, otherwise her makeup would've been smeared."

"Any other traces? DNA?" Bitter asked.

"Nothing on the body and Forensics hasn't finished processing the evidence from the scene."

"That's too bad. I was hoping that she'd managed to scratch her assailant."

Joe gave her a look, "Skin or blood under the fingernails, right?"

Bitter shrugged, "I can always hope."

"Not this time. Not yet anyway."

She took a long look at Candy's face, "It was one of us, Joe. It had to be someone in the department. No one else was in the building."

His face softened in sympathy, "I know, Bitter."

"It's hard to believe, but you just never know about people." She sighed, thinking of resignations after arrests for drunk driving, domestic violence, sexual assault, and other crimes. "Even cops can turn out to be evil human beings." Suddenly impatient with her lapse into the past, she forced herself back to business. "All the officers' DNA are in the secured database, correct?"

"Yes, of course. Ever since that series of sexual assaults a few years back." He took off his glasses and wiped them carefully. "I think everyone breathed a sigh of relief when the perp turned out to be a wannabe cop with a fake badge."

"Yes, I remember that case. It was just before I was promoted, so I didn't get to work that one." She picked up her purse and started toward the door. "Let me know when you get the results back on those tests, and if anything new turns up."

"Bitter?"

She turned back toward the little Coroner, "Yes?"

"I have a bad feeling about this one. First, she poisons you, and then she's murdered in your building." He shook his head as he peeled off his gloves. "And while you're still in the hospital."

Bitter smiled gently. "I'll be careful. Thank you, Joe, you've been very helpful, as always."

He shook his head as Bitter let herself out of the building and muttered, "I don't like it. And then they assign the case to you. It's just wrong."

Bitter sat on the top step of the bungalow, watching Chica race across the grass as Gato prowled the edges of the garden. A hint of a breeze touched her face and she turned toward the cooler air. *The weatherman said there'd be a break in this heat. It feels like the marine layer has finally kicked in. The wind is funneling up the river from the ocean.*

A drift of smoke carrying the scent of steak and barbecue sauce sizzling on the grill wafted over the fence, probably from the apartments next door. A bass riff competed with a popular Mariachi track from the house across the street.

A little brown hatchback stopped in front of the house. "*¿Tamales? Tamales* today?" the driver called over the fence.

"*Un momento. ¿Tienes elote?*" Bitter stood and carefully navigated down the steps.

Chica raced to the gate, barking like a shrill-voiced Rottie.

"Chica! Get away from the gate. Shhh...."

"You have a *perrito* now?"

"Ayyyy, *sí,*" Bitter grumbled. "Six cheese with *jalapeños* and six chicken, *por favor*. And two, no, three *elote*."

"*Bien,*" he said cheerfully as he put two packages of hot *tamales* in a bag and handed three foil-wrapped grilled corn on the cob on sticks over the gate to Bitter.

"See you next week?"

"*Sí, sí,* I'll be back on Saturday afternoon. *Gracias.*"

"*Gracias*. I'll see you then."

Her stomach growled as she trudged up the steps and into the kitchen. Chica and Gato followed at her heels, sniffing the air and hoping for a bite of the steaming *tamales*. As the streetlights came on, shadows trailed behind, gathering in the darkened hall outside the brightly lit kitchen. Bitter put two *tamales* and one *elote* on a plate before she poured herself a glass of wine.

Chapter 10 ~ Tuesday

Beep, beep, beep, the alarm kept going off. Bitter felt around the nightstand. *Where is it?* She fumbled for another minute before turning the light on. A cold little nose pressed against the back of her neck. *Oh,* she started, *I forgot about Chica.*

Bitter rolled over, only to see the little dog disappearing under the comforter. She pushed the covers back and swung her legs to the floor. The alarm clock lay upside down on the floor, just past her slippers.

"Chica, you are so spoiled," Bitter said to the little dog peeking out at her. "I see how you are, whining until you get your way." *I couldn't sleep for the whining until I let you come to bed with me. Silly little dog, you're so much like Lola's Coco.* She smiled fondly at the memory of the chocolate brown Chi that slept with her after Lola walked on.

Chica leaped off the bed as Bitter wiggled her toes into the fuzzy slippers. "Come on now, outside to do your business," Bitter said sternly as she slipped into her robe. She rotated her neck and shoulders. *Good. A little stiff,* she decided, *but I'm fine. No whiplash this time.* Chica danced in front of Bitter as she limped to the door. Gato was already waiting, ready to rush into the cool early morning air.

"Out you go now." Chica raced down the steps, barking wildly, while Gato leaped past her and darted across the tiny lawn to the shrubbery.

"Chica, Chica, shhh." Bitter tried to get the Chi's attention, but she was standing against the gate, barking and snarling.

Bitter started down the steps before she saw the filthy fingers groping through the gate. "Chica! No!" Bitter called firmly. Chica darted at the retreating fingers, snapping but not connecting as Jean jerked his hand back.

"Ayyyy, Bitter, *la perrita* is guarding you now?" Señor Suarez called from across the street. He held a small cooler in one hand and his keys in the other. He glanced to Bitter's left, behind the wall of shrubs and out of her sight. "Jean, go home. Now."

Bitter shook her head. "We need to do something about Jean."

"Bitter, you know he belongs to the *bruja*. It's too late to save him."

She looked briefly toward the sky and sighed. *There's no such thing as witches.*

"We could call social services for a welfare check, but I don't think they'll do anything," he said as he climbed into his battered truck.

Bitter considered his words as he pulled away from the curb. *Maybe if I call them myself.*

Chica and Gato ignored her as she went inside, until she leaned back out the door and shook the metal canister holding the cat food. It was a race to the front door and Gato won.

Bitter checked the video camera and tape recorder. Everything was a go, but she bit her lip, thinking of the erased surveillance footage. Carefully, she propped her iPad against the wall at the end of the table, so it could catch the interview. *I'll use it as a backup.*

The tiny interview room was stuffy. A table and two chairs nearly filled the space. It smelled like stale coffee and sweat, despite the lavender and vanilla-scented air freshener plugged into the only outlet. A power strip for the electronics filled the second socket.

Bitter checked the stack of mugs, coffee carafe, and a pitcher of ice water. Fresh coffee, clean mugs, the fixings. *Okay then. Let's keep this a friendly conversation and see what pops up.*

"Ms. Bitter?"

Bitter put on her public face before she turned toward the soft voice.

"Ms. René?"

"Yes. My supervisor sent me over to talk to you?" Her voice rose uncertainly, making the statement a question.

"Please come in, Ms. René."

"Vicki. Please call me Vicki." She blinked back tears as she came into the room. Bitter noticed that even with the high-heeled peep-toe pumps, Vicki barely reached five feet nothing.

Bitter shook Vicki's hand. "I'm sorry for your loss. Coffee?"

Vicki adjusted her sleek black dress carefully before she perched on the edge of the battered chair. "No thank you."

Bitter poured herself a cup and added cream and sugar. "It's safe. I made it fresh."

Vicki smiled wanly. "I don't like coffee."

Bitter warmed her hands on the hot cup before taking a sip. She never figured out how the interview rooms could get so cold and still be both stinky and stuffy.

She turned on the tape recorder, camera, and iPad. "I have a few questions for you." She looked at the clock as she sat down, across the table from the young woman. "Interview with Vicki René. Start time 8:25 a.m."

Vicki sniffed and nodded. Bitter handed her a tissue and gave her a gentle look before continuing.

"It's my understanding that Candy was your roommate."

"No. She was my girlfriend." Vicki smudged her mascara as she wiped away a tear. Her swollen eyes were bleak. "I was going to ask her to marry me on the Fourth of July—at the fireworks show."

Bitter blinked in surprise. *No one put this in the file.* She paused and stuffed her rage down into a dark place. It wasn't the time for anger, not with this vulnerable woman crying over her murdered lover. She took a deep breath before continuing. "I'm so sorry. I didn't know." *Why isn't this in the file? Surely, someone in the department knew that Candy had a girlfriend.*

"Not many people did. We worked different shifts. It was Candy's idea, so no one would know."

"Why did she want you to work on different shifts?"

"She said it was unprofessional for us to work together. It was too distracting."

"I see," Bitter said softly. "I'm going to have to ask a few questions about your relationship. We can take our time. You're not a suspect. We know you were still on shift when Candy—" she hesitated as Vicki let out a small gasping sob, and then continued, "when Candy passed."

Vicki looked down at the table. Her mahogany bangs fell forward to cover her face. The roots were black and curly, nearly as kinky as Bitter's own. Vicki brushed her bangs back as she looked up, and Bitter noticed her lipstick matched her gel-coated nails—a deep baroque red. The color suited her dark, melanin-rich complexion.

"Yes, I was on that call with the domestic violence hostage situation."

Bitter nodded gently. "I saw the transcripts. You did a good job of keeping the victim calm while she was hiding in the bathroom."

Vicki grimaced, "Candy texted me, but I couldn't answer. And then she didn't answer when I texted back." She paused as her eyes filled with tears. "She was already gone by the time I could reply."

Before Bitter could ask, Vicki pulled out her phone with a trembling hand and started scrolling through messages. "Here. See. She texted me at 4:30 a.m. and told me that she'd pick me up from work."

Bitter quickly transcribed the brief message and circled the time. A quick swoop and tap on the iPad captured a picture of the text. She saved the image to the case folder before continuing.

"Was she normally out at that time of night?" Bitter asked.

Vicki hesitated, "Sometimes."

"And?" Bitter prompted.

"Well, I didn't always know. I was at work. On my days off we went out dancing after Candy got off, she worked swing shift, and sometimes we wouldn't come home until the sun was up." Vicki smiled briefly before sadness overcame the happy thought.

Vicki scooted back a little in the chair and crossed her legs. Just then, the door opened a crack. A hand motioned to Bitter.

"Sorry Vicki, I'll be just a minute. Interview paused at 9:15 a.m." Bitter said before hitting the pause button on each of the electronic devices.

As she stepped to the door, Bitter noticed the red soles on Vicki's pumps. The red was lighter and brighter. It didn't match her nail polish. *Louboutin. About a grand at Saks. Pretty expensive pumps for a dispatcher.*

"What?" Bitter said impatiently to Morales as she gently closed the door, "What is so important that you need to interrupt an interview?"

"That's Candy's girlfriend?" he demanded; his face flushed.

Bitter glared. "Morales, I don't care what you think. It's not your business. Go watch the damn live feed if you want to know what she has to say. And don't interrupt me again."

"The Chief wants to talk to you before you leave."

A dark cloud surrounded Bitter as she turned to open the door. "Not now." She glanced back and said grimly, "Don't worry, you're on my list too. The interview time is in your email."

Morales' face got redder as he opened his mouth to reply. Just as Bitter shut the door in his face, she noticed his bloodshot eyes and swollen eyelids. *I wonder what's wrong with his eyes. Maybe he has allergies?*

She dismissed the distraction and managed to don her public face before she returned to the table, turned on all the electronics, and said, "Resume Vicki René interview at 9:19 a.m."

Bitter sighed. She'd gone through all the routine questions and verified where Vicki and Candy had met—like most night workers, nurses, and cops, it was on the job. The box of tissues was nearly empty. The trash was full. Vicki had a hard time answering some of the questions.

Thinking back, Bitter frowned. Vicki hesitated when asked about other relationships, and then rushed on to assure Bitter that they'd been exclusive for at least a year. Bitter's radar pinged steadily. She'd lay odds that Vicki was sincere, but Candy? Bitter remembered the bruising on Candy's arms and the entourage of blues, both male and female, who had gathered around the pretty woman at the potluck. *I need to talk to Sally. Today.*

The door eased open. "Detective Bitter?"

Bitter stood and shook the young officer's hand. "Officer Alfredo Vargas?"

"Yes, ma'am."

"Come and sit down. I have a few questions about Candy." She smiled gently at him. "Just call me Bitter. Would you like some coffee?"

"Yes ma'am. Thank you, ma'am."

Bitter poured two cups of coffee and waved him to the fixings. She waited as he added sugar and cream and took the first sip.

He smiled appreciatively. "Good coffee."

Bitter turned on all the electronics. Vargas was sweating a little, but that was no surprise. The interview rooms exuded pain and suffering and anger. She'd picked the lavender vanilla because it was a calming scent. A plus, it didn't make her wheeze.

"Interview with Officer Alfredo Vargas. Start time 10:40 a.m." With the formality done, her tone changed to soft and understanding, "Tell me about Candy. Were you friends?"

"We used to be. But then she met Vicki and she didn't have time for me anymore," Vargas said slowly.

"How long did you date?"

"Only a few months."

"When?"

"Well, I met Candy when I was first hired. She was flirting with the rookie at the front desk when I arrived."

"And that was?"

"April first, last year."

Bitter noted the date. "And when you broke up?"

He sighed, "We didn't really break up. She stopped answering my calls and texts. Then I went out one night, to this little club downtown, and she was there with Vicki. I'm not stupid." He looked down at his coffee cup. Bitter noticed that he bit his nails. The ragged edges of his cuticles were a darker shade of olive than his fingernails. "Well, maybe I was stupid that night. I got drunk after I saw them slow dancing and kissing."

Bitter nodded patiently. She'd looked up the reports and personnel records already, but she let him tell her what happened that night.

His voice got softer and acquired a hint of a Southern drawl that overlaid his Spanish accent. "I acted a fool, Bitter. Luckily, O'Malley was first on the scene. He saved my job." He took a deep breath, "I went to confession the next day. And started AA the day after that. I'd fallen into bad habits in college. The frat life—too many parties, too much alcohol. I was an athlete, so there were always girls. Lots of pretty girls."

He paused and sipped his coffee. "When I sobered up, O'Malley sat me down and recommended that I rethink my goals in life before leaping into bed with the next pretty young thing."

He looked up at Bitter, his face filled with anger. "Candy was a sweet girl. She didn't deserve to die in a stairwell."

Bitter sipped her coffee and pretended she didn't see the tears in his bloodshot eyes. After he had time to compose himself, she continued, "So, you were at work that night?"

"Yes. I was on the scene at the DV situation. The one where the wife was hiding in the bathroom."

"What time was it when you got back to the station?"

"About 6:30 a.m. We were in the break room. O'Malley was writing his report longhand, so we had coffee and waited for him to finish scribbling." A smile flashed across his face. "We were still pretty hyped from the incident. Got her safely out the bathroom window and found him passed out on the living room floor. Win-win. Wife saved and nobody else hurt, not even the suspect."

He frowned, thinking, "Sapp went off to the hospital to take her statement and the rest of us came back to the station. O'Malley met us there after he took the guy to jail. It didn't take too long. For once they weren't that busy. Got him booked in right away. So, we were just waiting on O'Malley to finish up so we could all clock out and go home."

"Did you see anyone at the station? Anyone that didn't belong there?"

He shook his head. "No one. Just the regular shift arriving for the morning briefing. The Chief came into the break room after the briefing and announced that you were getting out of the hospital that morning. The guys were all pretty stoked about it. You gave us a scare, passing out like that."

He paused. "One more thing. There was a delivery at the front desk for you when I clocked in that night. Somebody sent you a plant. It had white flowers." He tapped the table as he thought. "I can't remember who took it to your office. Somebody must have taken it upstairs and put it on your desk. It wasn't there when I left in the morning."

Bitter leaned forward. "Was there a card?"

Vargas nodded. "Yes, a big card. Pink envelope. I remember because O'Malley joked that pink wasn't your color." He looked at Bitter and his face darkened in embarrassment. "Um, yeah, it was a little tacky—"

Bitter leaned back and gave him a tight grin. "Cop humor. I understand." *O'Malley's already in sensitivity training. Not much more I can do.*

He looked at her curiously. "Didn't you get the card?"

"There were a lot of cards," Bitter deftly deflected the question. "I have to ask this: Did you see Candy again? After the scene at the bar?"

He avoided her gaze. "She did call me a few times, and, well, you know."

"No, I don't know. Tell me."

"We got together a few times. But she made it clear that it was just for fun, she wasn't leaving Vicki for a man." He paused again, before rushing on, "I had the impression that she had a thing for another woman, but it wasn't going anywhere. It seemed more like a crush than a relationship. She didn't really talk about it."

"Did she mention any names?"

"Never. She also let on that some guy was chasing her. She didn't like him. She didn't tell me who he was, just that he was a *dawg*." Vargas' vowels extended into a drawl with the last word.

"And the last time you two got together?"

Sadness spread over his face. "Last week. The night before you got out of the hospital. Before my shift."

"While Vicki was at work?"

"Yes." He rubbed the back of his neck guiltily.

"Was it consensual?"

Vargas jerked up, startled. "Of course, it was. She called me."

"And I have to ask," Bitter hesitated slightly, "did you two get a little rough sometimes?"

He blushed and looked down at his hands again, "Well, yeah. She liked it that way sometimes."

"And that night?"

"Yeah, she was really mad about that, I left marks on her arms by accident. She didn't notice until she was getting dressed. She told me that if I wasn't more careful, she wasn't going to come over anymore."

"And what did you do when she told you that."

"I got kinda mad. First, she wants it, then she doesn't, then she gets mad at me." He looked down again. "I never could figure her out."

Bitter waited silently for him to continue.

"I hope Vicki doesn't find out about this."

Bitter didn't answer.

Bitter sat back in her chair. The iPad was still downloading the interviews to her computer. She reached for the box of cards sitting on the corner of her desk. Slowly she sorted through the box. *No pink envelopes.*

She stood and hobbled to the window. *Too much sitting today. I have to do better than this, Doctor Leon wants to see me in a month.*

Flexing her knees, one at a time, she looked at the news crews hovering in the parking lot across the street. A young entrepreneur and her mother sat at a small table under a canopy. A pitcher of what looked like lemonade sat on the bright green tablecloth that covered the table. Reporters gathered in the shade, sipping from plastic cups. A cooler full of sodas and bottled waters sat next to the girl's folding chair.

Bitter frowned as a short, slightly balding reporter lit a cigarette. That didn't last long, the mom jumped up and shooed away from the patch of shade. He looked familiar, but Bitter didn't place him until the cameraman trotted up and pointed toward the river. The reporter tossed the cigarette on the ground, not bothering to scuff it out, and dashed for the dusty white and green van. It sported a large dent on the back corner, on the driver's side.

The girl darted out from the canopy and stepped on the lit cigarette, grinding its life out on the concrete sidewalk. She shook her head as she walked back to her table where another reporter waited for his lemonade.

The iPad dinged. Download complete. Bitter turned back to the computer and saved the interviews. She copied them to a flash drive, along with the rest of her files on the case. She dropped the drive in her bag. *It'll be safe in the gun safe at home.*

Though the heatwave had broken, it was still in the nineties as she pulled out of the parking lot. She rarely went home for lunch, but she had to check on Chica and Gato.

She pulled into the alley and tucked the sedan next to the garage, so there was room for another car to pass it and trudged up the back stairs. The misters inside the greenhouse cycled on again when she was halfway up the steps. *I need to fertilize the orchids.*

Chica was already barking, she could hear Bitter on the stairs. As soon as Bitter opened the back door, Chica raced down the stairs to do her business. The little dog did laps around the yard, yapping happily, while Gato rubbed against Bitter's ankles.

"Come on now. Time for lunch." Chica dashed back up the steps. She and Gato followed Bitter inside, hoping for a snack.

Bitter turned on the noon news as she fixed a sandwich and salad. The now-familiar voice of the reporter caught her attention. The makeup nearly covered his black eye, but when he turned to point at the river, the purpling next to his nose showed under the heavy layer of concealer.

Bitter flicked a piece of roast beef toward Chica. She leaped and caught it midair, then ran under the table to eat it.

The reporter was still talking, so Bitter hit the volume on the remote. "The body parts—" She hit the mute button. *Not my case. Not my problem.*

Before she left, she tucked the flash drive behind the .410 in the gun safe. "Just in case," she muttered as she locked the gun safe and put the key back in the lockbox hidden under the stairs, behind the freshly washed hockey gear. She sniffed carefully. *It still has a little hockey funk. Ugh. This weekend I'll put it all in for a long soak in the laundry sink with some oxy or baking soda and another run through the washer. That should help get the stink out.*

By the time she got back to the office and set up the interview room again, it was nearly 2 p.m. She looked at her notes. The next interview was with another relatively new officer. Bitter frowned. There were too many new officers on duty at the same time. She made a note to check the schedule and see if anyone had traded shifts or called in sick.

"Detective Bitter?" The crisp British accent echoed in the tiny room.

"Officer Peter Jones?"

"Yes."

Bitter stood and shook the tall blonde officer's hand. He squeezed too tightly. Her fingers ached after he let go of her hand. She didn't let the pain show on her face.

"Please sit down. Coffee?"

He shook his head as he settled into the old chair.

Bitter poured herself another cup before turning all the electronics on. "Interview with Officer Peter Jones." She glanced at her watch. "Time is 2:03 p.m."

Jones crossed his arms and leaned back in the old chair, tipping it back onto two legs. Bitter wondered briefly if it would hold him. Even metal chairs eventually crack and break.

"Officer Jones, please tell me about your relationship with Candy."

Jones tipped the chair forward and glared at Bitter. "I didn't have a relationship with the bloody bitch. She wouldn't give me the time of day."

Taken aback by his hostility, Bitter paused and took a sip of coffee while she gathered her thoughts. "I thought Candy was popular?"

He shook his head angrily, "No. She wasn't. And I was on the DV call when she was killed. You can check with O'Malley."

"I see." Bitter waited, letting the silence grow until it was clear Jones had nothing more to say.

"Can you tell me anything more about Candy?" she finally asked. "Did she have any enemies?"

"She had a lot of exes. She liked to flirt and play games, and then dump them without saying a word."

"So, she played that game with you?"

"No," he said, "she just brushed me off." His clenched fists and tight voice made it obvious he wasn't used to being brushed off by a woman. "She said she didn't like blondes. And then she took up with some Mexican guy. Vargas."

"Vargas' family is originally from Puerto Rico," Bitter said quietly, "not Mexico."

"Yeah, yeah, whatever. She dumped Vargas for that little Black dyke in Dispatch."

Bitter stood, put both hands on the table, and leaned forward into Jones' personal space as she took a long, hard look at him. He defiantly glared back. Shadows slid under the door and filled the corners of the room. The overhead light flickered as Bitter stared him down. She gritted out, "You will not use any kind of derogatory language regarding your coworkers or anyone else in or out of the department when speaking to me."

He finally dropped his eyes, his jaw still white with fury.

Bitter took a deep breath to regain control before she sat down and continued her questioning. In a tight voice, she asked, "What time did you leave the station that morning?"

He took his time before answering, "About 7:15 a.m. When everyone else left, right after the Chief came in and told us you were getting out of the hospital."

Bitter nodded and wound up the interview. As Jones stomped out, she checked him off her list and made a note next to his name.

Another one for sensitivity training. I'm going to have a word with Human Resources about him, he isn't a good fit in the department. Where do they find these guys?

One by one, Bitter checked off the list of officers that were in the station that night. Shift change had come and gone, with the usual thunder of boot-clad officers leaving the afternoon briefing, before she made it back to her office.

While the iPad downloaded the video onto her computer, she quickly scrolled through her emails. She'd already gone past the reminder from the high school when it registered. *Oh damn. That's tomorrow afternoon.* Quickly she looked over the interview list. All the officers had been on shift and out on calls at the time of the murder. *Rescheduling them works. I doubt they'll have anything I haven't heard already.*

She frowned when she got to Morales' name. She'd saved him for last. If she rescheduled the other officers, she'd have to interview him before the on-duty officers. She hesitated and then left him at the same interview time. *He'll probably no show anyway.*

She started at a tap at the door. It opened and Sally came in with a cart.

"Ready for some help?"

"Yes, thank you, Sally. Would you like to sit down for a minute?"

"No, I can't. I have to hurry. My grandson has graduation practice tonight. You know that Thursday is the last day of school?"

"Oh joy," Bitter groaned, "and I have a presentation tomorrow at the high school."

Sally looked at Bitter curiously, "A presentation?"

"Yes, for a criminal justice class."

"Oh, that shouldn't be too bad then," Sally chuckled as she loaded the potted plants onto the cart. "At least it's not an all-school assembly. The students will be squirrelly, with it being the next to the last day of classes."

Bitter gently took back the moth orchid. "I think I'll keep this one here. Moth orchids are tough. It'll tolerate the lighting in here, as long as I watch the humidity. I have a cool steam vaporizer that I can run when the air is too dry."

"Who sent that one?"

"I don't know. One of the blues said there was a pink envelope with it, but the card didn't make it up here."

Sally frowned, "That's odd. I didn't see this one and I'm the one that brought up the flowers and cards. I wonder who put it in here."

Bitter shrugged.

Sally glanced at her watch. "I don't want to rush you, but I need to hurry, or I'll be late picking Kenny up."

Bitter nodded briefly, "We can talk tomorrow. Let's get these down to my car."

She carefully locked the office door and tested the knob as Sally briskly pushed the cart into the elevator.

As the elevator door closed, Sally said, "I think you should know that Candy had a stalker."

"What? A stalker? Who?"

Sally made a frustrated face. "I don't know. I heard it through the grapevine."

"Who told you?"

The elevator door opened at the ground floor and before Sally could push the cart forward, Morales crowded inside, hitting the up button. Bitter glared at him as she pushed and held the door open button.

"What are you doing?" Morales demanded.

"In case you didn't notice, we were already on the elevator," Bitter said as Sally squeezed past him. "We'd like out."

Before Morales could step in front of the opening, Bitter released the button and slipped out. The elevator doors closed with a whoosh and Sally breathed a matching sigh of relief. "That man is so aggravating," she grumbled, "and rude. Just plain rude."

Bitter held the back door open, wincing at the blast of hot air, as Sally pushed the cart to the sidewalk. She pointed down the row of cars. "Down there. In the shade."

"Oh! Right next to my car. Good. Can I impose on you to take the cart back upstairs so I can pick up Kenny? That'll save me a few minutes." Sally said.

Bitter nodded absently, her mind back on Candy. "A stalker, huh? Do you remember where that rumor came from?"

"I wish I could remember. It was right on the tip of my tongue and then Morales distracted me. Now I can't think of the name. Maybe I'll remember later."

Bitter put on her gentle public smile. "If you do, would you mind leaving a message on my voicemail or texting me? It's important."

"Oh sure, Bitter," Sally said, glancing at her watch again. "I have to go."

Bitter shooed her away. "Go, go. I don't want you to be late."

Though she knew Sally was in a hurry, it startled Bitter when Sally peeled out, leaving rubber on the pavement, and roared out of the driveway.

I guess she was later than I thought. She watched as Sally gunned her bright yellow Mustang through the intersection just before the traffic light turned red. Bitter shrugged. *At least she was past the crosswalk.*

Slowly Bitter put the plants and cards into the Maverick's spacious trunk, then pushed the cart back into the building. She heard laughing as she passed the break room but didn't stop to see who was in the building. There were other things on her mind. She left the cart outside the Chief's locked door and walked back out to her car.

Halfway back to the Maverick, she stopped abruptly. A faded Confederate battle flag sticker, tattered by age and the hot valley sun, clung to the dusty glass of a lifted Chevy pickup.

What the hell? She shook her head. *I never would've noticed if he hadn't backed into the spot. Whose truck is this anyway?*

A memory of the evening news intruded, with Papá's voice echoing in her mind, "Nita, you can't fix stuck on stupid. You can't give *los babosos* facts. They just get mad and refuse to listen to anything that doesn't fit their worldview." He'd smiled sadly at her teenaged indignation and turned the TV off. They'd went out to the peaceful quiet of the lath house and fertilized the orchids.

Ah Papá, you were so right.

She put aside her disgust and went on to the Maverick. Despite the heat, she stood outside of the little car for a few minutes as she considered the possibility of a stalker and how that might've affected Candy's complicated love life.

Chapter 11 ~ Wednesday

Bitter glanced at her watch. *I'd better hurry up or I won't have time to set up for the class.*

Though traffic seemed unusually heavy around the high school, she finally pulled into the visitor parking lot with a sigh of relief. A tall, solidly built security guard in a reflective vest stepped up to the sedan.

"Ms. Bitter? We saved you a space, right over here." He pointed to the right before walking over to remove the orange cones blocking the last available space. As Bitter got out of the sedan, several students dressed in matching polo shirts and navy slacks, including Jennifer, dashed over to help.

"Here, Ms. Bitter, don't lift that." A pair of large hands reached past her and grabbed the box from the back seat. "I've got it."

More eager hands took her briefcase and the second box of supplies.

"Are you all enrolled in the criminal justice academy?" Bitter asked as she gently retrieved her purse. "Thank you," she said in an aside to the disappointed student, "I have some papers you can carry for me if you like." She handed him a folder.

"Yes, we're in the magnet school," Jennifer said eagerly.

"Okay, where is the office, Jennifer? I need to check in and then set up in your classroom."

Jennifer giggled, preening a little that Bitter remembered her name. "Oh no, Ms. Bitter, we have that all taken care of. The principal is waiting for you in the auditorium."

Bitter frowned slightly. "In the auditorium?"

"It's this way."

Before Bitter could reply, she glimpsed a familiar face. The little balding reporter bore down on the group of students with his cameraman trotting close behind. The security guard moved to intercept the pair before they reached the walkway that led into the depths of the campus.

"Let's make it quick. I don't want to talk to him," Bitter said quietly to the teen.

Jennifer glanced back and grinned as she guided Bitter into the campus. "My mom doesn't like him either." She confided as they walked quickly toward the auditorium. "He's not very nice. She says that he twists his interviews to make people sound stupid."

Bitter put on her public face and gently said, "That's not it, Jennifer. He wants to talk about the case I'm working on, and it would be unprofessional to discuss it with the media right now. That's why we have special public relations people. They act as spokespersons for the department and deal with reporters."

"Ohhh," said Jennifer.

"Now, where are you taking me?"

"Right here, Ms. Bitter, through this door." They entered the auditorium. A camera was set up at the back. The tech held a mic, obviously doing a soundcheck on the audio system. His voice echoed in the large room.

Before Bitter could say anything, the principal rushed over, "We are so happy to have you here today. We rearranged the entire assembly program for your presentation."

Bitter stopped. "The what?"

"The assembly." The tall, slightly balding man paused, his face flushing. "Didn't anyone tell you?"

Bitter pushed her annoyance aside and forced herself to smile. "Did you speak to someone at the station?" she asked.

"My secretary called your supervisor."

He looked at Jennifer, who inserted, "Captain Morales."

"Yes, Captain Morales. He said it would be fine."

Bitter closed her eyes for a moment in disbelief, and when she opened them, she reached out and shook the principal's hand. "I'm sorry, there must have been a miscommunication. I'll have to make a quick call. How long do we have to get ready? And I'm sorry, I didn't catch your name?"

He vigorously shook her hand, "Larry Peterson." He looked around at the bustling crew setting up chairs. "A half-hour."

"I'll step into the hall to make this call, if you don't mind."

"Sure, sure, whatever you need."

Bitter hit the speed dial for the Chief's office as she stepped out into the quiet hall.

"Sally?" Bitter interrupted Sally's greeting.

"Bitter? What's up?"

"I'm at the high school and they've set up an all-school assembly."

"Oh yes, the school called, and the Chief said it'd be fine." Sally stopped, puzzled, "Didn't Captain Morales tell you?"

Bitter sighed. "It's all right. I'll get it done. Thanks."

She limped back into the auditorium and looked around. Peterson rushed over, "We have about twenty minutes before students start arriving. Is everything okay?"

"Yes," Bitter said. "We have enough time if you have a high-speed copier. Jennifer, could you get the packet from the envelope there?" Bitter turned back to the principal. "I was only planning on speaking to the criminal justice class. How many more copies do we need for the students? It's only four pages total, front and back." She paused, "Also, are you set up to do a PowerPoint presentation?"

Bitter covered her ears quickly as the principal put his fingers to his lips. The piercing whistle cut through the noise of banging chairs and rumbling carts.

Silence ensued.

"Ronaldo," Peterson shouted, "we need a projector set up for a PowerPoint."

The tech on the far side of the room made a face. "Now?"

"Yes, now!"

Bitter could barely hear the cursing. She held back a smile at his creative use of the verbs and nouns to produce a suitably profane answer to the principal's request. It was in Spanish so only a few of the setup crew looked shocked.

"No news crews," Bitter said firmly.

"No, no. We don't allow them on campus." Peterson paused. "We can't keep them from talking to the students and filming from across the street though."

"That's fine."

"If I may ask, what's in the PowerPoint?"

Bitter smiled, a little grimly, "Highlights of the department and a couple of famous, or maybe infamous, cases I worked on."

Peterson grinned excitedly. "Perfect! Everyone has been talking about this since Jennifer told her instructor that you'd agreed to come and speak to the students. You'll be surprised how many hits your name has gotten on the internet this week."

Bitter nodded absently. She looked at the stage and then smiled, remembering a scene from the mystery novel she'd just finished reading.

"Can we also set up a small table, a light, and a couple of chairs on the stage," she asked abruptly.

"Sure, whatever you need."

"Hmmm, let's move the podium to the left, and put the chairs and table in the center front."

Peterson looked at her curiously.

"Don't worry, I have a plan. The screen rolls up, right?"

"Yes. It's on a remote."

"Even better," Bitter replied. She looked around, "I'll need a camera set up to project the scene at the table and chairs onto the screen so the students can see it clearly. Jennifer, I'm going to need you and a couple of your classmates for a little scenario. Let's pull out that AV unit with the TV and put it over on stage right with a couple more chairs. I'll need a light over there too." She pulled her car keys out. "I need a couple of things from the back seat of my car. Oh, and security. I'll need to speak to whoever's doing security for the assembly."

As Bitter and the students arranged the stage, shadows slid silently into the dimly lit corners. Only the spiders noticed as their webs swung gently in the breezeless room.

Students noisily filed into the auditorium. Two of Jennifer's classmates handed out Bitter's slender packets, three-hole-punched and stapled, still warm from the copier. Teachers directed their students to their seats. While most of the students excitedly chattered, Bitter noticed several young men slouched in their chairs with their long legs stretched into the center aisle. Arms crossed, legs blocking the aisle, their body language screamed defiance. One had red shoelaces on his white Jordans.

Bitter shook her head. *There's always one that ignores the dress code. No red allowed.*

As the students settled into the chairs, Bitter made her way up the steps and to the center of the stage. The lights dimmed as the principal introduced "Sacramento's best-known detective."

Bitter stood in the spotlight. Shadows crowded around and behind her, making the back corners of the unlit stage darker than a moonless night. She adjusted the microphone again as the students clapped politely.

"Thank you, Mr. Peterson," Bitter's voice echoed in the crowded expanse. "And thank you, Jennifer, for inviting me here today. I have some interesting cases to tell you about—"

All the lights in the auditorium came on as a bang rattled the windows. A dark figure ran screaming down the center of the room. Something flashed as the runner dodged a pair of Jordans sticking out in the aisle. Two more people dashed between the chairs, one brandishing a stick, while the other's face was obscured. The trio raced out the side doors as the students leaped to their feet to see what was going on.

Teachers scurried among the students, trying to calm the excited crowd as the screen slowly rolled down behind Bitter.

She waited until the volume dropped to loud chattering. Bitter held up a hand and the room quieted.

"Now, I need a volunteer to tell me what you just saw," Bitter said. "One of the students, please." She scanned the auditorium, then used her whole hand to indicate a student. "Young woman? In the third row, second seat. With the natural hair." She paused. "Yes, you. Come on up and let's talk about what just happened."

The teen's friends pushed her forward. Slowly she made her way up the side steps to the table and chairs next to Bitter.

"Now, a second volunteer please." Hands waved wildly in the air as Bitter scanned the students and motioned toward the back of the room. "Young man with the crutches, would you mind coming up and telling us what you saw?"

His bright red curls bobbed as he made his way down the aisle. He shook off help and hopped up the steps to the stage.

Bitter scanned the students and cracked a pleased grin. "You, young man, with your feet in the aisle."

The room slowly silenced as the students looked at each other.

"Yes, young man, you. With the red shoelaces. Please join us."

Two teachers began to move in on him, but Bitter waved them away, "No really, I would like the young man up here too."

Bitter shook each student's hand when they reached the stage.

"Now," she spoke to the crowd, "when we interview witnesses, we try to keep them from hearing what the previous witnesses said. Principal Peterson, could you escort the gentlemen out and down the hall, so they can't hear the young lady's story?"

She covered the mic with her hand when Peterson began to speak sharply to the tall young man with the red laces. "Not now please, let's not spoil the exercise."

Peterson gave her an exasperated look, then took the two teens out of the auditorium.

"Here. Sit down please." Bitter indicated the chair and adjusted the microphone. She turned back to face the students. "After an incident, we interview the witnesses. Sometimes it's out on the street and sometimes they come into the station to tell us what they saw. Or what they thought they saw."

Bitter glanced back at the huge screen. The little scenario was perfectly centered and easy to see. She nodded a "thank you" in Ronaldo's direction and took her seat.

"Please speak clearly into the microphone. Now Miss?"

"Williams, Miss Bitter. Tanisha Williams."

"Thank you, Miss Williams. Please tell me what you saw."

"The lights all came on and I was kinda blinded. I couldn't see," the teen said. "There was an explosion. Then somebody ran right past me. Something was flashing in his hand."

Bitter nodded. "In his hand? So, the person was a man?"

Tanisha hesitated. "I'm not sure. It was so quick."

"And then you saw?" Bitter prompted.

"Some crazy guy chasing him with a big shirt and a long thing in his hand. A stick or something."

"And the third person?"

"I just saw that one for a second, I was looking at the thing that the second person was swinging around."

"And they were all men?" Bitter asked.

Tanisha shook her head. "I don't know. It all happened so fast."

"What color were they wearing?"

"Dark clothes. The second one had on a big shirt. The last one had a hat or something on, I couldn't see his hair." She paused, thinking, "I think he had a stick too, but maybe not."

Bitter stood. "Thank you very much, Tanisha." She shook the girl's hand and a waiting teacher guided her to the chairs positioned on stage right. The auditorium buzzed as teachers tried to hush the excited students.

Bitter motioned for the principal to bring the red-headed student back in. He hopped excitedly back up the stage steps.

"Come," Bitter said. "Sit. And what's your name young man?

"Billy. Billy Boney. They call me Billy Bones because I keep breaking things." He patted his cast. "Like my leg. I fell off the roof this time."

Bitter nodded and made a quick mental note to have social services check on Billy's home life.

"Let's talk about what you saw, Mr. Boney."

"It was crazy," he blurted out. "There was a huge bang and then some girl ran down the center aisle. She had a flashlight or something in her hand, I saw it flashing as she ran."

"And then?" Bitter prompted.

He bounced excitedly on the chair. Bitter noticed a fidget spinner in his hand. It never quit moving. "Two more people were running really fast. One had a cape or something on, it was billowing. And a big stick. And the last one had a black motorcycle helmet on with a silver face shield." He paused. "I never saw a silver face shield on a motorcycle helmet before. Maybe it was a mask."

"Are you sure?" Bitter asked gently.

"Yeah, yeah, it was a mask. I'm sure."

Bitter stood and shook his hand. He kept the spinner moving constantly in his left hand as he moved to stage right, where Tanisha waited.

Bitter nodded to Peterson. He opened the door and motioned. It took a little extra time as the last student slouched through the door and up the steps.

"Good afternoon," Bitter said as stood and reached out to shake his hand.

He hesitated, then took her hand gently.

"And your name young man?"

"Luis."

Bitter gave him her public smile. "And your last name?"

"Otxoa."

Bitter gave him a larger smile. "Basque? It means wolf, right?"

For the first time, Luis looked her in the face. "*Sí*. Yes."

"Well, come and sit down." She motioned toward the chair. "Tell me what you saw, Mr. Otxoa."

"Well, the lights were dimmed and there was a loud bang. A girl ran up the center aisle and jumped over my feet." He looked sideways at the principal, who was hovering at stage left. "She had a cell phone in her hand. It was in flashlight mode."

Bitter looked at him in surprise.

"Then a guy in a hockey jersey and carrying a stick ran behind her. The other guy had a hockey helmet on with a silver cage. He was dressed in dark clothes."

Bitter smiled broadly, a genuine smile. "Very good, Mr. Otxoa. Maybe you should become a police officer, you have a good eye and memory for details."

He shrugged.

Bitter stood and motioned for the other students to join them at center stage.

"Now, let's have a show of hands. Who agrees with Miss Williams' statement?"

Half of the hands in the room shot up.

"Very good," Bitter said. "And now Mr. Boney's statement. Who agrees with him?"

Two-thirds of the remaining students raised their hands.

"Ah," said Bitter. "And Mr. Otxoa's statement?"

Only a few hands went up.

"Thank you all. Now, Mr. Peterson, will you have our trio come in please?"

Jennifer and her two classmates, Juan and Derrick, entered from behind the principal and faced the students. All three wore oversized black hockey jerseys.

"Jennifer?"

Jennifer raised her cell phone. It was covered with enough pink glitter to emit its own light, and when she turned on the flashlight and waved it above her head, sparkles followed the phone's movement.

Juan wore a goalie jersey that hung nearly to his knees and waved a defenseman's stick, long enough to hook a puck from ten feet out, while Derrick wore a black hockey helmet with a silver cage, just as Luis had described him.

Someone in the back of the room began clapping and others joined in until the sound rose in waves through the auditorium. As the clapping subsided, the lights brightened, driving the shadows back into the corners of the stage, out of sight.

"Thank you all," Bitter said. "While this scenario was taken from a mystery writer's classic novel, you can see the difficulty that we face every day. Eyewitness testimony is notoriously unreliable, although our friends did a pretty good job today. No Klingons or Storm Troopers. Or Bigfoot or sparkling vampires."

Principal Peterson snickered as the students burst into laughter. Bitter waited until it faded.

"Seriously, I've heard all of those descriptions, and not that long ago."

Bitter shook each student's hand one last time. "Thank you for helping with the scenario today. You all did a fine job, thank you."

She faced the audience and signaled Ronaldo to dim the lights again. "The PowerPoint please." She glanced at the clock. "We have time to look at a couple of Sacramento's well-known cases. The first was a reported kidnapping and Amber alert, but as we just demonstrated, things aren't always what they appear—"

As the students filed out of the auditorium, Bitter stopped Luis. "Mr. Otxoa, have you ever considered law enforcement? We could use your observational abilities in the department."

He hesitated, then pressed his lips together grimly as he shook his head no.

Bitter nodded, "Problem?"

"Maybe." He said reluctantly.

"You know, as long as it's small, like minor in possession or something like that, it's not insurmountable. No felonies." Bitter looked down, pointedly, at his shoes. "Lose the red. Suspensions hurt your grades and you'll need decent grades to get into the academy," she said sternly.

Luis' grim look faded and he flashed her a grin. "Thanks, Ms. Bitter. I'll think about it."

Chapter 12 ~ Still Wednesday

"Whew, it's hot out here," muttered Bitter as she put the last of the hockey gear in the back seat. The stick hung over the front passenger seat, wedged diagonally from back to front.

"Why do you have hockey gear in your car?" Jennifer asked curiously.

Bitter smiled. "It's some gear my son outgrew. I'm supposed to drop it off at," she hesitated, "at a friend's house on my way back to the station."

"Ohhh," Jennifer said, "that cute guy at the diner is your son?"

Bitter nodded.

"Wow. I didn't know you were that old."

Despite her irritation, Bitter held onto a strained smile. She turned to the little group of students. "Thank you all for your help today. I think the presentation turned out well."

She glanced in her mirror as she left the parking lot. The reporter was interviewing students across the street. *He never lets up. I hope this doesn't make the news.*

She turned the corner and got halfway down the block before her phone rang.

"Bitter."

"Hey, this is Harry. Sorry it took so long to get back to you."

"Hang on a minute, I'm driving."

Bitter pulled over into a shady spot under a stately Modesto ash. "Okay, I'm parked. How did the great salamander hunt go?"

Harry's voice reflected his disappointment. "Not well. The groundwater has dropped since you called me last winter, but we couldn't catch her. She's retreated into an underwater channel and we can't get at her. It's much too dangerous down there for a diver, and I'm not sure he could squeeze into the channel anyway. She's deep under the city."

Unsurprised, Bitter asked. "The babies?"

His voice brightened, "Oh we caught a bunch of them, they aren't as cautious as their momma. Or maybe it's the daddy." He chuckled, "The research students are having fits, they don't quite fit into the genus. Usually, this species is entirely aquatic, but these little guys seem to be comfortable on land, as long as there's a good water source nearby."

"Nocturnal?"

"Oh yes, definitely."

Bitter hesitated, "Food source?"

"Oh, they're carnivorous. Rats, mice, frogs, small fish, crawdads."

"People?"

It was Harry's turn to hesitate. "Well, I don't think they'd take on anything as large as a human, but they'd definitely take a bite if they had a chance. One of the graduate students was bitten when he grabbed a baby by its tail." He sighed. "No matter how many times I warn them, they just don't want to believe that a salamander will bite."

"Interesting." Bitter said, "I've noticed a huge drop in the rat population, especially downtown, near the underground city. Any sign of a mate?"

Harry huffed in frustration, "Not yet. But in their native habitat, their breeding season is August and September. The males often guard the nest, so this one might be the male and a female may be hidden somewhere else."

Before Bitter could ask, Harry said, "The students won't say anything. Nobody wants to make the *Weekly World News*. That's a career-killer."

Bitter smiled grimly. Harry would know. He'd run afoul of the tabloids early in his career. She paused, considering the latest media blitz. *It's not my side of the river.* "Have you heard anything about body parts in the river case?"

It was Harry's turn to hesitate. "Well, rumor has it that there's no sign of knife or saw marks on the bones. The damage to the remnants of flesh and the bones is more like teeth—and an acid."

"Hmmm, like digestive?"

"Hey, you didn't hear that from me."

Bitter said quietly. "I understand."

"Must go, time to feed the animals. Call me if you find any more exotic or interesting wildlife roaming the streets—or rivers."

"Will do. Thanks for the update, Harry."

She sat for a few minutes, considering body parts and carnivorous salamanders before she shook her head. *Not my case.*

Bitter wearily climbed the steep little steps to her back porch. The scent from the foil-covered plate evoked memories of Papá and his infectious laugh. He had always enjoyed grilling while family and friends gathered, eagerly waiting for the burgers and chicken.

Chica and Gato waited impatiently inside.

"Out, out, you two," Bitter said as two little noses lifted, sniffing the air. "Do your business now."

She put the plate in the microwave to keep it safe from her curious pets and nearly stepped on Chica when she turned. "Dog, go outside," she ordered. Chica danced, both front paws waving in the air.

"Chica, out!"

Gato, who sat twitching his tail and staring with unblinking eyes at Bitter until she motioned toward the open door, joined the tiny Chi. He leaped down the steps, taking three or four at a time, then strolled across the grass toward the old oak that dominated the back half of the garden.

Bitter sighed and left the back door open as she went to her bedroom to change clothes. Suitably dressed in old jeans and a T-shirt, she poured a glass of wine before she reclaimed her dinner from the microwave. Carefully, she sat down on the top step overlooking the backyard.

Unwrapping the foil revealed still-warm slices of grilled tri-tip, homemade potato salad, and a wedge of sweet potato pie. She smiled as she remembered Gema pressing the plate on her, insisting that if she couldn't stay for dinner, she could at least take a plate home.

She frowned, thinking of the coming weekend. *I wonder who's going to catch a case this weekend. Hot weather, celebrations, plus vitamin alcohol usually lead to trouble.* She sighed. *More work for me.*

She flicked a bit of tri-tip to Chica, and while the little dog was distracted, she gave a bite to Gato.

Dusk settled over the bungalow as she finished the last bite of the sweet potato pie.

"Speaking of work," Bitter said aloud, "I'd better get these orchids fertilized."

She turned on the cd player that sat on an old table next to the door. The soft sound of a Native American flute floated over the yard. The twinkle lights flicked on as the darkness grew deeper, giving the illusion of fireflies hovering under the old oak tree. Gato sat on a low branch, his eyes gleaming green in the reflected light, while Chica pranced across the grass.

Bitter unlocked the metal cabinet on the porch and carefully measured the water-soluble orchid fertilizer into a bucket. She added water and stirred gently to dissolve the fertilizer salts. Just as she lifted the bucket to pour it into the gravity-fed system that Papá had built a few months before his untimely death, Chica began barking madly.

"What the—?" Bitter looked over the porch railing. "Chica, hush."

A dark figure crouched on the grass below. "You!" Bitter shouted, "Get out of my garden!"

"Mine," Jean mumbled as he stumbled toward the tree.

Gato leaped from the branch and dashed for the porch steps, dodging the shambling figure. Jean turned and reached for the cat. Shadows poured out from the shrubbery and house and surrounded Gato, obscuring his body as he ran.

"No!" Bitter shouted and threw the bucket of fertilizer at Jean. The fluid splattered across his hand and arm.

A blood-curdling scream drowned out the music. Jean fell sideways and writhed in agony across the grass, clutching his arm. Bitter stopped in horror on the stairs as Jean's wet arm turned gray—and dissolved.

"Oh no," she gasped.

Jean staggered to his feet. He looked up at her, his pasty face twisted in pain before he turned and stumbled toward the alley.

Chica chased him, barking and snapping at his heels as he dragged himself up and over the fence, one-handed.

"Chica, Gato, in!" Bitter called. She shut them in the kitchen before she dialed, hands shaking.

"O'Malley," he answered crisply.

"This is Bitter. I have a problem."

"We're on our way. There was a 9-1-1 call from next door. Are you all right?"

"Yes," Bitter took a deep breath and regained her composure. "Come in through the alley."

"Will do. One minute out."

The growing sound of a siren cut off, but the blue and red lights were still flashing as O'Malley parked in the alley. A second unit pulled up, facing in the opposite direction.

Bitter made her way across the garden and unlocked the back gate. O'Malley and Sapp entered cautiously, hands on their weapons, and looked around the darkened yard.

"Wait, let me turn the lights on," Bitter said as she flipped the switch next to the garage door. The garden was suddenly stark in the bright floodlights.

"What happened?" asked O'Malley.

Bitter took another deep breath to ensure her voice stayed steady. "It was Jean. He crawled over the fence after Gato." She pointed up at the back porch. "I was mixing fertilizer for the orchids when I saw him. He grabbed for Gato and I threw the bucket full of liquid fertilizer at him."

She took another deep breath. "The liquid hit his arm, and it – it dissolved."

Sapp walked over to the porch, looking at the ground carefully. "Yeah, here's the spot." He said quietly. "Do you have some table salt?" He nudged the bucket with his foot, pushing it away from a mound of gray dust.

O'Malley gave Sapp a curious look. "You know what happened?"

Sapp sighed. "I meant to talk to Bitter about Jean, but she was in the hospital. The *bruja* hasn't been taking very good care of him lately."

"There's no such thing as witches," Bitter said firmly, pushing back the memory of Jean's dissolving arm.

Sapp eyed her but didn't argue the point as he continued. "Well, it'll kill the grass here, but we'll spread salt over the dust and then water it in. It'll be easier than trying to sweep it out of the thatch."

"Salt?" said O'Malley.

"Yeah. Salt breaks magic bindings. The fertilizer salts worked on his arm, but they were diluted in water. I want to be sure that there are no lingering effects after we leave." Sapp looked at Bitter somberly. "I'm not sure Jean will survive. If he got back to the old woman's house, she might be able to renew the bindings and keep him alive." He paused. "Well, as alive as he's been for the last who knows how many years."

He nudged the grass, careful to keep his toe out of the dust pile. "We'll pour salt over this mess, and water it in. Then we'll cover it with salt again and let it sit overnight. Soak the ground tomorrow. You can sod this area in a couple of weeks."

Bitter pursed her lips and frowned.

Sapp glanced at her. "Just humor me, okay?"

She nodded and slowly climbed the steps to the kitchen while O'Malley checked the garden and Sapp tested the lock on the garage and lath house.

"Catch!" she called from above.

Sapp deftly caught the flying cardboard container of salt and carefully poured a thin line around the perimeter of the dust, then sprinkled a layer of salt over the top. O'Malley turned the spigot and gently flooded the area with the garden hose. By the time Bitter reached the bottom of the steps, Sapp was adding a second layer of salt.

"So, water it down again tomorrow night. That should take care of it."

O'Malley glanced at his watch. "Gotta go. We'll write this up as a false alarm and do a welfare check on Jean tomorrow. After the sun comes up."

"Need any help with the fertilizing?" Sapp asked.

"No, Papá built a drip system when he'd collected too many orchids to fertilize them one at a time." Bitter pointed at the PVC pipe running from the porch rail to the lath house. "I'll just mix another batch of fertilizer and pour it in at the top. I can do it tomorrow. The orchids will be fine."

O'Malley looked pointedly at his watch again.

"Thanks," Bitter said. "I owe you one."

"No worries," Sapp said. "See you Sunday?"

O'Malley stopped looking at his watch. "Sunday?"

Sapp winked at Bitter before he replied. "Juneteenth celebration. Come over to my sister's place about one, we'll have more than enough food."

O'Malley grinned. "I'll be there. But we've got to go now."

The radio on his shoulder crackled. Bitter heard, "Fifty-one-fifty," amid the dispatcher's clipped words.

"See you then," Sapp said over his shoulder as they dashed to their units. "Don't forget to lock the gate."

Bitter muttered, "Like I would," as she turned the lock and turned off the floodlights.

Music drifted through the quiet garden as she climbed the steps, carrying the empty bucket. She locked the bucket inside the cabinet and went inside. The twinkle lights flickered on as she turned off the porch light.

BITTER

Shadows drifted toward the fence and gathered in pools of darkness under the oak tree. None passed over the circle of salt on the lawn.

Chapter 13 ~ Thursday

Bitter tapped her pen on the file. Her list of suspects was growing. Fair or not, Vicki's name topped the list. Bitter tapped on Vicki's name again, impatiently. *I don't think so, but I can't rule anyone out at this point.*

Vargas was next, followed by Jones.

But they were all at work. Bitter fumed. *I've verified every one of them.*

She turned to the keyboard and shot off a message to the techs working on the surveillance system and the key cards. *They should have something by now.*

Morales' interview was scheduled for 3 p.m., but Sally had called an hour earlier. He was taking the day off to "take care of some personal business." Bitter heard the sarcastic tone in Sally's voice but didn't ask what the rumor mill had to say about it. She shook her head as she hung up the phone. *Well, it's not like I'm surprised.*

A long morning of interviews produced a few new names for the suspect list. Vicki's ex was particularly bitter about being dumped for the pretty blonde. She wasted no tears on Candy, though she had plenty to say about Vicki's and Candy's relationship. Nothing good, of course. Despite her harsh words, Denise had wasted no time in finding a new girlfriend. Time-stamped receipts for the Reno hotel and ATM showed they'd been gambling when Candy met death in the stairwell. Bitter put a check next to her name.

I need to verify that they were actually together in Reno, she thought. *It wouldn't be the first time the new lover lied to cover up a crime.*

The computer chimed. A new message popped up on the screen.

Bitter's mood brightened when she opened the email. No luck on the cameras, yet, but the attachment contained a spreadsheet with a long list of officers and staff who had entered the building the morning Candy was murdered, neatly sorted by time of entry. She clicked on the print icon and reached for her highlighters and sticky notes.

I hope they caught all the key cards this time. It was a little too early to be holding the door open for a donut run.

One by one, she ticked off the names on the list. The officers out on calls during the crucial time period, check. Those interviewed and tentatively eliminated, highlighted in blue, check. Those with alibis not yet verified, marked in yellow, check. She highlighted a few names in green before she got to Morales. *What was he doing in the building so early?* She double-checked the time. *At 4:30 a.m.? Why would he be at work so early?* She put a star next to his name.

A few names down, she stopped abruptly. *The Chief? Since when does the Chief come in at 5 a.m.?* Frowning, she added a star next to his name.

There were a few more officers that had come in extra early that day, including the two rookies that were having a volatile affair. She shook her head and moved down the list, then paused. *Candy's entourage. Wasn't Cznik hanging around Candy too? Where was Adams?* She tried to remember if the handsome young officer was there or on duty, but the potluck was a fuzzy memory. She shook her head in frustration and put a star next to both names.

Bitter looked at the names and frowned. *I want the key card info for the entire week. Who else has been coming in early – and why?* She quickly typed the email and shot it off to the IT tech.

Then she scanned down the entire list. *Where is Candy?*

Candy's key card didn't appear on the list.

Damn.

Bitter glanced at the time, then dialed the Coroner's office. She wasted no time on preliminaries. "Joe," she interrupted, "Was Candy's key card on her when she came in?" Bitter listened intently. "No? Okay, thanks. I'll check the file and see what else might be missing. Talk to you later." She hung up before Joe could ask any questions.

She tapped her pen impatiently on her desk as she viewed the entire file again.

How did I miss that? And no purse found either.

Bitter shook her head. *Somebody opened the door for her. Maybe the murderer.* She stood and flexed her swollen knees a few times before she stepped away from her desk.

Time to talk to Sally.

Sally wasn't in the office.

"Oh, she took the afternoon off," the bright young woman at Sally's desk said. "I'm just filling in. Is there something I can help you with? The Chief is out too."

Bitter pursed her lips. "No. Could you just leave Sally a note that I was looking for her?"

"Sure," chirped the perky brunette.

"Thank you. I'm sorry, I didn't catch your name?"

"Oh, I'm Judy. And Sally won't be back until Monday. It's her grandson's graduation tomorrow night, so she's taking the rest of the week off."

"Ah, thank you, Judy," Bitter said.

Bitter sighed as she limped back to her office. *So much for that. It'll have to wait until Monday. Three and a half days shouldn't make a difference at this point.*

The phone rang as Bitter unlocked her office.

"Bitter."

"Hey Bitter, it's Sapp. I wanted to let you know that we drove past the old woman's house this morning before we got off shift."

"Yes?"

"It was empty."

"What?" Bitter sat down hard in her office chair. *Why didn't anyone call me earlier?*

"Yeah. Every light in the place on. The door standing open. Nobody inside. Smelled like death in there. But we couldn't find anyone inside. Called code enforcement and the health department, the place is a mess. Broken windows, mold in the sink, holes in the floors and walls, junk everywhere. We barely got through the first floor." He chuckled grimly, "Nobody wants to go down into the basement. We just got through over there for today, so I thought I should let you know before I head home. We'll have to go back out tomorrow." He sighed. "I didn't need the overtime."

"No sign of Jean?"

"None." She heard him hesitate. "Well, as far as we could tell in the mess."

"Thanks, Sapp. Keep me posted, okay?"

"Will do," Sapp said briskly. "Gotta get some sleep now. Talk to you later."

Bitter stared at the phone. The room grew dark as she sat thinking. The shadows drew closer.

"Well, hell." She got up and opened the blinds. The bright afternoon light drove the shadows back into the dark corners, away from the window. "I might as well go home, as much good as I'm doing here today." She glanced at the clock. It was only 4 p.m. She tidied up her desk, carefully putting the spreadsheet and her notes into the working file for Candy's case and locking it in a drawer.

The delicate, floating blossoms of the moth orchid on the shelf in front of the window caught her eye. *And where did you come from*, she thought, a*nd what happened to the card?*

A battered primer gray Ford F-100 blocked the alley entrance, so Bitter pulled around the block and parked in front of her bungalow. As she got out of the Maverick, she saw Señor Suarez puttering in his front yard.

"Bitter," he called, "Bitter, have you heard the news?"

"What news?"

"The old woman, she is gone."

"Really?" Bitter asked as she walked across the street.

"*La policia* were there this morning, and then there were men in and out all day. There was no one inside. *La bruja* has gathered her creatures and left."

"Did anyone see her go?"

He shook his head. "No. Not a sound." He looked at Bitter sharply. "There was screaming behind your house though. Last night, before the police came."

"Ah yes, Señor Suarez. Did you call 9-1-1?"

"Ayyyy, no. Was everything all right?" He leaned on his wrought-iron fence; his deeply tanned face wrinkled in concern.

"Jean crawled over my fence to get Gato."

"Ahhh." He nodded. "And Gato, he is safe?"

Bitter gave him a small smile. "Yes. Chica warned me."

"*Muy bueno*. The little dog earns her place en la familia."

Bitter's smile grew wider. "Yes. In her heart, she is a Rottweiler."

Suarez chuckled. "*Sí, sí*, that is true."

Bitter changed the subject. "Do you know who is blocking the alley?"

He frowned. "No. Someone is blocking the alley behind your house?"

"*Sí*. An old gray truck. A 1960s F-100."

"You should call *la policia*," he paused and gave her an amused look, a gold tooth flashing in his wide smile. "They will make him move or tow him away."

Bitter chuckled too. "Yes, Señor Suarez, I'll keep that in mind. Now I'd better go feed Gato and Chica, I can hear them carrying on all the way out here."

Chica's shrill bark continued until Bitter opened the front door. "Hush, Chica, it's me." Gato meowed nearly as loud as Chica's bark. "Here, out in front. I don't want you two messing around in that salt in the back."

Chica raced down the steps, yapping as she followed the fence line, warning off any intruders. Gato followed sedately, twitching his tail as he padded down to the walk.

Bitter yawned and went inside to change into her pajamas.

Bitter woke abruptly. She opened her eyes to a heavy, dark silence. The glowing numerals on the clock showed a few minutes before midnight. She rolled over carefully to avoid twisting her knees and snuggled back under the comforter.

Chica stuck her nose out from behind Bitter and growled at the midnight sky.

A bright light flashed through the window and a huge crack filled the air outside. The headboard slammed against the wall as the bed rose and fell with a thud. Flames exploded outside and lit the room in glowing yellows and reds.

"What the hell?" Bitter sat up as the bed settled back on the floor. She threw back the covers and looked out of the window. Flames shot from a house down the street, lighting the night sky. Burning bits of wood and shingles fell onto houses, cars, and the street.

Bitter called 9-1-1 as she was pulling on her jeans. It was busy, so she hit the preprogrammed number for the dispatch line. It was busy too. She jerked an oversized T-shirt over her head and reached for the tennis shoes tucked under the edge of the bed.

Sirens filled the air outside, rising as fire engines sped down the street and halting abruptly as the trucks stopped at the fire hydrants. Flashing blue and red lights streamed past the bungalow, lighting the bedroom. Bitter leaned out of the open window and saw police and ambulances positioned to block the street at the corner.

The cell phone rang.

"Bitter."

"Bitter, the old woman's house just blew up. Are you okay?" O'Malley shouted over the sound of sirens.

"Yes, yes, my house is fine. The explosion rocked the whole neighborhood." She paused, hearing people shouting outside. "I have to go. I need to tell my neighbors what's going on. Is the fire spreading?" she asked as she slammed the window closed to keep the billowing smoke out.

"Well, it blew chunks of the roof and siding all over, but the fire department is putting out the smaller fires now. The house is going up like a torch."

"All right, let me get out there, I hear Señor Suarez calling my name. I'll walk down when I can."

"Don't get too close. The fire chief said there could be more explosions."

"Will do." Bitter hung up and hesitated, then slipped the 9mm into its holster in the small of her back. The T-shirt covered it nicely. She stuffed her ID, business cards, and notepad into a small shoulder bag before she tied her hair back in a loose ponytail.

Chica woofed softly a few times but stayed shivering under the covers so Bitter left the little dog there. As she opened the bedroom door, Gato dived into the room and under the bed. She grabbed the box of N95 construction masks from the hall closet, where she'd stored them after last summer's fires. The breather valve helped, but she broke into a sweat as she put the mask on.

Shadows crawled above her head as she opened the front door, but in the dark, she didn't notice.

Outside, people milled in the street, cell phones raised to capture the blaze. Black and white units blocked the street and past them, she saw the inferno where the old woman's house had stood the day before. Smoldering chunks of siding and shingles lay here and there. Señor Suarez sprayed a smoking mass with a garden hose, flooding the street with water.

Bitter opened her gate as shadows scattered into the corners of the garden. Neighbors rushed over.

"What's going on?" "The explosion shook me out of bed." "Are we safe here?"

Bitter held up a hand to quiet her neighbors. "As far as I know right now, we're safe enough for the moment. Stay over here, away from the fire and out of the way." She shook her head at a shouted question. "No, I don't know what happened. It's the old woman's house."

The crowd quieted. *"La bruja,"* someone whispered.

"The house was empty yesterday. They don't think anyone was inside, they searched it." Bitter said loudly. "Here." She handed the box of masks to Señor Suarez. "Hand these out, please. You shouldn't breathe the smoke. It's probably full of toxins."

He nodded grimly and put on a mask.

Another fire engine pulled up in front of the blazing remains. Behind it, Bitter saw a familiar white and green van.

"Oh lord, that fool is going to get himself killed." She pushed through the onlookers, holding her ID high. "Move. Police, move out of the way." Before she got to the end of the block, she saw O'Malley intercept and herd the reporter and his cameraman away from the scene.

"No, you canna film from here. Get out of the way or I'll cuff you and take you downtown." O'Malley's accent thickened in anger. He pointed across the street, toward the black and whites and Bitter. "Over there. And get that van out of here. Park it at the corner, you can walk back and film from across the street. Yes, over there. And you better stay there, or I'll be arrestin' you."

Bitter ducked behind the milling group of onlookers.

"What should we do?" asked one of the apartment dwellers.

Bitter pointed down the street, away from the fire. "Right now, we need to stay out of the way. If you see anything burning anywhere else, let Señor Suarez or I know, and we'll get someone over to take care of it." She looked down the street, toward the blaze. "They're going to be working this fire all night."

"Miss Bitter?" A small voice at her elbow.

"Yes?" She turned and saw the little redheaded girl that lived in the corner apartments. The child wore a hospital mask that nearly covered her entire face.

Wow, time flies. She was just a baby the last time I talked to her mom. What is her name?

"Miss Bitter, I saw it."

Bitter glanced around, then motioned the child away from the fire. She sat down at the bus stop and patted the seat beside her. "Here, sit down, *mija*."

The child sat down primly and folded her hands in her lap.

"Tell me your name, please."

"Tabitha."

Bitter spoke gently. "Tell me what happened, Tabitha."

"I was in bed. Well, I was supposed to be in bed. I was looking out the window and a big flash of lightning hit the house and it blew up." She looked at Bitter, waiting for disbelief.

Bitter nodded. "I see. So, the lightning came out of the sky?"

"Yes," Tabitha said firmly.

Bitter looked up at the sky. Thick smoke obscured the moon and stars. If there were any clouds, she couldn't see them.

"And it hit the house and it just blew up."

"Yes."

Bitter waited for Tabitha to continue.

"It was the witch. She came back and blew up her own house."

Surprised, Bitter considered her next words before she spoke. "Did you see the witch?"

"Yes, I saw her last night when she took everything out of her house. She had pretty things, rugs, and curtains, and a huge mirror. Why did she leave, Miss Bitter?"

"I'm not sure," Bitter said gently, thinking guiltily of Jean's smoking arm dissolving into dust. "Was Jean with her?"

"The little man that didn't talk too good?"

"Yes, that was Jean."

Tabitha thought for a moment and nodded firmly. "Yes, he was with her, but I think he was hurt. He could only use one hand to move her stuff. She was mad at him."

"Did she yell at him?"

"No, but I could tell, she was tapping her cane on the dirt in the garden. I couldn't hear anything. They didn't make any noise at all."

"How many people were there?" Bitter asked, wondering who would have come to help the old woman move in the middle of the night.

"Oh, there were a bunch of guys. And a couple of women. They looked like witches too, all wrapped up in sparkly black shawls and scarves."

"And tonight, did they come back?"

"Just the witch, the one who lived there."

Bitter nodded. "And what did she do?"

Tabitha shivered, though the night was warm. "She stood in front of the house and pulled the lightning out of the sky. It hit the house," she pointed where the third floor had been, "right up there, in the middle of the star that was painted on the wall."

Bitter looked, but flames, smoke, and water from the fire hoses were the only things visible. "There was a star on the wall?"

"Yes. It was hard to see, the paint was peeling, but I saw it just before the lightning hit. But the light was so bright, I couldn't see anything more, and then the house just blew up."

"And the old woman?"

"I didn't see her anymore. She was gone."

"Tabitha! There you are!" A frantic voice intruded. "We've been looking everywhere for you."

Bitter stood. "She's safe here with me. Is everyone else all right?"

"Oh!" the young mother said, "Oh, it's you, Ms. Bitter. We were so worried about her. We couldn't find her."

"I understand," Bitter said calmly. "We were just chatting about what she saw."

Tabitha's mother rolled her eyes and knelt in front of the child. "Tabitha, what did I tell you about telling stories?" She looked up at Bitter. "Tabitha has a very active imagination."

Tabitha looked up at Bitter through a tangle of red curls. "I wasn't telling a story," she said precisely. "I was telling Miss Bitter what I saw."

Bitter pulled out a business card. "I'm sure the fire inspector will want to talk to Tabitha. I'm sorry we frightened you, Wendy."

The younger woman gave her child a tense look.

"No, no. It's fine. It's his job to talk to everyone who even thinks they might've seen something." Bitter scribbled a number on the back of the card before she held it out to Wendy. "Just call him in the morning, after you get up. Tell him that I said to call."

Hesitantly, Wendy took the card.

"After you all get up," Bitter repeated briskly before Wendy could speak. "And are you staying in your apartment tonight? Are you okay? Or do you need a motel for the night?" She motioned toward the opposite end of the block, where Red Cross volunteers were setting up a table and coffeepots. "They have coffee, hot chocolate, and tea. And if you need a place to stay, they have motel vouchers."

Wendy went limp with relief. "Thank you. I'm too afraid to stay there tonight. The fireman came and told us that we had to get out of the apartment until the fire was out."

Bitter took Tabitha by the hand. "Don't you have a brother or sister, Tabitha? Let's take your mom over to the Red Cross so you can go to the motel tonight." She leaned down and said in a stage whisper, "It'll be an adventure."

"But I don't have my toothbrush."

"I'm sure the nice ladies with the Red Cross have one for you. Maybe a hairbrush too."

Tabitha reached up and touched the kinky strands that had come loose from Bitter's ponytail. "Your hair is so pretty and curly," she said. "Why do you always put it up?"

Bitter held herself still instead of jerking her head back. *She's just a child*, Bitter told herself. *She doesn't know any better.*

"Tabitha!" Wendy hissed. "You don't touch other people's hair. It's rude." She looked apologetically at Bitter. "She's fascinated by curly hair. Especially Black hair." Bitter started to nod as Wendy continued, "Or is that a weave?"

"I see," Bitter said tightly.

Wendy didn't notice, she gathered her children from the hovering woman who lived on the other side of Bitter.

Bitter pushed back her irritation at the sight of the littlest one. *When did Wendy have a baby? I really need to pay closer attention to the neighborhood. With the boys grown and gone, I've lost track.* She resolved to invite Señor Suarez over for coffee to catch up on the neighborhood's doings. *Soon.*

Out of habit, she glued her smile back on, though no one could see it under the mask. "*Muchas gracias*, Señora Gutierrez."

"Thank you," said Wendy to the small, dark-haired woman, who smiled and patted each child on the head.

"*De nada*," she said.

Bitter delivered the little family—Wendy, Tabitha, and two siblings—to the Red Cross volunteers, who fussed over the children and made sure they all had goodie bags before the taxi arrived.

Tabitha turned and waved. "Bye-bye, Miss Bitter."

Bitter waved back and sighed with relief. *All right then, that's one family taken care of for the night.* She sat back down on the bench and pulled out the notepad. She didn't look up when a shadow floated over the paper. She kept writing.

Once the neighbors realized the house was empty, they settled in to watch the show. Lawn chairs and coolers appeared along the sidewalk, where the neighborhood could watch the burning house and firemen working to put it out.

"Not like we're going to get any sleep," said a young man as he sat down on the other end of the bench and offered Bitter a beer.

She looked up, startled. "Oh, sorry, I don't drink beer. Thanks anyway."

A crash and sparks flew up in a twisted cyclone of smoke and ash. Firefighters ducked back, then moved in again with water and foam.

Bitter stood and stretched wearily. *Coffee, I need some coffee,* she thought. *I'll make copies of these notes and give them to the fire marshal in the morning.*

The Red Cross volunteer handed her a full cup of coffee. It steamed in the night air. Bitter added cream and sugar and put the lid on the cup before removing her mask and sipping it cautiously through a straw. *Hmm, not bad.* She drank it quickly and settled the mask back over her face. *I should check the alley. If that truck is gone, I can put the Maverick back in the garage.* She slowly walked down the block, away from the fire, and around the corner.

The streetlights glowed yellow, dimmed by the smoky haze that settled over the neighborhood. Shadows followed Bitter, but she didn't notice. The truck that had blocked the alley earlier was gone. A fire truck blocked access at the far end, preventing traffic from entering the narrow lane.

She walked halfway down the alley, toward her garage, before she saw the dark shape huddled on the ground, across from her back gate.

"Are you all right?" she asked cautiously, standing well back. Drunks and drug addicts occasionally staggered down the alley and curled up under the neighbor's garage overhang, where there was a little shelter from the hot sun and rain. There was no rain tonight, only smoke and barely a breeze.

"Are you all right?" she repeated loudly. "Do you need help?"

Nothing moved in the alley.

She couldn't hear any breathing over the noise of the fire.

Bitter pulled out her cell phone and hit the speed dial. She interrupted the dispatcher, "This is Bitter. I have someone on the ground behind my house, in the back alley. I can't tell if he's breathing. He's not responding to questions. Can you get someone over here?" She listened intently. "Yes, the alley. Behind my house. Yes, where I live. By the fire. Send an ambulance too."

She shook her head as she hung up. Dying sparks fell from the sky as she carefully circled the body, looking for signs of life, one hand on the 9mm. Instinct warred with training, she knew better than to disturb a passed out drunk or druggie until backup was handy. She rubbed the long-healed knife scar on her forearm against her jeans. *A rookie mistake, I was lucky.*

"Bitter?" A soft call echoed in the night.

"Yes, O'Malley, down here."

O'Malley closed the distance in long strides. He stopped and looked carefully around before he turned his flashlight onto the huddled form. With one hand on his taser, he cautiously nudged the body with a toe. It didn't move.

"Hey, are you okay?" he asked.

Bitter padded closer. In the bright light of O'Malley's flashlight, she saw a dark stain under the body.

"O'Malley, I think he's hurt. That's blood."

He angled his flashlight to get a better view as Bitter leaned over and gently pulled back the hoodie. He, no, she didn't react. Blonde hair spilled out as her head lolled back.

O'Malley stepped back in surprise.

"Sweet mother of god, it's Sally." He paused. "Bitter?"

Bitter felt Sally's neck for a pulse. She caught a faint flutter.

"She's alive. Barely."

O'Malley fumbled for his radio. "Dispatch, I need EMTs and an ambulance in the alley behind Bitter's place. We have a victim down, injuries unknown."

Bitter rolled Sally onto her back with an effort. Blood covered the front of Sally's white silk blouse and welled up through the tattered fabric. Bitter quickly put pressure onto the gaping wound and with her free hand fumbled for her keys. "Here." She tossed the keys to O'Malley. "Open the garage door. The light switch is just inside on the right. There are clean rags on the bench."

A few quick steps took O'Malley to the garage. Light spilled out into the alley.

"Quick," Bitter said, "Give me a rag." She wadded up the cloth and placed it over the wound. Blood covered her hands as she applied more pressure.

"EMTs are on the way."

"I already called," Bitter said as an ambulance pulled up at the far end of the alley, away from the fire. Two EMTs from the fire department rounded the opposite corner and trotted toward

Bitter and O'Malley. Bitter kept both hands on the wound until the first EMT knelt over Sally and took her place.

"More light," the short, stocky woman demanded while her partner checked Sally's vitals.

Bitter opened her gate and flipped on the garden lights. The bright white light washed over the fence and into the alley.

"I've got a pulse."

"Shit, somebody shot her."

"Get that bleeding stopped."

"Jeez, look at the size of the exit wound. Get her on her side, quick, let me get a dressing on the entry hole."

Bitter stayed back, out of the way, and looked around. "We'll need to tape off both ends of the alley. Get Forensics out here. Let's try not to disturb the scene too much." She watched the EMTs work on Sally, frowning, as the ambulance backed down the alley. O'Malley wet a rag in the garage sink and handed it to her. She wiped the blood off her hands.

O'Malley directed the ambulance as it backed down the alley until he motioned for it to stop. A third EMT leaped out of the back and pulled out the gurney.

The EMTs loaded Sally up and into the ambulance. The driver barely gave O'Malley time to slam the doors before she gunned it. She skidded a little, then the wheels caught, and she sped down the alley, lights, and siren blaring. One of the other EMTs handed Bitter some alcohol wipes before they trotted back toward the fire.

More blues spilled into the alley, flashing lights into every crack and cranny along the lane.

"Get back," O'Malley ordered. "Forensics is on the way. Tape off the other end of the alley and," he pointed, "you two, Jones and Cznik, go keep an eye on it. Don't let anyone but Forensics through. And start a log," he called after them.

Bitter examined the ground around and on each side of the bloodstain. "O'Malley, I think she was dumped here. There's not enough blood on the ground."

He looked at the dark stain carefully. "I think you're right. Some of that is oil."

"Yeah, from Mr. Christenson's old bucket," Bitter said disapprovingly. "It leaks a quart a week."

He frowned and focused the flashlight on the bare ground. "Were there any strange cars around? She's a big woman, they must have dumped her out right here or there'd be drag marks in the gravel."

Bitter stopped and looked back up the alley, toward the fire. "A beat-up old F-100 was blocking the alley when I got home from work."

"You didn't call it in?"

"No," Bitter said sharply as she walked back into the garage. She began soaping up her hands and arms in the utility sink, washing off the remaining blood. O'Malley looked at her and bit off his next question.

"What was she doing here?" Bitter continued as she rinsed and dried her hands on a clean rag, "Why would someone dump her behind my house?" She ripped open an alcohol wipe and carefully wiped her hands and arms, then used a second wipe to clean the gate latch and light switch.

He nodded. "I was wondering about that. Did she even know where you live?"

"It wouldn't be hard for her to look it up. She has access to all our personal information."

Headlights lit the alley as the forensics van pulled up. The driver spoke to Jones, then backed up and pulled across the entrance of the alley to block it. Techs spilled out, pulling out a canopy, lights, and the other tools of their trade. Bitter stepped aside and motioned toward the dark stain where she'd found Sally.

"Have your supe send me the report when you're done," she told the nearest tech.

He looked at her blankly. Bitter impatiently jerked out a card and handed it to him. He glanced at it, looked at Bitter, and looked at the card again.

"Oh." He stuttered, "Oh, sorry Bitter. I didn't recognize you." He motioned toward his face. "The mask."

O'Malley snorted, then looked away when the tech gave him a sharp glance.

"Yes, I'll let Sgt. Franks know. We'll get that to you as soon as we process the scene and get it written up." His voice changed from professional to concerned. "Is she still alive?"

"When they left," Bitter said.

He nodded, "Hope she makes it."

"Me too," Bitter said softly.

She turned back toward O'Malley, all business. "Call the chaplain. Somebody needs to go tell her grandson and get him to the hospital. As far as I know, he's her only family member in the area." She softened her tone. "And we need to get some officers together for his graduation tomorrow night. I don't want him to miss his graduation or graduate alone. Ask around, see if there's anyone who knows the boy who is willing to take him."

O'Malley stared into a dark corner, next to Bitter's garage.

"O'Malley?" Bitter said sharply.

"Yes, I heard you. I'll pick the lad up and take him to his graduation. Don't worry, I'll make sure he gets there." O'Malley said absently, still looking at the shadows gathering in pools of darkness just outside of the portable lights the techs had set up. He finally shook his head and got out his notebook. "Well, Bitter, you were first on the scene, so what did you see and when?"

Dawn touched the horizon as Bitter wearily climbed the steps to her porch. She left the front door slightly ajar as she padded down the hall. Gato and Chica raced out to the garden when she opened her bedroom door. She followed them back outside. Ashes covered the peacock chair. She frowned at the mess and shook the cushion over the rail to knock the ashes off before she sat down.

"Ayyyy, Papá, what would you do now?" she said aloud as she looked over the ash-laden landscape. Even the apple green of the Maverick lost its brilliance in the soft amber light. She leaned back and closed her eyes, ignoring the faint wisps of shadows hovering amid the haze of smoke that still covered the neighborhood.

She slipped into sleep, but it didn't last. A heavy thump into her lap woke her. "Gato!" she grumped. "Okay, okay, everybody back to bed. I won't make any sense at all if I don't get some sleep."

She pulled out her cell phone and hit the speed dial. "This is Bitter. Tell the Chief and Captain Morales I won't be in the office today. After I get some sleep, I'll go talk to Sally's grandson. Any word on how's she doing?" Bitter listened intently. "She's in surgery? They think she's going to make it?" She sighed. "That's one bit of good news today. Thanks."

She dropped the mask onto the chair before she went inside. The kettle was already on the stove in the kitchen. She turned on the burner to boil water for mint tea. *It's not like I'm going to need it to relax, I'm so tired I think I'd sleep through another explosion.*

While she waited for the water to boil, she pulled out the 9mm and laid it on the table so she could safely take off the holster and strip out of her blood-stained clothes. She dropped the T-shirt and jeans in the laundry sink to soak. *A quick shower, then sleep. I'll wash my hair later.*

Gato and Chica beat her back to the bed.

Chapter 14 ~ Friday

The cell phone's shrill trilling brought Bitter out of a deep sleep. She blinked and focused on the clock. It said 10 a.m. She'd only been asleep a couple of hours.

"What?" she barked into the phone.

"Mom, are you all right?" José asked anxiously. "I just caught the noon news and saw the fire."

Bitter sighed. "Yes, son. I'm fine. I'm sure O'Malley or Sapp would've called you if something had happened to me."

"Yes, but—"

"Son. I'm fine. The house is fine. I've only been asleep a couple of hours."

"Sorry, Mom, I was worried. It made the national news."

Bitter blinked blearily. "Must be a slow news day."

José chuckled. "Yeah, I guess so." He paused. "It was *la casa de la bruja*, wasn't it?"

"There's no such thing as witches," Bitter said automatically.

"Okay, Mom," José said slowly. "But it was her house, right?"

"Yes, it was the old woman's house."

"And who got hurt? They said there was a body in the alley."

Only the hovering shadows could see her expression. "Yes son, I found Sally lying on the ground in the alley behind the house. Somebody shot her."

"Sally?" José's disbelief echoed in his voice, "The secretary that works for the Chief? What was she doing back there? Who would shoot her?"

"We don't know yet. She was alive when they rushed her to the hospital."

"Damn. That's weird."

Bitter rubbed her eyes. "Son, do me a big favor please?"

"Sure, what?"

"Don't call your brother. I'll call and leave him a voicemail, so he knows everything is fine. He'll pick it up when he can. I don't know where he is right now. Some hush-hush job again."

"As long as you're going to call him."

"I will," Bitter said testily. She took a deep breath. José didn't deserve her grumpy tone. He was just worried. She gentled her tone. "Thank you, son. Now I need to get some sleep. Love you."

"Love you too, Mom. Be careful."

"I will."

Bitter shook her head slowly after José hung up. She sat up and reached across the nightstand to pull the blackout curtains closed before she snuggled down into the bed and drifted off into a light sleep. The acrid stench of the smoke in her hair slowly filtered into her consciousness and Bitter found herself staring at the wallpaper in the dim room. Finally, she pushed back the comforter.

"I'm awake now. I might as well get up and wash the stink out of my hair," she muttered.

Bitter poured herself another cup of coffee as the washer churned. All her bedding smelled like smoke, so she'd put it in the washer before she showered.

As she took the first sip, her cell phone rang again. She muted the noon news and reached for the phone.

"Bitter."

"Nita, are you all right?"

"Yes, Julio," she said wearily, "I'm fine, the house is fine, the animals are fine."

"I saw the fire on the news. Rosalia's mother has called three times already asking about the little dog."

Bitter chuckled sourly. "She didn't ask about anything else, did she?"

"Oh, she wanted to know about the car too."

"Chica is fine. The mechanic has a rebuilt engine for the Honda, but it'll take some time. There's a lot of damage so he's waiting on the rest of the parts before he starts the repairs. Where is Rosalia anyway?"

Julio hesitated, "Well, she had a failure to appear on something from several years ago, so she got scooped up at the ER." He rushed on, "Nothing for you to worry about, we're helping her take care of it. She was extradited to Merced County. Some mess that involved an ex-boyfriend. I guess he told her that it was all taken care of, and then he threw away all the court papers after she broke up with him. She missed the last court date because she didn't know about it. The lawyer said it shouldn't be much longer."

Bitter frowned.

"The little dog hasn't been a problem, has she?"

"No, no. She's fine. Gato seems to like her."

"I'll let my wife know, so she can tell her cousin."

"Okay, thanks, Julio."

Bitter hit the end button and contemplated the silent television. The noon anchor looked somber before the screen switched to video. Bitter hit the sound button.

"While rumors of arson are circulating the Alkali Flat neighborhood, fire investigators are working with local law enforcement to determine the cause of the fire. The property had recently been vacated by its long-time owner." The video of the charred remnants of the old woman's house panned to the alley as the anchor continued, "Meanwhile, Chief Brown refused to comment on the investigation into the shooting in a nearby alley, just around the corner from the fire. A thirty-year police department employee was found shot behind another employee's home. The identity and condition of the victim have been withheld pending notification of relatives."

Bitter sighed deeply and hit the off button.

"At least they didn't say my name," she said to Chica and Gato as she glanced out the kitchen window. Just beyond the back fence, she saw the rust-streaked white top of a van.

"Well, hell," she muttered. "That blasted reporter's waiting for me to leave for work." She smiled grimly. "He can wait a while longer."

Just then, the phone rang. She eyed it and contemplated dropping it in the trash before she finally answered. "Bitter."

"Detective Bitter?" chirped an unfamiliar voice.

"Speaking." She kept an eye on the van as she poured another cup of coffee.

"This is Judy. The Chief wants to talk to you."

"Well, put him on."

She barely recognized the Chief's voice. "Bitter, I need you to work this case." With a sinking feeling, she knew what he was going to say before he continued. "Sally. I need you to find out who shot Sally."

Bitter knew better than to argue when she heard that tone. The Chief wouldn't take no for an answer, and she wasn't sure she wanted to say no anyway. "Yes sir. Please write up the memo and shoot me an email. I'm already committed to attend Sally's grandson's graduation tonight, so I'll start putting it together in the morning." She thought for a moment. "Actually, I'll see the boy tonight, probably at the hospital. If I have a chance, I'll talk to him and see what he remembers."

"Fine. That's fine. I'll have the temp draft the memo."

Bitter paused, "Chief, let's be sure and look that draft over carefully before you circulate it. Remember what happened the last time a temp distributed an official memo."

A chuckle filtered through the pain in his voice, "Yes, I haven't forgotten. 'Pubic' instead of 'Public.' And Sally," he choked a little, "Sally read me the riot act about letting temps do her work."

"Chief, could you email me a list of the on- and off-duty officers for last night?"

She heard the hesitation in his voice, "Do you think one of us might've shot Sally?"

"I want to cover every base, sir. Has anyone gone out to check the area and see if there's any footage of the cross streets? I think some of my neighbors have those new doorbell cameras. And I'll talk to the neighborhood watch captain, I'd mentioned to him that there was a truck parked across the alley earlier. He might've checked it out already."

"Good. I'll have Morales assign someone to check for cameras and I'll have Judy email you the schedule for last night." He sighed heavily, "Thank you, Bitter. We're depending on you."

Bitter disconnected the call. *He's putting me in a bad spot. It's all a conflict and I shouldn't be working either of these cases. But what choice do I have?* She picked up her coffee cup and padded into the hall. "What would you do, Papá?" she asked the picture on the wall. She closed her eyes, not seeing the shadows gathering around her in an invisible embrace. After a moment, she sighed, "Yes, you'd do what needed to be done. I'll take care of it. One way or another."

While the sheets turned in the dryer, Bitter polished her practical black shoes to a high gloss. For a brief moment, she considered pumps, but her knees protested even as she thought about wearing heels. She put fresh sheets on her bed and washed up the dishes while the comforter finished drying.

Bitter glanced at the clock. "Whoops, gotta go." She slipped into her dress uniform and tucked the .45 into its holster. She slung her purse over her shoulder and shooed Gato and Chica into the kitchen.

Just as she reached the front door, her cell phone rang.

"Bitter."

"I've got Kenny, we're already at the school."

"I'm leaving now. I have to make sure the coast is clear, there's a reporter staked out in the alley. Do we need tickets?"

"We're good. The principal approved us. Just tell security your name."

Bitter paced up and down the short hall, in and out of the living room, as she spoke. "Any word on Sally?"

"She's holding her own. Still unconscious. We'll take the boy over to the hospital after we get him graduated."

"Good job. I want to talk to him, but I can do that at the hospital."

O'Malley hesitated. "Um, Bitter. He's nonverbal."

"What?"

"He doesn't talk."

Bitter sat down on the living room sofa. "He doesn't talk?"

"No."

"He writes? Types?"

"Oh yes. He's a very bright young man. He just doesn't talk."

"Oh," Bitter thought for a moment. "Well, we'll work it out."

She stood and went back to the front of the house. Slowly, she barely cracked the front door. A peek to the left and right revealed an empty street.

"No sign of reporters. See you at the school."

The lingering smoke had dissipated in the light breeze that sprang up after sunrise. Bitter frowned at the layer of ash on the Maverick, then shrugged. *I'll take her to the car wash on Saturday and have her detailed.* She whipped the little car around the corner and accelerated toward Midtown before the reporter and his cameraman realized that she'd slipped away.

A row of black and whites filled the red zone in front of the Memorial Auditorium. Bitter nodded as she turned into the driveway. *Good,* she thought, *the department turned out in full force for Kenny.* The same security guard she'd seen at the assembly waved Bitter through and pointed left to an empty spot amid the reserved spaces.

The seats quickly filled with proud parents, grandparents, and siblings, while the officers stood along the wall. Clad in their dress uniforms, the blues made a statement by their presence. Most of the parents and guests were ready for the occasion, and the few attendees dressed in the local "colors" slowed their strut and lowered their voices when they spotted the officers lining the perimeter of the auditorium.

The graduation, like all ceremonies, dragged on until the graduates finally proceeded across the stage.

O'Malley nudged Bitter when a tall, olive-complected teen stepped up to receive his diploma. Loose light brown curls escaped from under his cap.

"Kenny," O'Malley muttered.

As Kenny received his diploma, the crowd burst into applause. The blues stepped forward and high-fived him as he walked back toward his seat. He paused in front of Bitter and moved his hands rapidly in sign language. She smiled gently at him, not understanding until O'Malley whispered loudly, "He said 'Thank you.'"

Bitter looked up and nodded. "You're welcome, Kenny. We're glad to come and see you graduate."

Kenny smiled sadly and nodded back. Before Bitter could react, he stepped forward, bent down, and threw his arms around her. He shook slightly and she realized he was trying not to cry. She hesitated for a fraction of a second as she pushed back her own emotional memories, then hugged him tightly.

O'Malley waited politely until Kenny stepped back. "Kenny, you'd best get back now." The teen signed again and went on to his seat amid the other graduates.

"What did he say?" Bitter asked quietly.

"He'll see us after the graduation. I'm taking him to the hospital."

"I didn't know you knew American Sign Language."

"My youngest is hearing-impaired. Aiden played football with Kenny last year before he graduated. The boys spent a lot of time together before Aiden went off to college." O'Malley smiled proudly, "Aiden's on the college team. A wide receiver. He says he doesn't need to hear to catch a pass—just so he catches it. He's waiting for Kenny to join him. The lad got a full-ride football scholarship."

Impressed, Bitter watched Kenny rejoin his classmates.

"Why doesn't he talk?"

O'Malley looked away uncomfortably before he replied softly. "His mother, Sally's daughter, died in an accident when he was a baby and after a couple of years, his father remarried. Child Protective Services got involved when his preschool teacher noticed that he had stopped talking and there were bruises on his face. When they got him to the hospital, the doctor found more bruises, cigarette burns, and partially healed rib fractures. They think his stepmother abused him, but they couldn't pin it on either parent."

Bitter nodded, her eyes still on Kenny. "So, he was placed with Sally." It wasn't a question.

"Yes," O'Malley said. "He hasn't spoken since he was four."

She sighed. "Is he eighteen?"

"This coming weekend. And he's going to stay at my house. I've already talked it over with his social worker."

Bitter pursed her lips. "Kathleen?"

"Aye, she and Sally are friendly. It'll be all right."

Bitter looked doubtfully at O'Malley. His wife was notorious for her temper—she had once smashed the windshield of his unit in a fit of rage.

He chuckled as he met her gaze. "No, really. She likes the lad. He'll be fine."

The hospital sighed with pain and suffering. It was after visiting hours and the daily bustle had quieted into the slow rhythms of the night. Muted footsteps echoed through its dim halls and shadows crowded into darkened corners. The elevator rose, floor by floor, the numbers flashing on and off. Bitter stood silently, thinking, as it stopped and let visitors and staff on and off. Finally, the bell dinged, and the door opened at the correct floor.

Bitter stepped out and turned right, toward the Intensive Care Unit waiting room. The scent of coffee and hot chocolate wafted from the carrier in her hands. O'Malley sat across from Kenny, their flying fingers filling the silence. He nodded as Bitter entered and motioned for her to sit down.

"Sally?" she asked as she set down the drinks. She handed the hot chocolate to Kenny and took a coffee for herself.

"Still unconscious but holding her own. She's on a ventilator now, but the doctor thinks they may be able to take her off it tomorrow." O'Malley replied before sipping the hot coffee gingerly. "We have a blue stationed in front of her bed. You can't see him from here. She's in the back corner where they can keep a close eye on her."

Bitter nodded, glancing toward the nurses' station. The light from the computer screen lit the nurse's face as he worked. Someone was snoring softly nearby, drowning out the gentle beeps of the monitoring equipment.

"Who's been by?"

O'Malley gave Bitter a sharp glance. "The Chief, of course, and most of the office staff. A few blues, mostly women. Why?"

"Who's keeping the log?"

O'Malley pointed with his chin toward the nurses' station. "Everyone has to sign in. And they aren't letting anyone but family and the Chief in anyway."

Bitter turned toward Kenny. "How are you doing?" He shrugged unhappily. "Are you up for a few questions?" He shrugged again and looked at O'Malley. The officer nodded gently.

Bitter pulled a chair closer to Kenny and sat down. She pulled a small notebook out of her purse. "If you think of anything later, you can always email me. Right now, I just have a few questions."

O'Malley translated as Kenny signed reluctantly, "What do you need from me?"

"Do you know when Sally left the house last night?"

"It was about 8 o'clock. Grandma said she had a date."

Bitter looked up from her notebook in surprise. "A date? Did she say who?"

"No, she never tells me who she's going out with. She always drives, so I never see who he is."

"Is it the same person?"

"I don't know. She never tells me anything about her dates."

Bitter frowned. "Does she meet them online?"

Kenny shook his head. "No."

"Church? School? Work?"

"She used to date some old guy, but I think she broke up with him." Kenny's fingers made emphatic motions. "She was pretty mad at him. I heard her on the phone telling her friend that he lied to her, that he was still married."

Bitter held in her groan. The odd hours and stress were hard on a marriage, and some cops enjoyed the thrill of the chase, both on and off the job. She took a slow sip of her coffee before asking, "Did he work for the police department?"

"She never told me, but I think so."

"Did you have any idea where she was going?"

"I thought they were going out to dinner. She made dinner for me, but she didn't eat. She said she'd be home by midnight." Kenny paused and rubbed his face with both hands to hide the tears welling up in his eyes.

Bitter gentled her voice, "She's tough, Kenny. She's going to be all right."

He flashed her a broken smile while his fingers danced, "If anybody can make it through this, it's Grandma. I just wish there was something I could do." He paused while O'Malley translated. "I need to take a walk or something. I can't just sit here." He abruptly stood and began pacing. The nurse looked up at the sudden movement, then turned back to his work.

In the silence that followed, Bitter heard a distant sobbing. She stood and turned away from O'Malley and Kenny, holding up a hand as O'Malley opened his mouth. "Shhh."

Kenny looked at her, puzzled, before he caught the thin thread of sound. He glanced toward the nurses' station, then back toward the hall.

Slowly O'Malley unfolded himself from the chair and rose. "Who's crying?" he asked.

"I don't know," Bitter whispered. "I heard it when I was here before."

Kenny quietly stepped into the hall, then turned back toward the two adults. "Let's go find her." He bit his lip as he signed. "I have to do something, or I'll go crazy."

"Let me peek in at Sally, and then we'll go look around," Bitter said. Painful memories of waiting anxiously in the ER while doctors worked on Papá intruded for a moment. She pushed them back. *No time now,* she thought. She drank the rest of her coffee and dropped the cup in the trash.

The nurse looked up as she quietly signed the log. "ID?" he asked. Bitter showed her ID and he nodded. "Show the officer, too." He pointed toward the back corner before focusing on the computer screen again. Bitter noticed that the soft sounds of the ICU drowned out the distant sobbing.

The blue put down a book and stood, one hand on his weapon, as she rounded the corner. Bitter held up her ID. He pulled out a penlight and examined it carefully before moving out of the way. Bitter paused. "What city?" she asked, peering in the dim light at his uniform.

"Bakersfield," he replied. "They wanted someone from out of the area to keep an eye on her."

She nodded, satisfied, as she gently pushed the curtain back. Sally lay in the hospital bed, her hair scattered over the pillow, eyes closed, pale and quiet except the rise and fall of her bandaged chest. The monitor beeped steadily. Bitter stood for a moment next to the bed, fury rising into her throat. "I'll find them for you, Sally," she vowed in a bare whisper, "They aren't going to get away with this."

She touched Sally's pale, plump hand lightly before turning away. The blue adjusted the curtain as Bitter slipped past him. "Nobody but Kenny, the Chief, and me," she said firmly.

"Those are my orders," he said.

"Right," Bitter snapped. Then she stopped herself. He was just doing his job. "Sorry. I know you know what to do."

"I understand. Tough case. I'll keep them out."

"I'll be back later," she said as he sat down in the institutional wood and foam chair and picked up his book. The tiny book light made a bright spot in the darkened room. *They must've dragged that chair in from the waiting room*, Bitter thought, *It's the same fabric.* She turned and walked back to the waiting room. "Ready?"

Kenny stood in the hall, his head cocked as he listened to the faint sobs. He glanced right and left before turning to the right and leading Bitter and O'Malley toward the emergency exit. Shadows slipped along the walls behind them.

"Wait," whispered Bitter as Kenny opened the steel fire door, "We'll wait on this side, O'Malley, you go on through and make sure the door opens from the inside."

Kenny gave her a crooked smile and signed, "It does. I used the stairs the last time I was here."

Bitter nodded and said gently, "Let's double-check anyway."

When O'Malley opened the door from inside the stairwell, she gave Kenny a thumbs up. "You were right, of course. But we can't be too careful."

He grinned at her before he slipped through the door.

Bitter looked up and down the stairs. The sobbing echoed in the dusty silence. She couldn't tell where the sound was loudest. "Which way?" she asked. Kenny pointed down. "Are you sure?" He nodded. She grabbed his arm as he started down the stairs. "O'Malley, you first. Kenny and I will follow." Kenny frowned at her until she looked down at her knees. "Sorry," she said reluctantly. "Bad knees."

With an understanding nod, Kenny signed. "Go down backward."

Bitter looked at him questioningly.

"It's easier on your knees. Hold the rail and go down backward. I'll guide you."

She shrugged and turned at the top of the stairs, gripping the inner rail tightly. Kenny put a hand lightly on her shoulder as they took the first step down. Bitter focused on the battered gray steps as they went down, one step at a time. Not being able to see where she was going put her off balance. Kenny patted her shoulder at the last step before the landing.

"Better?" asked O'Malley.

"Yes," Bitter said. She looked at Kenny. "Thank you. I never would've thought of that. But it works."

Kenny shot her a brief smile, then tipped his head and turned, listening intently. He pointed down.

At the next landing, when O'Malley opened the fire door to listen, the sobbing sound was louder. Bitter frowned as she looked down the stairs.

"It sounds different," O'Malley observed.

She nodded. "Let's go down another couple of floors."

Two more landings and Bitter stopped. "I need a break."

Kenny turned toward her, his expression stricken with concern. "No, no, I'm okay. My knees just need a little rest." She smiled to reassure him, "Backwards is better, but my neighbors may think I'm crazy."

Kenny raised an eyebrow.

"She lives in a high-water bungalow," explained O'Malley. "Her front door is a whole floor above ground level."

Kenny's mouth shaped an "O" before he nodded in comprehension.

Bitter looked down the stairwell. "How many more floors," she asked, "I thought we only had a couple more floors to go."

"Basement," said O'Malley. "Three more flights before we hit the bottom."

Kenny shook his head.

"Kenny?"

He held up four fingers.

"Four?" asked Bitter.

He nodded.

O'Malley gave Kenny a sharp look. "Two levels in the basement?"

Kenny nodded again. His fingers flashed. "Morgue in the basement, then one more below. Mechanicals and storage."

"How did you find it?"

The fluorescent light reflecting off the stark white walls lit Kenny's face in harsh contrast. He closed his eyes for a moment. When he looked at Bitter, his eyes glittered with unshed tears.

"When I was little, Grandma used to bring me to appointments with the psychiatrist. While she was talking to the doctor one day, I snuck away." His face twisted in a sour grimace. "Took them five or six hours to find me. I was hiding on the very bottom level, in a storage room. There were lots of blankets, so I made a nest and hid."

Bitter softened her voice, "Why did you hide?"

"He asked too many questions."

"I see."

"He wasn't mean. He was nice to me. He always had candy and toys for me, but I didn't want to talk to anybody about my dad or his wife. I didn't want to talk. I just wanted to forget everything." He looked at Bitter with sad brown eyes. "After that, Grandma didn't make me go anymore. We learned ASL together, so I didn't have to talk."

Bitter thought for a moment. "Did you hear anything down here before? When you were little?"

She saw his resemblance to Sally when he furrowed his brow, thinking. "There were a lot of scary noises. And shadows." He looked around uneasily, "There's still a lot of shadows."

O'Malley opened his mouth, glanced at Bitter, and closed it. She knew he'd talk to Kenny later about shadows, but for now, he was quiet.

"Well," she said, "Let's go down then."

The echoes changed as they descended. Kenny stopped, opened the fire door, and listened in the outer hall at the first basement level and slowly signed, "That doesn't sound human."

"Yeah," said O'Malley, peering through the door into a dimly lit hallway. "Almost like a cat. But not quite. It's a deeper sound. Throaty."

"Down," signed Kenny, motioning toward the stairs.

They crept down the steps, Bitter facing forward despite the pain in her knees. *I'd rather face it, whatever it is*, she thought. The stale air was cool on the lowest level, cooler than in the stairwell. The two adults fanned out in the hall, Bitter on the left, O'Malley on the right, and looked in each doorway. The sound grew softer as they flashed a light into each room before moving on to the next.

Kenny trailed behind, head cocked as he listened. Suddenly, he rapped on the wall to catch Bitter's and O'Malley's attention. He stood in front of an open door. "Here."

O'Malley put a hand on his weapon. "Wait there, Kenny. Let me check it first."

Kenny stood to the side as O'Malley edged through the doorway. His flashlight darted through the room, as he checked between the shelves.

"Well now," he said. "Guess the hunt is over for now." He motioned for Bitter and Kenny to come in and pointed down. A thread of sound rose from a floor grate. As O'Malley knelt to look at the opening, it faded slowly away.

"Definitely not human," said Bitter.

"Nope," O'Malley said as Kenny nodded.

"Well," Bitter said, "That's that for now. Let's go back upstairs." She looked down the hall at the fire door that led to the stairs and her knees twinged in protest. "Kenny, is there an elevator?"

Kenny nodded and pointed left, around the corner.

The elevator door slid open just as O'Malley reached for the up button. The trio paused in surprise as the hospital psychiatrist stepped forward. He stopped abruptly and glared at them, his ice-blue eyes narrowing as he scanned their startled faces. "What are you doing down here?" he demanded.

"Looking for ghosts," Kenny slowly signed as O'Malley translated.

"There are no such things as ghosts," the psychiatrist snapped. "What are you doing down here?" he repeated.

Bitter stepped forward, "Well, maybe, and maybe not, Doctor Kezar," she said. "There's something out there, and we don't know what it is. Yet."

O'Malley gave Bitter a quick side-eye. She had lectured him often enough that no supernatural creatures or ghosts roamed the city so she must have an ulterior motive. He relaxed his face into a broad smile and his Irish accent deepened. "And Doctor, why would you be roaming the lowest levels of the hospital, now? Didna you hear something that brought you down here? Could it be that you were doin' a bit of ghost hunting yourself?"

Doctor Kezar took a half step back. The elevator door closed behind him, he had nowhere to go. His eyes darted beyond O'Malley, down the darkened hall where shadows waited.

"Did you hear something too?" Kenny signed.

The doctor peered at the young man. "Is that you, Kenny? It's been a long time. Your grandmother stopped bringing you to see me." He paused and softened his tone, "You heard something too, Kenny? Is that why you're down here?"

Kenny nodded somberly.

The psychiatrist's hostility evaporated as he lost his usual tight control and sagged against the wall. "I'm not going mad then." He glanced at Bitter and his thin lips twitched. "Occupational hazard. After a while, the doctor starts analyzing himself. And then I started hearing things."

"A woman sobbing at night?"

He looked around the dim space, avoiding Bitter's steady gaze, before he finally gave a quick nod.

Bitter hesitated, remembering his persistent questioning after Sal poisoned her. Being a cop, she had to know. "How long have you been hearing these sounds?"

Again, he avoided her eyes. "Years."

Her voice grew stern, "How many years, Doctor?" The shadows in the hall slid closer and rose menacingly behind her.

He looked away. "Since you were poisoned by the shrooms and came under my care." He stood straighter and looked her in the eye. "The night you were brought in hallucinating and screaming about monsters and dead people crying in the night." He took a quick breath, regaining control of himself. "I thought you were having a mental breakdown. After we finally got you sedated and the allergic reaction to the mushrooms under control, I was walking the halls, checking on my other patients, and I heard sobbing in the distance. I tried to follow it, but it faded away."

"Did you hear it again?"

"Occasionally, through the years. When it hadn't happened for a couple of years, I put it out of my mind. Until I saw that you'd been admitted again."

"And you heard it that night?"

He turned abruptly toward the elevator and pushed the up button, then looked back, reverting to his usual demeanor. "Yes," he snapped.

Before Bitter could speak, the door opened and Doctor Kezar disappeared into the elevator. O'Malley gave a long, slow whistle as the door slid closed.

"Do you suppose that's why he was after you?" He turned toward Bitter, "He wanted to know if you heard the sobbing woman too." It wasn't a question, though Kenny turned toward O'Malley and raised an eyebrow.

Bitter turned so Kenny could see her expression and sighed. "I had to see him, Kenny, after I was poisoned by shrooms and was brought in nearly dead from the allergic reaction—and hallucinating." She gave him a small, sad smile. "He asked me too many questions too."

"About monsters?" he signed.

"Yes, *mijo*, about monsters."

Kenny grinned at Bitter's little endearment. She nodded in satisfaction and her smile grew a little happier. *He's a smart kid. He'll be fine at college, even if he doesn't talk.*

O'Malley pushed the up button. The door opened and before they could enter, the little nurse that looked like Lola stepped out, nodded to Bitter, and turned left, down the hall toward the storage rooms. O'Malley gave Bitter a sharp look when she returned the nurse's nod. He cleared his throat as they entered the elevator. "I'm off on Sunday, so Kenny and I will be at Gema's at ten." He glanced at the teen. "We'll set up the tables and chairs. Sapp said they have a big canopy too, so I'm sure she can use the help."

Bitter nodded, lost in thought as the elevator ticked up, floor by floor, to the first floor.

"Kenny," said O'Malley as the elevator door opened, "Sally won't be waking until morning at the earliest, so there's no need for you to sit there all night. Let's get you something to eat and then to the house for some extra clothes. Kathleen has already made up the bed for you at my house. And Aiden left the Xbox, so you can put in some time on that video game you two were playing."

Kenny's fingers flew.

"No, she'll be fine," O'Malley said firmly. "You'd be better off to get some rest. We'll come back in the morning to check on Sally, and then we'll go find something to do. Too bad Bitter's sons aren't here, they'd take you to play hockey." His face brightened. "Wait, Gema's kids play. I'll bet they have enough gear for you too."

Kenny frowned and shook his head.

"You don't play?" asked Bitter.

He nodded.

"Well, don't feel alone. I can't even skate."

Kenny's face lit up at her revelation. He turned to O'Malley and signed. "Okay. Food, clothes, video games. Sounds good."

O'Malley threw an arm over the teen's shoulder. "Come on, son. Denny's?" Kenny looked back at Bitter and made a face as they exited the lobby. She choked down a laugh as she made her way through the parking lot to the Maverick.

Chapter 15 ~ Sunday

The hot oil spattered as Bitter lowered the last of the lumpia into the fryer. She glanced at the clock. *As soon as this is done, a quick shower and I'll be ready to go.*

Steam rose from the hot lumpia as she deftly lifted it out of the oil and stacked it with the rest of the fried treats in the pan. She quickly covered the pan with foil and slipped it into the carrier. Several bottles of sweet chili sauce were already packed in a second carrier, along with a tray of *yema*, ready to go. She unplugged the fryer before she dashed to the shower.

Summer heat radiated from the gravel as Bitter opened the garage door and quickly loaded the food into the little car. *Whew. It's going to be another hot one today.* With the air conditioning blasting, she pulled out into the alley, leaving the engine idling as she closed and locked the garage door. She took a long look around the alley to make sure the battered white and green van was nowhere in sight before she set out toward Midtown

The blackened remains of the old woman's house got a glance as she turned left, away from the river. The yellow hazard tape hung limply from the remnant of the battered picket fence that once enclosed the front yard. A quick movement and a flash of coppery red beyond the fence caught Bitter's eye. She braked hard, then pulled over. "I don't have time for this," she muttered under her breath as she got out of the Maverick. With her left hand behind her back, grasping the grip of her carry gun, she walked slowly down the filthy sidewalk, a puff of ashes rising with each step.

"Hey," she called out sternly as she approached. "What do you think you're doing?"

A small voice answered. "We're trying to catch a kitten."

"Get out of there right now," Bitter ordered, taking her hand off her pistol as two small heads appeared. "Tabitha, does your Mom know you're out here?"

No response.

"Tabitha," Bitter said sharply.

A reluctant response, "No."

"You need to go home right now. Do not go back on that property. It's too dangerous."

Tabitha looked stubbornly at Bitter, her eyes bright under her tangled red mop of hair. "The kitten was crying."

Bitter motioned toward the sidewalk. "Now."

"But Miss Bitter, I—"

"Tabitha, do I need to talk to your Mom?"

The little girl crawled through a gap between the pickets and an ash-covered bush, followed by a tow-headed boy. Her face crumpled as she tried to brush the ashes off her shorts. Grime covered her hands, knees, and face, and the little boy was even dirtier.

Bitter sighed again.

"Tabitha, if I put some food out for the kitten, will you promise to stay out of there?" She didn't wait for the child to reply. "Now go home. I don't want to see you out here again. Understand?"

Both children nodded unhappily. Bitter stood sternly with her arms crossed and watched as they crossed the street.

It only took a few minutes to walk back to the bungalow and get a can of cat food, two bowls, and a bottle of water. Bitter waved at the dejected pair sitting on the apartment stairs after she put the food and water just inside of the fence. She walked back to the Maverick and got in slowly, hissing at the heat rising from the black vinyl seat. After turning the key in the ignition, she adjusted the vent, so the cold air blew on her face. Then, she checked the side mirror to make sure the children were safely on the grass in front of the apartment building before she put the car in drive.

She shook her head. *I should check on those kids later. What were they doing over there? And where is Wendy?* A loud shriek broke into her thoughts.

"TABITHA!"

Whoops, there she is. Despite the heat, Bitter quickly rolled down the window to listen.

"Tabitha, I told you to stay inside while I took a shower. What are you doing out here?" Wendy's shrill voice was clear over the purring of the little I-6 engine. "And Toby, oh-my-god-look-at-you! Get inside right now and get in that bathroom. Don't touch anything!"

A door slammed and silence filled the neighborhood. Bitter waited a moment. *Okay then, no more screaming. I'll check on the kids later.*

She glanced back toward the two bowls nestled under the tattered shrubbery, blackened with smoke and covered with ashes. *I'll refill the food and water later, so the kids stay out of there.* She shook her head and sighed. *I wonder what the old woman was doing with the cats?*

She pondered the question as she made her way into Midtown. Tall Modesto ash trees shaded the short street, providing relief from the hot sun. Smoke was already rising from the grill in the front yard when she pulled up in front of the tidy Victorian. As she parked, Gema's daughter bounded through the gate, smiling broadly. "Ms. Bitter! You came! Do you need help?"

"Yes, thank you, Tasha." Bitter handed her the heavy carrier. "Careful, the lumpia is still hot."

"Mmm, lumpia!" Tasha beamed. "I love lumpia. Grandma didn't make any today."

"Grandma?"

"Yes, she and Grandpa got here last night." She smiled happily. "They always come for Juneteenth. The whole family comes to celebrate with us."

"The whole family?"

"Yes. Uncle Jasir will be here too. Grandma is looking forward to meeting you. She wanted to know where your family is from."

Bitter followed Tasha through the gate. "My family?"

"Your family in the Philippines."

"Bitter! You made it!" Gema bustled down the front steps with a covered tray. She set it down on the table next to the grill before giving Bitter a quick hug. "Tasha, is that the lumpia? Take it into the kitchen and put it on the counter. Don't tell the boys what's in it or we won't get any." She called after the teen as she started up the steps, "And don't tell your uncle either!"

"Your family is here?" Bitter asked cautiously.

"Oh yes. We all gather for Juneteenth. It's our family reunion weekend. Then everyone goes off on their separate vacations. Dad and Mom are going on a cruise to the Bahamas next week. The only person missing is my kid sister, Jesie. She's in basic training, so it's not like she could come this year."

Gema looked at Bitter's pensive face. "We invite a lot of other people too. It's not just family."

"Okay," Bitter said doubtfully. She looked around the garden, cool in the shade of the huge tree in front of the house. "This is lovely."

Gema smiled. "I try to keep it looking nice. If I didn't, Mrs. Mitchell would be complaining."

Before Bitter could ask about the sweet-smelling pink flowers by the gate, her phone rang. "Bitter."

"Nita? Where are you? We're at your house and no one is home. Are you working?"

Bitter shot Gema a guilty glance. "I'm at a, um, friend's house. I'll be there in ten."

Gema put her hands on her hips stubbornly as Bitter hung up. "Oh no, you don't. You just call them right back and give them the address here. We finally get you to come over to relax and you aren't running off now."

Tasha set another pan next to the grill. "Ms. Bitter, you're leaving?" Disappointment rang in her voice. "But you just got here."

The teen's obvious dismay made Bitter stop a sharp retort. She turned and when she saw the girl's stricken expression, quickly put on her public smile. "Are you sure, Gema?" Bitter said over her shoulder. At Gema's nod, she hit redial, "Julio, my friends want to meet you. Do you have time to come to Midtown?"

"Plenty of time. I brought tri-tip and chicken for the grill. And Liz made a pot of adobo."

"Oh good! Their grill is ready." She glanced at Tasha, whose sad face transformed into a brilliant smile at Bitter's words.

"All righty then! Where are you?"

After Bitter gave Julio directions and hung up, Gema said softly, "Thank you, Bitter. Mom would've been really disappointed. She's been asking about you."

Bitter gave her a sharp glance and Gema threw up her hands. "No worries, Jasir only mentioned that you're Filipina and you know how moms are. You are famous, you know. People want to meet you."

Bitter sighed.

Gema grinned mischievously. "You know you have a Wikipedia page."

"I what?" Bitter's voice rose a little.

O'Malley strolled from the side yard and across the lawn, trailed by a pair of off-duty rookies, Cznik and Adams. "Hey, Bitter, you made it. Gema, we have the canopy set up. Your boys said that you want those folding tables and chairs set up now?" He took a second look at Bitter, puzzled at her frown. "Bitter?"

"O'Malley, a Wikipedia page about me? Really?"

He held up both hands in denial. "Don't look at me. I didn't do it." Behind his back, Cznik snickered while the other rookie's eyes widened in surprise.

Before Bitter could say more, a bright red Camaro pulled up behind the Maverick. Julio jumped out and stepped quickly around the car to open the door for his wife, Liz. Once the adults were out of the car, the bucket seats flipped forward, and two teenage boys piled out of the car. Bitter heard Tasha suck in a deep breath behind her. "Ohhh, they're cute, Ms. Bitter. Are those your nephews?"

"Don't you two disappear," Julio said loudly. "Get back here and help with the food."

Liz left him to organize the teens. "Bitter, it's so good to see you." Under the carefully applied makeup, Bitter could see the remnants of a sunburn that rivaled the red of the car.

"Liz, a little too much sun?"

Liz grimaced, "We went to the beach last weekend and I forgot the sunblock."

Bitter smiled sympathetically but her thoughts were less charitable. *How many times is she going to get fried before she learns to keep sunblock in her bag? It's not like Julio is going to think of it. He's never had a sunburn in his life. Good thing the boys take after him.*

Liz tossed back her blonde hair, a platinum shade a little too pale to be natural in an adult. "And these are your friends?"

Amid the introductions and arranging of an assortment of aluminum pans filled with marinated meats, the teens discreetly slipped into the backyard.

Sapp brought yet another covered dish from the house and eyed the full table. "I'd better get busy with this."

"The tri-tip first," suggested Julio.

Sapp gave him a friendly slap on the back, "Sounds good. You've got this?"

Julio grabbed a pair of bright green, elbow-length silicone gloves from the box he'd put under the table. "Sure!" He expertly checked the grill and turned down the heat on the right side before placing a drip pan filled with water on the bottom rack. With the tri-tip arranged on the upper rack over the drip pan, he started adding marinated chicken to the other side.

Music burst from the backyard in a heavy bass beat. Sapp gave a worried glance toward the neighbor's house. Bitter followed his look and frowned.

"I know it's the middle of the day, but Mrs. Mitchell is pretty testy if she thinks the music is too loud." He hurried down the walk and after a moment, the volume dropped.

Bitter stopped and turned toward the river. Sirens echoed in the distance. The bass had obscured the sound. Gema and Liz were still chatting, but O'Malley walked toward the street, his head cocked to one side.

"Do you hear that?" Bitter asked.

O'Malley nodded. "It's getting closer."

A tall, dark-complected man with a tight silver 'fro leaned over the porch railing. "Hey, the TV says there's a police chase."

Bitter glanced up. The resemblance was unmistakable. "Mr. Sapp?"

"That's me," he said loudly. "There's a live feed from a news chopper. It's coming this way."

"What happened?"

"Drive-by shooting down by the river."

"Damn." O'Malley turned and called to Gema. "Make sure the kids stay in the backyard." He ran toward his new Dodge pickup, parked two houses down and across the street.

"Julio," Bitter caught his attention. "Turn the grill down and get everyone into the backyard. Quick." The sirens were growing louder. Over them, revving engines and screaming tires punctuated the throbbing bass from the backyard.

"Bitter!" O'Malley shouted. She turned in time to see a brown Ford LTD backing slowly into the street. The white-haired driver could barely see over the wheel.

"Mrs. Mitchell, stop!"

It was too late.

The old, well-kept car was halfway out of the driveway when the chase screamed around the corner. A vintage white Caprice swerved and clipped the rear quarter panel and bumper of the Ford before careening into the massive tree across the street, just missing O'Malley's prized pickup. The impact pushed the LTD sideways into the wrought iron fence.

Bitter grabbed one of the rookies, Cznik, by the arm and pointed toward the corner. "Wave them down." Wide-eyed, he hesitated, but at Bitter's firm push in the right direction, ran toward the oncoming sirens, waving his arms wildly to slow the oncoming police cars. Bitter rushed to the Caprice with Adams on her heels. Before she reached it, a red-clad teen rolled out of the front passenger door, got to his feet, and ran. Sapp passed her at full speed, "Check the car!"

A second teen popped out of the back and ran in the opposite direction, with O'Malley in hot pursuit.

A third teen leaped out of the back door of the crumpled car but sprawled across the sidewalk when he put his weight on his right leg. Smoke rose from the crumpled hood as Bitter pulled her carry gun from its holster and approached the car cautiously. The first flicker of flames licked up over the hood and a shrill scream echoed from inside the car.

She glanced at the teen on the ground. He wasn't going anywhere. "Watch him," she ordered Adams as she holstered her 9mm and took four quick steps to the driver's window. It was open. Bright red curls and blood obscured the teen's face, but her stomach churned as she recognized him. She tried the door. It was jammed shut. As she stepped back, ready to dash around the car, a voice rang out, "Nita."

She ignored Julio.

"Nita. I've got it." When she looked up, Julio tossed a fire extinguisher to her, over the car. "Keep the flames off him if you can." Still wearing the silicon gloves, he leaned in the passenger door and grabbed the boy by the shoulders. He pulled, but the seat belt held the teen in place. Julio tried to unfasten the belt. It was jammed. He pulled out a pocketknife and began sawing at the tough nylon as Bitter sprayed the flames licking over the dash. The teen struggled as the belt tightened against his hips.

"Billy," Bitter shouted over the boy's screams, "Hold still." Heat washed over her as she swiftly ducked into the back seat, wedged her hand between the door and seat, and pushed on the tilt adjustment. *If I can drop the seat back, it'll loosen the belt and we can pull him over the seat and out the back door.* It didn't move. She pushed against the seat and tried the lever again. It stayed stubbornly stuck.

Julio kept hacking at the seat belt. It finally parted as Bitter sent another spray of fire retardant over the back of the seat and into the flames. Julio dropped the knife and pulled the teen out of the driver's seat. The cast on Billy's left leg caught for a moment on the steering wheel, but Julio jerked him loose and dragged him out of the door. Adams abandoned the injured teen on the ground to help Julio carry Billy away from the burning car.

The street filled as units from every jurisdiction pulled up and blues spilled out.

Bitter slid out of the back seat and dropped the empty fire extinguisher on the sidewalk. She turned toward the teen still lying on the ground and stepped on his hand as he reached for the pistol lying just past her foot. He looked up at her, wide-eyed as she caught her balance and smoothly pulled her carry gun out. "Don't move," she snarled. He froze, staring up at the blue-black barrel.

"Here," Bitter called to the nearest blue. The teen lay on the sidewalk until the officer knelt and cuffed him. Two more blues helped pull the teen to his uninjured foot and half-carried him away from the flaming car. One leg hung at a crooked angle.

Bitter caught the eye of the Sergeant and motioned toward the pistol on the ground. The tall woman turned and barked orders at a random blue. He nodded and pulled on disposable gloves before picking the pistol up and walking briskly away from the burning car. After quickly removing the magazine and checking for a round in the chamber, he dropped it into an evidence bag.

As the fire department pulled up, the crumpled side of the LTD caught Bitter's attention. She walked toward the car. With the car pinned against the fence, the driver couldn't open the door. Despite Gema's orders to stay in the backyard, her sons were helping a tiny senior citizen dressed in red capris and a brilliant red- and yellow-flowered blouse out of the passenger door.

"Aaaaaack," the woman growled at the boys and shook her cane at them, "What do you think you're doing? And where is my hat?"

Bitter's nephew picked up a bright yellow sunhat that fluttered to the ground when she exited the car. He tried to hand it to her, but she stayed focused on the two boys in front of her. After he brushed the hat off, he handed it to Bitter before retreating to the relative safety of Gema's front yard.

"Thank you, boys, let me talk to Mrs. Mitchell please." Bitter waved the teens away from the irate woman. "Mrs. Mitchell, I'm Detective Juanita Bitter, with the Sacramento police department. Are you all right?"

"Nothing like this ever happened until those people moved in," ranted Mrs. Mitchell, shaking her cane toward Gema's house. "Who hit my car? How am I going to get to the golf course?"

"You play golf?" Bitter couldn't stop herself from asking.

"Yes, I play golf. Didn't I just tell you I'm going to the golf course?"

Bitter persisted. "Mrs. Mitchell, you should let the EMTs check you over first."

"Tell those boys to get my golf clubs out of the trunk. I need to get to the golf course. I'm going to miss my tee time."

Bitter paused, then pasted a polite look on her face, "I'll tell you what Mrs. Mitchell, I'll call my favorite taxi driver if you'll let the EMTs look you over while he's on his way. I'll put the taxi on my account. When is your tee time?"

Mrs. Mitchell looked at Bitter suspiciously. "You don't look like a cop. What are you, a secretary?"

Someone snorted behind her. Bitter didn't look around. She focused all her attention on the woman, who barely reached her shoulder—and Bitter was only five foot two herself. "No ma'am, I'm a homicide detective. It's my day off." She got her official ID out and handed it over.

Mrs. Mitchell examined it carefully, peering through her bifocals at the picture, then at Bitter's smoke-smudged face. "Weren't you on the news the other day?"

Bitter sighed. "Yes, I'm afraid so."

"Well, I guess I can do that. Hurry up and call the taxi. I'm going to be late."

Relieved, Bitter waved an EMT over. While he checked the tiny woman over, a blue tried to take her statement. "I told you, I was backing out of my driveway and some idiot ran into me," she told him testily. "No, I didn't see him coming, are you deef? He hit my car."

Bitter hit the speed dial. "This is Bitter. I need Gian, please. I have a lady who needs to get to the golf course right away. Put it on my credit card."

By the time Gian pulled up in his yellow taxi, Gema's oldest son had pried open the trunk and retrieved the golf clubs.

"My shoes," demanded Mrs. Mitchell. Instinctively, both the teen and Bitter looked down at her gold lame sneakers. "My shoe bag. Why didn't you get it? It's in the trunk. It was next to the golf bag."

"Oh, just a minute, Mrs. Mitchell. I'll get it." He dived back into the trunk and pulled out a leather bag.

"Yes, that's it." Mrs. Mitchell stopped abruptly as Gian got out of the taxi. She looked him up and down, scowling at his wiry, gray-streaked beard and dark blue turban. "Who are you?"

Bitter stepped forward quickly. "Mrs. Mitchell, this is Gian Singh. Gian, this is Mrs. Mitchell. She needs to get to the golf course right away."

"John Sing?" Mrs. Mitchell peered at Gian suspiciously. "He doesn't look Chinese."

Gian glanced at Bitter. She grimaced in embarrassment, but he just winked at her before turning back to his passenger. "I'm Sikh, Mrs. Mitchell. My people are from India, but I was born in West Sacramento," he said as he opened the taxi door. "What time do you tee off?"

Mrs. Mitchell looked at her watch. "At 11:30. We only have twenty minutes to get there."

Gian smiled at her, "I'll get you there on time." He put her golf and shoe bags into the trunk.

"Thank you, Gian." Bitter said gratefully, "Can you pick her up too? She'll need a ride home."

"No problem, Bitter." He leaned a little closer and whispered. "She still drives?"

Bitter nodded. He frowned and gave Mrs. Mitchell a quick side-eye, then put his professional smile back on. Bitter heard him say, "Trust me, Mrs. Mitchell, we'll be there in a few minutes," as he climbed back into the taxi and started a Y-turn. Bitter waved blues away as Gian carefully maneuvered between the units and past the fire engines and ambulances.

With Mrs. Mitchell on her way, Bitter stopped and looked over the scene. The Caprice, smothered in fire retardant, was still smoking a little. A pair of EMTs lifted a gurney, with Billy securely strapped down, into the waiting ambulance. A blue waved Bitter over.

"The driver wants to talk to you. He said he knows you?" she said doubtfully.

"Yes," Bitter gave the blue a stern look, "I met him at the high school the other day." She walked around to the back of the ambulance, where the EMTs waited impatiently. "Billy, they need to get you to the hospital."

"Ms. Bitter, I need to talk to you," he whispered hoarsely. "It's not what you think."

"Billy," Bitter said incredulously, "What do you mean? What else can it be?"

He moaned and the nearest EMT gave Bitter a look. She ignored it as she climbed into the ambulance and gently put her hand over Billy's bandaged fingers. Blood still oozed from his nose and both eyes were already turning purple.

"Billy, I'll come to the hospital later."

"Wait. Wait."

Bitter waited.

"I took my Mom's car. We were just going to cruise around. Tag a few fences over in Broderick. Just having a little fun."

"Billy, this can wait."

The light in the ambulance dimmed a little.

"No, no. Ms. Bitter, I have to tell you. There was something in the river. Something big. I saw it from the I-Street Bridge. It was swimming upstream, toward the park." His labored breathing was loud in the sudden silence. "That's why I drove by the park. I wanted to see what it was. I didn't know Sammy had a gun until he saw some guy he had a beef with. I didn't know he was going to shoot someone." A tear trickled down his cheek, leaving a track through the smudges. "It hurts, Ms. Bitter."

"I know it hurts, Billy, it'll be all right."

"Don't go near the river." His voice rose an octave. "Promise me, Ms. Bitter."

Bitter looked at his tear-stained face and gently patted his shoulder. "I promise, Billy. I'll come and see you tonight if I can, okay?"

The nearest EMT scowled at Bitter as she climbed out. "Was that really necessary?"

Bitter ignored the question. "First- and second-degree burns?"

The EMT, still unhappy, slammed the doors shut. "Mostly. Probably a broken nose from when he hit the steering wheel. I don't know about that leg though. It was already broken, and the impact broke the cast. It probably reinjured his leg. It looks bad."

"I see," Bitter said as the ambulance began slowly weaving its way through the crowded scene and as it turned the corner toward the hospital, its lights and siren suddenly filled the smoke-filled air.

Sapp appeared at the far end of the block, marching a cuffed teen to a unit. A second teen stared defiantly from the back seat. Sapp shook his head and led the boy to a different unit. Bitter couldn't hear what he said as he tucked the boy into the black and white, but the teen's freckled face spoke volumes.

Sapp was still breathing a little hard when he joined Bitter. "Chased him halfway to the river. That kid could run!"

Bitter nodded silently, thinking of Billy's frantic demand that she stay away from the river. She noticed that Julio was back at the grill, wearing a fresh T-shirt and minus his gloves. His normally crisp curls were a tousled mess. A blue took notes while Julio expertly flipped the chicken breasts. He caught her gaze and waved her over. She started toward the garden, but Sapp began cursing under his breath.

She looked back and saw Sapp's frown. "Figures he'd show up," he muttered, "and look who's right behind him." When she turned back toward Gema's house, Morales was at the gate and a familiar white and green van was backing into the spot just vacated by Gian's taxi.

"Well, damn," Bitter growled.

Sapp's frown lightened. "Hey, do you have the Chief's cell?"

Bitter paused. "Yes. Why?"

"Give him a call. Tell him there's an incident right in front of my sister's house and by chance, we're grilling. Invite him to join us before the blues eat up all the food. Be sure to tell him you brought lumpia."

Bitter flicked a glance at Morales, who was already talking to Julio at the grill.

Sapp nodded encouragingly. "I heard the Chief is having some marital problems. Don't tell him I told you, but he needs to get out of the house on the weekends. And he can quash you-know-who." He tipped his head toward the grill with a mischievous grin.

Bitter looked over at the cameraman filming the scene while the reporter hovered near the units, talking excitedly into the mic. "All right. While I call the Chief, you get Public Relations on the horn. We need someone to talk to the press ASAP."

Chapter 16 ~ Still Sunday

The pack of teens made quick work of the cleanup, wiping down the tables and chairs while Sapp and Julio presided over the grill. O'Malley kept the reporter and his cameraman at bay until the department's spokesperson arrived. She had the reporter well in hand at the end of the block, where he couldn't see Gema's house without passing the police barricades.

Bitter washed her face inside the house and reapplied her makeup. The remnants of the bruises had faded to barely visible. Once she touched up with bronzer and blush, they didn't show at all.

Tables and chairs filled the gardens, front and back. Gema's and Sapp's family, guests, and blues who "just happened" to be in the area filed along both sides of the heavily loaded buffet tables. Amid the clink of beer bottles and hiss of newly opened sodas, newcomers got the story of the car chase, with full descriptions of the wreck and Julio's quick action in saving the driver.

Sapp's race "halfway to the river" wasn't neglected, nor Adam's failure to secure the loose pistol. Adams took it in stride, laughing and tossing back another beer before reminding his fellow officers that he was off-duty at the time, and thus not responsible for Bitter's mistake in telling him to "'watch the teen,' instead of 'secure the scene.'"

At the end of the garden, shaded by a huge orange tree, the teens had their own table. Kenny grabbed a can opener to pop open a fruit-flavored Jarritos, while Tasha cracked open an ice-cold Zesto Calamansi with honey. "Mmm, I haven't had one of these since we visited Grandma Sapp." She beamed at Julio's oldest son, "She has to order them from a Filipino importer. You can't get these from the store." The teen nodded in agreement as he pulled another Zesto from the cooler hidden under the table.

Bitter, Julio, and Liz sat with the Sapps in the shade, well away from the street and possible intrusion by the reporter.

"So Jasir tells me your Lola was from a little town near Clark Air Force Base?" asked Mrs. Sapp, who immediately insisted that Bitter call her Riza.

Liz opened her mouth, but before she could speak, Julio nudged her and shook his head slightly. "She doesn't need your help," he whispered. Liz gave him a wounded look but sat back instead of showing off her expertise in family history and genealogy.

Bitter took a sip of her soda before replying. "Yes. He met her after the war when he was stationed at Clark. She worked at the base hospital. She was a nurse and according to Abuelito, even the doctors stopped to listen when she was in charge of the ward." She smiled a little at the memory. "He said she always let him think he was in charge—until he wasn't."

Julio laughed, "Yes, our Lola was a bit of a thing, but she kept us all busy after she retired from nursing."

"Ah, we might be related. Some of my aunties married servicemen after the war." Riza said.

"Really?" Bitter asked, "I'll have to get out Lola's notebook. She wrote down all of her family's names and where they were from." Liz went on alert at Bitter's words, but at a second nudge from Julio, she stayed silent. Bitter didn't miss the look on her face. Liz would want copies of Lola's notes later.

Julio leaned forward. "Where did you meet Mr. Sapp?"

"I met Vic, Sgt. Sapp, at Clark. I was Jasir's and Gema's teacher at the elementary school."

"Oh?"

She patted Vic's hand. "He was always there for his kids. And so handsome. The dashing young airplane mechanic, a widower with two young children." She smiled and winked at Bitter. "I let him chase me until I caught him. We stayed at Clark until our youngest, Malaya, was born. Then the volcano erupted. After we were evacuated, we moved to Travis—"

Before Riza could say more, Morales' mocking voice rose above the chatter, "So Bitter, any hot suspects in Candy's murder?" Silence fell over the tables as everyone looked at Bitter.

She set down her forkful of tri-tip slowly and stood so her voice would carry over the crowd. Though her expression and voice remained controlled, tension filled her words, "At this point, everyone is a suspect. Including you, Captain. I'll expect you tomorrow at 9 a.m. for your interview." She nodded to the open-mouthed rookies, gave Morales her deceptively gentle public smile, and sat down.

"Whew," Gema's stage whisper carried across the garden, "You just told him, huh?"

A loud chuckle from the Chief, who arrived via Uber just in time to hear Bitter's tight-lipped response, broke the tension. "I suppose I should expect an appointment too? I'm available tomorrow and Tuesday after 2 p.m. if I'm on the interview list."

Bitter nodded. "Thank you, Chief. Tomorrow works for me too. At two then?"

"Let's make it three, if that's all right with you, Bitter. I have some paperwork to clear out in the morning." He looked pointedly around at the continuing cleanup efforts in the street and the bumper-to-bumper row of units outside of Gema's gate.

"I'm sure I'll have reports to review, especially regarding this weekend's crime wave."

Before Morales could respond to the Chief's jovial remarks, his radio sputtered. He regained control of his expression, rose, and nodded to Gema. "Back to work. No rest for the wicked."

As he strode back to his car, someone whispered loudly, "No worries about that. The wicked get plenty of rest. They dump all their work on their staff." Morales' back stiffened, but he kept walking. With lights flashing and siren blaring, he burned rubber and nearly hit Gian's yellow taxi as it turned onto the narrow street.

The reporter and his cameraman abandoned the police spokesperson when Morales skidded past their van, and by the time Gian finished parking, they were hot on the unit's exhaust.

Several blues hastily rose amid the crackling noise of tin foil. With quickly wrapped to-go plates and low-voiced thanks to Gema and Sapp, they sped off in their black and whites.

"Mrs. Mitchell, Gian, please join us," Gema called as Gian opened the taxi door for his elderly occupant. "We have tri-tip and chicken," she said persuasively as she walked swiftly to the gate, "macaroni and cheese, potato salad, and all kinds of pies and cakes."

Mrs. Mitchell stopped and looked at her empty driveway. "Where's my car?" she demanded.

"We had it towed to the body shop," Bitter called as she made her way across the garden. "The driver's mom has insurance. She'll take care of everything. I hope you don't mind, I had them take it to the same shop that works on my cars." She handed the fuming woman the shop's business card. "We can have it taken somewhere else if you have a favorite mechanic. At no cost to you, of course."

Mrs. Mitchell peered up at Bitter. "Well, since it isn't going to cost me anything," she said suspiciously.

"Won't you join us?" Gema repeated.

Gian nodded enthusiastically. "It's actually past my lunch break, Mrs. Mitchell. Aren't you hungry? You did play eighteen holes today." He held out his arm to escort the tiny woman to a table. "A chair for Mrs. Mitchell?" he called.

Gema's oldest son vacated his chair at the pleasantly shaded table by the orange tree. "Here!" He shooed the other teens away while Tasha quickly wiped the plastic tablecloth. As Mrs. Mitchell settled into the chair, the Chief pulled out the chair next to her.

"You don't mind if I join you?" he asked as he set down a fully loaded plate, with a half dozen lumpia balanced on top. "I'm Chief Brown, Sacramento Police Department. My top homicide detective, Bitter, called and invited me to the party." He held out his hand. "Call me George."

"Nice to meet you, George," she said as she shook his hand. "But don't you have anything else to do?" She looked pointedly at the tow truck removing the wrecked Caprice.

He smiled and sipped a Dos Equis. "Fortunately, the young fools managed to only hurt themselves. Lousy shots, thank goodness. They scared the people at the river and wrecked the car. Other than a broken leg, some minor burns, bruises, and smoke inhalation, it looks like they're fine." He waited while Mrs. Mitchell accepted the plate offered by Tasha, filled with grilled meats, potato salad, macaroni and cheese, greens, lumpia, and other treats, before he continued, "So I only have to read over the reports and forward them to the DA tomorrow."

Mrs. Mitchell sipped fruit-filled sangria from a wine glass, hastily brought out from the house after Gema glared at her son.

He'd started to offer a plastic glass. With each sip, Mrs. Mitchell relaxed a little more.

"This is good," she said to Gian as he sat down. He'd put her golf clubs and shoe bag on her porch before filling his plate at the buffet. "John, did you have some wine?"

Gian shook his head. "Oh no, Mrs. Mitchell, I'm driving. No wine for me."

"This wine is pretty good. Gema, where did you find this?"

The nearest teen opened his mouth, but at Gema's stern glance he stopped and cleared paper plates and cups from the table. "Oh, at the store," Gema said evasively.

Riza winked at Bitter and whispered, "It's Señorial Sangria. Don't tell her it's nonalcoholic. We put it in the punchbowl with a fruit-and-ice ring."

Bitter dropped her fork and covered her mouth with both hands to hide her amused surprise. "Oh no!"

"We make sure there's plenty of nonalcoholic drinks for the teens and our friends in recovery," Riza smiled at Vic as he set a fully loaded plate in front of her. "Thank you, dear."

Vic sat down with a second plate for himself, "Like me," he said as he popped the top of a soda. "Twenty years clean and sober now. I don't even miss it." Riza gave him a quick kiss on the cheek, pride shining in her eyes.

Bitter nodded. For a moment, the memories of Papá and Mamá, smiling and surrounded by friends, overshadowed the happy faces of Vic and Riza. For the first time since her sons left home, the dark clouds that filled her days subsided as the memories of her parents and the joy of friends and family swept through her. A tear formed, but she quickly wiped it away. *I miss them all. I wish my sons could be here.*

Riza saw Bitter's angst and patted her hand. "Don't let the job take over your life. You can have fun too." She looked understandingly at Bitter. "Life goes on."

Her kindness pierced Bitter's old wounds, and she fought back the unshed tears that flowed out of her damaged psyche. Fiercely, she regained control of herself.

Stop feeling sorry for yourself. Your life is fine, she thought angrily and pushed the memories and pain back into the dark place where she hid her emotions. When she glanced at Julio though, she caught the worried expression on his face before he looked away. For a moment, she regretted how she'd pushed him away after Papá died. She couldn't share her pain and grief with him or their brothers. She'd focused on her boys and the job. And then the fiasco with Sal, right before they lost Mamá—

When Julio looked back at her, she gave him a small smile and a quick nod. The look of relief on his face eased her mind. *Mi familia es todo and Julio never stops trying to take care of us all. It's time to stop living in the past.*

From the corner of her eye, Bitter caught a glimpse of the Chief as he scanned the tables. He focused on her and rose. "Excuse me, Mrs. Mitchell, I need to touch base with Bitter." He sighed. "Duty calls."

Gian finished his meal, rose, and bowed, "Alas, I too must go." He handed Mrs. Mitchell a business card. "My customers are waiting."

Vic put a napkin over his plate, then got up and slipped into the empty seat before she noticed that she'd been left alone. "Mrs. Mitchell, I'm Gema's father. My grandsons told me that you're a pilot?"

Flattered, she nodded, "Yes, I owned a little biplane when I lived on the coast. I had to sell it after the cows ate the fabric off the wings. They were after the salt from the ocean spray." Vic made an encouraging noise and she continued, "But I was thinking of getting another plane. They say the new Cessnas are much easier to pilot than my old biplane."

Bitter lost the thread of their conversation when the Chief loomed over her.

"Yes?" she said warily.

"Candy's funeral is Wednesday. The family would like you to attend." He looked around. "This probably isn't the time or place, but I wanted you to know as early as possible." He lowered his voice, "Her father is a friend. We went to the academy together."

"What time?"

"It's at 3 p.m., in the downtown cathedral." He leaned closer and Bitter smelled the alcohol on his breath. "Thank you, Bitter. It means a lot to the family that you're working on her murder." He blinked a few times and looked around, his blotchy face highlighted by the afternoon sun. "I should go home. My wife might worry if I'm not there—if she calls."

Bitter held back the pity that surged forward at his sad expression.

"Are you going back to the hospital tonight?" At her nod, he said, "Tell Sally I'll see her after work tomorrow."

"She's conscious? Why didn't anyone tell me?" snapped Bitter in a sudden burst of anger at Morales, the Chief, and her memories of the long hours of waiting and praying for good news.

"No, no. Not yet. But the doctor was hopeful when I spoke to him earlier. She's a strong woman, she'll be up and around soon."

Bitter struggled to choke down her rage. *Let it go. He doesn't need that right now. None of this is his fault.* She stopped at that thought. *Could it be? What was he doing at the station that morning?*

Was it a coincidence? She pushed back the sudden surge of questions. *Now is not the time. Tomorrow.*

Feedback from the stereo system echoed through the garden in an ear-bending screech. Bitter jumped at the sound and turned toward the house, where she could see Sapp and his father standing at the top of the porch steps. Sapp held a wireless mic up in the air, away from the speakers perched on each side of the porch, then handed it to Vic with a flourish.

Vic waved for silence as the teens moved through the tables, refilling glasses from pitchers filled with juice and sangria. Gema and Riza hastily poured wine for the adults, while Julio passed out a few more beers to his new friends. Bitter noticed Cznik and Adams sitting together, both with brimming plastic cups. Foam spilled over the lip of Adams' cup and onto the tablecloth.

"Thank you all for joining us today," Vic said. "As we celebrate Juneteenth, let us give thanks for the joyous news that reached our ancestors in Texas on this day. For today, we were set free, all of us, from the evils of slavery. It's been a long road since then, and it hasn't been easy. Though we have come far, we still have many miles ahead. We're in this together, family and friends. This is our Independence Day, make it a good one!"

Sapp raised a mug. "A toast: To family, friendship, and freedom," he shouted and downed his beer.

Flanked by Julio and Riza, Bitter picked up her glass and held it high, the sense of belonging breaking through her hard-won barriers, and, for a brief moment, the joy of the celebration sang in her heart. "To freedom! ¡Salud!"

Shadows slipped through the trees and gathered under the old Modesto ash, its bark newly scarred by the Caprice's bumper. A dark shadow in the center bowed his head in silence.

No one noticed.

Chapter 17 ~ Sunday Night and Monday

Dusk settled over Alkali Flat as Bitter pulled into the alley. She sighed as she opened the garage door and looked at the Maverick. "I just had you detailed, and look at you, you're all dusty again," she scolded the little car before she pulled it in next to the Dart.

With the Maverick safely locked in the garage, she carried two trays of leftovers up the back stairs to the kitchen. Gato and Chica met her inside, sniffing the air greedily. "No, no, out you go." She leaned on the rail and watched as the pair dashed downstairs. Both avoided the bare spot in the lawn. "I'll have to patch that before the rainy season," Bitter said aloud, "Otherwise you two will be tracking mud into the house."

She went back into the kitchen and poured a glass of wine, then settled in the old chair on the porch to contemplate the day.

When the party broke up, Sapp packed the Chief into an Uber and sent him home before he embarrassed himself. Bitter shook her head sadly. She wasn't the only one with memories of happier days with family and friends.

Liz, who only drank diet soda, took Julio and the boys home. Julio hugged Bitter tightly before they left and assured her that they would visit more often. Bitter smiled a little at his sudden display of affection. She hadn't realized how dark her life had become—or maybe she hadn't wanted to think about it.

Gema was right, I need to get out more and away from the job. Be with good people who care about each other and the world around them. Spend time with my family.

There were several designated drivers, though Sapp still had to call Gian to take several guests home, including Cznik and Adams. Both men were wasted when they stumbled to the taxi. *I wonder what will happen if their wives see them together? They looked pretty amorous at the party. Maybe they got a room?* She shrugged. *Maybe they have one of those agreements that nobody talks about. Not my business unless it affects the job.*

Much to her surprise, near the end of the party Jones appeared from the backyard. His date, a dark olive-complected young woman with flowing black hair, led him to a waiting Uber. Upon reflection, Bitter decided that he'd avoided her during the celebration. If his date hadn't needed help guiding him to the street, Bitter might not have noticed him at all.

After pouring Jones into the back seat, Sapp walked back to her, ruefully shaking his head. "I'm not sure he's going to make it to work tomorrow." He'd glanced over his shoulder to make sure they were gone before he said, "If looks could kill, you'd be dead, Bitter. He really doesn't like you, does he?" She'd shrugged and went back to helping Gema clear the tables. Between Gema's teens, Kenny, O'Malley, and Sapp, they'd cleaned up the mess in record time.

Stopping at the hospital on the way home was unproductive. Billy was sedated in the burn unit and Sally was still unconscious. The kid with the broken leg was in surgery.

"Oh! I forgot to check on that damned kitten." Bitter stood wearily and got a bottle of water and a can of cat food from the kitchen. The fading rays of the sun cast deep shadows in the wreckage of the burnt house. There was no sign of a kitten, but the food was gone. As Bitter emptied cat food into the bowl, something rustled in the bushes. She stood and stepped back, one hand on her carry gun. The bushes rustled again, the soft ashes floating above the dead grass and blackened soil for a moment, then settling. Cautiously, she poured water into the second dish. She backed away from the bowls and scanned the garden, searching for any other movement.

She was nearly back to her house when a faint squeaking rose from the wreckage behind her. She turned and walked back to the corner, but the thread of music from the apartments and distant traffic obscured any other noises. After pausing for a few minutes, she crossed the street again and stood in front of the ash-laden garden. It was nearly dark. The streetlights clicked on, the dim, yellowed light barely illuminated the black and gray ruins. The nearest light remained dark. She looked up, but in the gathering gloom, she couldn't tell if it had been damaged when the house exploded, or if it was just burnt out.

Nothing moved, so she continued around the block and down the alley behind the old woman's property. Only the tattered bushes, chimney, and remains of the foundation were visible under a thick layer of ash.

I'll call animal control, she decided. I'm not setting foot in that mess if I can help it.

A breath of air lifted ash in a gray swirl, then dropped it. Bitter, on high alert as soon as the ash moved, stood on tiptoes and peered at a gap in the foundation. Though it was twenty feet or so from the sidewalk, the ground sloped downward, and she could see a deeper black within the crumbling stones.

Sapp did mention a basement. I wonder what's down there. She paused. *A well perhaps? Or a cistern?*

She took another hard look at the property. It's full of ashes and debris. *I'd better warn Wendy to keep Tabitha and, what was his name?* She smiled a little, remembering Wendy's shriek at seeing the ash-covered children. *That's right, Toby, away from here.*

As Bitter crossed the street in front of the apartments, she noticed that Wendy's apartment was dark. She climbed the stairs and tapped lightly on the door anyway. No one answered. After tucking a business card into the crack between the door and its frame, she walked around to the parking lot behind the building. Wendy's little yellow Toyota was nowhere to be seen.

By the time Bitter climbed the steps to her own house, Gato and Chica were waiting eagerly for their dinners. She sighed as she filled their dishes. *I'd better leave Harry a message. He needs to know that Billy saw something strange in the river.*

The alarm went off at its usual 6 a.m. Bitter rolled over and slapped the snooze button.

"Too early," she muttered as Chica dived off the bed and began dancing next to the closed door. When Bitter didn't move fast enough, Chica yipped excitedly two or three times to remind her that little dogs have small bladders. "Yes, yes, I'm coming."

With her robe thrown over her shoulders, Bitter opened the bedroom door. Gato sat outside, his tail twitching. The pair dashed down the hall as Bitter followed and opened the back door. Cool morning air rushed in—a relief from the heat of the past few weeks. She left the door open, took a deep breath, and pushed the "ON" button on the coffeepot. "Time to get this day started."

While the coffee brewed, she sat down at the table and mentally reviewed Candy's case.

Killed in the police station.

No key card used or found with her.

Lovers, former lovers, and rejected suitors all appear to have alibis.

People in the building, but no one heard anything.

Cameras didn't record anything that morning—or it was erased after the fact. Who has access?

The murder weapon was my carry gun, which had been put in Property when I was rushed to the hospital.

Sally said Candy had a stalker but didn't tell me who. And then someone tried to kill Sally. Why?

What am I missing here?

As Bitter poured her first cup of the day, she went over it all again. While she was adding sugar and creamer to the steaming coffee, she paused, spoon suspended above the cup.

Wait. Was my Walther locked in Property, or just put in my office? Didn't O'Malley tell me he'd locked it in my office? I picked it up from Property before we knew that Candy was dead in the stairwell. How did it get there?

And who put the white orchid in my office and where is the pink envelope that Vargas mentioned during his interview?

She noticed that she hadn't stirred her coffee when she put the spoon down and started to pick up the cup. The pale swirl of creamer floated, still separate from the dark liquid—much like the questions that whirled through her thoughts.

A quarter past nine and he's not here yet. Why am I not surprised? Bitter thought as she waited for Morales in the interview room. She resisted the urge to call the Chief's office. Instead, she took off her suit jacket and hung it on the back of the battered metal chair. Before she sat down, she flexed her knees. *They're feeling better,* she thought in surprise at the nearly pain-free movement.

Maybe the doctor was right. Meds and those exercises seem to be working.

She got out her notes and began reviewing the key card information that had arrived in the morning emails.

The door crashed open.

Bitter didn't look up. "Sit down please," she murmured as she slowly closed the file folder and tucked it into her briefcase.

"You bloody bitch!"

Startled, she looked up into Jones' beet-red face, twisted in fury.

"It was you that turned me into Human Resources, wasn't it?" He slammed the chair to the side, against the wall. "They called me in this morning. This is your fault."

Bitter pushed her chair back and stood, ready for action. "We have standards, Jones. If you're unable to work with everyone in the department, then you have no place here," she said sternly.

"That's not up to you," he shouted. The stench of alcohol wafted from his pores as he swayed. Behind him, she could see blues gathering curiously, peering in the door.

She tensed as he took a step closer. "That's right. It's not up to me. It's up to HR to decide if you need training or a different job. But you aren't helping your case right now."

With Jones towering over her, the small room felt claustrophobic. Bitter took a deep breath and centered herself, raising both hands in the stance Papá had taught her. Through the door, she saw an older blue nudge one of the rookies. She couldn't hear what he said, but the rookie grinned. Just then, Jones lunged over the table. Bitter sidestepped and grabbed his arm, using his momentum to pull him the rest of the way over the table and dump him headfirst onto the floor. Before he could get up, she stepped daintily past him and out of the door. She stood poised for his next move.

The nearest blues moved back, giving her room.

A voice in the back, "What's going on?"

"Later," she said softly. "No time now."

Jones staggered to his feet, shaking his head. Blood trickled from a cut on his forehead. He wiped it and looked at the red stain on his hand.

"Shit, he's bleeding." O'Malley's voice boomed. "Move out of the way."

Before O'Malley could reach Bitter, Jones charged. Despite her protesting knees, she danced to the side, ducked under his outstretched arms, and as he passed, turned and kicked him behind the knee with her sturdy black shoe. As he staggered, she punched him twice, then stepped back out of reach. He roared as he caught his balance, then turned to charge at her again.

Moving quickly, O'Malley grabbed him in a bear hug from behind. Jones threw his head back, but O'Malley had fought in the bars of Ireland in his misspent youth. He kept his head tipped to the side, ready for that move. O'Malley used Jones' momentum to pull the enraged man backward, to the side, and down. Before Jones could react, O'Malley had him pinned face down on the floor.

"Cuffs."

A blue stepped forward and smoothly cuffed Jones.

"Just until he calms down," Bitter said quietly. "No need to make this worse than it is."

"Worse than it is?" Morales' voice carried, "You hit him, Bitter."

She turned toward the Captain as he pushed past the blues.

"Yes, I did. It's all on video," she pointed up at the camera and shrugged. "And plenty of witnesses." She looked at Jones. "Can someone call for an ambulance? He's bleeding."

An old-timer hidden behind the younger blues chuckled at an unheard comment, "That was nothing. You should've seen her when she was a rookie. See that scar on her arm? A meth head slashed at her when she was checking to see if he was alive. The blade caught her on the arm as she dodged it. She knocked him into the next week before we could stop her. Now me, I'd have just shot his scrawny ass. But he lived to tell his jailhouse lawyer buddies all about it when he went 'home' again."

The salt-and-pepper head nodded sagely at the blues who turned toward him. "Her Papá made sure she could defend herself." He sighed, "We lost him after she joined the force. Ayyyy, it was a sad day. He was a good cop."

O'Malley hauled Jones to his feet. "Jones, what were you thinking?" he asked, his accent thickening as he fought to control his temper and speak reasonably to the enraged man.

"Easy for you to say," Jones spat in disgust, "She had you put in sensitivity training too."

"And what if she did? Maybe I needed a refresher course on how to act like a decent human being." O'Malley retorted. "Times have changed and sometimes old dogs need to learn new tricks. Or retire. And I'm not ready to retire yet. Bitter might be harsh, but she's not vindictive. She must've thought you were redeemable, or she'd have done more than report you." He paused for a long minute and looked around the room to make sure he had everyone's attention. "She and I had a chat about it over coffee and she explained how something I did was inappropriate. We agreed that I should take the class—"

Bitter interrupted O'Malley before he could finish. It was past time to clarify the situation for the avidly listening blues.

"It's not like you gave me any choice, Jones. Using a derogatory slur toward a member of the department, a dispatcher, when you know you're on video and being taped," Bitter shook her head in disgust, "What part of that did you think was okay? How could I let it slide? And how could you expect me to do just that? Let it go?"

The tension was palpable until the light bulb above them blew out with a pop. Jones flinched.

O'Malley looked up. His eyes widened slightly, then he looked away from the shadows gathered above and shook Jones slightly. "Come on now. Let's get you sitting down so the EMTs can take a look at that cut." He glanced up again and pushed Jones toward the furthest interview room. "We'll sit you down in here, where you can calm down."

"I don't need to calm down," Jones shouted, "That bloody bitch is going to ruin my career. And that nosy old biddy that works for the Chief is just as bad. I hope she dies," he spat as O'Malley dragged him away.

Before Bitter could follow them, the EMTs bustled in and shooed the onlookers away from the interview room where O'Malley kept Jones restrained. It didn't take long for them to secure Jones to the gurney and roll him out the door.

"Add alcohol, instant asshole," O'Malley muttered under his breath as Jones, still shouting insults, disappeared with the EMTs.

"Well, Bitter, it looks like we'll have to delay that interview," said Morales. He puffed up a little as he looked around. "Show's over. Don't you all have work to do?"

"Oh no," Bitter said gently, "We have more than one interview room." She pointed with her chin across the waiting area. "Sit down and I'll get my briefcase and electronics."

Blues scattered as Morales strode into the opposite interview room. A couple of rookies helped Bitter move her things, while Morales made himself comfortable.

"What's his problem?" Cznik whispered to O'Malley.

"Old news and not my business," replied O'Malley, "and if you're smart, you'll get some Visine for those eyes and handle your problems. Bitter can hold her own. She's tough." He looked around at the curious stragglers. "The Chief will expect incident reports from all of you before the end of your shift."

Groans floated down the hall as the blues dispersed.

Bitter ignored everyone outside of the interview room and busied herself making more coffee and preparing her electronics. Luckily, both the tablet and coffeepot survived Jones' dive over the table. She fixed herself a cup of coffee and nodded toward the coffeemaker. "Have a cup," she invited Morales.

"I don't think so," Morales replied as Bitter sat down, "I don't expect to be here long."

Bitter looked up from the notes she'd started studying and frowned. "Really? Why would you think that?"

"I have better things to do than to waste time on this." Morales sneered. "I was in my office early to do some paperwork. Just like the Chief. We were going to meet later that morning to go over the budget and the incident report from your allergic reaction in the break room. We were also going to discuss the impropriety of your relationships with O'Malley and Sapp."

"My what?" Bitter's voice rose a little in surprise. Rage at the implication forced her to battle her temper. "What do you mean relationships?"

He shook his head, as if she should know what he was talking about, "You think no one has noticed that you three have been thick as thieves ever since that murder last winter? The headless man? You even went to a party at Sapp's house this weekend. And O'Malley was there too."

She managed to keep her voice even. "There were a lot of cops at the Juneteenth celebration, including you and the Chief. And, for your information, it was at Sapp's sister's house. She invited me. In any case, I'm not here to discuss office gossip with you. Perhaps you should wait until Sally is out of the hospital. I'm sure she'll have the latest release from the rumor factory," she finished smoothly.

Bitter didn't miss that Morales stiffened slightly, then struck a pose of studied indifference when she said Sally's name.

She flipped the file folder open, "What were you doing in the building at 4 a.m. on the morning that Candy was killed?"

Morales leaned back in his chair, his body language relaxed. "Paperwork. I already told you that."

Bitter made a note. "Did you see anyone else enter or leave the building or in the stairwell?"

"Nope."

"What time did you hear I was being released from the hospital?"

He scowled, "At the morning briefing, like everyone else."

"How long had you known Candy?"

His eyes flickered, "I didn't know Candy personally. She was just a dispatcher."

Bitter looked up from her notes, surprised at his reply. According to rumor, his last three conquests had also been young, beautiful, and blonde. Candy fit the profile. She gave a mental shrug and filed the discrepancy away for the moment.

Abruptly she asked, "What did you do with my carry gun?"

Surprise filled his expression, "Your carry gun?"

Bitter repeated, "What did you do with my Walther after I passed out in the break room?"

A bare hint, his pupils widened, "I didn't do anything with it. O'Malley took it."

Bitter's voice reflected her exasperation. "Morales—"

"That's Captain Morales to you."

"Captain Morales, you were the senior officer present at the incident. It was your responsibility to secure my weapon."

He shrugged. "O'Malley took it. I don't know what he did with it."

She saw there was nothing to be gained from this line of questioning, so she changed direction. "I see by the key card records that you've been in the building early every day. Why?"

"I told you, I have work to do. And speaking of work, I have a meeting with the Chief," he glanced at his watch, "in ten minutes. So, we're done here."

Before Bitter could speak, Morales was up and out the door. It slammed behind him. She sat for a moment, then took a deep breath and spoke for the record, "Interview with Captain Morales ended, 9:50 a.m."

She rubbed her forehead in frustration. *I didn't even have a chance to ask any questions about Sally.*

By the time the Chief arrived, Bitter managed to interview the remaining on-duty officers, including O'Malley and Sapp. She poured herself another cup of coffee while she reviewed her notes. She didn't mention Morales' insinuations to O'Malley or Sapp—they weren't relevant to the case and it wasn't appropriate to repeat them anyway. The recording picked them up, so good enough for now. She'd handle Morales and his nasty remarks later.

She circled the connections between the interviews. *Morales said O'Malley had secured my pistol. O'Malley confirmed it. He put it in the bottom drawer of my desk and the office door was locked.*

O'Malley kept my keys, so he and Sapp could feed my cat. They told me they had the keys at the hospital.

Who else has access to my office? The Chief? Morales? The janitor? Who?

And when I picked my pistol up on the morning I got out of the hospital, it was in Property. How did it get there?

She made a note to check the log in Property. After consideration, she added a second note to check the log for the entire week, and who was on shift from the time O'Malley secured the Walther in her office to when she picked it up at Property the morning of Candy's death. She tapped the pen on her notebook, then wrote a third note to make sure that the pistol was still there. She couldn't pick it up until after the investigation was complete.

She rubbed her throbbing knees. *I didn't do them any good with this morning's antics. I'll pay for it tonight when I try to go to sleep. So much for feeling better.*

The door opened slowly. "Bitter?"

"Come in, Chief. Coffee?"

He sank into the chair. It creaked when he settled his bulk on it. "Please."

As she handed him the steaming cup, she noted the dark circles under his eyes. He took the cup and sipped it, then sighed in relief. "Good coffee. Better than the sludge in my office."

Bitter put on her gentle public smile. "Hopefully, Sally will be out of the hospital soon, and you can stop depending on temps."

He sighed again. "Before we begin, Bitter, you should know that my wife has left me. I'd prefer that this stays off the record,

I'm hoping she'll reconsider after a few weeks at her sister's house."

She maintained her smile despite her surprise at his revelation. "Well, Chief, do you think it's relevant to the case?"

"No. And HR knows because I set up spousal support voluntarily. That means a garnishment from my paycheck."

Bitter's eyes widened. "You're that far along in the divorce process?"

"No," he said sadly, "It's supposed to be temporary, but her lawyer filed the paperwork so it's officially a legal separation."

She hesitated, but the question and its answer were important. "May I ask why?" she asked politely.

He nodded, "She was sure I was cheating on her."

Taken aback, Bitter blurted out, "With who?"

He blushed a little. "Sally."

"Sally?" Bitter leaned back in her chair and looked hard at the Chief. Her voice grew stern, "And?"

"I wasn't. I've never cheated on my wife."

Bitter heard the truth in his voice. She thought for a moment, reviewing her plan for the interview. "All right then. I can't promise that it won't come out in the course of the investigation, but as far as I know right now, my questions today won't involve you and your wife's relationship." She paused. "Do you happen to know if Morales and his wife are still together? I noticed that their wedding picture isn't on his desk."

The Chief looked at her, surprised at the question. "As far as I know they're still together. Sally," he choked a little, "Sally would know."

Bitter nodded and picked up her pen. "Shall we begin?"

The late afternoon sun slanted through the blinds in Bitter's office as the day's interviews downloaded to her computer. She reviewed her notes on each interview and highlighted points she wanted to explore further.

"The Chief was here early because he couldn't sleep," she said aloud, "He was supposed to meet with Morales, but when Candy's body was found, they postponed the meeting. So how did Candy get in the building? And why was she here?" She thought for another minute before checking her notes on Morales' interview. "I thought Morales said he and the Chief were meeting early?"

The moth orchid caught her eye, the delicate blossoms floating above the tiny pot. The aerial roots looked a little shriveled. *Oh, you need water.*

She picked up the orchid and stepped into the hall, carefully locking her office before she went into the ladies' room. With a few paper towels blocking the drain, she adjusted the water temperature until it was room temperature and filled the sink halfway. While the orchid's pot sat in the water, absorbing the moisture, she handled her business and washed her hands thoroughly in the other basin. As she left the restroom, the little flowerpot wrapped in paper towels to absorb any dripping water, she saw Morales shaking the knob on her office door.

"What are you doing?" she asked sharply.

Morales stepped back and gave her a startled look. "Where were you?"

Bitter looked at him incredulously, pointedly at the ladies' room door, and back at him. "Where did you think I was? Gallivanting around town?" she asked, "What do you need?"

Morales regained his composure, "I want to look at the files on Candy's case."

She frowned. "Why?"

"I need to verify a couple of things."

Bitter looked at him sternly. "No." As he began to speak, she interrupted him, "No, I haven't ruled anyone, including you, out of this case. If you need to verify something, you can put in a formal request in a memo to the Chief." She paused for effect. "You insisted that I work this case, despite my objections. So, I'm running it. If you have a problem with that, take it up with the Chief."

Red washed up over Morales' face. He turned and stalked to the elevator, his back rigid and fists clenched. As the elevator door closed, a loud bang echoed into the hall. *Punching walls again. He needs to get a grip on his temper.* She unlocked her office door and put the orchid back in its place.

After she contemplated Morales' demand and access to her office, she made a quick decision. *I need to keep everyone out of my office and these files until this case is closed.* She reached for the phone.

"Building Maintenance, this is Jontay."

"Oh good. Jontay, this is Bitter."

"Hey girl, what's up?"

Bitter sighed. Jontay was incorrigible. "I need a new lock on my office door. ASAP, please. And nobody else with a key."

"Oh dang. Today?"

"Please."

"I'll be up in fifteen minutes. Do I need to know why?"

"Best if you didn't. I don't want anyone to know that I've changed the lock right now."

"Ohhh. I'll bet it has to do with Candy's murder. Well, do a work request for me and I'll make sure it's the last one inputted this month. Will that work?"

"Thanks, Jontay. I appreciate your help. Bring me the spare key, please. I'll keep it for now."

"Will do. See you in a few." The phone disconnected.

Bitter looked around her office. Everything seemed to be in place, but she suddenly felt exposed. O'Malley could be trusted, yet someone had moved her Walther from the locked office to Property. She got out her key ring and laid it on the desk, impatient with her sudden bout of paranoia.

I'd better get that incident report on Jones written up while Jontay changes the lock. It's not going to write itself.

Chapter 18 ~ Monday Night

The setting sun's golden glow lit the front of the bungalow as Bitter wearily unlocked and opened the gate. Chica's shrill barks echoed from the kitchen. The little dog heard the Maverick's engine as Bitter pulled up and the squeak as the front gate opened.

As she entered the garden, she looked automatically toward the burnt shell of the old woman's house, past the end of her block. A chain-link fence surrounded the property and large yellow signs warned of the dangers of trespassing.

I need to talk to Wendy. She needs to keep the children out of there.

Something fluttered in the evening breeze. The deepening dusk made it hard to see what was moving on the other side of the ruins. She closed the gate before she walked to the end of the block and across the street. When she peered through the fence, she couldn't see anything at first. Then the streetlights flickered on in a burst of yellow light and she saw a dark, shambling figure duck into the alley.

"Hey," she shouted, "Jean! Come back here!" Her knees protested as she rushed toward the alley that ran beyond the chain-link fence. When she reached the alley and looked down the rough gravel road, there were only shadows. It was empty.

Bitter walked slowly back to her house. *I'll feed Chica and Gato before I go to the hospital to check on Sally and Billy. And I should call Harry.*

She patted the Maverick as she passed it. *No rest for the weary.* She grinned a little at the memory of that unseen blue, safely anonymous in Gema's garden, contradicting the Captain. *That sure made Morales mad.*

Two cups of coffee later, Bitter gathered her purse, notebook, and keys. Chica and Gato lay snuggled together on the plush pet bed under the kitchen table. "I'll be back," she told the sleepy pair as she closed the kitchen door. She tucked the .45 into its holster and put her suit jacket back on.

It was still warm outside, with a breath of air moving from the river inland and over Bitter's house. She stopped for a moment to enjoy the bit of breeze before carefully navigating the front steps. When she opened the Maverick, she rolled down the window.

After making a Y-turn, she turned left in front of the apartments on the corner, heading east toward the hospital. Automatically, she looked up toward Wendy's apartment. The silhouette of a child appeared in the window, backlit by the light inside. The profile looked like Tabitha. Bitter waved and the child returned the wave. The shape of her hand looked odd. *Maybe she has a glove on?* Bitter wondered why she would be wearing a glove, then dismissed the thought. *They're probably playing a game of dress-up. I'll talk to Wendy and the children tomorrow about staying away from the old woman's property.*

Bitter signed in and produced her ID for the nurse. Above her name, she saw that Kenny, the Chief and, she paused in surprise, Morales had signed in. "Who let Morales in?" she asked the nurse sharply.

He looked at the log, surprised at her reaction. "I don't know," he said. "I was off last night." He leaned over the counter and caught the attention of the blue sitting in the chair, "Hey, Charlie, were you on duty last night?"

The blue put his book down. "Yes, why?"

"Did this guy, Morales, get in to see Sally?"

Charlie unfolded his long legs and stretched, then walked over to look at the log. "Oh, yeah, that guy. He said he wanted to see Sally, but he wasn't on the list, so he didn't get in."

"You turned him away?"

He chuckled a little, "No, that cute little nurse that was in charge last night took care of it. He never made it back to me."

"Oh?" Bitter let her tone ask the question.

"He was pretty persistent, but she wasn't having it. She was a bit of a thing," he said reflectively, "but she didn't have any trouble telling him to step out of the ICU."

"Thank you," said Bitter, relieved. "Has anyone else tried to see her?"

Charlie used his chin to point at the nurse. "There's been a stream of people, but only the Chief and Kenny were allowed in. Tony here, and the rest of the nursing staff, have been careful to keep everyone out. They barely need me."

She looked back at Tony. "Has Sally regained consciousness?"

He shook his head no. "Not yet. She's still sedated, but they expect to finish bringing her out of it tomorrow or the next day."

Sally was sleeping, but she seemed closer to consciousness. Her color looked better, though it was hard to tell in the dim light. When Bitter patted her hand gently, she stirred a little and her eyes fluttered, but she didn't rouse completely.

On her way out, Charlie caught her attention. "What's up with Morales? He didn't want to take no for an answer. I thought I was going to have to interfere until the nurse took care of him."

Bitter sighed, "It's a long story, but he's my supervisor. We have issues."

Charlie's eyes quickly flicked up and down Bitter's shapely figure. "I see," he said. "Well, he didn't get in."

Bitter heard the unspoken question in the tone of his voice and ignored it. "Good. Thank you."

The halls remained quiet and dim as Bitter made her way to the burn unit. Soft moans followed her footsteps past the nurses' station, where the Filipina nurse that looked like Lola was monitoring vitals on a computer screen. She gave Bitter a quick nod and kept working.

After a moment, Bitter saw Billy's distinctive curls, bright against the white pillow. A bandage covered the bridge of his nose and both eyes were blackened. Bandages covered his hands and the wrappings extended to his elbow on his right arm. A light blanket covered his body, and Bitter noticed that the cast on his broken leg was gone. As she approached, her staid shoes tapping on the linoleum floor, his eyes opened.

"Ms. Bitter," he whispered, "you came."

"I came last night too, but you were sleeping."

"I thought it was a dream." His voice was soft and hoarse. "I was drifting on a cloud. I couldn't open my eyes."

"How are you feeling?"

"It hurts, but it hurt worse when I fell off the roof," he whispered. A slow tear gathered in one eye, "They said my leg is pretty bad. They took the cast off."

"I see that. Did Julio hurt you when he dragged you out of the car?"

"No, I'd already messed it up when I hit the tree," his voice broke, "They don't know if I'll be able to walk again without crutches."

"Billy," Bitter said in a low, firm voice, "They said they don't know, right? That means that it's up to you to follow the doctor's orders and do your rehab. It might not be perfect, but you're a strong, stubborn young man. I'm betting that you'll walk and run on that leg again."

For the first time since he opened his eyes, Billy's face brightened a little. "You think so?"

"I do." In fairness, she qualified her answer, "But you do have to follow the rehab plan. And that means no walking on it until the doctor gives you the okay." She touched his arm gently, her fingers dark against his pale freckled skin, "No climbing on roofs, no more driving your friends around, no more of that foolishness. Do what your mom tells you." She looked around the dim room and frowned. "Where are your parents?"

Billy closed his eyes.

Bitter waited for a moment before she asked, "Billy, is there something I should know about your family?"

He shook his head slightly. "No. Mom is at work. She'll be here when she finishes her shift. I wrecked her car, so she has to take the light rail and the bus. She's not too happy with me right now."

Bitter gripped his unbandaged arm and shook it lightly as she replied, "You know, sometimes parents yell at a kid because they're scared and relieved that their baby is alive. They yell so they don't cry."

An olive-complected nurse entered the unit and nodded his head, the short, curly ponytail bobbing to add emphasis to his words. "That's right, son, they're so afraid of losing their child, they sometimes show it with anger. They don't know how to show you how much they care."

Billy sighed. "She was really mad, Amir."

"Well, you can face that when you get out of the hospital. Right now, you need to focus on getting well." Bitter said gently. "How are your hands?"

He lifted his hands and looked at the bandages. "Better, I think. They don't hurt as much as they did last night."

"Good." Bitter watched Amir until he moved to the other side of the unit and began checking the patients' charts, one by one. "Billy, do you remember what you told me? About the river?"

He shuddered. "Yes."

"Tell me what you remember."

His eyes widened as he whispered. "There was something big swimming in the river. It was long," his voice rose a little, but at Bitter's glance toward the nurse, he quieted, "It was really long, like a sea serpent."

"Not like a shark," asked Bitter, as she remembered stories of bull sharks in the delta.

"No, for sure not like a shark. More like the Loch Ness monster, but it didn't have a long neck like the pictures I saw on TV. I didn't see the head. It didn't go up and down in the water like Nessie. It moved side to side, like an eel or a snake. It was too big to be an alligator." He stopped for a moment. "Do they have alligators here?"

Bitter smiled a little at him and shook her head no. "Not around here. The winters are too cold for them."

"Oh. Okay." He lay back against the pillow, then raised back up a little. "But what about New York? I read that alligators live in the sewers there. New York is colder than Sacramento."

She stopped and looked at him, thinking of the giant salamander under the city. "No. No alligators. Not in New York and not here in Sacramento. That's just an urban legend."

He caught at her sleeve with one bandaged hand, "Are you sure? I thought I heard something slithering across the floor. It hissed." His hand dropped. "Maybe I was dreaming."

At the motion, Amir bustled back to his bedside. "Are you getting tired, champ? Are you hurting? You're due for your meds."

Bitter touched Billy's shoulder, "I'll be back tomorrow night, okay?"

He nodded. His eyes closed, then he forced them open, "Mom will be here later."

Amir brought over a cup with a couple of pills and a glass of water. "Let me sit you up a little, son, and we'll get these pills down you. Then you can sleep until your Mom gets here." The bed hummed as it raised Billy's head and shoulders.

"Billy," said Bitter, "remember what you made me promise in the ambulance?"

He looked at Amir uncertainly, then at Bitter. "I remember."

"Promise me the same thing. Don't go in the river, ever."

He nodded nervously, two swift jerks of his head, "I promise." Then he threw her a mischievous smile, "I can't swim. I never go in the river."

Amir handed Billy the pills and water, "Here son, take these." He leaned toward the teen and whispered, "I can't swim either. And I never, ever go in the river. Not even knee-deep."

Bitter shook her head at both of them. "We need to fix that. Swimming is good therapy for that leg. But the river is too dangerous."

Two heads, one dark and the other red, turned toward her.

She sighed. "Yes, I can swim. That not-swimming thing is a stereotype and definitely not true." She patted Billy's shoulder, careful to avoid the bandages, "I swim in the pool at the gym."

Billy's eyes drooped as the bed lowered to a more comfortable position. Amir gently pulled up the blanket to cover the teen's chest and arms. "He'll be out of here tomorrow. Check at the front desk, he should be in a regular room by the end of the day," he said over his shoulder. "He's a good kid, just a little hyper. His parents need to keep him busier."

The image of the fidget-spinner flashed into Bitter's memory. "Do you have anything for him to do? It's not good for him to be confined to a bed."

"His friend came by earlier," said Amir. "Spent a couple of hours with him."

"His friend? Which friend?" Bitter's tense questions came quickly.

"A tall kid. Older. Didn't talk but they did fine." He looked at Billy's bandaged hands. "Billy talked, and the other kid signed."

She went limp with relief. "It's all right, I know who he is."

"Sad to see such a young kid getting into trouble."

Bitter had turned to leave, but at his tone, she turned back. "Young? How old is Billy?"

Amir looked at her oddly, his dark eyes filled with questions. Surely, she knew Billy's age? Then he gave a tiny shrug. "He's thirteen."

Bitter's mouth dropped. "He's what?"

"Yes, he's only thirteen."

"He was at the high school."

Amir gave her a crooked smile, "You didn't know? The boy is too smart and much too hyper for his own good. They promoted him to the high school two years ago because he'd already passed all the classes for middle school. He told me all about it while I was changing the bandages on his hands." His smile faded, "Obviously school isn't keeping him busy enough either."

She gave Billy an evaluating look, *I think I know something that will keep him busy. And thirteen, huh? That's good, the public defender can probably keep him out of Juvenile Hall.* She pulled out a business card and scribbled a note on the back. "Please give this to his mom. Ask her to call me before he gets out of the hospital."

Amir took the card with a wry grin. "You like this kid." She gave him a look and his smile widened. "I like him too. I'll talk to his mom and make sure she gets your card."

Bitter gave him her small public smile. "Thank you."

A soft snore interrupted her. Billy was sound asleep. Bitter gave him one last look before she left. The Filipina nurse was gone and Bitter realized that she still didn't know the woman's name.

Shadows filled the hall. Bitter didn't notice. She walked to the elevator, lost in thought. After the elevator door closed, a faint thread of sobbing echoed from somewhere deep in the building. Amir leaned out of the unit, looked up and down the hall, then closed the doors against the sounds of the night.

Chapter 19 ~ Tuesday

Coffee dripped into the carafe as Bitter busied herself at her desk, preparing for the day. The computer hummed, then pinged, indicating new emails waiting for her review.

The early morning sun highlighted the tops of the trees lining the street across from her office window. The bright light would reach into her window later when the sun dipped toward the western horizon. For now, the sky was still pink and blue with a light breeze from the river cooling the area. As she stirred cream and sugar into her coffee, she stood in front of the window and gazed out at the reporters loitering in the empty parking lot. A cluster of young men and women dressed in camera-friendly outfits held steaming cups decorated with the local coffeeshop's logo. A battered white and green van straddled two parking spaces, garnering glares from latecomers trying to park in the few remaining spots.

She turned away from the window and sat down at her desk. One by one, she opened each email, working from the top to the bottom. Several received a quick tap of the mouse to send them into oblivion. "Blasted spammers," Bitter muttered, "How do they get my email address? And why can't IT block this garbage?"

At the crack of eight, the telephone rang.

"Bitter."

A pause, "Oh, you're there."

She looked at the caller ID on the phone. *Ah, it's the techie. What's his name? Dan? I hate it when I can't remember a name. Well, it'll be on the emails.* "Yes, I'm here. Did you have any information for me?"

The hesitant voice on the other end gave her the bad news. "No. I couldn't get anything from the video. It's gone."

Bitter huffed before she replied. "Can you tell me how it was done?"

His voice grew firmer, "Without a backup on the server, basically it was just a matter of erasing the tape."

She dug back into memories of the last time she'd ruined a VHS tape. The machine had eaten it. "So, the tape is gone. And there are no backup or computer files. Right?"

"That's right," his confidence in the answer showed, "There's no hard drive. The upgraded camera system that will be connected to our servers is in next year's budget. This system was a basic video recording system. Running a magnet over the videotape, probably a neodymium rare earth or other industrial strength magnet, took care of it. The tapes are destroyed."

"Oh." Her disappointment showed.

"I do have all the key card information for you. I sent you an encrypted file."

"And the password?"

He hesitated.

"Don't tell me, you sent it in a separate email?"

Indignantly, "No. I sent it by interoffice mail."

Bitter didn't let her eyes-raised-toward-heaven, Lord-give-me-patience response show in her voice. "Thank you. I appreciate your help. Do you have anything else for me?"

"No, that's it."

Before he could escape, she asked, "Did you check both Candy's and Sally's emails for the last ninety days? I'd like to know if they received any personal emails, particularly from other employees."

"We looked at their emails."

She forced herself to be patient, "Did you send me the files?"

"Well, no. There was nothing out of the ordinary."

"I would like a printout of who sent them emails, especially any that were deleted. They should be on the backup server."

Silence answered her question.

"You do have a backup server? Right?"

"Well, we had some technical difficulties and the budget—" His voice faded.

She closed her eyes and sighed. "Send me what you can, as soon as possible. Will just the last two weeks of emails make it easier?"

Relief filled his voice, "Yes, I can get those to you."

"We haven't located Candy's phone. Has anyone requested their cell phone records? Who called them, voicemails, and texts?"

"Yes, the Chief called and had me start the process while you were out on sick leave. The phone company required a subpoena. We're still waiting."

"I understand. Thank you for taking care of that."

She sensed his relief as she let him go. *I'll bet he was planning on leaving a voicemail. I caught him by surprise. Nobody likes to admit that their equipment is less than adequate for the job.*

As she poured herself another cup of coffee, she contemplated the two cases. Instinct and experience told her they were connected.

Candy died. Sally survived. Two departments in the same agency. What is the link?

She made herself comfortable in front of the computer and sipped her coffee as she continued scanning her emails. An email from Forensics took her full attention.

Well hell, they didn't find the bullet. She sighed in frustration. *Sally was shot somewhere else and dropped off, just like O'Malley and I thought. So, no bullet and no ballistics report to compare to the bullets that killed Candy. Sally was damn lucky. She lost a lot of blood. If we hadn't found her until morning, it would've been too late.*

She made a mental note to stop by the hospital on the way home to check on Sally's condition and talk to Kenny again. The printer clicked and whirred as she printed out the email and added it to Sally's file.

By lunchtime, Bitter had already sorted the emails into files, printed and filed relevant information, and reviewed the interviews again.

Her stomach growled. Time to run home for lunch.

On her way down in the elevator, Bitter changed her mind and hit the "B" button. The doors slid open at the first floor. Morales stepped in. He pushed the third-floor button. He glared at the down arrow above the door.

"Where are you going?" he demanded.

"Down," Bitter replied.

"Obviously," His voice oozed sarcasm.

The elevator dinged and the door slid open. When she left the elevator, he followed her out. As the doors slid closed behind them, she walked to the far end of the short hall. The brisk tap, tap, tap of her shoes echoed in the bare space, with Morales' footsteps adding a separate cadence. She stopped in front of the Dutch door that secured the Property room. A thick plexiglass window covered the upper portion of the door. A tarnished counter bell sat on the narrow shelf next to the pass-through locker, where it had probably been since the building opened.

Bitter tapped on the bell.

"One minute," a voice called from the bowels of the underground space. She waited patiently until he appeared. "Detective Bitter," surprise filled the technician's face, "How can I help you?"

"Checking on my pistol. The Walther PKK/S .32."

His expression changed, "You can't take it out of Property. It's part of," he stumbled over the rest of the sentence, "of your case."

She put on her public smile, always useful at putting victims, witnesses, and fellow officers at ease. "I know that. I just want to be sure it's still here."

Morales grunted behind her. "This is a waste of time. It's here. Where else would it be?"

She ignored Morales. "I'd also appreciate it if you'd check the log, please, and see who turned it in after I had the allergic reaction in the break room," she looked at his nametag, "Mr. Lee."

He paled. "I can't do that."

Her smile tightened, "Why not?"

"I already reported it to my supervisor," his voice cracked.

She leaned forward and examined his expression through the plex. "Reported what?"

"I was on vacation."

She raised her eyebrows and stopped smiling, "And?"

He glanced at Morales and nervously licked his lips, "When I came back to work the log was damaged."

"Damaged?"

"A whole section of pages was missing. Someone ripped them out of the book. I had to get a new logbook and we're working on recreating the missing pages."

She pinched the top of her nose with a thumb and forefinger. "Is my Walther checked in or not?"

"I don't know." He saw the expression on Bitter's face and rushed on, "We're still recreating the log entries and verifying that all property is still here. We have to check every locker manually, then enter it into the log and the new computer program."

She closed her eyes and got her rage under control. "So, you don't know who checked my pistol in. We know it was here because I checked it out after I was released from the hospital. Then it was checked back in as evidence after Candy's body was found, correct?"

"Yes, ma'am." He stuttered a little. "Well, as far as I know, it was checked in. I wasn't here. I was on vacation." At her expression, he rushed on, "I'm about halfway through the lockers. My supervisor ordered me to check the money in the safe first. It's all there, so I could move on to the weapons. We don't store narcotics here. They're transported to a secure warehouse up on Sequoia."

"This is a waste of time," Morales muttered. "I checked it in myself after you turned it over to me last Friday."

Bitter whirled and took a step toward him before she regained control of herself. "Why didn't you say so?"

He smirked, "You didn't ask."

"Where's the receipt? That will tell us the locker number where it's secured."

Morales shrugged. "I put it in my desk."

Lee piped up, "I'd appreciate a copy of that, Captain. There's only two of us working here right now. The third evidence tech is out on maternity leave."

Bitter turned back to the tech, "You said there's also a computer log?"

Lee gave her an indecipherable look before he answered her question, "The old computer crashed, and we lost everything. IT could only save part of the data, and some of that was corrupted. The new system just arrived last week, so we've been entering all the property and evidence into it as part of recreating the computer log. We're long overdue for a full inventory."

Bitter nodded briskly and turned toward the elevators. Before she took a full step, she looked up and stopped, then slowly scanned the upper levels of the hall. "Lee," she said over her shoulder, "Don't you have cameras down here?"

Both Lee and Morales looked at her, then up toward the ceiling over the elevator doors. "I thought we had cameras," Lee said. "I remember looking up at them when I was hired."

Bitter took a few steps forward to look closely at the wall and ceiling. "I think there was a bracket up there," she pointed, "and another over there. I see a hole where a cable must've connected it to the video recorder upstairs."

"Next year's budget," said Morales. "The city decided it could wait another year."

"That's ridiculous." Bitter scowled, "After the fiasco with missing evidence that cost us that big narcotics case, I thought the department was going to upgrade security through the whole building."

Lee interrupted, "That's why narcotics are stored in the secured warehouse now. They had already budgeted for that location, so it was cheaper to move the narcotics storage over there. I just log the evidence in and then notify my supervisor. He arranges for secure transport to the other facility."

Bitter looked back up at the hole in the wall. The fluorescent lights seemed dimmer and the upper corners of the room darker than they were just a few minutes before. "Please notify me as soon as you locate my pistol. An email would be good, with the locker number."

"I'll find it," he assured her with confidence that she didn't share, "I spent eight years in the Army. I ran the warehouse and trust me, if I can't find it, it's not here."

"Thank you," Bitter forced the words out, "But 'it's not here' is not an option."

She stalked back to the elevator, furious with the inadequate security that interfered with her case.

This is why we need to overhaul the technology and security in this building. It's insane that someone can simply destroy the logbook and we're left searching for property and evidence in our own Property room. She fumed, *And they'd better find my Walther.*

The elevator door opened just as she pressed the button. Cznik stepped out. He carried a locked bag under one arm and absently nodded to Bitter as he passed her. The elevator doors closed behind her and it started rising before she realized that Morales was still downstairs.

Chapter 20 ~ Tuesday Night

Drawn back to the old woman's house, Bitter stared through the chain link at the ash-filled property. The late afternoon sun left dark shadows, obscuring the deep hole within the foundation walls. She looked at the bowls at her feet, just inside the fence. "Empty again," she muttered. "Something is eating the cat food anyway."

She carefully pulled the bowls under the fence, refilled them with dry cat food and water, and pushed them gently back under the metal links. "Sorry kitten, it'll have to be dry food until I get to the store."

She paced along the perimeter of the property and peered down the alley where she'd seen Jean. On impulse, she pulled out her cell phone and started to call Sapp. Before she finished dialing, she remembered Morales' insinuations about Sapp and O'Malley. She breathed deeply a few times to calm the fury that the mere thought of Morales and his snide accusations brought on. *Screw him*, she thought as she hit the last button.

"Sapp," he snapped.

"Are you busy?"

His voice changed, "Not that busy. What's up, Bitter?"

She looked back down the alley. "Have you seen Jean hanging around the old woman's house?"

"No, but I've been pretty busy with the teens out of school. Plenty of traffic stops, underage drinking, and vandalism right now. Why? Is he trying to get Gato again?"

Bitter laughed a little. "Not with Chica ready to guard her good buddy. But I thought I saw him the other night in the alley. Not the one behind my house. The alley that runs east to west, on the far side of the old house."

"Do you think he's trying to retrieve something from the house?"

"I don't know, but the little girl that lives across the street was trying to catch a kitten in that mess."

Silence met her, then Sapp sighed. "I'll get a couple of bags of salt."

"What?" asked Bitter.

"Salt. I'll put a line of salt around the whole property. That should keep him out and whatever's in there inside. There's no rain in the forecast, so it should work for a good while."

She hesitated before asking, "You think there's something supernatural going on?"

Sapp heard her disbelief, "Not necessarily, but salt discourages more than just magic, and we know it affects Jean, so that's good enough for me."

Bitter looked back at the filled dishes. "I think there might be a cat or something in there. I put food out and it's gone. There's a fence up now, so that might keep Jean and the kids out of there."

Sapp chuckled, "Since when did a fence keep a kid out of an interesting place?" He abruptly stopped laughing. "Who put a fence up? It wasn't the city, I just talked to the inspector this morning. The old woman's lawyer isn't answering the phone and not returning calls either. The inspector is not happy and that's never good."

"I don't know. I came home from work and it was up." She walked back to the nearest warning sign. "There's no name on the sign." She glanced up and down the fence line, "I don't see any contractor signs up either. That's odd."

"Well, I'll—"

She heard his radio in the background. Something about graffiti at the elementary school and the perps still on site.

"Gotta go. I'll call later tonight or tomorrow. And Bitter?"

"Yes?"

"You stay out of there too. It's not safe." She heard his siren wail through the phone. "I'm out. Talk to you later." The phone went dead.

The bushes rustled, but when she looked, nothing was visible. A tiny sway in the lower branches faded to stillness. She paced the perimeter of the property again. Nothing else moved.

Bitter walked across the street toward her house. She changed direction when she saw Tabitha and Toby sitting on the steps that led to their apartment. Her expression changed when she saw the thick bandages wrapped around the girl's forearm, hand, and fingers.

"Tabitha, what happened to your hand?" Bitter's concerned voice echoed in the stairwell.

Tabitha looked down, her tangled red curls catching the light. "I, well I—"

Bitter looked sternly at Toby, who tried to hide behind his sister. "Toby, what happened?" His eyes grew larger, but he didn't answer.

"Do I have to ask your mother, Tabitha?"

Her rosy lips trembled as she brushed her hair back and looked up. "No," she whispered. "I went to find the kitten. It was crying."

Bitter motioned for the children to move over. "Let me sit down."

After they scooted over and Bitter made herself as comfortable as she could on the hard concrete step, she said, "Tell me what happened."

Tabitha gave her a sideways look. "Are you mad at me?"

"Disappointed, yes, but not mad." Bitter kept her voice soft but firm, "I told you to stay away from the old woman's house. Why did you go back? I fed the kitten."

Tabitha looked down again. "I was in my bedroom and I heard the kitten crying, so while Mommy was in the bathroom, I went outside."

Behind Tabitha, Toby nodded, his eyes wide.

"And what happened, Tabitha? What did you do to your hand?"

"I saw the food that you put out. The kitten was hiding, I saw his eyes shining in the bushes. So, I stuck my hand under the fence." She sniffled, "And then it grabbed me." Tears ran down her plump little cheeks.

"The kitten grabbed you?" questioned Bitter.

Tabitha sobbed.

"Tabitha?"

"It bit her," said Toby, his voice quavering as he lisped the words, "It wasn't a kitten."

Bitter hauled herself up off the step, her knees protesting the sudden motion, and leaned over the children protectively. "What was it, Toby?"

"I don't know."

"Tabitha?" Bitter said in a low voice, "What bit you?"

As Tabitha sobbed, she reached out and Bitter took the child in her arms. Her tone softened as she lifted and hugged the little girl. "Sweetheart, what bit you?" she asked again.

"I don't know," Tabitha wailed. "It just bit me."

"She screamed," said Toby. "And Mommy ran out and picked her up." He raised his eyes to meet Bitter's, "She was bleeding."

The door above them opened and Wendy came out onto the landing. "Oh!" she gasped when she saw Bitter. "What are you doing here?"

Bitter gave a deep sigh. "Well, I was going to warn you to keep the children away from the old woman's house, but I think I'm too late. I caught the children trying to catch a kitten in the mess over there. I also saw Jean prowling around the neighborhood two nights ago. "

"Tabitha, Toby, get inside right now," Wendy said firmly. Bitter put Tabitha onto the step and steadied her. Still sniffling, the child began slowly climbing the stairs. Toby followed, but not without a last lingering look at Bitter.

"I'm going to put a childproof latch on that door so I can keep these kids inside," Wendy said as she came down the steps. "Every time I shower or try to rest before I go to work, they're sneaking outside. Maybe this will teach them a lesson."

Bitter, taken aback by her hostile tone, went right to the point. "What bit Tabitha?"

"I don't know, and I don't care," said Wendy, "I'm tired of CPS coming by to check on the kids and having my ex's mother blame me for every little thing. It's not like she watches the kids so I can go to work."

She took a deep breath and her voice changed, "No, I do care what bit Tabitha. We went to the ER. They saved her fingers, but she was in surgery for hours." As she approached, Bitter could see her bloodshot eyes and exhausted face. She sat on the step, so her face was level with Bitter's and her voice grew fearful. "What bit my baby girl, Bitter? What's going on? I'm afraid to take the trash out at night. Strange noises and weird people are wandering the streets. The other night someone was screaming behind the apartments."

Bitter smothered her flinch at the mention of screaming. It was Jean in her backyard who had woke the neighborhood with his anguished cries. "I don't know what's going on, but I'll find out," she promised.

Looking at the dark circles under Wendy's eyes, Bitter flashed back to a fateful night. The screams that had her out of bed and on her feet, grabbing the Glock and racing out the door before she was fully awake. The cold, rough cement of the sidewalk under her bare feet. A single dim streetlight that lit the scene as she rounded the corner. The sharp, medicinal smell of the meth he'd been smoking that lingered on his clothes.

She'd grabbed his arm and jerked him away from the cowering young woman on the lawn. How he rolled to his feet and made a move to lunge at her, then froze when he saw the barrel of the Glock pointed at his face. Her rage and the .45 in her hand as she held him at gunpoint, ready to shoot him if he made a move. The sirens and flashing blue and red lights as O'Malley roared up and secured the scene.

O'Malley probably saved his life.

The ambulance, the reports, the night would've been even longer if she'd shot him, though it might've made life a little easier for Wendy. Fortunately, the children were at Wendy's mother's that night, so they didn't see him beating her. Oddly, they hadn't asked about Wendy's black eye and split lip.

It wasn't the first time he'd beaten her.

Bitter's thoughts returned to the present. Wendy stared past Bitter, lost in her own memories, and hadn't noticed Bitter's brief silence.

I need to pay closer attention to Wendy. The kids are growing up so fast and she's pretty much alone. Being busy is no excuse.

Mentally running back over what Wendy had said, she focused on another issue. "Is your ex giving you any trouble?"

"Just in court," Wendy said bitterly. "He's trying to get custody."

"He's out of jail already?" The thought that he might be out caught Bitter by surprise. "He shouldn't be out for at least a couple more years."

"No, but his Mom is trying to take custody away from me. She'll give him the kids as soon as he's out."

Bitter patted Wendy gently on the shoulder. "It doesn't work that way. She can't just take the kids and then give them to her son." She sighed. "California standard is joint legal custody, one parent has primary physical custody, and the other has a visitation schedule. Grandparents can get visitation too."

"But she said—"

"Oh, I'm sure she did." Bitter smiled just a little to reassure Wendy. "Do you have a lawyer?"

"Yes. He's taking care of the divorce."

"And your house is clean, there's plenty of food, and the children are being watched by an adult while you're at work, right?"

Wendy sniffed and nodded. "Señora Gutierrez watches them."

Though Bitter usually avoided getting involved in the neighborhood dramas, her mind was still filled with the stark memories of him hitting Wendy. She made a sudden decision. "Let me know when you go to court again. I'll come with you."

Wendy gasped, "You will?"

"I have a personal interest since I was the first officer on the scene when he was beating you." Bitter's smile grew grim. "I thought I was going to have to shoot him. I can't do anything to influence the court, but a little moral support can't hurt your case."

A small sound upstairs, a squeak as the door opened, caught their attention.

"I have to check on the kids."

"It's okay. I have to take Chica and Gato out again, and I have some things to do before I go to bed. Go check on the kids and get that latch on the door ASAP. You can't have them running around unsupervised, especially since Tabitha was bitten by something." Bitter patted her on the shoulder again. "Go take care of your family."

Wendy abruptly stood and hugged Bitter. "Thank you," she whispered before she let go, turned, and trotted up the stairs.

"You're welcome," Bitter said as Wendy disappeared inside.

What am I doing? Now I'm going to court for my neighbors? Wasn't it enough when I arrested her ex and then testified against him? We got him put away for both felonies: domestic violence and possession of meth.

She stared up the stairs for another minute, thinking, then shrugged and walked back around the corner to her house.

I'm getting soft, she thought as she trudged up the steps and let herself inside. Chica and Gato were waiting impatiently as she opened the back door and let them out to do their business. The twinkle lights glowed amid the tree branches and the automatic misters in the lath house hissed as they added much-needed moisture to the air.

Chica and Gato dashed back up the steps when Bitter whistled, ready to crawl into bed. The thought of Tabitha's tear-streaked face kept Bitter awake for a while, until she finally got back out of bed and made herself a cup of mint tea, sweetened with local honey.

If it wasn't a cat, then what bit her?

The question worried her until she finally fell asleep. Dark visions of crying children haunted her dreams. She moaned a little as she tossed and turned. Finally, Chica snuggled up and licked her face. Bitter turned over, only half awake, and muttered, "Can you not lick me," before she drifted into a dreamless sleep.

Chapter 21 ~ Wednesday

Cars lined the streets near the huge cathedral. On K Street, black and whites took up every inch of space in front of and behind the waiting hearse.

"Good thing I called you," Bitter said to Gian as he pulled up and double-parked next to the hearse. "Otherwise, I might as well have walked. There's no parking for blocks."

Gian, his face somber, twisted in his seat to look back at her. "Watch your back, Bitter. Somebody hated that young woman enough to kill her and they're probably in there like a two-faced snake, waiting and watching for their next victim. Don't let it be you."

"Thank you, Gian," Bitter said as she slowly climbed out of the taxi. Her dress uniform was too warm in the bright afternoon sun, but it suited her bleak mood and the sad occasion. The shoulder holster chafed a little under her right arm. She preferred her other holster but changed her mind at the last minute. Sitting in a wooden church pew would become uncomfortable with the Glock tucked into the small of her back.

"Call me if you need a ride home. I work late tonight."

"I will. Thank you, Gian."

With a wave, he pulled away, his radio already crackling with directions to his next fare.

Candy's father stood watching outside the double doors of the cathedral. "Bitter," he called as he walked down 11th Street toward her, "Thank you for coming."

"I'm sorry about your loss, Captain Soto," she replied as she shook his hand.

He blinked back tears. "Me, too." He cleared his throat. "Anything new?"

She shook her head. "Not yet. I'm still compiling all the statements and going over the evidence."

"Before I forget, we'd like you to join us after the funeral. It's a family tradition, to eat and drink together before we have to face another night without her." He sighed. "The Chief and Candy's," his voice broke, "Candy's girlfriend, Vicki, will be there."

"Yes," Bitter said reluctantly, "I'll be there. And later, when you have time, I'd like to talk to you. I need to nail down the timeline, and I'm sorry, but I need your input too."

"I never thought I'd lose one of my children. My baby—" He choked up.

Bitter pulled a package of tissues from her purse and offered him one.

He wiped his eyes, wadded it up, and stuffed it into a pocket. "Thank you."

An usher motioned from the doorway, "It's time," he said in a voice just loud enough to be heard over the passing traffic.

Soto offered his arm to Bitter as they climbed the steps. When they reached the top, he led her to the priest waiting just inside the massive double doors that led into the cathedral. "Bitter, meet Father Flores."

Rich Irish vowels filled his words as he greeted Bitter, "I'm sorry we had to meet under these circumstances, Detective Bitter. Thank you for coming." He smiled at her briefly, then turned to the next mourner.

"The Chief said you'd want to sit to the side, where you can see everyone. O'Malley saved you a seat," Soto pointed to the left, "Over there, in the front." He motioned to the usher, who took a good look at Bitter and nodded at the whispered instructions.

"This way please," the young usher said and offered his arm. She noticed the freckles that stood out against his pale skin and his eyes were swollen and red. When he turned, she saw the family resemblance in his profile. *A brother or cousin perhaps?*

A few of the mourners turned as they made their way to the front of the church. When they saw her, a wave of murmurs rose from the packed pews and intensified as more people turned to look. Her escort looked nervously around as the attention of the church focused on her. He increased the pace, his back stiff as he concentrated on getting Bitter to her seat.

O'Malley stood in the front row of the pews on the north side of the cathedral, set with their backs to the side wall. He motioned to the corner seat next to him, closest to the altar, where she could view the family in the front row, and the friends and relatives that filled the pews behind them. A plump seat cushion sat on the hard wooden pew beside O'Malley.

Blues in dress uniforms filed in and filled the pews behind Bitter, Vargas among them. He gave her a quick head bob and then sneezed several times in a row. The usher handed him a packet of tissues and after a few more suppressed explosions, he got the sneezing under control. He wiped his red, swollen eyes with a fresh tissue.

Allergies?

"Thank you," Bitter said gently to the usher before he returned to the main doors, ready to escort the next group of mourners waiting beside the bénetier. Several dipped their fingers into the holy water and crossed themselves before he took them to their seats.

As she faced the altar, the back of her neck itched with tension.

I hate sitting with my back to anyone, even blues. I still don't know who killed her, or why.

A pearly white urn stood at the front of the church, on an antique mahogany table covered with a white satin cloth. Ethereal flowers in a pale metallic silver flowed up the sides and decorated the top of the urn. Deep wine-colored roses circled the base of the urn and a fan of greenery behind emphasized its small size. Shimmering hints of pink, blue, and lavender flickered across its satin surface.

After standing silently for a moment, head bowed in respect, Bitter sat down next to O'Malley and looked over the mourners. Captain Soto and his wife were front and center in the first row. Beside them sat an older woman, about Soto's age, dressed in black with a black veil covering her face. Bitter nudged O'Malley. When she had his attention, she pointed with her chin and gave him a questioning look.

"Candy's mother. Soto's first wife," he whispered. "She's Catholic. That's how they were able to use the cathedral."

Bitter raised her eyebrows slightly.

"Oh," O'Malley evaded the question, "her mother set it all up. I don't know if the Bishop is aware." He lowered his voice even further until Bitter could barely hear him. "I think Father Flores knows. Rumor has it that he heard Candy's last confession. Candy and Vicki attended Mass here on their days off."

Trust O'Malley to have the gossip, Bitter thought.

Dressed in a demure black dress with long sleeves and a scoop neck, Vicki sat on the other side of Candy's mother. Her hair and face were also covered with a lace veil, but Bitter could see her shoulders shaking as she wiped her eyes with a matching handkerchief. The older woman wrapped her arm around Vicki and hugged her.

Soto's current wife glanced at his ex and scowled.

"No love lost there," O'Malley observed in his near-silent whisper. "Candy was his youngest with the first wife. He and the second wife had no children. She died several years ago. Cancer, I think. This is wife number three," he paused, "or is she number four? I can't keep track. They keep getting younger—or maybe I'm getting older."

"Where's your wife?" she whispered back.

O'Malley frowned. "Kathleen and Mrs. Soto aren't friends." Before Bitter could ask, he added, "None of the Mrs. Sotos. They don't speak and I don't ask why."

"I see," Bitter's low voice stayed neutral.

He changed the subject. "There's the Chief. He's a friend of the family."

The Chief shook Soto's hand first, then greeted the ex with a hug. Mrs. Soto frowned at him as he took her hand to express his sympathies. Captain Morales was close on the Chief's heels.

"I don't know how friendly Morales is with the Sotos, but they seem to know each other," O'Malley muttered.

They don't look that friendly to me. Bitter thought uncharitably as Morales took his turn at greeting and extending his condolences to the family.

As the organist began to play, the Chief and Morales took their place in the third row, behind the Soto family. At an unseen signal, everyone stood and turned toward the rear of the church. Bitter followed, rising a little slower than the other mourners. Her knees protested, though she slid forward and used the prayer rail to take some of the weight off her joints as she rose.

As the priest and altar servers proceeded up the center aisle, O'Malley filled in the details of a Catholic funeral. "There's usually a procession, but the current wife had a fit about Soto escorting Candy's mother up the aisle, and then when she found out that Vicki was going to walk with the urn to the altar, it got ugly. So, they consulted with the priest and decided that they'd omit that part of the service."

Bitter nodded, her attention focused on the Sotos, as O'Malley crossed himself and fell into the familiar routine of the Catholic service.

A few people slipped into the cathedral midway through the service, including Denise and her new girlfriend. Bitter wouldn't have noticed the pair, except the usher rushed to seat them with the blues. After a whispered argument, Denise shook her head firmly and pointed at the pews closest to the entrance. The usher shrugged and led them to the last empty seats in the back. Bitter didn't miss Denise's dirty look, though the girlfriend seemed oblivious. The pair left sometime before the mourners stood for the final prayers.

By the time the funeral was over, Bitter was grateful for the cushion that O'Malley had brought for her to sit on. The dark, polished wood of the antique pews was lovely, but hard as a rock after an hour or so. The urn with Candy's ashes was going home with Vicki, so the priest gave the final blessing and released the mourners.

"Ride over with me, Bitter?" asked O'Malley.

She sighed. "I hate funerals and receptions." She looked up at O'Malley, her eyes black with memories. "Yes, if you don't mind."

"I can't stay too late. Kathleen will expect me home early."

"That's fine," Bitter replied, "I can always call Gian for a ride home if it gets too late. I need to talk to Soto if I can."

O'Malley's voice sharpened, "Today?"

"Hopefully what I need to know will come out in conversation. Otherwise, I'll have to have him come in for an interview," Bitter said softly. "I'd like to keep it informal as long as possible, for his sake." She glanced toward the elder Mrs. Soto and pointed with her chin, "I'll have to talk to her mother too, but probably not today."

The mortician passed them as he slowly rolled a cart carrying the urn out to the hearse. He carefully loaded and secured it, then solemnly spoke to Candy's mother. Bitter could hear her giving him the address in a quavering voice filled with tears. Vicki stood next to her, silent.

After the hearse pulled away, Mrs. Soto took Vicki's arm. The pair slowly walked toward the cathedral parking lot. They stopped for a moment in front of Captain Soto and the Chief. The sudden flutter of pigeons fleeing some unknown menace distracted Bitter, and the opportunity to eavesdrop on their conversation disappeared.

"Let's go," she said to O'Malley. "I want to get this over with."

Cars filled the driveway, three deep in front of the garage, and a long row of vehicles lined the street. O'Malley dropped Bitter off in front of the house and slowly eased down the street as he searched for a parking place.

The hearse was already gone.

Bitter waited in the shade of an old oak. It took several minutes for O'Malley to maneuver his truck into a tiny space near the bottom of the hill and walk back up to the house.

"Shall we?" he asked and shortened his stride to accommodate Bitter's pace. The young usher was waiting on the porch of the mid-sixties three-story split-level. He opened the door and waved them inside. Candy's mother appeared from the hall and took Bitter's hands.

"Thank you so much for coming. I've heard so much about you." She smiled sadly at Bitter as she spoke, "Cattee was a fan, you know. She followed all your cases." Tears sparkled in her hazel eyes.

A pang of guilt hit Bitter. *Candy meant well when she offered the tea. Maybe she really didn't know it could kill me.*

"No, I didn't know, Mrs. Soto."

"Please call me Grace. Mrs. Soto sounds like," she glanced over her shoulder toward the living room, "like I still belong here." She took a shuddering breath. "I live downtown now. It's better that way." She looked at O'Malley and her voice grew frigid. She transferred a hand to Bitter's arm before she spoke. "O'Malley."

"Good to see you again, Grace," his voice was polite though the undercurrents between them felt old and dark. "I'm sorry it was under these circumstances."

Grace didn't respond, though her grip grew tighter.

"Please come inside, Bitter, and meet the family." Soto's voice carried across several conversations. Grace tugged gently at Bitter's arm and led her into the depths of the home. O'Malley followed.

On the right, several teens sat on the steps leading up to the third story bedrooms, blocking the path of any interlopers into the private areas of the house. Bitter could see the family resemblance in several, though two or three could be cousins or perhaps friends. Their dark eyes followed her as she passed.

Ahead the entry opened into a spacious living room, crowded with Soto's peers, all in dress uniforms, young men and women dressed in varying shades of black, and boisterous children.

The custom tiles that surrounded the fireplace reflected the emerald green grass of the park-like garden outside. Off-white drapes framed huge, floor-to-ceiling windows. A bar height table placed in front of the windows held the urn, carefully centered on a shimmering silver lame tablecloth. Vicki sat on a matching chair next to the table, one small hand placed protectively on top of the urn.

Even as Grace and Bitter started toward Vicki, a small blonde child dashed across the room and bumped into the gracefully arched table leg. Vicki quickly grabbed the urn with both hands to keep it steady as the table shook under the impact.

Soto's voice boomed, "Josephina, stop running in the house."

The little girl looked up at his stern face and tears trickled down her cheeks. Soto's wife scooped her up and carried her toward the buffet on the other side of the room. "Shhh, shhh," she crooned to the child, "Mommy will get you some candy."

A hint of Spain flavored Grace's bitter words, "You see what I deal with? She does not teach the children respect. Instead, she feeds them sweets while," her face showed the strain of her tight control, "while my baby waits for justice."

Castilian, thought Bitter. *But she's been here a long time, or she's good at languages. Maybe both.*

Bitter put a hand over Grace's hand, the one that was still gripping her arm tightly.

"Grace," Soto called from in front of the fireplace, "Bring Bitter over here." He stood next to the Chief and Morales. The glass in his hand was nearly empty.

"Ayyyy," hissed Grace as she turned her face away so Soto couldn't see her expression. "I am not his to call like a servant.

He can call his *wife*," her angry voice made the word a slur, "if he wants something."

Bitter glanced over and caught the Chief's eye. She tipped her head toward Vicki. He responded with a quick nod and spoke quietly to Soto. It took more than a few words before Soto finally nodded. He set his glass on the counter and refilled it with the dark liquor from a half-full decanter.

"Grace," Bitter kept her voice soft and gentle, "I should pay my respects to Vicki before they get me involved in cop talk."

"Ah yes, you have met?" Grace also lowered her voice as she moved through the guests toward Vicki.

"Yes, we have, thank you for asking."

Grace shot a hard look toward the buffet, where Josephina and her mother were selecting sweets from the candies scattered amid the chafing dishes and serving platters. "She cannot even cook. A caterer brought the food." Her voice revealed her outrage. Bitter couldn't tell if it was because the latest Mrs. Soto couldn't cook or that a catering crew was working in what was once Grace's kitchen.

Bitter tugged at her arm gently.

"Perhaps we should speak to Vicki for a moment?"

Grace sighed. "Yes. Nothing can change what has been done. Even if I still lived here, he would not be any different." She looked toward Soto, "His child sleeps in heaven, but he laughs with his friends."

"He cried at the funeral," Bitter tried to comfort her.

"Ayyyy, yes, he cried, but was it for my Cattee or for his own mistakes that led to her murder?" Bitter opened her mouth, but Grace continued, "He could never be bothered with our children, not until it was too late. Not even when Cattee was sobbing that she had killed you, not even then could he just accept her as she is. No, he was not kind to her. He told her that if you died, it would be her fault because she was too stupid to ask anyone if that tea was safe."

Laughing at some joke that Soto had told, Morales turned toward the two women. He lost the smile and glared at Bitter before he turned back to his cronies with a fake laugh.

"And that one, he is no good," Grace's vowels rounded and her Castilian accent thickened.

"Morales?" asked Bitter.

"Ayyyy, he is always pretending to be everyone's friend, while he tries to, to—" she hesitated, searching for the right word, "How do you say? Get next to their wives."

"Ah, and did he try to talk to you too?" Bitter glanced at the circle of men. None of them were looking her way.

"He was a friend of my husband. I told him to leave my home and never come back."

"And?"

"He was there the next weekend when my husband and his friends were watching *fútbol* and drinking *cerveza*." The words burst from Grace, "He has no respect. He sat in my house and smirked at me, while my husband treated me like a servant, not worthy to decide who could and could not come into my home."

"Is that when you left Soto?"

"Yes. Not long after. I think he was most angry that I took the children with me. It made him look bad. But he could not care for them. Who would watch them while he was at work?" Grace dabbed at her eyes with a lace handkerchief. She looked back toward the men and pointed at Morales with her chin. "You know him?"

Bitter huffed in frustration. "I know him." She lowered her voice so it wouldn't carry to anyone else's ears. "We don't get along."

Grace gave her a sharp glance and finally started moving toward Vicki, still perched on the chair. Several women surrounded her. One turned and saw Bitter. With whispers and side glances toward the advancing pair, they each solemnly pressed Vicki's hands. One smartly dressed woman wearing a black silk hijab kissed Vicki's cheek before the group scattered. As she passed and gave a bare nod to Grace, Bitter realized that she was one of Vicki's coworkers. The other women ignored Grace and Bitter as they left en masse.

"*Mija*," Grace greeted Vicki, "You know Bitter?"

Vicki held out a trembling hand, "We've met."

Bitter took Vicki's small, cold hand and held it for a moment. "I'm so sorry."

Delicately, Vicki pulled her hand from Bitter's. "I don't believe you." Tears welled in her dark eyes. "How dare you lie to me? They put you on the case and I have to tell you about our life together?" her voice grew louder, "And all the time you knew that she was cheating on me? My beautiful Candy is dead, no thanks to you."

Shocked at her vehement words, Bitter stared at the grieving woman. Before she could respond, Grace swept Vicki into her arms.

"*Mija, mija,* our Cattee is gone, but you are still family. I will not abandon you."

Vicki's hysterical sobs fell into a suddenly quiet room.

"Shhh, shhh, *mija*. Come, it has been a terrible day. I will take you home." Grace looked about the room. Before she could speak, O'Malley stepped up.

"I'll carry the urn out for you, Grace. You take care of Vicki."

She nodded once, regally, and turned back to help Vicki down from the chair. "Come, my car is parked in front." She looked at Bitter over Vicki's lace-covered head with graceful dignity. "We will speak of this another day. Now is not a good time."

As she supported Vicki's wavering steps to the door, O'Malley carefully picked up the urn and looked around the room. Soto suddenly appeared from the hall with a small box and packing material. "Here, you'll need this."

Bitter shook off her surprise and took the box from Soto. O'Malley quickly wrapped the urn in tissue, then bubble wrap and packed it into the box.

"I've got it," he muttered to Bitter, "Let me get this out to Grace, and then we can leave."

"You go ahead," Bitter replied, "I need to talk to Soto for a minute."

O'Malley didn't pause as he stalked outside.

"She's on meds, you know," said Soto.

"Who? Grace? Vicki?"

He grimaced and nodded. "Both. It's been a terrible shock to us all. Poor Vicki, you know she was going to ask Candy to marry her. And now," he paused, "now it's too late."

"Maybe it's not the time, but Grace mentioned—"

"Yeah, I know. Candy told her mother that I said it would be her fault if you died." He looked out the window, avoiding Bitter's eyes. "That's not exactly what I said." He sighed, "But close enough."

Bitter softened her voice, "Why?"

He sighed again. "I always thought she'd come to her senses and stop fooling around. Marry a nice young man. Spanish maybe, or Italian. Even an Irish lad. A good Catholic. Vicki's a nice girl, but—"

When he paused, Bitter said, "But she's a girl. Right?"

Soto flushed, "Yes."

"I understand that she's a good Catholic though. Goes to church. Made Candy go with her. Even planned to marry her."

Negation screamed in every muscle of his tense body.

Bitter took a deep breath before she spoke. She knew that he probably wouldn't appreciate her input, but she had to try—for Candy's sake if nothing else. "If I may, I'd like you to think about something. Did you ever have to wonder about your gender or sexuality?"

Soto's head jerked up and his eyes widened in surprise.

"No, no, don't answer," she said quickly, "Just consider that maybe Candy never wondered about hers either. She was who she was, just the way she was born. It was the way she was meant to be."

Soto opened his mouth to reply, but Bitter pressed forward before he could say anything that might haunt him later. "So, Candy called you when I collapsed in the break room?"

It took a few seconds for him parse the new question and reply. "Yes. She was hysterical. She said that she'd killed you. I could hear the ambulance siren and then the EMTs in the background, so I knew you weren't dead. At least, not yet."

Bitter looked up at him, "I realize she must've been pretty upset, but wasn't her reaction a bit extreme?" She was missing something important about Candy, but the knowledge floated just outside of her comprehension. It wasn't clear yet, but it felt so close, like the finely spun silk of a spider web brushing against her mind. She looked around and realized that everyone had left after Vicki's outburst. Only Soto remained in the room. His wife's voice rose, her tone sharp, in the kitchen amid the clinking of dishes and ripping sounds of plastic wrap.

He shot a glance toward the kitchen door and evaded the question, "Vicki needs some time to process all this."

"Yes, that's true. But why did she blame me? I didn't even know Candy."

He turned back toward the window, away from Bitter. She could only see his profile, "She thought you knew Candy and lied to her about it. Someone told her that you and Candy had a thing going on."

Bitter stepped back, her surprise visible, and stumbled as she stepped on a toy. She grabbed the edge of the table to catch her balance. "She what?" Her voice rose a little.

"Shhh, I don't want the wife to hear. She never liked Candy and she hates Grace. We don't need anything else to fight about. Not right now."

"Vicki thinks I was having an affair with Candy?" Disbelief filled her voice. "Are you kidding me?"

He bowed his head, "No."

"Who told her that?" Bitter's voice grew stern. "It's important."

He couldn't look at her, "I don't know. Vicki was pretty upset when we were making the arrangements," his voice broke again, "for Candy. Especially when my wife had a fit about the procession, so we had to change the original program. But when Vicki arrived at the church today, she wouldn't even speak to me."

"But why would anyone think that we were having an affair? I didn't even know Candy. I met her for the first time at the potluck."

He finally looked Bitter in the face, "The room was full of cops, and nobody gossips like a cop with an audience."

"And?"

"Her reaction, like you said. She was screaming something about how she'd killed you and she'd never had a chance to tell you that she loved you."

The room spun as Bitter grasped the implications. Soto grabbed her to help her keep her balance as she stepped back onto that damned toy a second time. She clutched his arm for a moment until he helped her sit in a nearby folding chair. Shock made her knees weak, and then fury rose in her throat like bile.

"Everyone was there in that room and heard her," she said. It wasn't a question.

"I think so."

She took several deep breaths to control her rage.

"Are you all right?"

She took another breath and stuffed her anger back into the dark place where it belonged. "Yes." She gazed up into his concerned face, remembering how Candy had held her hand for a little too long when she'd handed over the cup of tea. "I was just shocked. I had no idea she had a crush on me."

Relief entered Soto's voice, "So it wasn't true?"

At first indignant, Bitter tempered her response as she realized that Soto really didn't know anything about his daughter's personal life. "No," she said gently, "It wasn't true. Please convey my apologies to Vicki." She smiled bitterly, "I don't think she'll talk to me again."

"I'm not sure she'll speak to me again either. She thinks we all knew about Candy's affairs and were lying to her. I'll ask Grace to talk to her. The girl seems to trust her."

A light knock at the door caught Bitter's attention. One of the teens that lingered on the stairs slouched to the entry. "It's Officer O'Malley," he called into the living room. "He wants to know if you're ready to go."

"One minute," she said to the teen before she shook Soto's hand. "Thank you for inviting me. It's been a hard day."

He squeezed her hand, "Just find out who did it."

She put her other hand over his in an unspoken promise. He closed his eyes to hide his pain, then let her go.

O'Malley waited on the porch. "Ready?"

"Yes. It's been an illuminating day."

O'Malley waited for an explanation, but Bitter stayed silent all the way to Alkali Flat. As he pulled up in front of the bungalow, she abruptly asked, "Can you make a list of everyone who was in the break room when I collapsed?"

"Sure."

"Thank you."

She climbed out of the truck before he could get around to the passenger door to open it. He opened the gate for her instead.

"Thank you for the ride. See you tomorrow?" Bitter said absently, already walking toward the house.

"Yes, I'm on shift tomorrow. I'll have that list ready for you."

She nodded, lost again in her thoughts, and climbed the steps up to the porch. He waited until she unlocked the door before he got back in the truck and started toward home.

"What was that all about?" he muttered. "And why is it important who was at the potluck?" He glanced back as he turned the corner, but a cloud of shadows obscured the front of the bungalow. The dark figure at the top of the steps raised a hand in farewell.

Chapter 22 ~ Wednesday Night and Thursday

The night air was still warm, but Bitter shivered a little as she slipped into fresh pajamas. "Come," she patted the bed. Chica perked her ears up and gave a sharp little bark. "Really? You want to go out again?" Chica danced on her hind legs as Bitter opened the bedroom door, then dashed for the back door.

"Come on, Gato. One more time, then to bed we go." Bitter flicked on the porch light as she opened the door. "Do your business."

Chica raced down the stairs, then stopped abruptly and began barking wildly at a dark figure that peered over the back gate. Bitter snatched up Papá's Maglite that still hung from a hook just inside the door and aimed the bright beam across the yard.

"It's me," Sapp's voice rose over Chica's yapping. "Will you please turn that thing off?"

Bitter turned off the Maglite and flipped the outside switch for the garden floodlights. She slipped on the old sneakers she wore when gardening and slowly went down the steps. As she picked her way across the brightly lit yard, she asked, "What are you doing?"

"Shhh, I've got a bag of salt. I was pouring it along your back fence when I heard the door open. So, I looked over the fence to make sure it was you."

"Salt?" she questioned as she opened the back gate.

"Yes. It breaks the bonds of magic and kills weeds too. Win-win."

Bitter frowned. "There's no such thing—"

"Yes, yes, I know. No such thing as magic." His voice sobered, "Just because you don't believe in it, doesn't mean it's not real. I also put a good layer around the *bruja's* property. It's an unbroken line, so it will keep Jean out and whatever's hiding in there inside." He walked over the patch of dead grass where the ashes of Jean's arm had fallen and prodded it with his toe. Slowly he poured another thin layer of salt over the dead grass. "Just in case." He murmured.

"Assuming whatever is out there isn't a cat," Bitter's voice was dry.

Sapp grinned at her. "Yes, assuming it's not a cat or some other natural creature. Except for slugs and snails. They won't cross it either."

"And the old woman?"

"Oh, she's human—at least as far as I know—so she can cross it." He shrugged. "I could be wrong about her though."

"What about salamanders?"

"Hmmm, I don't think salt is good for salamanders. Dries their skin out." His forehead creased in thought as he considered the question. "Do you think the mother salamander might be roaming the neighborhood? It's pretty dry this time of year."

Bitter shook her head, "You're right, it's too hot and dry. No, I'm quite sure she, or maybe it's he, is holed up for the summer, down in the underground city or in an old well or cistern."

"All right then, let me get back to applying salt along the alley. I thought I should get this done tonight while I was thinking about it and I wasn't too busy with calls."

He started back toward the gate when Bitter had a sudden thought, "Sapp. Do you remember who was in the break room when I collapsed?"

He looked at her and several emotions skittered across his face, too quickly for Bitter to identify. "Yes. I'm fairly sure I know who was there."

"Can you make a list? It's important."

His face brightened, "Are you getting closer to solving Candy's murder?" he asked eagerly.

"Not yet."

For a split second, his face fell, then he gave her a little secretive smile. "I should know better than to ask that question. I'll have the list for you tomorrow. Let me know if you need anything else."

She considered the questions that still lingered even after interviewing all the staff who'd been in the building the day of Candy's murder. "Where was Jones before the DV call came in?"

He squatted down and held out his hand for Chica to smell while he reflected on the question. "I'm not sure. I think he was at the station. He came in early to cover for Adams." He shook his head ruefully, "I should've told you before, but I forgot. Adams had covered for him the day before when he was two hours late for work." He shrugged. "Jones said he had an appointment, so Adams stayed late to cover. The next day, the day Candy was killed, Adams went back to the station at about 4:30 a.m. when Jones texted him that he was in the building."

"So, they might've both been there when Candy was killed." It wasn't a question.

He frowned, "Maybe, but the call came in right after Adams left. Adams, O'Malley, and I were having coffee at the Denny's right around the corner from the station."

Bitter huffed in frustration. "I'm not sure there was enough time for Jones to meet, confront, and kill her and then make it across Midtown to the DV call. And why was Candy in the building at all?"

Chica nudged Sapp's hand. He looked down at her like he'd forgotten she was there and gently patted her head. "I have to go, little dog. 'Miles to go before I sleep' and all that."

Bitter stopped him with a question. "Hey, while you were pouring salt on the ground, did you see anyone hanging around the area?"

He considered the past hour. "Not really," he finally said. "The fence looked bent outward and up a little over by the alley. Nothing big enough for a human."

"What about a child?"

"Hmmm, a kid would have to be pretty small to squeeze under there. And it's filthy over there. I didn't notice any scuffs in the ashes, but they're pretty light and could've floated over any marks. I'll check it again before I leave." He glanced up with a mischievous look at Bitter as he scratched Chica behind her ears. "I'll add an extra layer of salt, just in case."

It took some effort, but Bitter managed to stop her frown at his little jibe at her disbelief. Instead, she asked, "Did you notice if the dishes were empty?"

He stood and Chica danced around his legs, trying to regain his attention. "Now that you mention it, yes. If you have a can of cat food, I'll refill them now."

As she turned to get the food, he said, "Be sure not to disturb the salt when you refill them tomorrow." She gave him a look as he continued, "It's important that the circle stays unbroken. If you see a broken place, pour more salt over it, and give me a call. I know someone who can check it out."

Bitter did frown at that. "A *bruja*?"

"Not exactly. More like a spiritualist familiar with witches and their practices. There's more than one tradition, and it's important to know which one so we know what we might be dealing with. Salt is pretty universal in breaking magical bonds though." Sapp grinned at her, "Don't worry, I'll be sure to introduce you."

She didn't reply. Once she reached the kitchen, she got a can of cat food and leaned over the porch rail. "Here," she said and tossed the can to Sapp in an underhand throw. He snatched it out of the air.

"I'll get the gate, no need to come back down." He looked down at Chica and pointed at the steps. "Chica, up!" he said firmly.

To Bitter's surprise, Chica gave a little high-pitched woof, turned, and trotted up the steps.

"That's the girl," Sapp said approvingly. "But you'll have to call Gato. I don't have any luck with cats. They like me, but they won't obey me." He gave a little snort of laughter, "They remember when they were gods and we humans were just staff."

Bitter whistled for Gato as Sapp secured the back gate. Gato dropped from the tree and strolled across the lawn. With a second whistle, he dashed up the steps and into the back door.

Sapp raised a hand and disappeared into the dark alley as Bitter turned off the garden lights and closed and locked the door.

"To bed now," she told the furry pair. By the time she reached the bedroom, Chica was under the covers while Gato kneaded the throw that covered the foot of the bed. When the bunched-up fabric satisfied him, he turned and snuggled down for the night.

Bitter adjusted the blackout curtains to ensure that the streetlight didn't shine into the room. She slid into between the sheets and made herself comfortable with her book. After a few minutes, her eyes drooped, and the book slipped from her hands. She'd barely read three pages before she fell asleep. An hour later, the timer on the lamp clicked and darkness filled the room.

"Doctor's orders," Bitter muttered grumpily as she paced around her office. "Fifteen minutes and I have work to do. No time for this." She looked at her watch and sighed. "Two minutes gone. I might as well go get some coffee." She shuddered at the thought of break room coffee and looked toward the window.

Maybe I'll make a fresh pot. It might shake loose some of the cobwebs.

She paced back and forth a few more times. Reluctantly she thought, *My knees are feeling better today though. Maybe the exercises and walking are helping. Or maybe it's the meds.*

She'd found O'Malley's list of officers who had attended the potluck slipped under her door that morning. Sapp had dropped his list off after she'd had a chance to look over O'Malley's list. Both lay on her desk, with names highlighted in green, yellow, and blue. She had remembered correctly, Cznik was in the break room during the potluck, but Adams was off duty that day. After double-checking the key card list for both the day of the potluck and Candy's murder, she started to draw a light pencil line through Adams' name, then stopped. *Maybe. Maybe not.* She added a question mark.

Jones? Where was Jones? And was Vicki's ex there?

Neither name appeared on O'Malley's and Sapp's lists. Jones' key card didn't appear on the list until he and the other blues returned from the DV. She checked the weekly schedule again.

Nope, they didn't bother to officially adjust their schedules. Why am I not surprised? She made a note to discuss this issue with HR. *We need to know exactly who's on duty, where and when. These new guys always seem to take a few months to understand why we always need to know who's out on the streets.*

Back and forth, she paced, thinking about Candy and Sally and the gossamer threads that seemed to connect her two cases. *Sally?* Bitter stopped pacing and looked at the list again. Sally hadn't been at the potluck either.

She looked up from the list, thinking, and saw the delicate blossoms of the orchid flutter in the breeze from her fan. Gently, she reached out and touched the white petals. "I still don't know where you came from."

Her phone rang.

"Bitter."

"I only have a minute," O'Malley said. "I got a call from Grace this morning. After the funeral yesterday, she took Vicki home. They were going through the mail and opened Candy's credit card bill. She'd bought something from a florist."

Bitter went on alert. "What was it?"

"Don't know. They called the florist and couldn't get an answer. He wouldn't tell them who ordered or if it was picked up or delivered." O'Malley sighed heavily, "I guess he's had some problems with his customers' and the recipients' spouses, so now he doesn't give out any information at all."

"When did she buy it?"

"The bill shows it was the late afternoon, the day before she was killed."

She hesitated. "Why didn't Grace call me?"

O'Malley sighed, "Vicki doesn't want to talk to you. In fact, Grace said that she's leaving the department and moving to San Francisco. I guess she has family there. So, Grace thought it'd be best if she called me and asked me to pass the info on to you. They'll leave the bill at the front desk tomorrow."

"No," Bitter said quickly, "Please ask Grace to hold onto the bill until we can arrange to meet somewhere, away from the station. I don't want anyone else to know about this yet."

"Okay?" O'Malley's tone made it a question.

"It's important that no one else knows. Tell her not to tell anyone, not even Candy's father."

The crackle of the radio in the background interrupted Bitter.

"Oops, gotta go," said O'Malley. "I'll let Grace know. Hang onto the bill and you'll get it from her. Don't tell anyone."

"Correct. Thank you."

The blaring siren filled the phone before the line went dead.

She paced a few more times, back and forth, considering Candy's purchase. *My orchid? We'll have to get a subpoena to get that information from the florist.* She made a note to get the paperwork started.

When she glanced out of the window, the canopy across the street caught her eye. Business had slowed a bit after the heatwave broke, but several reporters loitered in the shade, drinking ice-cold bottled waters and sodas. She smiled, remembering the summer Roberto and José had manned a lemonade stand on the corner. Most of the boys' customers were neighborhood children and their parents. They'd done well. Their little stand made enough money for new skateboards. And then she'd invested in helmets and knee and elbow pads. The boys complained, but she'd insisted. They knew better than to defy her.

Shaking off the fond memories, she looked at her watch again. "Eleven minutes. Okay, I need to do something other than pace this office. Maybe the Chief is in. I can check and see what Sally was doing that morning."

She locked the door behind her and jiggled the door handle to make sure the latch had caught. The emergency exit sign at the end of the hall drew her attention. *I haven't had a chance to look at the stairwell. Well, now is as good a time as any.*

The steel fire door opened easily. She slipped inside and closed the door quickly before anyone could see her. The air smelled dry and stale, overlaid with disinfectant and a slight metallic tang—the scent of old blood. The fluorescent light overhead cast a greenish glow over the battered concrete landing. She stood at the top of the stairs and gazed at the damaged wall across from her. Chipped paint and gouged concrete walls revealed the marks the bullets left after they'd exited Candy's body. Someone had scrubbed the wall, but dark stains marred the gray steps and landing below.

They might be feeling better, but her knees protested at the thought of descending the stairway, so she turned around and grasping the metal rail firmly, began slowly going down backward. Step by step, she examined the walls and concrete. *Forensics already went over this with a fine-toothed comb,* she thought. *I don't know what I'm looking for in here.*

At the bottom of the stairs, she turned and looked up, toward the second-floor doorway. Oddly, the light didn't seem as bright as it had when she entered the stairwell. She looked toward the fluorescent fixtures. One bulb flickered, creating intermittent pinkish shadows on the ceiling and walls. A blowfly buzzed, adding a tiny echo somewhere above the lights. She shaded her eyes and gazed into the corners at the very top of the stairwell, then at the underside of the steps that led further up into the building.

She again examined the steps, one by one, as she slowly climbed back up. Nothing. On impulse, she kept climbing, though her knees hurt, up to the third floor.

No one noticed when she stepped out of the stairwell in front of the Chief's office. The smell of burnt coffee drifted into the hall. *Ugh. I hope the temp turned the coffeemaker off.* She limped halfway to the elevator before she noticed the shred bins at the far end of the hall. The narrow openings were too small for a pistol, even the PPK/S.

I'll bet no one looked inside those.

The bins required a key, but Bitter knew where to find it.

An hour later, Bitter sat at her desk, gazing at the computer screen. She'd enlarged the digital image of the large pink envelope lying on top of a pile of papers and discarded mail. The card was missing, but the stained envelope had her name on it.

The calm voice of the young man who answered the phone at Forensics speeded up a little when she identified herself and told him where she'd found the envelope. The Forensics team wasted no time in storming the third floor and taping off the end of the hall. She'd managed to get a picture of the envelope lying in the scattered papers before they'd shooed her away.

The dainty cursive with a tiny heart dotting the "i" in her name was a sad reminder of the young woman who'd tried so hard to get her attention.

Is it my fault that she's dead?

A light knock at the door interrupted her gloomy thoughts.

"Detective Bitter?" The soft voice sounded uncertain. "Are you in there?"

"Who is it?"

"Sgt. Franks from Forensics. We spoke earlier."

Bitter limped to the door and unlocked it. "Sorry. I needed a little quiet time to think."

He put on a professional smile nearly as good as Bitter's as she let him into the office. "I understand."

"Have some coffee. Sit down." She motioned toward the chair. "I have a few questions."

He made himself comfortable. "Thank you, but I've probably had enough coffee for today."

She poured herself a fresh cup of coffee, with all the fixings, and sat down before she asked the question burning in her mind, "Blood?"

"We think so. I put a rush on it and the techs are working on the envelope right now. They're doing a full workup on it, including DNA. The stains are too smudged to pull out a fingerprint—we think. But I'll know more soon."

She sat back in her chair as she considered the possibilities. "No sign of the card?"

He shook his head, "No. But I have guys checking every shred bin in the building. Good thing you looked. They're usually emptied every two weeks. The contractor has been short-staffed, otherwise the bins in this building would've been emptied last week."

Bitter gazed at him over the rim of the cup as she sipped her coffee. She noticed the deep lines on his face and how the glare from the window reflected on his forehead and scalp. The remains of his receding hairline were mostly gray.

"You said that you think it came with a plant?"

She motioned with her chin toward the orchid next to the window. "That one."

Eagerly, he stood and stepped over to examine the pot. "Damn. No wrappings or tape."

She shook her head, "No, not there," and opened the bottom drawer of her desk. The hot pink foil wrapper sparkled in the clear evidence bag.

"Holy sh—" he stopped himself. "That was wrapped around the flowerpot?"

"Sally and I touched it before I realized that the card was missing. After that, I only touched the edges when I took the foil off."

"How did you know?"

She handed him the evidence bag, "I didn't. But nobody knew where it came from or how it got into my office. So, I saved it." She gave him a crooked little smile, "And honestly, I didn't want you to take my orchid."

His grin spread across his face until it threatened to touch his ears. "I'll get this to the lab. With luck, we'll find some prints. I should have something for you later today or tomorrow."

He started toward the door, but Bitter cleared her throat. "I think," her throat was suddenly dry, and she cleared it again before she forced the words out, "Could you let me know as soon as possible if the handwriting matches Candy's?"

A sudden realization blossomed in his face as he made the connection between Bitter's hospital stay, the orchid, and the stained envelope. "You think—"

Bitter saw him making the connections. "I don't know. I didn't know her. We only met once, at the potluck. And I don't know if this is even connected," she admitted. "I need more solid evidence than a missing and now found envelope. All I know right now is that Candy was murdered in this building and somebody didn't want that envelope and card found."

Franks stuck out his hand. "We'll do our best to get you what you need." His eyes glistened as he shook Bitter's hand. "Candy was one of ours—and we take care of our own," he finished firmly.

"I'd appreciate it if you didn't share any suspicions with the other officers. I haven't ruled anyone out yet." Bitter said softly.

He nodded briskly. "You can rule me out. I was on a cruise with my wife to the Bahamas—second honeymoon." His face turned grim as he continued, "And yeah, I'll keep it quiet."

She closed the door gently behind him. As he strode down the hall he muttered, probably louder than he realized, "Shit, they were right. She is psychic. How did she know to check the shred bin? And to keep those wrappings, and properly bagged and tagged too." He shook his head in disbelief as he pressed the up button on the elevator.

Bitter sat back down and reached for her coffee. Before she could take more than a sip, her door opened.

"Morales," she said.

He frowned, "Captain Morales."

Her lips twitched as she replied, "Okay. Captain Morales. Can I help you?"

"Why is the third floor taped off and filled with Forensics techs?" His grumpy tone told her that he had been out and about and hadn't heard the news.

She pushed a little, "Oh, found some evidence." Then, with a shrug, "I don't know if it's going to be anything important." She took a slow sip from her mug. "Coffee?"

He changed the subject. "How is Sally doing?"

"When I was at the hospital, she was still unconscious, but they're going to start bringing her out of it soon." After another sip, she added, "She might not be able to talk for a while. She was having trouble breathing, so they've kept her on the ventilator."

He still frowned, but something changed in his expression as he looked toward the orchid by the window. "Did you hear about the Chief?"

Bitter opened her eyes a little wider and added a curious tone to her voice, "What about the Chief?"

"His wife left him because of his affair."

She saw the opening and went for it, "His affair? With who?" She put a hint of disbelief in her voice as she raised her eyebrows slightly.

With Bitter's words floating in front of him like an iridescent fly on a fishing line, he bit, "Well rumor had it that he was sleeping with Sally."

"No!" Bitter emphasized her surprise at the thought.

He continued, "But I think he was cheating with someone else. One of the younger staffers. Or maybe a blue."

"Really?" Her questioning tone asked for more information.

Morales left the question hanging as he ran his eyes over her desk. He paused, but he couldn't see the image on the screen from where he was standing. "Yeah. Well, that was the rumor." He started to turn toward the door, then turned back. "If I can't get upstairs to do my work, I might as well go home." Abruptly, "I need to use your phone."

Bitter stood and pushed the desk phone toward him. "Help yourself." While she distracted him by handing him the receiver, she stealthily turned the monitor off.

"Chief? This is Morales. You know the entire third floor is taped off?" He listened for a couple of minutes. "Well, I can't get anything done if I can't get to my office. I'm going to head out. See you tomorrow?" He hung up and looked at the orchid again.

"Where'd the flower come from? You know I'm highly allergic to pollen."

"It was a gift," she said, "and you don't have to worry about orchid pollen unless you handle the flowers."

He looked at her doubtfully.

"No, orchid pollen doesn't float so it doesn't usually cause allergic reactions. It's sticky so it sticks to a bee or other pollinator when they visit—"

"Yeah, yeah. I'll ask my allergist." He interrupted with a dismissive wave of his hand. "The Chief wants a report as soon as possible."

"Fine," Bitter said to his back as he went out the door.

She fixed a fresh cup of coffee. The first had gone cold while she baited Morales. Just as she sat down, the phone rang.

"Bitter."

A tumult of sound exploded from the earpiece. She pulled the phone away from her ear, looked at it, then held it far enough away that the noise didn't completely deafen her. Somewhere in there, she heard a voice. "Bitter?"

"Yes, it's me. Who is this?"

"Hang on a minute." The noise level suddenly dropped, as if the caller had closed a door. "Can you hear me now?"

"Harry," Bitter said, "What on earth is going on over there?"

He laughed in delight. "You'll never believe this. We caught the big one, and yes, it was a male."

"And the babies?" She held her breath, waiting for the answer.

"Well, not all of them. And the female is still out there somewhere."

She let out her breath in a whoosh. "Where did you find him?"

"It was actually near your neighborhood, on the northwestern end of the underground city. He was holed up in an old cistern near Alkali Flat."

"Really?"

"Yes, just a couple of blocks from that house that exploded last week." The noise level increased again, and something about the noise caught Bitter's attention.

"Harry?"

"Yeah?"

"Do those creatures make a lot of noise?"

He laughed. "Oh yes, can't you hear them in the background? Sounds like a pack of cats in heat when they really get going. Those are just the babies."

"And the daddy salamander?"

"You'd swear he was a woman sobbing her heart out." In her mind, she could see Harry shrug, "His voice is deeper, more like someone who'd smoked too many cigarettes and drank a few too many whiskey shots over the last thirty or forty years."

Cautiously, Bitter said, "I might know where the female is hiding."

He went on point like a bird dog, "Where?" he asked eagerly.

"You'll have to be discreet. Go talk to Doctor Kezar at the hospital. He's the head of the psychiatric department. And then go all the way to the lowest basement at night and see if you hear anything."

Doubt entered Harry's voice, "A shrink? Are you kidding me?"

"Tell him I sent you and that I asked you to keep it quiet." Bitter added, "Seriously, he might hug you after you explain that you're looking for an animal. Anyway, I think the female is down in the storm drains somewhere near the hospital."

"Bitter, if I find the female, I'm going to owe you forever," he said eagerly.

Bitter's lips quirked into a smile. "Well, I do have a favor to ask. I know a young man who doesn't have enough to keep him busy."

"Oh?"

"He's young, a genius, has an interest in cryptozoology, and is nearly as hyper as you were at that age."

"Really?" Harry's voice sounded uncertain.

"Yes. I'll talk to his mom and bring him by if that's okay with you? He's still in the hospital right now," she thought guiltily that she owed Billy a visit. "But he should be out soon. He's gotten himself into a bit of trouble, but I think it'll be all right. He needs something to occupy his time."

Harry chuckled at her tone of voice, "You like this kid. Okay then, let me know when and we can see how he does when he sees the salamanders. We'll go from there. He'll have to keep his mouth shut though. We don't need any publicity."

A sudden thought hit Bitter. "Hey, Harry? Do you know what the creatures have been eating?"

"There was fur floating in the water where the male was hiding. Several different colors."

Nausea rose in Bitter's throat. "Cats?"

"We're having it tested, but yes, part of it looked like cat fur. Some of it was definitely from rats. Apparently, the tails aren't as tasty as the rest of the rodents, so there were a lot of bits and pieces scattered around down there. Why?"

She didn't answer his question. "Any sign of people?"

"Not that I noticed. And we made a mess capturing him, so I doubt you'd be able to tell if anyone else had been down there now."

"You said the babies bite?"

The long pause let Bitter hear the faint mewing in the background. "Yes. That's right, I did tell you about the student that was bitten. It was ugly. He'd grabbed it and it twisted right around and took a big chunk out of his hand. I told the ER that he caught it in a trap. I don't think the doctor believed me though." The noise grew louder, "I have to go. Feeding time for the cryptids."

"Before you go, are they venomous? Anything to worry about if a person was bitten."

Harry's voice grew cautious, "Someone was bitten?"

"Yes, a child. She didn't see what bit her. She thought it was a kitten."

"Oh, no, there's no venom to worry about," relief filled his voice, "No more dangerous than a cat bite." He rethought that statement, "Cat bites can be bad though. Puncture wounds are easily infected. Did she see the doctor?"

"Yes," Bitter said, "It was a bad bite, but they saved her fingers."

"Oh man, that's not good. Do you need me to check on her?"

Bitter thought for a moment, "I'll see if her Mom is okay with talking to you. She's pretty upset about it." She considered the question, "The brother said it wasn't a kitten, so they know that something is out there. They just don't know what."

"I'm free tomorrow. Let me know and I'll come and interview her. And I need to get an exact location. We'll try to catch it, whatever it was." The noise level in the background continued to grow.

"It was at the house that burnt down. Something is in there. It's eating the cat food I put out."

"Oh, shit, *la casa de la bruja*? Didn't you say her minion was trying to catch your cat? Look, we'll be out tomorrow morning with a crew. It'll take me that long to gather everything we need.

Will you be home?" Harry paused and Bitter heard another voice in the background. She couldn't make out what Harry said to the other person, his voice was muffled. He came back on the line. "Gotta go. I'll call you first thing in the morning."

"All right then, I'll let you go. I can hear the animals getting restless. Thanks, Harry."

The phone clicked off and with it the not-quite-human crying. Her stomach churned at the thought of the carnage Harry and his team must've found in the cistern.

What the? Wait. La bruja? Who has he been talking to? she pondered, then remembered his little idiosyncrasy. *Oh, wait. He watches the news in Spanish. Says it's more interesting than the local newscasts.* She sighed, *I guess I'd better start catching the Spanish news now. Like I need one more thing to do.*

She spent a few minutes worrying about Tabitha. Harry could be overwhelming when he was on the trail of a new beast. He'd been obsessed with the salamanders since last winter's unsolved murder. She resisted the urge to open the files on that murder and go over them again.

Sal is gone, one way or another. He's dead, he's back in Las Vegas, or he's hiding under whatever rock he crawled out from under before he slithered through my life.

She shook her head, impatient with her wandering thoughts. The memories of Sal made her skin crawl—at least what little she could remember. Most of those days were a blur. Mamá had told her that it was a blessing that she couldn't remember more than brief flashes between the night in the Las Vegas casino when she met the tall, charismatic man and when she woke screaming in the Sacramento hospital, only a week later.

I need to focus on something else.

Resolutely, she put the murky past behind her. After a few sips of coffee, she opened the case folders and turned the monitor back on. The pink envelope filled the screen.

I wonder what happened to the card? She pondered the question while staring at the image, then began reading the entire case file again. After a few pages, she grabbed green sticky notes and began tagging the items that caught her attention. She added more notes to some of the tagged pages.

The sun was setting by the time she emerged from the whirlwind of thoughts, speculation, and collating random facts that consumed the rest of the afternoon. She looked through the files one more time before she locked them in her bottom drawer.

Now if we could find my Walther. I sure hope it's down in Property.

Chapter 23 ~ Thursday Night

The streetlights flickered on as Bitter pulled up next to her garage in the alley. A stray bit of yellow hazard tape flapped in the light breeze, caught on the rough wood of the fence. She opened the garage and pulled the Maverick in, then closed the garage door and locked it.

The lock on the back gate stuck, but after a minute of jiggling the key and cursing under her breath, it opened. She carefully stepped over the line of salt that extended along the fence line and went into the side door of the garage. After a short search, she emerged triumphantly with a can of dry silicone spray. Lubricating the lock took a few seconds. After testing her key several times, she closed and locked the gate and returned the spray to the garage workbench.

The back steps seemed twice as steep as she wearily climbed up and let Gato and Chica out of the kitchen. They raced down the stairs, Chica yapping happily.

After she stripped out of her suit and did her daily exercises, she showered off the day's sweat and cares. Once changed into her pajamas and robe, she made a cup of mint tea and grabbed her new book, a steamfunk by an indie author. The comfortable old chair on the back porch awaited her foray into an adventure story set in an alternate America.

Carefully, she sipped the hot tea and watched Chica frolic around the yard. Gato found his usual perch in the tree and surveyed his domain. *He remembers when he was a god.* Bitter smiled as she remembered Sapp's joke about cats not obeying. "That's the truth," she said aloud.

After another sip of tea, she set the cup on the little table next to the chair. With her head resting against the back of the chair and her feet propped up on an old wooden crate, her eyes grew heavy. The book lay open on her lap as reality faded into dream.

"Miss Bitter, Miss Bitter," a small hand shook her awake.

"Tabitha?" Bitter's dream wove into the tapestry of the night and then she woke up to the towheaded little boy shaking her. "Toby, what's wrong."

"Tabitha went back for the kitten. I can't find her." Toby's ash-covered face was streaked with tears.

Bitter shook herself fully awake. "Toby, how did you get in here?"

He tugged at her hand, trying to pull her toward the alley. "We have to find Tabitha."

"One minute, Toby." She pulled her hand free and pulled on her gardening sneakers. "I have to get something," she said as she hurried into the kitchen. He followed her inside. She unlocked the gun safe in the hall closet and contemplated for a split second, then pulled out a box of shells, marked with an "R," and her Remington .410.

Wide-eyed, Toby watched her load four shells into the shotgun. She dropped a handful of rock salt-loaded shells in the right pocket of her robe, then considered and dropped several steel buckshot loads in her left pocket. On the way out, she grabbed her keys and cell phone from the table, next to her purse, and the Maglite from its nail next to the back door.

"Come on Toby, show me where she went."

As they went back outside, a growl from under her chair revealed Chica's hiding place. "Chica, in." The little dog dashed past her and at Bitter's whistle, Gato followed.

Toby trotted toward the fence between the apartment parking lot and Bitter's lath house. "No, Toby, I can't—" She stopped herself, thinking quickly, then grabbed the step stool she used in the lath house from under the stairs. "Okay, Toby, you came over the fence?"

"Yes," he lisped.

She followed him over the fence, holding the Remington out and away from her body as she dropped to the ground. She winced. Her knees protested the landing on the hard ground.

"Toby, where's your Mom?" she asked as they rounded the corner of the building.

He sniffled, "I don't know. I couldn't find her."

Bitter hit the speed dial. She started talking as soon as the call connected. "O'Malley, are you and Sapp on duty? I need you here at the burned house, no lights or sirens. Right now. Neighbor and her young child are missing."

"Five minutes out. I'll call Sapp, he might be closer."

"Hurry." She disconnected the call.

"Toby," she stopped and grabbed the little boy's shoulder, "Did Tabitha crawl under the fence?"

He started crying.

"Damn." Bitter looked around, then up at the apartment across from Wendy's. The window still shed light across the Bermudagrass in front of the building. She tugged Toby up the steps and banged on the door.

"Who is it?"

"It's Detective Bitter. Have you seen Wendy?"

The door opened a crack. "Oh my god, Toby." The young woman threw the door open and gathered up the crying child.

She stared over Toby's tousled head, her light brown eyes wide at the sight of Bitter and the shotgun tucked under her left arm.

"I don't know where Wendy and Tabitha are, and I think the baby is alone in their apartment. Can you stay with Toby and the baby while I try to find them?"

Bitter barely waited for an answer from the startled woman. She darted across the landing and found Wendy's door unlocked. After quickly checking the apartment, she ushered the pair inside, looked in on the peacefully sleeping baby, and rushed back downstairs.

As she descended, she pointed the Maglite at the burnt remnants of the house. The bright light flashed over the construction fence and settled on a break in the chain-link. *Oh no.*

Heart pounding in fear for the little girl and her mother, Bitter crossed the street and checked the break. The soft ash hid footprints, but she saw a scuff in the middle of the encircling line of salt. She paused and picked up a pinch of salt from the outer edge and sprinkled it across the broken line. *There's no such thing as magic. But it can't hurt. I'm pretty sure it'll keep Jean out if he tries to cross it.*

Carefully, she stepped over the salt barrier and entered the property. A flash of pink caught her eye. She tested the ground at every step, aware that there was once a basement below the old house. Slowly, she closed the distance to the bit of fabric dangling from a blackened shrub. As she centered the light on it, a rustle in the bushes made her abruptly step back. Ashes rained down on her as she brushed against a large shrub. She examined every inch of the foliage with the Maglite, but the ash-covered bushes hid any trace of an intruder. A little further, a bare patch of soil lay in front of a gap in the stone foundation. She paused to glance at the pink bit of flannel, then side-stepped up to the gap with the shotgun ready.

"Tabitha?"

A whisper hissed from the black depths beyond the foundation walls. "Miss Bitter?"

"Tabitha, is that you?"

"Miss Bitter, I can't wake Mommy up."

"Stay still, Tabitha, help is coming. Can you climb up?"

Her little voice quavered, "I can't leave Mommy alone. There's something down here."

Bitter flashed the light along the foundation walls before she carefully leaned over the broken edge and aimed the bright beam toward Tabitha's voice, nearly straight down from where she stood. She saw Wendy first, sprawled across the remains of what had once been the basement stairs. When the light touched Wendy's eyes, her eyelids fluttered but stayed closed.

"Miss Bitter, be careful. That funny little man is here. I saw him right before Mommy fell."

Jean.

The light caught Tabitha's pale face next. She sat on the step next to Wendy, her bandaged hand filthy with gray and black ash. Tabitha's fingers were white with the grip she had on her mother's hand.

Bitter kept the shotgun pointing into the basement, away from the trapped pair. The broken treads above Wendy told the story, she tried to reach Tabitha and the burnt steps collapsed under her.

"Tabitha, don't move. Just stay right there with your Mom." She examined the void below, but the debris hid most of the basement floor. What remained of the house had collapsed into the hole.

Something with a V-8 engine pulled up and stopped outside of the property. *A Ford,* Bitter thought, *Probably O'Malley or Sapp.* The car door opened with a soft squeak and closed with a click, distinct in the still night air.

A second Ford pulled up.

"Bitter?" A soft voice called her name.

"O'Malley, we need some help here," she said in a tone calculated to barely reach the sidewalk. She kept the light centered on Tabitha. Something moved in the bushes behind her, but Bitter stayed focused on the child. "O'Malley, that had better be you creeping up behind me."

"No, it's me, Sapp. O'Malley is checking the perimeter."

"Keep an eye out, Tabitha said Jean was here somewhere." Bitter whispered.

"Just what we need. What's the situation?"

Something scuffled along the wall, a barely visible movement within the black on black scene. Bitter redirected the light. "A rat, maybe."

"Maybe." Sapp's voice echoed his doubts. "We need to get down there."

"We're going to have to call the fire department. Wendy fell and she's still unconscious. She's going to need an ambulance." Bitter held the light on Wendy's leg, twisted in an unnatural position under her body.

Sapp stepped away from the foundation and spoke softly into his radio as he surveyed the surrounding shrubs and fence.

"Dispatch has them on the way. Ten minutes out."

"Ten minutes? The station is right around the corner." The tension in Bitter's voice revealed her worry.

"They're on the way back from another call."

A frightened little voice rose from below. "Miss Bitter, something is down here. I hear it moving."

"Keep an eye on her," Bitter ordered. "I need to think for a second." She glanced at Sapp, who had his flashlight focused on Tabitha, then closed her eyes, recalling the old house as it stood just a few days before. She bit her lip, thinking, then opened her eyes and looked around. "There was a cellar door." She slowly turned her head left to orient herself, then right, and left again. "Over there." She pointed to the left.

"I'll look," Sapp said, "Keep that shotgun ready. I can hear something rustling down there." He took a step, then stopped. "What's that loaded with?"

"Rock salt. I have more shells in my right pocket. Hot loads are in the left." Bitter said, never taking her eyes off Tabitha.

"Good. Let me find these steps." Sapp snapped open his baton and using it as a probe, started working his way to the left. The light from his flashlight lit the broken walls surrounding the hole in the ground. Barely fifteen feet away, he said, "Got it."

Bitter didn't move. "Can you get it open?"

"It's already half-open. Someone's been down here already." Sapp's voice grew muffled. "Don't shoot me, I'm going in. I've got to get this door open a bit wider." The sharp crack of breaking wood accompanied his words.

She stayed poised, with the .410 resting on the edge of the foundation wall, ready to swing right or left. "Tabitha," she called softly. "Officer Sapp is coming down. I want you to get as close as you can to your Mom and cover your face with both hands. Don't look up, no matter what happens."

"What about Mommy?"

"Scoot as close as you can to her. She'll be okay." *I hope,* Bitter thought. "We have the fire department coming to help get her out."

Sapp's voice rose from below Bitter, "Careful when you come down. There's an old cistern down here somewhere, according to the city inspector. It's probably covered with debris." He came into view, gingerly testing each step before he put his full weight on the unstable surface.

"Do you see anything down there?"

"No, not yet." He reached the stairs and knelt to check Wendy's pulse. "Slow and steady, but she's got a nasty bump on her head."

Tabitha stood up.

"Stay there, Tabitha," Sapp snapped, "Don't move. I don't want you to fall in this mess."

A brick fell somewhere in the basement. Sapp looked right, toward the sudden scrabbling of claws on stone, "Bitter," he shouted, then rose and turned toward the sound. Tabitha screamed as a dark shape materialized from the depths of a hole in the floor, hidden by the black-on-black of ash and darkness. Sapp wrapped an arm around the child, pulling her down and back, behind him and next to her mother. "Don't look. Cover your eyes, quick."

The hulking form was fast. Bitter was faster. She swung the barrel right, away from the trio, and aimed at the charging beast. The shotgun barely kicked as she took a deep breath and breathed out slowly as she fired, once, twice, three times, paused and then fired again. Just like Papá had taught her.

The giant salamander reared back and screamed with pain—and rage—as the rock salt peppered her slime-covered hide. She stopped, one eye oozing blood, and swung her blunt nose up toward Bitter, then took a step toward the broken stairs where Sapp guarded his helpless charges. He readied his 9mm in a two-handed stance.

"Stay down," Bitter shouted as she reloaded with the hot loads. "These aren't rock salt."

A bright beam highlighted the creature from the other side of the foundation walls, across from where Bitter stood. Blinded, the salamander shook her head, spraying blood and slime across the ashes, and bellowed. The deep moaning roar echoed through the night, and Bitter heard windows slamming open in the quiet neighborhood.

Slowly the beast turned and lumbered back toward the hole in the floor. Bitter stayed poised to shoot as the salamander crawled out of sight.

"About time you showed up, O'Malley," Sapp said. He faced the hole as the salamander's tail disappeared, ready for another attack.

The distant sirens grew louder.

"Well, it looks like I missed all the excitement," O'Malley said cheerfully. "Jean was skulking about. I almost had him, but I heard shots." He peered across the open basement. "Bitter, is that a .410?"

Sirens drowned out Bitter's reply. The fire truck screamed around the corner, lights flashing, with an ambulance on its tail. The driver killed the siren as he pulled in next to the units, but the flashing lights lit up the apartments and surrounding houses.

"O'Malley, could you lead the firemen in? I need to watch that hole. The steps are over here, to my left."

As the EMTs clattered down the stairs, Bitter kept watch from above, the .410 at the ready.

Harry's going to have kittens if I killed that thing. I'd better call him once we get Wendy and the kids taken care of. She huffed as she kept a bead on the dark hole. *At least now he knows exactly where to look.*

A one-armed figure dressed in black crouched in the alley amid the dead weeds and watched as the EMTs brought Wendy up the steps on a backboard. A rat ran over the scuffed toes of his boots. He didn't move.

As the EMTs secured Wendy on the gurney, she opened her eyes. "What, what happened?"

The nearest EMT, a stocky, dark-complected woman, patted her gently on the shoulder. "You fell. We're taking you to the hospital."

Wendy closed her eyes.

"Oh no you don't," the EMT told her. "You have to stay awake now."

Sapp carried Tabitha up and put her in the ambulance. "You're going with your mom to the hospital, Tabitha," he said firmly. He searched in his pocket, pulled out a pen, and scribbled on the back of a business card before he tucked it into Tabitha's pocket. "Bitter will come and get you in a little while. You stay with your mom in the ER until she gets there."

He turned to the EMT. "She needs to be seen. She was down in the ashes and debris and her hand should be checked. Tell the nurses to keep her at the ER, Bitter will be there shortly to pick her up and take her to her babysitter." The EMT didn't question Sapp's military-sharp orders, but when he turned away, she rolled her eyes in exasperation and checked Tabitha over quickly, then belted the child into the jump seat inside the ambulance.

"We'll get you cleaned up, sweetie," she said to the bedraggled child, "and you need those bandages changed."

"Tabitha," Wendy whispered.

"I'm here, Mommy."

The EMT patted Wendy's shoulder again, "We've got her. Officer Sapp said that Detective Bitter will pick her up and take her to the babysitter after she's checked out at the ER."

Wendy tried to sit up, "Toby. The baby."

"Lay still, we have to get you to the hospital."

"Miss Bitter will take care of everything," said Tabitha serenely, her little hands folded with her left protectively over the bandages on her injured hand. "She chased the monster away."

"Tabitha," Wendy said sharply, then her voice faded in pain. "That child and her imagination," she sighed as she let the EMT push her back down onto the gurney.

Bitter appeared out of the dark. The nearest fireman jumped at the sight of her in the ash-covered black robe and pajamas, carrying the .410 under one arm. "Damn," he muttered, "She gave me a start. I didn't see her until she was right here."

Sapp looked over and snorted. "Do you know what you look like?" he asked Bitter.

"Probably a hot mess," she said ruefully. "I need to take a fast shower and change out of these filthy pajamas. You told them I'll pick up Tabitha at the hospital?"

Sapp replied as the ambulance driver hit the lights. "Sure did, and that you'll take her to the babysitter."

"Good. I'll go see Señora Gutierrez right now. I'm sure she'll stay with the children tonight."

"You should see your hair."

She patted what remained of her usually smooth bun with her free hand, smearing more ash across the kinky curls. "I don't want to."

"O'Malley and I will make sure that the fence is secure, then meet you at the station?"

She nodded and turned toward her house. Two steps away, she stopped and looked back. "Sapp, the salt line was scuffed right where the fence was breached."

He glanced at the opening in the fence. "I have two or three containers of salt in the car. I'll be sure to take care of it before I leave."

O'Malley strolled up in time to hear Sapp's words. "You're carrying salt now?"

Sapp flicked him a quick, disapproving glance, "I'll use whatever works to keep people safe."

O'Malley guffawed and smacked Sapp on the shoulder. "I have three containers in my go bag in the unit. Never leave home without it. Come on, I have some steel cable ties in the trunk. If we can muscle that chain link close enough to the post, we can tie them together until the contractor can get out here and fix the fence properly."

Bitter ignored their byplay as she hurried to Señora Gutierrez's house. Light peeked through a crack in the curtains. *Oh good, she's up. Or the creature's bellowing woke her.* The door opened immediately at her soft tapping.

"Ayyyy, what happened to you? You are covered with the filthy ashes."

"Wendy had an accident. She and Tabitha are on their way to the hospital. Can you watch Toby and the baby?"

Before Bitter finished speaking, the tiny woman gathered her purse, keys, phone, and a book. "You will bring Tabitha back from the hospital, *sí*?"

"*Sí.*"

"Who is with the children now?"

"Wendy's neighbor."

Señora Gutierrez nodded briskly. "Good. I will go now. You go bathe and then go to the hospital to get Tabitha. I will bring the children here *mañana*." She shooed Bitter out the door, "Go, go. I will take care of everything."

"If you need anything—"

"Nada. Go."

Bitter watched her bustle down the sidewalk, past the bungalow, toward the apartments. She waved behind Señora Gutierrez's back and attracted O'Malley's attention. With the classic motions of pointing two fingers at him, at her own eyes, and then at the tiny woman, she ordered him to keep an eye on the woman as she went around the corner to Wendy's apartment. Bitter stood next to the gate and watched until O'Malley gave her the high sign.

Despite his silent assurance, she took three sideways steps toward the street, so she could see the back of the building over the hedge and waited until she saw the bedroom curtains twitch open. Señora Gutierrez waved. She knew Bitter would wait until she was safely inside.

"Okay then," Bitter muttered. "Let's do this." She opened the gate, and carefully closed and locked it after she was inside the yard. Her hand left black marks on the rail as she climbed the steps. She noticed when she reached the top and looked back at the trail of filthy footprints on the walk and steps. "Oh damn. What a mess."

After checking the doors to be sure they were locked and emptying her pockets, Bitter stripped in the laundry room. She dropped her pajamas, robe, and sneakers in the laundry sink. As it filled, she squirted several tablespoons of Dawn dishwashing liquid over the clothing and pressed them under the water. *Good enough for oil-covered seagulls, good enough for ashes. They can soak overnight. I'll deal with them tomorrow.*

Wrapped in a towel that she retrieved from the laundry basket, she put the .410 and shells away, then plodded to the bathroom. While the shower warmed, she took her hair down. A look in the mirror generated a muttered curse word or two about cryptids roaming her city.

With a generous squeeze of her favorite body wash and a quick scrub with a loofah sponge, she managed to remove the smudged ashes from her skin. She sighed and poured conditioner into her hand. *I'll have to wash my hair properly tomorrow and probably deep condition this weekend,* she thought as she finger-combed it gently through her hair. *Ugh.* Slowly the water turned black, then gray, and finally ran clear down the drain. As she rushed, it brought back memories of the days when she had to get two boys and herself out the door. "Hurry, Mommy, hurry," she chanted softly as she whipped a towel around her wet hair.

Jeans, a fresh blouse, and sneakers only took a minute. She unwrapped her wet hair and frowned. "A headwrap it is," she muttered as she pulled her hair into a high ponytail and wound it into a loose, tangled bun. With her hair safely covered by the brightly patterned fabric, she tucked the .45 into the holster in the small of her back and grabbed her purse, cell phone, and keys. "Let me go get this child."

Shadows followed her out the door and down to the garage. She glanced right toward the ruins of the old house. Both units were gone, and the fence secured. Except for the purr of the I-6 engine, the night was as quiet as it ever got. She whipped the Maverick left, toward the hospital. She didn't notice the indistinct figures hovering over the sidewalk. None crossed the salt line that surrounded the old woman's property.

As the little car zoomed east, a dark figure appeared from the alley. He shambled around the property twice, peering at the unbroken line of salt, before giving up. He headed south, paralleling the river and away from Alkali Flat. A few blocks away, a black sedan with dark-tinted windows pulled up and stopped in front of him. The back door swung open and he climbed inside. As soon as the door closed, the car sped off into the night.

The automatic doors swished open. The scents and memories spilled out—disinfectant, blood, pain, and death.

Bitter stopped abruptly and prepared herself to go inside to look for Tabitha and Wendy. Before she could step into the crowded waiting area, a voice rang out. "Bitter?"

With relief, she saw it was the blonde nurse. *What was her name?* "Angie?"

"Oh good, it is you. I didn't recognize you with that scarf wrapped around your head. They called me down to help with the little girl until you arrived." Angie parted the sea of patients and visitors with nothing more than the look on her determined face as she led Bitter through the ER to the nurses' station. Tabitha sat on a chair in the corner, with her freshly bandaged hand resting on her lap. She wore a clean oversized T-shirt and a plastic bag lay at her feet. Her curly hair looked damp, so Bitter assumed that someone had bathed her.

"They're really busy down here tonight," Angie looked worried, "I had to wash Tabitha up before they could redo the bandage on her hand. Luckily, she didn't get any of those nasty ashes inside the old bandage. Or worse," She sighed, "in the stitches. It was a mess."

"I can see it's busy. Anything special going on?"

Angie looked around to make sure no one was listening, then bent closer to Bitter's ear. "The sobbing was so loud tonight that even I could hear it upstairs."

"Oh?"

She nodded nervously, "Yes, it started just before the ambulance arrived with Tabitha and her mother." She flushed. "When they asked for a volunteer, I said I'd come and help out down here for a while."

Bitter changed the subject, "How is Wendy doing?"

Tabitha looked up from the handheld game balanced precariously on the corner of the desk. "Mommy has a broken leg and a concussion," she said in her precise voice. "The doctor said she can come home in a couple of days." She faltered, "Who's going to take care of us, Miss Bitter?"

Bitter smiled gently, knowing she couldn't fool this bright and stubborn child, "Señora Gutierrez is at your apartment right now and tomorrow she's taking you all to her house until your Mom goes home."

"Are you taking me home now?" Tabitha asked. Exhaustion settled over her face.

"Yes, I am," Bitter replied. "Angie, did Wendy give you permission to let me take Tabitha home?"

"It's in the pile of papers here," Angie sniffed indignantly, "I double-checked. The head nurse made sure she signed everything before they took her into surgery to set that leg."

"Is she out yet?"

"Let me check," Angie said. She picked up the telephone and punched in a number.

Bitter turned to Tabitha. "How are you feeling?"

The little girl's eyes were huge in her pale face. "I'm tired. My hand hurts." She looked up at Bitter's head. "Oh, that's a pretty scarf. Why did you cover your hair?"

"It's called a head wrap." Bitter gently corrected her. "I didn't have time to fix my hair properly, so I decided to wrap it instead. It's a traditional head covering. My great grandmother used to wear head wraps when she went out."

"Oh," Tabitha said, "I like it. Can I have one?"

Bitter gave her a little smile, "When your Mom feels better, I'll come over and show you how to wrap your hair properly." She grew serious, "We're going to have a chat about minding your Mom and police officers. Not tonight, but when your mom gets home. You need some consequences for disobeying her."

Tabitha's lip trembled, "I heard the kitten crying."

"Tabitha," Bitter said quietly but firmly, "It wasn't a kitten. You know that now. You are not to leave your apartment again without your mother's permission. Do you understand?"

The child ducked her head and peeked out under her tangled curls at Bitter's stern face.

"Tabitha?" Bitter's tone demanded an answer.

"Yes, Miss Bitter. I won't go outside again without Mommy's permission."

Angie hung the phone up, oblivious to the conversation. "She's almost ready to go to recovery. It took longer to sedate her than to set that leg. I'll make sure she knows that you took Tabitha home."

"Good. Any idea when she'll be released?"

"Not yet. They want to keep her for observation until at least tomorrow. She was unconscious for a while."

"Thank you. We'll check tomorrow and make sure she gets home safely." Bitter held out her hand, "Ready?"

'Yes." Tabitha slid off the chair. "Thank you, Nurse Angie," she said politely as she took Bitter's hand.

Bitter led the child to the Maverick. "Oh, you brought the green car?" Tabitha brightened up. "I always wanted to ride in your car."

"You'll have to sit in the back seat."

Tabitha pouted, but when Bitter ignored her pique, nodded silently. Bitter opened the passenger door and flipped the front seat forward. After she buckled Tabitha in, she wrapped a plush blanket around the child and tucked a pillow between her and the side of the car. "In case you're tired."

"Thank you." Tabitha snuggled against the pillow.

Bitter put the plastic bag with the dirty clothes on the floor mat under Tabitha's feet. By the time she got into the driver's seat and started the engine, Tabitha was already nodding off.

Soft jazz filled the car as Bitter drove carefully through the darkened streets. The moon's bright silver rays lit the road home.

A unit sat outside of the apartment when Bitter pulled up.

"Any trouble?" she asked Sapp as he opened the passenger door.

"No, it's quieted down, so I thought I'd chill out here and write the report." He unbuckled Tabitha and lifted her out of the car. "Your blanket?"

"Yes, but I'll get it later. Wendy's apartment is upstairs and on the left." She picked up the bag of dirty clothes.

Sapp carried the sleeping child upstairs and tapped gently on the door. It opened immediately. Señora Gutierrez must've been awake and waiting. "*Muchas gracias,*" she said as Sapp disappeared into the apartment. "And her *mamá?*"

Bitter looked at her watch. "She must be in recovery by now. We can check tomorrow to see when they'll release her. It might be tomorrow, or it could be a couple of days."

"Bien. I will keep the children until she gets home."

Bitter took her hand, "Muchas gracias, Señora. Let me know if you need anything."

"*Ah, de nada. Vamanos a mí casa mañana. [It is nothing. We will go to my house tomorrow.]*"

"*Gracias,*" said Sapp as he went out the front door. He handed her a business card. "Call me if you need anything."

Bitter stopped just outside of the door, "Be sure to lock the door. Tabitha told me that she wouldn't go outside again without permission, but she doesn't always do what adults tell her to do."

Señora Gutierrez frowned, "I will sleep right here on the sofa. I am a light sleeper. She will not sneak past me." Her expression lightened. "I will hang the baby's noisy bell toy over the door. If she tries to open the door, it will jingle and wake me."

"That should work," Sapp said over his shoulder as he led the way down the stairs. When they reached the sidewalk, Sapp stopped next to the Maverick. "Bitter, we can finish the report tomorrow. You look like the cat dragged you in after the Sandman beat you up." Her hackles rose, but before she snapped at him, he grinned and added, "Get some rest. Tomorrow will be a busy day. I'll slip the report under your office door before I get off shift."

He walked down to the alley and watched as Bitter put the Maverick in the garage. After she carefully stepped over the salt and closed the gate, he climbed into his unit. The radio crackled and he stood on the gas as he peeled out, heading east toward Midtown.

Chapter 24 ~ Friday Morning

The early morning light leaked around the blackout curtains in Bitter's bedroom. She rolled over to face away from the window, squirming around carefully to avoid disturbing the little dog curled up next to her shoulder. Drifting back into a soft cloud of dreams, the sudden pounding on her front door abruptly brought her back to earth.

"What the?"

She pulled on her second favorite robe and stumbled down the hall. A dark form filled the old window in the front door. "Who is it?"

"Bitter, are you in there?" Señor Suarez's anxious voice echoed on the porch.

She hurried to unlock the door. "What's wrong?"

"You need to see this, Bitter. *La bruja,* she has been here."

She rubbed her forehead. "What?"

"*Por favor*, come."

"*Un momento,*" she replied.

He paced back and forth on the porch as Bitter stepped back, away from the door.

"Do I have time to dress?" she called from the hall.

"*Sí, sí*, but quickly. You must see what *la bruja* has done."

He waited at the bottom Jof the stairs, and when Bitter appeared, dressed in last night's jeans, blouse, and sneakers, he hurried to open the gate. "Come, come."

A growing crowd of neighbors stood between Bitter and the corner. As she worked her way through the group, they slowly parted. When the last man moved over and she could see the empty lot, she stopped.

"What happened?" she asked, dazed at the sight.

From behind her, Señor Suarez said, "*No sé*. I thought you might know."

Before her lay the empty lot, literally a flat rectangle with nothing to be seen but dirt. The chain-link fence, the charred debris, and even the hole where the basement had been the night before were gone. Nothing remained. Not even a blade of grass broke the surface of the soil.

"Holy shit," said a deep voice to her right. "I'd think I was dreaming, but I already pinched myself twice."

"It was *la bruja*," Señor Suarez said firmly. "Bitter battled her creature of the night here and won, so the witch has moved on."

"There's no such thing as witches," Bitter said automatically as she stepped off the curb. Someone grabbed at her arm, but she shook off the restraining hand. No one followed as she slowly walked to the opposite sidewalk. Along the concrete edge, she could see the white line of salt. A solid ring the night before, the grains of salt were scattered, and the ring was broken every few feet around the entire perimeter. Tire tracks led from the street and across the gray-brown, silty soil, crisscrossing the lot.

She surveyed the scene, legs spread, and hands on her hips, for several minutes. Finally, she shook her head and pulled out her cell phone. "Dispatch, this is Bitter. I need the city inspector and arson investigator down here as soon as possible. Yes, I'm at the lot where the house burned the other night, just down from my house." She listened for a moment. "Yes, I'm sure you're going to get more calls. I can't tell you what happened here, I'm looking at a bare dirt lot." As the dispatcher continued to question her, she grew irritated, "Yes, of course, I'm sure I'm looking at the right address. I think I know my own neighborhood."

A unit pulled up. O'Malley wearily got out and walked over to Bitter. "Well?" he asked, "What do you think?"

She kept scanning the lot, looking for any sign of last night's battle. "I don't know, O'Malley," she finally said. "Nobody heard anything, nobody saw anything, but it's just gone as if it had never been here at all."

He nudged the broken line of salt. "Well, I guess Sapp was right. *La bruja* is human anyway. She had to break the protective barrier before she could clean up the mess."

"There's—" Bitter started.

"Yes, I know, there's no such thing as witches. You keep saying that." O'Malley said in exasperation. "But I don't have any other explanation of how the house, the basement, the fence, and that damned lizard disappeared. Do you?"

"She's a Chinese giant salamander," Bitter corrected him absently, not paying attention to his tone.

"Okay, whatever." O'Malley's irritated voice broke into Bitter's train of thought. Surprised, she looked up at him. He stared across the property and muttered, "It's as if the ground just swallowed it all up and smoothed itself over." He shook himself.

"Are you all right?" Bitter's concern penetrated his anger.

He sighed. "No, and neither are you," he swept an arm back toward the crowd across the street, who were staying well away despite their curiosity, "or your neighbors. But I don't know what we can do to fix this."

"Hazard tape?"

"What?"

"O'Malley, do you have hazard tape? We don't want anyone walking across that lot until it's been looked at. It could cave in." Bitter looked back across the street. "Though I doubt any of my neighbors will set foot on it now."

He looked past her, down the street. "I don't think we'll need to worry about it. Here comes the city inspector and the fire investigator is on his tail." His voice changed, "And that blasted reporter is right behind them. Like I needed one more thing to do before I can go home and get some sleep." He looked down at Bitter. "You'd better get out of sight before he parks, or he'll have you on the news. Again."

"I'll pass on that, thank you very much," Bitter said over her shoulder as she briskly walked toward her fascinated neighbors. "Shhh," she said as someone started to ask a question. She slipped into the middle of the group, behind the tallest and widest onlooker. "There's a reporter in that van and I don't want to talk to him."

Several older and wiser heads nodded, but two teens from down the street pushed to the edge of the sidewalk, eager to talk to the reporter.

"Well, I'm sure they'll be happy to talk to him," Señor Suarez appeared at her elbow. "Those kids are always telling tall tales, I'm sure they'll have a story about how *la bruja* called in the fairies, who filled in the hole with good river bottom soil. And now it's ready for her and her coven to dance naked by the light of the full moon."

Bitter chuckled at his sarcasm.

"On second thought, *un momento*, let me talk to those boys," he said as he pushed his way forward. "*Hijos*, come back here. *Necesita hablamos.*"

The teens swaggered back slowly, each holding a battered skateboard. They knew better than to defy Señor Suarez. He'd been in charge of the neighborhood watch since before they were born, and he never let them forget it. He peppered them in rapid Spanish, reminding them that they were not to talk to reporters about the neighborhood and especially Bitter. *"Comprende?"* Though a full head taller than the silver-haired man, the blonde boy bit his lip while the shorter, olive-complected teen nodded somberly.

He repeated himself in English for those who didn't understand Spanish. "We do not tell the tales of Alkali Flat to reporters or policemen." He glanced behind him. "Except Señora Bitter, of course. She is one of us. She knows our secrets." He looked around, "The city will say that *la bruja* came with heavy equipment and many men and illegally cleaned up the lot. We will not say anything different."

He gave the teens a sudden flash of a smile. "You can tell the reporter that the owner is a witch." He held up a hand to stop their questions, "But, he will not believe you. So, you might not want to do that because then you will not be on the television tonight."

Bitter smiled at the teens' obvious dismay at the thought of missing an opportunity to mug on the news for all their friends. Then she remembered Harry. She looked toward O'Malley, but all she could see were her neighbors' backs. She shrugged, he didn't like reporters, so he'd probably roust the man in a few minutes. Or at least make sure that the reporter and his cameraman stayed down the block, away from Bitter's house, when they filmed their story.

She hit the speed dial as she walked back toward her house. The voicemail came on with a brief message that Harry wasn't available, please leave a message. Bitter took a deep breath before she began, "Harry, this is Bitter. You need to call me before you bring your crew over. The situation has changed. I have some bad news about locating that salamander. And Harry, a reporter is sniffing around." She hung up.

I might as well make some coffee and get ready for work. There's nothing more I can do here.

She almost made it to the gate before she heard rapid footsteps approaching from behind. She whirled, one hand on her carry gun.

"Bitter," Señor Suarez said, ignoring her defensive stance, "Do we need to check the basements? They once connected to the buried sidewalks of the underground city." He looked at her tidy bungalow. "I think your Papá bricked up the entrance, but there was a tunnel under your house."

She made a swift decision. Señor Suarez could keep secrets. He'd proved himself as trustworthy through the years. "No, I know someone who will come and check for tunnels. He was supposed to try to collect the creature today," she glanced at the crowd at the corner, "but obviously that won't happen with a reporter and the inspectors snooping around."

"Ah, *bien,* I should look for him?"

"I'll give him your number. It's still the same, right?" At his nod, she continued, "He'll call and coordinate with you, hopefully later today." She reached into her pocket and pulled out her key ring. The key she wanted was the brown one—the one that matched the color of the basement door tucked under the front porch. Señor Suarez took it and put it in his pocket. "Don't try to search alone. Wait for Harry."

The gold tooth glinted in his smile. "I saw what happened last night. Do not worry, I will wait for your expert."

Bitter gave him a sharp look and continued, "The door that leads from inside the house and down into the basement is locked and dead-bolted. If anything is in there, don't try to escape by the inside stairs, you'll be trapped." She looked at the porch, a full story above the ground. "Papá did wall up the tunnel, but there's a cistern in there too. I haven't seen or heard anything moving around in the basement but be careful."

One calloused brown hand covered Bitter's. "I will be careful. I have not lived this long by taking chances with *la policía, las brujas,* or the many creatures that walk the night."

"I don't know that it is one of hers." She glanced up and down the street, "But I think that Jean was feeding it. That's why he was collecting cats and I think maybe other stray animals too."

"Ah, then it might come back, looking for food." He took a step back and gave her gate an appraising look. "Cold iron and salt will keep it out—or in—if it belongs to *la bruja.* I will make sure that our neighbors know to watch out for strange things, especially at night." A movement at the corner caught his attention. He turned toward the now-empty lot, "Bitter, you must go now. I see that reporter's van creeping this way."

"*Gracias,*" Bitter said hastily. "I'll call Harry when I'm inside."

"*Bien.* Go." Señor Suarez stepped off the curb and sauntered across the street, directly in front of the slow-moving van. It stopped. He looked at the driver and passenger, nodded somberly, then continued slowly walking to his own house. By the time the van moved forward to where they could look past the hedge and into Bitter's garden, she was nowhere in sight.

"Coffee?"

Bitter's stomach churned at the thought of the bitter sludge in the Chief's office. "No thank you," she said politely.

"Trouble in the neighborhood last night?" The Chief leaned back in his chair and sipped from his coffee cup. It smelled a little better than the usual brew.

"A bit. We got it under control. Two to the ER, a mother and child. Child snuck out, Mom fell through the stairs while trying to collect her and take her home."

"Do I need to know if you shot anyone?" He raised an eyebrow.

Bitter gave him a reassuring look, "Not officially. I used the .410. It was loaded with rock salt. No humans involved. I called in an expert. The head of the neighborhood watch will coordinate with him."

"So, it's just the facts in the report, right? Nothing to attract any media attention?"

"That's correct, sir, a simple missing child case. She was recovered safely, still in the neighborhood. No perps." She paused, "A reporter was sniffing around though. I can't promise that he won't dig something up."

He leaned forward, lowering his voice, "Before you go, I saw a news report about a mysterious clean up at the fire scene from last week."

"The city inspector believes it was an illegal clean up by the property owner."

"Hmmm," the Chief grunted, his face a picture of disbelief.

"I honestly don't know how it happened with no one noticing, sir. I was sound asleep and woke to the neighborhood watch leader pounding on my door. He was the first to notice."

"Mmm-huh," he responded. "Reliable?"

"Yes, sir. He's been the head of the Alkali Flat neighborhood watch since before Papá passed. In fact, he and Papá started it." She stopped and corrected herself. "Actually, more like he and

Papá formalized the group. There's always been those who watched and protected our neighborhood."

"Very good. Be sure to document your hours." He watched as Bitter pushed herself up, using the arms of the chair. "You didn't hurt yourself, did you?"

"No sir, just a little stiff."

He eyed her suspiciously. "Are you sure?"

She forced a smile. "Yes sir. I'll be fine."

The Chief stood, picked up his coffee cup, and took a step toward the outer office. "Keep me posted on any new developments."

Bitter qualified her reply. "Yes, sir, as much as I can."

He frowned but didn't push the issue. "And your cases?"

"Nothing I can prove yet. I have some ideas that I'm working on. They're coming along slowly. I'm waiting for results on the envelope found in the shred bin."

He sighed. "Well, stay out of the news if you can. I know that reporter is stalking you." He motioned toward the office door. "We're all depending on you, Bitter. We can't keep looking sideways at each other, wondering who killed our Candy. You need to find the murderer soon. "

"I understand."

"Plans for the weekend?" he asked as he followed Bitter out of his office door.

"The usual. Check in with my sons, take care of the orchids, work on my cases, read, and relax. Visit a friend. Nothing special." She shrugged. "And you?"

His face grew sad. "Nothing special. I'll try to call my wife. Hopefully, she'll talk to me. I'll stop by the hospital to see Sally."

"I'll be sure to stop on the way home and check on her. Is an officer still assigned to guard her?

Startled, the Chief looked at Bitter. "Yes, why?"

"I just wanted to be sure."

The perky temp that Bitter met in her previous foray into the Chief's office interrupted before he could ask any more questions, "More coffee, Chief?"

"Yes, please." He held out his cup.

"I'll let you know as soon as I have something. Hopefully later today or early next week," Bitter promised as she slipped past the temp and into the hall.

Her footsteps echoed in the hall. A fragment of yellow tape hung limply on the wall, near the recycling bins. Though the midday sun's rays lit the windows over the bins, the hall seemed dim as she approached the elevator.

She glanced at Morales' office door, stopped, then looked up and down the hall, before she pulled a tissue from a pocket, covered the doorknob, and tried to turn it. Locked, of course. *Well, it was worth a try,* she mused. *I don't know what I thought I'd find anyway. Forensics checked every office on this floor after I found the envelope.*

Bitter turned and went back to the Chief's office. The temp looked up with a bright smile. "Can I help you?"

Bitter put on her public smile. "Is Captain Morales in today? He's not in his office."

The temp's smile faded, "He called in sick today."

"Thank you," Bitter said to the young woman reassuringly, "It's no problem. I'll talk to him next week." She lost the smile after she left the Chief's office and fumed as she made her way back to the elevator. *Why didn't the Chief say something about Morales being out?*

Back in her own office, Bitter sat down and unlocked the bottom drawer of her desk. She pulled out the files and laid them in a neat row across the well-worn wood. One by one, she reviewed each file and the notes she'd jotted in the margins. The highlighter pens stayed busy as she marked her prime suspects.

"I still can't rule out Jones or Vargas," she muttered to herself, "even if Vargas has an alibi. And Jones hated Candy—did he have time to kill her and still make it to that DV call? And Vargas, he knew he was Candy's second, or maybe third choice. Some men can't accept being last in line."

She put another sticky note on the transcript of Denise's interview. "Then there's Vicki's ex. No love lost there and I'm still waiting on verification from the casino in Reno."

Deep in her notes about the interpersonal relationships of the interviewees and the victim, she jumped when the cell phone rang.

"Bitter."

"It's Harry."

At his tone, Bitter sat up straight, "What happened?"

He sighed heavily, "Nothing. No sign of her at all."

"Well damn."

"I think she's retreated into the underground city. We won't see her again until the rainy season."

"I'm sorry, Harry, I didn't have any choice."

"Yeah, I know. Señor Suarez filled me in with the details you left out."

Surprised, Bitter said, "He wasn't there."

Harry snickered, "Neighborhood Watch. Of course, he was there and saw what was happening. He was on his way to your front door when you went out the back and over the fence. When he saw the police cars, he knew you were already out there searching for the child. He saw the whole thing from across the street. He told me, '*La casa de la bruja* is out of our jurisdiction.' And that's why he didn't follow you to help."

Bitter stared at the wall, remembering a quiet summer night when she was still a child. She'd overheard Papá and Mamá talking about something in low tones in the kitchen. Then Señor Suarez arrived. He said, "We must do something." And Papá agreed. A few days later, signs for the neighborhood watch went up. Though they were posted on every block, the street in front of the old woman's house was the border of both Alkali Flat and the neighborhood watch. Her house was just outside of the neighborhood watch boundaries.

"Bitter, are you still there?"

She shook off the memories. "Yes, I'm here. I was just thinking."

"I didn't have a chance to examine the property, but the city inspector was there with his crew. The soil looks like it's solid fill, so unless the old sidewalk and tunnel are still under there, there's no chance of her entering your neighborhood. Señor Suarez assured me that Alkali Flat is protected from 'the creatures of the night.'"

"So, there's no chance of capturing her now?"

"Nope. Not until the weather cools and the rains start. Then she'll be out looking for her mate. I hope to catch her then. We're going to need a bigger cage. She's nearly twice as big as the male."

"Did you make it to the hospital?"

"Oh yes, I talked to the doctor. He wasn't too happy that you'd sent me over to talk to him. At least until I told him that he wasn't hearing things." He chuckled bitterly, "Now I'm going to have to call him and tell him that he'll be hearing her sobbing down in the storm drains until winter."

Bitter winced. "Yeah, that's going to be problematic."

"Actually, he seemed relieved. A few more months may not bother him, now that he knows that it's an animal and not a ghost. I left my card, just in case he sees or hears anything new or different."

"By the way," Bitter interjected, "Remember that young man I told you about? I got a text from his mom. He's out of the hospital. He has a long stretch of physical therapy ahead of him, but his mom said that if he follows the exercise regime and can walk on that leg, then she's willing to bring him out to the university."

Harry's voice turned cautious, "Do you think she's going to be a problem."

"Actually," Bitter said, "her exact words were: 'Anything to keep that boy busy and out of trouble.' I think she'll be fine. If you can forward me any reputable books about biology, strange creatures, and cryptozoology, I'm sure his mom will appreciate it. It's going to be a while before he can walk and he's going to need something to keep him busy while he recovers."

"Sure," Harry cheered up, "I have a whole list that I recommend to my students. I'll get that to you as soon as possible."

"Harry, send it to my home email, please. I don't want our IT techs to be wondering what I'm up to now. Or for whoever set up my Wikipedia page to find out and add that I'm currently researching cryptids when I should be investigating a murder."

He burst into laughter at her dry tone. "I was wondering how long it would be before you found out about that page."

"Harry?"

"No, no, it wasn't me. It was one of your fans. A young woman."

Bitter's heart sank as she thought of Candy. She kept her voice even. "Thank you, Harry. I assume you're monitoring it?"

"Naturally."

"Well, thank you."

"You're welcome," his amusement rippled through the phone, "I have to dash back to the university now. Time to feed the cryptids. The salamanders aren't my only creatures—and I have to monitor feedings so none of my students stick a finger or hand into the cages."

"Talk to you soon."

"I'll be around. Señor Suarez and I are going fishing."

Bitter paused, "You aren't going out on the river, are you?" she asked suspiciously.

"Not after what Billy saw. No swimming anywhere except for the college pool."

"Okay then. Be safe."

After Harry hung up, she sat staring at the sparkling bits of dust that floated in the late afternoon sun's rays. Finally, she picked up the top file and began sorting through the photographs of the crime scene. Fanned across the desk, they painted a picture of violent death, with Candy crumpled in a pool of blood in the last image.

She stood and paced back and forth in the office, her agile mind fitting the pieces together. *I can't prove anything until I get the results back.* She looked at the clock on the wall. The second hand stood at a minute before five.

Just as she turned back to her desk, her cell phone rang.

"Bitter."

"Hey, girlfriend. It's Friday night. Past time we went to that little bar down by Improv Alley," Gema said. Before Bitter could beg off, she said, "Appetizers are half off before ten and they make the best avocado rolls you'll ever taste in your life. And it's old-school night, so it's Motown 'in the house' and 'the best of the best' of the sixties to the eighties. None of that mumble rap stuff."

Gema's infectious enthusiasm spilled out of the phone. Before she could stop herself, Bitter asked, "What time?"

"How about 8:30, so we can have a drink and enjoy some appetizers before it gets too crowded?"

Bitter surrendered to the inevitable. "Which club? I'll meet you there."

"It's that new place right on the corner of 6th, just down from Improv Alley. It looks like a hole in the wall until you get inside."

Bitter looked at the scattered files. Candy's picture from the morgue lay on top, her blue eyes fixed on something, someone she'd never see again. Bitter closed her own eyes for a moment, saddened by the image of the young woman who would never dance with her lover down at the club again. She sighed and looked at the orchid bobbing gently in the breeze generated by her desk fan. "I'll be there."

"Not that I need to tell you, but dress to impress. They have a strict dress code."

Bitter laughed out loud at the thought, "No jeans, huh?"

"Or doo-rags, gang attire, or hats—unless they're proper old-school fedoras. You know, like twenties and thirties gangster or Indiana Jones styles." She paused, "Well, satin or velvet doo-rags might pass muster, especially if they match the outfit. The bouncer decides who gets in and who doesn't, and he doesn't play."

"I'll take a taxi. Parking is impossible in that part of town." Bitter mused. "Safer too."

"No drinking and driving for me," Gema agreed, "I'll take a Lyft."

Bitter disconnected the line. Putting the files back in order didn't take long. She stopped sorting and took out the printout of Candy's face. She gazed at the young woman's expression for a few more minutes, running over the possible suspects in her mind. Finally, she slipped it back into the folder and put the stack in the bottom drawer of her desk. She tried the drawer twice after she locked it. The latch had caught, and the files were secure, but she tested it anyway.

The empty hall lay before Bitter as she left the hospital elevator. The waiting room was also empty, and the same nurse sat in front of the computer.

"Bitter," he greeted her, "How are you tonight?"

"I'm fine, Tony. How are you?"

"Almost off shift," he grinned, "so all is well."

She signed into the log, right below Kenny's name. "Is he here?" She tapped on his name with the pen.

"Not right now. He stepped out with that Irish cop to get something to eat. They should be back soon."

She nodded her thanks as she made her way back to Sally's bed. Once more, the blue on guard duty took the time to examine Bitter's ID. She didn't complain. Better to be too careful than to have another attempt on Sally's life.

Sally seemed restless. When Bitter gently touched her hand, she stirred a little. Then she settled back down. Someone had brushed her hair. It lay smoothly across the pillow. *Not much longer*, Bitter thought. *Maybe I'll have some answers tomorrow.*

She met Kenny and O'Malley at the elevators. The door slid smoothly open and Kenny nearly ran into her before she could step out of the way.

His fingers flashed.

"Sorry, I didn't see you," O'Malley translated.

Bitter patted Kenny on the arm, "It's all right, I shouldn't stand right in front of the door."

He smiled broadly and signed, "Grandma should wake up soon. The doctor said any time now."

"That's great news, Kenny. Hey, do you still have my card?"

He shrugged and gave her a sheepish look.

She pulled a business card and pen out of her purse. "Let me know as soon as she wakes." She quickly wrote her cell phone number on the back of the card. "I'm going out with a friend tonight, but you can call—" she hesitated, "sorry, text me any time. I'll come as quickly as I can."

He gave her a quick hug and made shooing motions toward the elevator.

"Have fun," O'Malley said as he pushed the down button. "We'll be here for a while if you have time to stop by later."

She stopped, halfway into the elevator, and frowned. "Won't Kathleen be upset if you're not home soon?" She remembered a few notable incidents before Kathleen's meds had kicked in.

"Don't worry about that." He grinned mischievously, "Kenny was tasked to keep an eye on me." He leaned forward and continued with a stage whisper, "And it's her Bunko night. She won't be home until late, so as long as we make sure we bring her Dutch Bros coffee and a treat, we'll be fine."

Kenny fumbled in the plastic bag branded with a local gourmet foods logo and triumphantly pulled out a large box of truffles, wrapped with a red bow.

"Keep them cool or they'll melt," Bitter warned. Kenny bowed with a dramatic flourish, then dropped the gift box back in the bag before elevator doors closed.

Chapter 25 ~ Friday Night

Bitter rubbed gel on her hands and pulled her hair up into a high ponytail, then braided it tightly. Carefully, she wound the braid into a bun and pinned it in place. She turned her head one way, then the other, looking for escaping curls in the bathroom mirror. A few baby hairs curled in front of her ears and around the edges.

After she patted her face dry with a towel, she applied a protective spray and then the foundation. Blush, eyeliner, and eye shadow followed. She brushed a light coat of powder over her face. Mascara and lipstick finished the look.

The black silk pantsuit fit perfectly. The rose shell under the snug black jacket set off her coloring and picked up the hint of blush on her high cheekbones. She sighed as she pulled on the low-heeled, glossy black ankle boots. She'd had the pants shortened when she realized that high heels weren't an option anymore. She checked in the mirror, turning side to side to see every angle of her right leg. *Nope, can't see the ankle holster.*

Bitter shifted her keys, ID, and cell phone to the matching black beaded purse. She eyed the 9mm and sighed. *Not a good idea to carry a gun in a purse.* Alcohol and guns—never a good mix, even for a cop. *The Sig is too big for my bag anyway. The Alleycat will have to do. If I can't hit something in seven shots, I need a refresher course at the range.*

"All right then." She grimaced in the mirror as she slung the purse over her shoulder, "I guess this will be okay for tonight."

She locked her 9mm inside the gun safe before she turned off all the lights, except a small lamp in the living room, and went out on the porch. Her timing was right, Gian pulled up in his yellow taxi just as she reached the front gate.

"Gian, thank you."

"You're my last ride of the evening, Bitter. Call dispatch for a ride home. My cousin is working tonight, so he knows to keep an ear out for you," Gian said. His voice seemed deeper than usual.

"Are you feeling all right, Gian?" Bitter asked, concerned about his exhausted voice and bloodshot eyes.

He gave her a tired smile. "Yes, I'm just tired. It's been a long week. Between my customers and finishing the final draft on my book, I've been burning the candle at both ends."

She wanted to ask about his book, but authors tend to get testy during the final stages before publishing. She decided that sticking to work questions might be safer, at least until he finished the new novel.

"Grumpy customers?"

He chuckled, "Yes, a few. And Mrs. Mitchell plays golf at least twice a week. I'm picking her up in the morning."

"Oh my," Bitter gave a short laugh, "I'll bet she needs a ride home too."

"Of course," he looked at his GPS, "Where did you say you were going?"

"I'm meeting a friend at a new club near Improv Alley. She said it's at the corner of 6th."

"Ah, I know where it is. I went to college with the bouncer." He nodded, "It's very safe." He glanced up into his rearview mirror and chuckled again. "But then again, you're a detective. You've probably seen all the seamy sides of town at one time or another."

"At one time or another," she agreed.

She fastened her seat belt. Two blocks later Gian slammed on the brakes as a shambling figure stumbled in front of the cab. Before Bitter could react, the familiar figure disappeared down a walkway between two brick buildings.

"That was close," Gian commented calmly. "He didn't even look."

Bitter twisted in the seat, looking back, "Do me a favor, Gian. Please go around the block."

"A suspect?" he asked as he swung around the corner and down the next street.

She frowned, watching for the space between the buildings where Jean should emerge. "Not really. But I'd like to see where he goes."

Gian stopped across from the narrow space and pulled out a flashlight. The bright beam washed between the buildings, but no one was there.

"Where did he go?" asked Bitter. "He wasn't moving fast enough to get through there and across the street before we came around the corner."

"The underground city is below. Maybe there's a way to get down there." Gian put his flashlight away as he considered his answer. "No. I've been down that path and there's nothing. No doors, no windows, just bare bricks."

She thought back to her rookie days. "You're right. I've been through there too. Not that I had time to thoroughly inspect it. I was chasing a suspect at the time." She sighed. "Oh well, off to the club. I'm meeting a friend there."

As they pulled away, a dark figure peeled away from the wall. A slight bulge in the bricks and black clothing had hidden him from the questing light. He turned east, then north onto side streets until a narrow alley took him in the right direction. A ramshackle Victorian stood amid the crumbling brick edifices, remnants of the Industrial Age of the West Coast, hidden by the overgrown shrubs and trees that spilled into the alley. A flickering yellow light, perhaps a candle, glowed in a small window in the tower. He tapped three times on the front door. It opened into black emptiness and the one-armed figure disappeared inside.

Two quick turns and several blocks away, Gian pulled to the curb in front of a door that could've starred in a 1930s era gangster movie. A line of partygoers waited, two abreast, along the sidewalk behind a velvet rope. Bitter scanned the line, looking for Gema, but she wasn't among those waiting to go inside. She frowned when she saw a tall blonde man.

Is that Jones? In a full Super Fly outfit?

Bitter stared in disbelief at his audacity, until he glanced over and saw her in the taxi. He glared at her and turned back to the petite young woman dressed in a vintage forties tiered skirt cocktail dress in ivory with black gloves and shoes. She had a large tropical flower in her golden hair.

They can't even get their colors coordinated, let alone match their eras, Bitter thought uncharitably.

The bouncer who stood in front of the main door wore a tailored black suit, red silk shirt and matching tie, and a sharp black fedora adorned with a silk ribbon and blue speckled feather. At least six feet tall and a muscled two-hundred pounds plus, he made it clear with a glance that there'd be no trouble on his watch. The traditional facial tattoos adorning his chiseled features added to his confident air of "don't mess with me."

"Please wait here," Gian said as he climbed out of the cab. Bitter watched as he greeted the bouncer with a manly hug and slap on the shoulder. Just as she reached for the door handle, Gian returned and opened the door with a flourish. He offered a hand to Bitter. Surprised, she took his hand and let him help her out. He escorted her up the three steps to the platform where the bouncer waited. "Ms. Bitter, this is my old friend and classmate, Jon. Jon, meet Ms. Bitter. She is meeting friends here tonight."

The bouncer held out a large, long-fingered hand, and Bitter flinched inside as she took it, expecting him to crush her fingers. Instead, he gently squeezed and released her hand as he said in a charming New Zealand accent, "It's very nice to meet you, Ms. Bitter. Welcome to our club." He opened the door and waved a second man, tall, slim, and dressed in an identical black suit, over. "Ms. Bitter, this is my husband Barry."

"Pleased to meet you both," Bitter held out her hand. Barry took it just as gently as Jon had as he shook and released her hand. His royal blue silk shirt set off his delicate olive complexion and crisp dark brown curls. The red of the speckled feather on his fedora caught her eye. It matched Jon's shirt.

"Thank you," she said to Gian as the inner door opened and the bass rhythm spilled out into the warm evening. The line on the sidewalk outside rippled in anticipation, but Jon crossed his arms as he broadened his stance and the partygoers' excitement subsided.

Barry waved her inside with a slight bow. "I hope you have a good time tonight."

The small entry opened into a large ballroom, complete with a hardwood dance floor. A full bar filled the right wall and several bartenders busily served customers. The DJ mixed the next selection smoothly into the bumping music, slipping from classic Motown into early eighties electro-funk. The floor quickly filled with dancers.

Gema was waiting just inside. "Bitter," she beamed as she hugged the shorter woman. "I'm so glad you came out tonight. This DJ is amazing. I have a table in the corner where we can see the whole place." She grinned at Bitter's surprised look, "I know how it is. I don't like having my back to a door either. Remember, I'm a lawyer. Not all of my former clients like me."

To the left, three steps up led to a platform filled with several small tables, each with two or three chairs. Bitter scanned the room and noted an exit a few feet away, behind the huge speakers that dominated the DJ's booth. An old-school disco ball hung over the dance floor, turning slowly so a rainbow of lights danced over the faces of the lucky customers who had passed the bouncer's muster.

A server appeared as soon as Bitter and Gema sat down.

"A Shirley Temple and a glass of water with no ice, please," Bitter said.

Gema leaned forward, "We're running a tab tonight, Lucy. Please bring me a fuzzy navel, two orders of avocado rolls, sweet chili sauce on the side, and extra napkins." She looked at Bitter, "Calamari?" At Bitter's pleased smile, she added it to their order.

"No alcohol?" she asked after the server left.

Bitter shook her head no. "I never drink when I go out." She smiled to take the sting out of her words. "I've been a cop too long."

"So, where's your carry gun? That outfit wouldn't hide a standard holster." She laughed at Bitter's look. "Don't kid me, my brother's a cop. He always packs one. I wouldn't think you'd be any different."

Bitter glanced around, but no one appeared to be watching them. She leaned closer so no one else could hear. "Ankle holster."

"A derringer?" Gema's surprise showed in her raised eyebrows.

"No, a mouse." At Gema's inquiring look, Bitter expanded her answer. "An Alleycat."

"Oh. A .32 Beretta. Nice." Gema crooned. She caught Bitter surveying the room and flicked a glance across the club, "If you're looking for admirers, that guy at the bar hasn't taken his eyes off you since you walked in."

"Oh, no. Seriously?"

"Yes, seriously."

Bitter turned her chair so she could view more of the club's interior. As she scanned the bar, she recognized the man at the bar. "Well, damn."

"What?"

"That short guy, right? The one with a bald spot? He's a reporter."

Gema sighed in frustration. "Do you want to go somewhere else?"

"Oh no. I wouldn't give him the satisfaction—or the time of day either. He can stay right where he is and spy on me." She leaned closer to Gema, "He and his cameraman have been cruising the neighborhood. The day after the big fire, he was posted up in the alley behind my house, hoping to catch me when I left. Too bad I'd parked the Maverick in front."

They both rolled their eyes at the same time and burst out laughing just as the food arrived. The divine smell made Bitter's stomach growl. Gema arranged the plates so they could both easily reach the avocado rolls and a mountain of breaded calamari.

Though the club was half empty when Bitter arrived, the tables rapidly filled with patrons. Leather and lace, satin and silk, lacy hose and black fishnets dominated the attire of the evening, intermixed with a few vintage velvet suits that were probably exhumed from the back of a parent's closet. The music got louder as the crowd packed the dance floor.

"How can she walk in those," Bitter marveled as a spandex-clad woman in six-inch heels swayed by, "let alone dance?"

Gem paused mid-bite, "She's a professional dancer. Watch her make this guy look sick." As she finished the avocado roll, a new beat filled the room.

The dancer struck a pose, then proceeded to dance the legs off her partner. Two songs later, he staggered off the floor as she tossed back a drink and the next victim stepped up to ask her to dance.

"Notice how she never lets them touch her?" Gema sat back in her chair and sipped her drink. "One night some fool tried to manhandle her while they were dancing. Barry warned him to leave her alone." She shrugged. "All the regulars know better. New guys only get one warning. He didn't listen. Jon bounced him off the sidewalk outside."

Another familiar face caught Bitter's eye. "What is he doing here?"

"Who?" Gema leaned forward to scan the crowd.

"Captain Morales." Bitter twisted and leaned forward a little to see around someone blocking her view. Surprised, "I think he's alone."

"That's unusual?" Gema craned her neck to check.

"Yes." Bitter bit off the word. She sat back and turned so she could watch from the corner of her eye. "I don't want to be obvious, but I'd like to know why he's here tonight. He wasn't at work today."

"Maybe he's on the prowl?" Gema stood and stretched. "I don't think he's realized you're here."

Bitter shrugged, "It doesn't matter. I'm off duty."

A snort of laughter answered her. "Cops are never off duty, they just like to pretend they have time off. If anything happens, you'll be in the middle of breaking it up and arresting people." Gema's eyes sparkled in amusement. "And I'll be handing out business cards."

A tall, handsome man with a mane of locs bounded up the steps, "Gema! You're here." He took her hand, "Will you dance?"

As he tugged on Gema's hand gently, Bitter waved toward the floor. "Go on, dance. I'll guard the table."

They were several steps away when he glanced back at the table. His eyes widened when he saw Bitter and he stopped. "Gema, is that Detective Bitter?" he asked in a whisper loud enough to be heard two tables away, over the music.

Gema led him back to the table, "Bitter, this is my friend Alejandro. Yes, Alejandro, this is Detective Bitter."

He bowed to Bitter. "I am honored to meet you. You are more beautiful in person than on television." She nearly expected him to kiss her hand.

Before Bitter could reply, Gema punched him in the shoulder, just hard enough to catch his attention. "Knock it off. Let's go dance before the song is over."

He bowed again, then let Gema lead him to the dance floor.

Bitter waved the server over. "Another fuzzy navel and Shirley Temple, please." She reached into her bag and pulled out a bill.

"You're running a tab," the server said hastily.

Bitter searched her mind for the server's name. *Lucy*. "No, Lucy, this is for you. Thank you."

"Oh! Thank you, Detective Bitter."

"Please, just call me Bitter."

Lucy hesitated, "Thank you, Bitter. I'll get your drinks. Tall?"

"Yes, please." She looked toward Gema, out on the dance floor. "I think Gema will be thirsty."

Lucy gave her a huge grin. "Yes, and Alejandro too."

"Are they a couple?" Bitter asked.

"Gema and Alejandro? Oh no! He's a prosecutor in Vallejo, down in Solano County. She's a defense attorney. That would never work." Lucy's shocked look satisfied Bitter's curiosity.

Bitter sipped her drink and monitored the customers from her seat. A few uniformed blues came in and circulated through the crowd before disappearing back out the main door. A figure in a black leather trench coat caught her attention. She sat up straight and leaned a little to the left for a better look. It was Vargas. He sashayed past the bar with a beautiful brunette dressed in a black leather and lace outfit with matching thigh-high boots.

He didn't notice Bitter at the corner table.

Vargas escorted his date to a table near the dance floor and motioned for a server. Bitter kept a half an eye on him and breathed a little sigh of relief when she saw the server bring him a duplicate of the glass in front of her. *Good,* she thought, *He's learned to go out and have fun without getting drunk.*

A new surge of partygoers emerged from the entrance, among them Jones and his date. Only a few seats remained empty, and some were at Vargas' table. Jones' face soured, though his companion didn't hesitate to lean over the table and ask a question.

Vargas stood and shook Jones' hand before motioning toward the available chairs. Bitter continued scanning the room but kept half an eye on the table. With Jones' attitude toward Vargas and his propensity to violence, especially toward women, a fight before the end of the evening wouldn't be a surprise. Jones might be taller, but she'd put her money on Vargas for the win.

A server appeared next to the table with a tall frosted glass garnished with an umbrella. It smelled of rum with hints of pineapple and coconut. She pointed with her chin as she set the drink down in front of Bitter. "From the gentleman at the bar."

Bitter looked in the direction indicated and saw Morales. He nodded and held up his drink. "No," she said emphatically. "I don't accept drinks and I don't drink hard liquor anyway. Please take it back to him." She pulled out a bill and handed it to the server. "Thank you for bringing it over, but I won't accept drinks from anyone."

"He already said he won't take it if you refuse it."

Bitter gave him a dirty look, but he just gave her a snarky smirk. "Fine, you can leave it here. But I won't drink it."

Just then, Alejandro and Gema returned from the dance floor. She sat down and finished the drink she'd left on the table. Before she could motion to the server, Bitter said, "I already ordered more drinks." Gema gave the fruity drink on the table a pointed look, and Bitter shrugged.

Inspiration struck.

"Alejandro, someone sent me a drink, and I don't drink when I go out." She gave him her public smile. "There's no need to waste good alcohol, are you thirsty?"

He didn't miss the implication. With a broad smile, he picked up the drink and tossed the umbrella on the table. "Sure. Who am I pissing off?"

Bitter gave a little nod toward the bar. Alejandro held the drink up to say, "Thank you," to Morales and downed it. Morales glared at Bitter, then turned toward the bar and waved to the bartender for a refill.

"He can still watch you in the mirror behind the bar," Alejandro observed.

Bitter shrugged. "Oh well."

"A stalker?"

She scanned the room, "No, the stalker would be the reporter over there, at the other end of the bar." She looked back at Morales. "That one is my supervisor."

"Ohhh," Alejandro said, "Totally inappropriate then."

"I'm afraid so." Bitter agreed.

"Cops and lawyers," Gema took a sip from the fresh drink delivered by the server, "Some things never change."

"Well, some do," Alejandro waved to the server, "We don't drive drunk anymore."

Bitter thought of a few notorious incidents, not that far in the past, and the unsuccessful attempts to hush them up. Alejandro didn't miss her raised eyebrow.

"Well, most of us anyway," he amended his statement, "there's always some knucklehead who thinks he's fine before he gets behind the wheel."

"Sadly, there's a lot of people who don't think before they try to drive home after an evening out," Gema agreed. She raised a glass in a mock salute. "Makes the house payment every month."

Bitter and Alejandro raised their glasses in response.

"By the way, Alejandro, you aren't driving home tonight, are you?" Gema asked.

He gave her an assessing look, "Why, are you inviting me over?"

Gema put on a shocked face, "Are you kidding? With four teenagers in the house?"

He shook his head, pretending that it was a disappointment. "You're just teasing me again." He glanced sideways at Bitter.

"Seriously, I have a room at the hotel around the corner. I don't drink and drive."

"Don't look at me. I came by taxi." Bitter protested. "And I don't drink when I'm out anyway." Though her words were joking, for a moment she flashed back to a fateful night in Las Vegas.

Gema saw her expression change. "Hey, whatever you're thinking, don't," she said. "I see that look. We're here to enjoy the evening, not dwell on the past."

"Speaking of the past, neither of you ladies have mentioned my carefully assembled outfit for the evening," Alejandro joshed, trying to brighten Bitter's suddenly dark mood. When both women looked at him blankly, he said, "Shaft. Remember the movie?"

"Which one?" Bitter asked as she pushed back old memories with an effort and took a long look at him. "You're missing the oversized sideburns. And Shaft didn't wear his hair in locs."

"And on top of that, your jacket is the wrong type and era." Gema joined in. "That's an eighties motorcycle jacket, though the black leather is correct. And that turtleneck is one-hundred percent cotton, isn't it?"

Alejandro looked sheepish, "Polyesters make me itch."

"It could be worse," Gema scanned the room again and pointed with her chin at Jones. "Check out the blonde Super Fly wannabe."

Alejandro turned his chair and scanned in the direction Gema indicated. "Oh no," he put on a distressed face at the sight. "And she's dressed like she's at a forties jazz club. Wrong era."

They laughed and Bitter's mood brightened. Even the glare that Jones shot at Bitter as he led his date to the dance floor couldn't ruin her evening.

The music slid into a Latin-infused eighties hit. Alejandro stood and held his hand out to Bitter. "I'll bet you can salsa."

She hesitated, "It's been years."

"Well?"

She took his hand and let him lead her to the floor. Space opened amid the dancers as he led her into the first classic steps of salsa. As she followed his lead, he increased the complexity of the front to back and side steps to match the rhythm of the music. By the time the DJ allowed the music to fade and transitioned to the haunting vocals of Lisa Lisa, Bitter realized that the doctor-ordered exercises were having a positive effect on her body. Though her knees protested the vigorous dance, it was a suggestion, not a demand, to sit down. Alejandro's body language asked her for the slow jam, but he saw the answer in her face during the final steps of the salsa and let her lead him back to the table.

She stood next to her chair and looked over the crowded dance floor. Beyond the swaying bodies, she saw Morales standing near the door, talking intently to Jones. Behind them stood Vicki's ex, Denise. *When did she get here?*

Bitter couldn't read Morales' expression, but when their eyes met, she felt a sudden chill. Denise caught her eye and glared across the room, while Jones flicked a look her way, then turned toward Morales. The lights dimmed for a moment and she glanced up at the disco ball. When she looked back, all three were gone.

The last tinkling notes of the piano faded into silence. The DJ allowed a few seconds to pass before the soft notes of the cymbals and drum filled the empty space, followed by the horn section and the clear voice of the lead singer smoothly enunciating the mournful lyrics of another eighties slow jam.

Bitter felt her phone vibrating in her purse. She took the phone out and glanced at it. "Duty calls. I'll be right back," she told Gema as she picked up her bag. The exit door opened easily, and she stepped outside. A loitering couple dressed in less-than-their-best outfits started for the open door but stopped at Bitter's hard look. "Don't think it," she snapped as she allowed the door to close behind her.

Slowly, favoring her right knee a little, she made her way to the corner where the alley emerged onto 6th Street. The night air felt cool after the overheated club, despite the air conditioning and fans that kept the air moving inside the building. She stumbled where the asphalt of the alley met the sidewalk. The uneven surface scraped against her shoe, but she caught her balance. The moon lit the streets and, in the distance, the never-ending flow of traffic on I-5 provided a low rumble of background noise.

Once under the streetlight, she punched in her security code and pulled up the text message. She read it twice, her face grim, before she hit the speed dial and put the phone to her ear.

Voicemail. Damn. At last, the beep came, "Chief, this is Bitter. Call me as soon as possible. I know who killed—" She stopped talking, startled, as Morales materialized from a darkened doorway.

"Hang up," he said softly, holding an all-too-familiar Walther in the approved two-handed stance. She hesitated. "Hang it up now."

Slowly she moved the phone away from her ear and hit the disconnect button.

"Keep your hands where I can see them."

Though she held both hands out to her sides, in his view, he kept the pistol pointed at her. She took a few deep breaths to calm and center herself. *Be ready.*

He motioned with his head toward the alley she'd just left.

"Why?" She kept her voice low and calm.

He didn't answer.

Bitter took a step back, toward the alley. "Why? Why would you throw everything away? Your career? Your wife? Your family?" She took another step back, carefully feeling the concrete under her foot to ensure it was level before putting her weight on it. She kept her center of gravity slightly forward, ready for any opportunity before he had her cornered in the dead-end alley.

Silence met her questions. The moon and streetlight backlit Morales, she couldn't see his expression. One slow step after another, she moved backward into the alley, careful to keep her balance when the ground level changed.

Her care paid off. Morales stepped from the sidewalk to the asphalt and stumbled on the edge. Distracted, he lowered the pistol slightly and put one hand on the brick wall to keep his balance.

The muzzle was already rising as Bitter dropped her phone and leaped to the side and forward, into the dark shadows cast by the buildings. He pushed off the wall and turned, too late, as she hit the pistol with her purse. The shoulder strap caught the muzzle and pulled it down and to the side. The flash of two quick shots showed his twisted face as he fought to bring it back toward Bitter.

A shrill scream echoed behind Bitter in the alley.

Time slowed as adrenalin took over and she used every ounce of weight and momentum to slam Morales into the wall. He twisted to shake her off as she grabbed him by the arm and used his own movement to pull him sideways and down. Height and weight gave him the advantage. He wrenched himself from her grasp.

She took two steps back and came in again with a short nerve punch to the bicep, knocking his arm and pistol up. He kept his grip on the pistol, but the shot went high and wide. Dust and fragments of brick rained down on the cowering couple next to the exit door. Though alcohol slowed his reactions, he pushed Bitter hard and her knee betrayed her. She slipped and before she could catch her balance, he punched her in the chest with his free hand. Gasping for air, she fell backward to the ground, momentarily stunned. He lowered the pistol, swaying, then resumed his two-handed stance and aimed at Bitter, ignoring the screaming woman pounding on the back door of the club.

As the emergency exit burst open, shadows boiled into the alley from every direction, surrounding Morales in a deep nothingness. Inside the cloud of darkness, a figure solidified in front of the enraged man. When it raised its glowing eyes to his face, Morales roared in rage and fear as he emptied the Walther, then threw it at the shadow and ran.

Bitter caught her breath and sat up, reaching for her ankle holster as Morales disappeared around the corner. She left the Beretta in its holster, rolled to her feet, shook the dirt off, and scooped up the cell phone glowing in the darkness at her feet. "Call 9-1-1," she shouted as the terrified couple pushed their way inside the club. Before Alejandro could get out of the door, with Vargas and Barry on his heels, she was gone.

Chapter 26 ~ After Midnight

Bitter ran down the street after Morales. The I Street Bridge loomed overhead as he leaped onto the railroad tracks. He stumbled in the gravel, then caught his balance and kept running.

"Foot pursuit," Bitter panted, "I Street Bridge. He's heading west, toward West Sacramento." Her cell phone crackled urgently, but there was no time to reply as Bitter followed Morales, running on the metal grate between the two sets of rails.

She lost ground, both knees throbbing as she pounded across the bridge. Overhead, a warning siren, and the rumble of cars slowing to a stop filled the night air. In the distance, slivers of moonlight appeared between the overhead sections. The bridge slowly swung out as they raced toward West Sacramento. Morales beat her to the edge by fifty feet or so, and teetered there, undecided. Across the widening gap, on the other side of the river, flashing red and blue lights were approaching rapidly. The sirens grew louder. He looked over his shoulder at Bitter, measured the distance between them, and backed up a few yards.

"No!" she shouted. "Don't—"

He built up speed as he raced toward the gap and leaped. His body hung in the air, arms flailing like a long jumper, reaching for the opposite side. His hands touched the edge, but he wasn't quite close enough to get a grip. Fingers slipping, he fell out of sight. One, two, three heartbeats later, a loud splash echoed from the dark water below.

Bitter dashed to the downriver side of the bridge and leaned out to see if he surfaced. Long moments passed before she saw a hand, an arm, and then a pale face rise from the muddy depths.

"Damn," she muttered, "he's going to make it."

She heard the thunder of footsteps behind her and quickly turned. Sapp was running like a track star toward her as she waved her arms to catch his attention.

"No!" She yelled, "No! Stop! Don't go in the water." She leaped in front of him. With no time to slow down, he plowed into her, knocking them both to the graveled path between the tracks. Sapp rolled over her and jumped up to help her stand. She staggered as he pulled her to her feet.

"Come on." She picked up her cell phone and stuffed it into a pocket before she limped heavily back to the rail, peering out into the darkness. The bright beam of Sapp's Maglite flashed out over the water and caught Morales stroking freestyle downstream as he angled toward the Tower Bridge. Sapp kept Morales spotlighted as more blues raced to the edge of the bridge on the West Sacramento side.

Bitter clutched the rail, her knuckles white against the dirty black metal. A V-shaped row of ripples rose from the river's depths, following Morales as he swam. She grabbed Sapp's arm and pointed, "There! Over there!"

"Shit! What is it?" breathed Sapp, as he trained the beam on the water.

"I don't know. It's big."

The light caught Morales' face as he lost his concentration and his steady strokes faltered. The maw of something huge rose from the water. It surrounded him and sucked him back down. All Bitter could see were the pale scales glittering for a moment as a fin turned and a black eye caught the silver light of the moon. A long, narrow-finned tail splashed through the water and disappeared. Morales didn't have time to scream.

Sapp kept the light pointed at the spot where Morales went under. The ripples disappeared into the river, smoothing into the larger waves of the ever-flowing current.

The cell phone chimed. It was the dispatcher.

"It was Morales. He went into the river. Call out Search and Rescue." Bitter said quietly. "Yes, Captain Morales. He went under between the I Street and Tower Bridges."

Sapp gave her a somber look before he turned back to the river.

She disconnected the call. "My great grandmother, *mi Abuelita*, told us to stay away from the river. Papá laughed at her tales, but we never went swimming in the river. Ever." Bitter said quietly. "There are legends of monsters in the rivers of California. I have a clipping of an 1880s news article about a monster in the Mokelumne River."

"Not bull sharks? Do you know they found a shark two-thousand miles up the Amazon? And one up the Mississippi, all the way to Illinois."

Bitter shook her head. "That didn't look like a shark. But yes, anything is possible. I wouldn't be surprised to see a bull shark, especially out in the delta. But that thing was bigger and shaped wrong. The mouth looked more like a bass rising to engulf a lure. But that coil of body, it was more like a snake than a fish." She paused, remembering Billy's words at the hospital, then turned and looked up at Sapp. "I'll write the report. He went under, and we didn't see him again. Nobody on the other side could see him. The bridge was in the way."

Sapp nodded slowly before looking back down at the river flowing smoothly toward the delta.

"How did you know it was Morales?"

Bitter hesitated, "He had access to my office and carry gun. O'Malley put my Walther in my desk drawer, and yet when you and Gema took me to work to pick it up, it was in Property. No videos and a few days later, I found out that the logbook in Property was damaged. We don't know when it was checked into Property. It was supposed to go back to Property as evidence, but remember, he was the one who took it from me in the waiting room. He said it was because I'm the only one in the department that carries a .32 as a personal carry gun."

Sapp's eyes darkened at the memory.

"And right after Candy was killed, I noticed he was having an allergic reaction to something. It wasn't until yesterday when he told me that he was highly allergic to flowers, that I made the connection. It was the orchid that Candy had bought for me. I think," Bitter stumbled a little over the words, "I think she wanted to apologize for poisoning me with the mushroom tea. He had to have handled the flowers to have a reaction to the pollen. I'll bet that by Monday Franks will report that his fingerprints are on the wrapper and the pink envelope."

She took a deep breath, "And then he tried to direct my attention toward Candy's flings with a couple of other officers. He even insinuated that the Chief was having an affair with her." She stared at the river. "Like I cared what she did in her private life. That was her business, not mine. It wasn't anyone else's business either."

"So, why?"

"He was jealous. She refused him."

Sapp looked at her. "And?"

"And what?"

Sapp sighed, "There's more to the story than that. Why was he out to ruin your reputation? Why did he assign you the case and then undermine you at every step?"

"He was always a jealous man."

"And?"

"Mamá chose Papá over him."

Sapp raised his eyebrows, "Ahhh, and he never forgot?"

He quickly erased all expression from his face as Bitter glanced up at him and replied softly, "Yes."

"Okay, and why else?"

Bitter looked up at Sapp's impassive face. He waited, not looking at her, giving her time to decide what she wanted to tell him—if she told him anything at all. She hesitated, and slowly let the dark secret rise from the hidden place where she stuffed her rage.

"I refused him too." She said bitterly, her eyes darkening in anger. "He approached me after my husband died. Offered to be a father to my boys. I said no, I had Mamá and Papá to help me raise them and I didn't need a married man as a sugar daddy. Then Papá died and Mamá never recovered. And then there was Sal…"

Sapp started to look down at her face, but glimpsing her expression, jerked his gaze forward again, pretending he hadn't noticed. Instead, he just shook his head and took a deep breath. "A man scorned, huh? Some guys don't take that too well."

"And then my carry gun disappeared from the station." She smiled grimly. "He thought it was Papá's and I let him keep thinking that. Except Papá's Walther is safely locked in my gun safe at home. I always carried the matching pistol that Papá gave me the day I got my POST certificate." She sighed at the memory. "Papá was so proud."

Bitter took a deep breath, "It started coming together after Candy's funeral. Her father told me how she was devastated when she accidentally poisoned me." She paused, waiting a long moment, wondering if she should tell him the rest, and then went on, "He said that Candy was so upset because she had a crush on me, and she thought she'd killed me. And when she blurted out that she loved me in the break room, Morales was standing there, listening to her sob on the phone to her father—"

She looked across the river at the gathering crowd at the opposite end of the bridge. "So, who else could it be then? But there were still unanswered questions. Vargas, Vicki, Vicki's ex, even Jones. I couldn't be sure. At least, not until tonight, when Sally regained consciousness. She couldn't talk yet, but she could sign. She made sure Kenny knew."

Her smile was grim. "That young man may not talk, but he can text just fine. Morales lied to her. That's why she was so angry with him. He hadn't left his wife and he wasn't getting a divorce. He was just on the prowl again. He sweet-talked her into meeting him and then they went for a ride. They argued and when she started to get out of the truck, he shot her with my Walther and dumped her in the alley. But then she didn't die.

"He couldn't get to her to finish her off, not with the officers guarding her. He was running out of options, so I think that when he saw me in the club tonight, he decided to finish old business and kill me. He emptied my own pistol at me," anger touched her voice, "when I came outside to call the Chief about Kenny's text—and then he ran."

She paused. "He always was a lousy shot."

Sapp nodded.

"We need to search the area. He dropped my Walther before he took off. I didn't have time to pick it up."

Just then, Sapp's smartphone chimed. He read the text out loud. "Tell Bitter we found her bag and the pistol. G."

Bitter sighed in relief, "Thanks. Now, I need to make a call before anyone else arrives."

She pulled out her cell phone. *It's a wonder I didn't smash it when I dropped it*, and dialed. *Voicemail, as usual.* "Harry, this is Bitter. Billy was right about something in the river. I just had a sighting. You aren't going to like this one. Give me a call tomorrow."

Bitter looked up at Sapp. He was staring at the river again, shaking his head in disbelief. "Harry is over at UC Davis. Specializes in exotic animals and on the side, a bit of cryptozoology." She paused, "He'll want to interview both of us. Are you okay with that?"

Sapp nodded, his face solemn. "As long as it doesn't make the news."

Bitter responded with a dark chuckle, "Oh no, he has his own reputation to consider. He's already had one close encounter with the tabloids. Nearly ruined his career."

She started to take a step away from the railing and her knee buckled as she grimaced in pain. Sapp jumped forward and caught her by the elbow before she fell.

"I think I'll need a little help."

Sapp cracked a tiny smile and lifted her back up. In silence, she hobbled back toward the Amtrak station, with Sapp supporting most of her weight. The red and blue flashing lights ahead grew brighter as more black and whites pulled up and blues thundered up the rails toward them.

"You might want to see the doctor. You didn't do your knees any good tonight." Sapp said gently before the leader of the pack reached them.

Bitter almost smiled at his cautious appraisal.

"Yeah. I might."

"Well, the ambulance just pulled up."

"Yeah, I saw." She huffed as a white and green van pulled in behind the ambulance. "That damned reporter was at the club. He must have a police scanner in his van."

"So?" Sapp asked gently.

Bitter sighed. "I don't think I can drive right now. And my car is at the house anyway, I took a taxi tonight. I was considering walking home. It's not that far and I needed to think." She glanced down at the torn silk fluttering over her bloody knees. "Oh damn. I skinned my hands and knees. The EMTs are going to have fits." She hesitated. "I guess I'll have to see my doctor. He's going to want a full workup on my knees," she sighed, "and they were just starting to feel better. I'll go see him tomorrow."

Sapp shook his head at her. "Bitter, you can't even walk right now. You know the EMTs are going to insist on taking you to the hospital."

"Keep that reporter away," she ordered. Then she looked up at Sapp sternly, "And don't let O'Malley call my sons."

A shadow slipped into the darkness behind Bitter as the first blue reached them and leaned down to support her on the other side. One by one, more shadows slipped away from the bridge and into the night as the two officers helped her to the ambulance.

Epilogue

The squad car sat sideways across the narrow street, blocking traffic, its blue and red lights highlighting the trees and shrubs as they flashed. O'Malley stood on the sidewalk, watching the enraged woman throwing clothes out of the second-story window, most of them flashing into flame as she held the lighter to a dangling sleeve or pants leg, then tossing it to join its fellows on the growing bonfire.

Shadows gathered in the shelter of bushes, sliding between the circles of light thrown by the streetlights.

Neighbors huddled together to watch the spectacle, safely across the street and out of range of unidentified flaming objects.

A second squad car pulled up and Sapp leaped out, ready to race into the house.

O'Malley nodded cordially and flicked a glance at the sidewalk beside him.

Sapp stopped and walked quickly over to view the fire. "Aren't you going to do anything?" he asked.

O'Malley's accent thickened. "Nay, it wouldna do any good. Kathleen's out of control. I think she's off her meds again."

"What set her off?"

"Ayyyy, she found a message on the voicemail from another woman."

Sapp gave O'Malley a side-eye but didn't speak.

"T'was the travel agent—" O'Malley paused, "I thought I'd surprise her with a vacation."

"But your clothes?"

O'Malley gave Sapp a sly grin. "Didna ye ever notice that my work locker is full of uniforms? And I have a storage unit around the corner where I keep my parents' heirlooms and good clothes. Those rags are just for working around the house and yard."

Sapp looked at the ground and shook his head in disbelief.

"My grandmother warned me about messing with crazy women, no matter how pretty they are. I shoulda listened." He shrugged. "Now it's too late."

The flames grew higher as Kathleen started tossing bedding onto the fire.

Sapp nudged O'Malley. "At least you don't own a white Bimmer, huh?"

O'Malley frowned, "A BMW?"

Sapp rolled his eyes. "Surely you remember that movie? I think every woman in the country saw it." He pointed at the raging woman with his chin. "Bet she did. More than once."

Before O'Malley could reply, a dark blue Dodge Dart Swinger pulled up. Bitter got out and walked slowly over to the watching officers.

"Well?"

"The neighbors called the fire department." O'Malley glanced at his watch. "They're about a minute away. What are you doing here? You're off duty."

"I got a call, so I came over," Bitter replied, watching Kathleen closely as the distant sirens slowly grew louder. "You know, we're going to have to get her out of there so the fire department can save your house."

O'Malley shrugged.

The sirens suddenly intensified.

Bitter's lips twitched as she turned away. She might've been holding back a smile. "Stay here," she ordered.

Sapp and O'Malley looked at each other as Bitter walked slowly up the walk and stopped where she was fully visible in the flickering light of the fire. Silhouetted against the flames, she shook her head, tossing back the kinky black curls tipped with flickering red and gold highlights.

She waited.

Kathleen threw a lamp out the window and watched it smash onto the concrete below before she noticed Bitter standing halfway between the street and the fire.

"You!" Kathleen shrieked. "What are you doing here?" She disappeared from the window.

Crashing sounds emerged from the house before the raging woman charged out the door, a vintage baseball bat in her hands. "I'll get you for this, Bitter. You owe me. You owe me for this miserable life. If it wasn't for you—" She screamed incoherently in rage, running down the sidewalk as she raised the bat.

Bitter watched calmly until Kathleen stopped and swung the bat awkwardly. Stepping neatly out of the way as the bat swung toward her head, Bitter hit Kathleen in the ribs with a stun gun. The bat flew into the bushes, scattering the watching shadows.

"Holy mother of—" Sapp took a step forward as Kathleen convulsed and fell twitching. The momentum of her swing carried her onto the grass. He paused before looking back at O'Malley. "Did you know Bitter had a stunner?"

O'Malley stepped out into the street and waved the fire engine to park behind the units. He shrugged. "Nope."

A fireman trotted over to Kathleen and waved the EMTs in as Bitter tossed her hair back and walked slowly to the curb.

Sapp started to say something but thought better of it and closed his mouth. He looked back at the paramedics tending to Kathleen. "The hospital for a seventy-two-hour hold?"

O'Malley nodded. "That'll give me time to get this mess cleaned up."

"So, what are you going to do?"

"Nothing. Father Flores said it's 'til death do us part or she leaves me."

Sapp rolled his eyes, expressing his opinion without a word.

Bitter looked at Sapp first, then O'Malley. "You'll have to write the report. I'll look at it when I come in tomorrow."

They both watched as Bitter walked back to her car, a cloud of shadows rushing in from the foliage and surrounding her as she opened the door.

"She isn't limping," O'Malley observed.

"Yeah, after she took that fall on the bridge, the doctor told her that he wouldn't release her for full duty until she let him do a full workup and start a treatment plan." Sapp shrugged. "Gema said it was some kind of lingering allergic reaction from the mushroom poisoning and the inflammation had settled in her knees. So, she got shots to reduce the swelling. And started taking allergy meds. Finally."

O'Malley waited until Bitter got into the Dart and started the engine before he continued, "You heard Morales' wife had filed for divorce."

Sapp nodded, "Maybe that's what drove him over the edge. We'll probably never know."

Bitter slowly pulled away from the curb, looking in the rearview mirror at the two tall officers standing on the sidewalk, backlit by the dying fire. Behind them, the EMTs were strapping Kathleen to a gurney.

"Ayyyy, Papá, you were right, karma does take her revenge eventually," She smiled grimly. "If you just give her enough time to work."

The dark figure riding shotgun nodded solemnly, but she didn't see him.

It's only a shadow.

~ *Until Next Time* ~

A MOKELUMNE RIVER MONSTER.

Upon the highest Celestial authority there is at the present time habiting the Mokelumne river, only a few miles from this place, a short distance above the Big Bar bridge between Jackson and Mokelumne Hill, a water monster that has spread consternation and terror among our entire Chinese population. They assert that one day this week a number of them were on the river just below the old Boston mill site, when they saw what they supposed to be a large fish near the top of the water, and one of their party made a leap into the river to capture the prize. But no sooner had he struck the water than the monster turned upon its would-be captor, and instantly drew him under, and from whence he had not arisen at last accounts. The monster is said to have teeth like a dog, and to have powerful strength, as the man was as nothing in his grasp. The Chinamen who witnessed the tragical fate of their unfortunate countryman, concluded that the thing was the devil, and fled for their lives. It is also claimed that another Chinaman lost his life in about the same manner, near this place, several years ago, and it is thought that this is the same monster returned, if indeed he has not inhabited the Mokelumne ever since. While we are not prepared to vouch for the truth of this story, yet it is evident that something has occurred or been seen on the river to excite our Chinese denizens and put them ill at ease. Some of our daring and curious citizens talk of getting up a party to investigate the matter, and if possible capture the monster, which they believe to be the Calaveras *Chronicle's* long lost snake, which has not been heard of since Higby went into the Internal Revenue Department.—[Amador Dispatch.

Sacramento Daily Record-Union, Sept 8, 1881

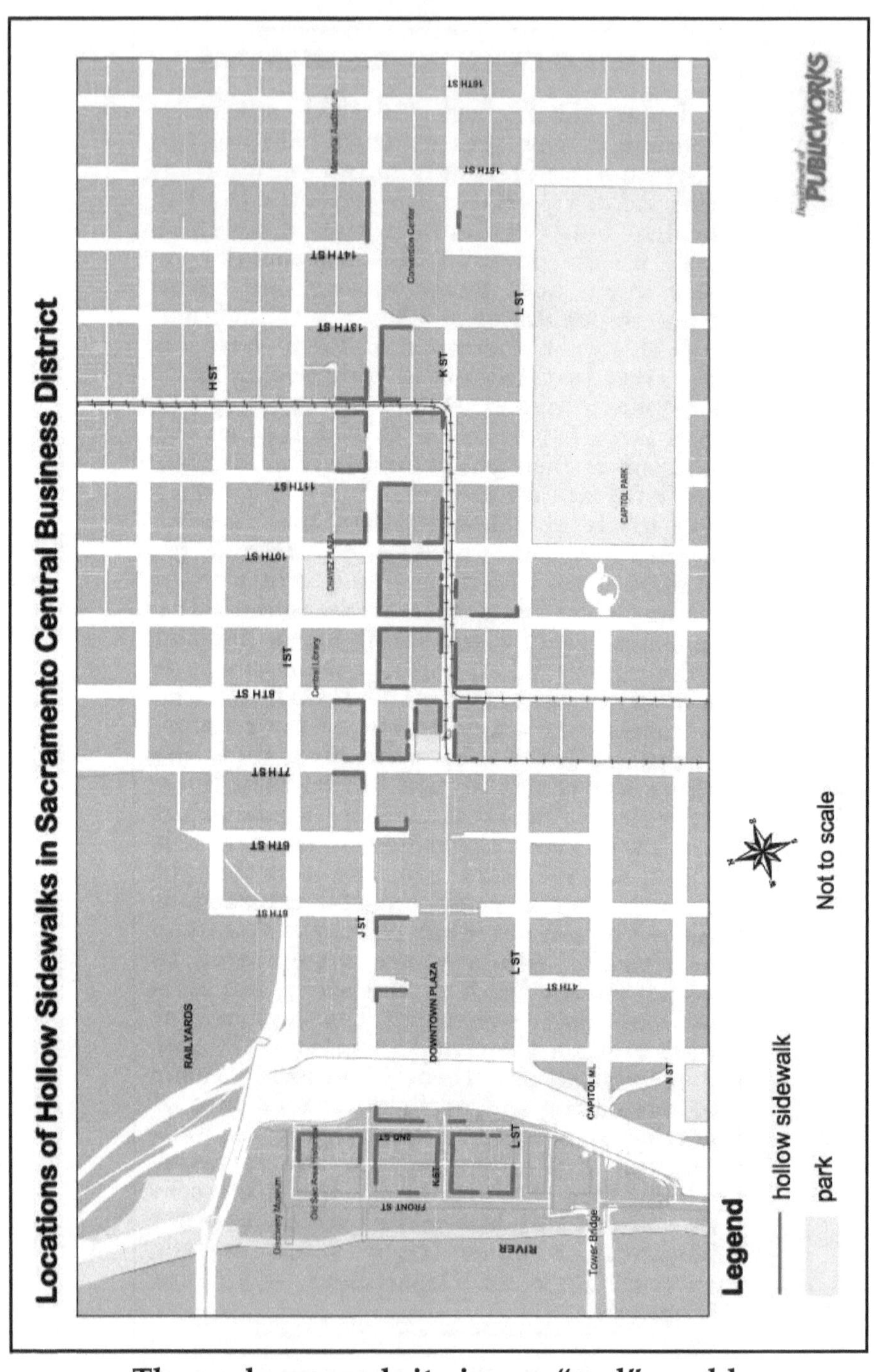

The underground city in our "real" world.

Acknowledgments

First, I'd like to thank my mom, Hazel Griffith, and my late father, Don Griffith, for all the support and encouragement that I've received through the years as I've raised a family, worked in a variety of jobs, and followed my dreams.

I'd also like to thank my family, friends, and fellow writers who read the first bits of the Bitter saga and helped me make it a better story. Without the input from Karen Blaettler, Joe Bonadonna, Bertha Chambers, Brynne Chandler (Emmy-nominated for Batman and well-known for her work on Gargoyles, Teenage Mutant Ninja Turtles, and He-Man and the Masters of the Universe), Lianna Costantino, Lofeeya Darden, Arthur Greene III, and all the others who've encouraged me over the last five years, this writing journey would've ended before it began. The knowledge that I've gained from the founders and members of the Black Science Fiction Society, Cherokee Indians – Genealogy/Research, Reading in Black, The State of Black Science Fiction, and Writers Detective Q&A Facebook groups was invaluable to the evolution of Homicide Detective Juanita Bitter, the storyline, and building a diverse world.

Of course, I can't forget my de Jauregui family, thank you so much Papá and Mamá, Frank, and everyone else. Thank you too, my dear children, who have put up with my sporadic immersions into writing and obsessive book collecting for all these years.

Just so you all know, it was a conversation with Neal Litherland about the bitterness and difficulties of an author's life that led to the concept of Bitter and her world. Once she coalesced in my mind, she pushed all my other projects aside and demanded that her story be told. Many thanks, Neal!

And last, but not least, all mistakes are mine and mine alone. No one else can claim them.

The Cast of Characters

La Familia and More

Juanita "Nita" Bitter – Homicide detective, Sacramento PD

José Magiting Bitter – Bitter's youngest son

Roberto Banoy Bitter – Bitter's oldest son

Julio Santos – Bitter's older brother

Elizabeth "Liz" Santos – Julio's wife

Julio's and Liz's two teenaged sons

Rosalia Perez – Liz's cousin's daughter

Papá – Juan José Santos

Mamá – Sofia Sakki Santos

Lola Sakki – Bitter's grandmother

Abuela and *Abuelo* Santos – Grandmother and Grandfather

Abuelita Santos – Great Grandmother

Gato – Bitter's old tuxedo cat

Chica – Rosalia's Chihuahua

The Police Department (and More)

Sgt. O'Malley – Longtime street cop

    Kathleen – O'Malley's wife

    Aiden – O'Malley's son

Officer Jasir Sapp – Street cop, US Air Force (Retired)

Cattee (Candy) Maria Soto - Dispatcher

Chief George Brown – Chief of Police

Captain Morales – Bitter's supervisor

Captain Soto – State Police and Candy's father
>   Mrs. Soto (current)
>   Josephina Soto - Daughter
>   Mrs. Grace Soto (ex-wife) – Candy's mother

Officer Kahlid – Street cop
Officer Vargas – Street cop
Officer Jones –Rookie
Officer Adams – Rookie
Officer Cznik – Rookie
Sgt. Franks – Forensics
Vicki René – Dispatcher and Candy's girlfriend
Sally – The Chief's secretary
>   Kenny – Sally's grandson

Denise – Dispatcher and Vicki's ex
Lee – Property Room tech
Jontay – Building Maintenance
Joe – County Coroner
Judy – Temporary employee
Charlie – Bakersfield police officer

Friends, Neighbors, and Acquaintances
>   Harry – UC Davis professor and cryptozoologist
>   Gema Sapp – Jasir's older sister, Defense attorney
>   >   Tasha – Gema's teenage daughter, ice hockey goalie
>   >   Gema's three sons
>
>   Vic and Riza Sapp – Jasir's and Gema's parents
>   >   Jesie – Kid sister
>
>   Gian Singh – Bitter's favorite cab driver and novelist
>   Señor Suarez – Neighbor, Neighborhood Watch
>   Señora Gutierrez – Neighbor, Daycare provider

Wendy – Bitter's neighbor
    Tabitha
    Toby
    Baby

Other Characters
    Sal Salomon– Bitter's ex-husband (deceased)
    Jean Petit
    La Bruja – the witch
    Doctor Leon – Bitter's doctor
    Angie – Nurse
    Rosie – Nurse
    Antonio – Nurse
    Amir – Nurse
    Tony - Nurse
    Doctor Kezar – Head of the Psychiatric Department
    Jennifer Black – Teenaged fan
    Billy "Bones" Boney – Teenager
    Luis Otxoa – Teenager
    Larry Peterson – High school principal
    Ronaldo – Audiovisual tech at high school
    Father Flores – Catholic priest
    Mrs. Mitchell – Gema Sapp's neighbor, golfer, and pilot
    Jon and Barry – Owners of the nightclub on 6th
    Alejandro – Solano County Prosecutor
    Reporter – Freelance, ambulance chaser
    Cameraman - Freelance

A Sneak Peek at Bitter Sins

Gato patted Bitter's face.

"What?" she muttered as she tried to push the big tuxedo cat off her chest so she could roll over and catch a few more minutes of sleep.

Claws pricked her cheek with Gato's next effort to wake her.

"Ouch, ouch, okay Gato, I'm awake."

Chica crawled out from under the comforter and stood at the foot of the bed, her ears perked up. She stared at the closed bedroom door and whined.

A tap, and then another on the front door echoed down the hall. Bitter sat up and rubbed her eyes. The clock said it was 3 a.m.

At the second series of taps, she reached for her robe. With the .32 in her hand and her cell phone in her pocket, she padded down the dark hall barefoot. A dark silhouette backlit by the streetlight filled the old-fashioned window in the door. She instinctively pressed her back to the wall when she realized the porch light was out. That light was never turned off, ever.

She took a few light steps back and slipped through the kitchen door, out of the direct line of the front door, before she asked, "Who is it?"

No one answered.

She peeked around the edge of the doorframe, heart pounding, just in time to see a figure turn away from the door. She waited until she heard a creak from the porch steps, then she slipped back across the hall, into the living room. The streetlight's rays filtered between the heavy curtains, where they didn't quite meet, and filled the center of the room with a dim light. Cautiously, she crept along the wall next to the bookcase, where the soft yellow light couldn't reach, and shadows reigned.

When the wrought iron gate slammed closed with a metallic crash, she pushed the side of the curtain over just enough to see the front yard. Nothing moved outside.

Slowly, Bitter made her way back to the hall. Before she stepped into the hall, she stopped and peered around the corner at the front door. The window remained empty, but her instincts screamed at the silence.

She waited.

The minutes dragged on.

Maybe I'm being paranoid.

Just as she prepared herself to cross the hall again, to the kitchen, the sound of quick steps on the porch stairs filled the quiet night. A bright light flashed through the window and someone knocked.

Bitter readied the Walther. "Who is it?"

Bullets crashed through the window and down the hall. An instant later, the door flew open, kicked in by a dark figure. It slammed into Bitter, knocking her down. The world went black and a crushing silence descended.

Before You Go

RE de Jauregui

Coming Soon!

How do you say it? "they-how-rrr-hey-ghee" *(Be sure to roll the rrr!)*

A lifelong speculative fiction fan, designer, artist, and writer, de Jauregui has finally stepped out of nonfiction and into fiction. In her new books, *Bitter* and the upcoming *Bitter Sins*, she melds crime and urban fantasy into a murder mystery.

You can find her books on Amazon at amzn.to/3bFm5gi or check out her websites at www.ruthdj.weebly.com and www.AlienStarBooks.com

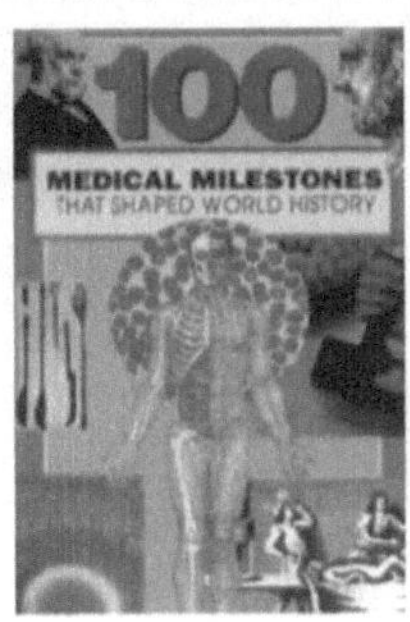

What awaits beyond the door that leads you to the next plane of existence? KG Blaettler explores the possibilities in this collection of short stories.

https://www.amazon.com/dp/B088GYKZK7

Joe Bonadonna

Take a trip into the wildly imaginative worlds of Joe Bonadonna. From mysterious fantasy to outer space to pirates, Bonadonna delves into his vast knowledge of classic movies and the golden age of science fiction to create his fantastic tales.

Bonadonna is also a contributor to a number of anthologies, including Janet Morris' well-known "In Hell" series.

Find Bonadonna's books on Amazon amzn.to/3fXpKJu

The Best of Black Fantastic
MVMediaATL.com
TERMINUS
MILTON J. DAVIS
TALES OF THE BLACK FANTASTIC FROM THE ATL
Amber and the Hidden City
BLACKTASTIC!
BLACKTASTICON 2018 ANTHOLOGY
LINDA D. ADDISON
MILTON J. DAVIS
MEJI
MILTON J. DAVIS
Ten years ago MVmedia was established to provide exciting science fiction and fantasy based on African/African Diaspora culture, history and tradition. Stop by and browse titles that range from Afrofuturism to Black Scifi. Welcome to the best of the Black Fantastic!

Kai Leakes
KAI LEAKES
A UNITY ISLES NOVELLA
ONI'S TEARS
KAI LEAKES
KAI LEAKES
SIN EATERS
DEVOTION BOOK ONE
SIN EATERS:
RETRIBUTION
DEVOTION BOOK
LOVE TRUST, & Pleasure
BROTHERS OF KEMET SERIES
KAI LEAKES
-When the Light and Dark are at war, sometimes the Gray can only be your salvation-

Action, passion, romance, and fantasy, swirled into touch of darkness—Kai Leakes leads you into dream worlds filled with handsome heroes, evil demons, vampires, evocative prose, and action-packed adventure.
Visit Leakes at Kaileakes.com or
https://www.amazon.com/Kai-Leakes/e/B00884BO0A

CRIER'S
KNIFE
NEAL F.
LITHERLAND
New Avalon
Love and Loss
in the
City of Steam
Neal F. Litherland
The
Rejects
Neal F. Litherland